GIFTS
RETURNED BY
THE RIVER

———

EDITED BY

IAIN SINCLAIR

GIFTS
RETURNED BY
THE RIVER

—

EDITED BY
IAIN SINCLAIR

ALICE ALBINIA | RENCHI BICKNELL | JAVIER CALVO
B. CATLING | JACK CATLING | GARETH EVANS
ALLEN FISHER | JÜRGEN GHEBREZGIABIHER | JARETT KOBEK
STEPHEN MCNEILLY | MICHAEL MOORCOCK | LOUIS PETIT
VICTOR REES | ANYA REEVE | JOHN ROGERS
ADOLFO BARBERÁ DEL ROSAL | MATTHEW SHAW
IAIN SINCLAIR | BEN WICKEY | CAROL WILLIAMS

SWEDENBORG
HOUSE PRESS

2025

PUBLISHED BY:
SWEDENBORG HOUSE PRESS
SWEDENBORG HOUSE
20/21 BLOOMSBURY WAY
LONDON
WC1A 2TH

EDITOR: IAIN SINCLAIR
BOOK DESIGN: THE QUINN FIZZLERS

ISBN: 978-0-85448-235-1

BRITISH LIBRARY CATALOGUING-IN-PUBLICATION DATA.
A CATALOGUE RECORD FOR THIS BOOK IS AVAILABLE
FROM THE BRITISH LIBRARY.

PRINTED BY TJ BOOKS

CONTENTS

CONTENTS

APPENDICES

INSERT

GIFT, Iain Sinclair

PART I

HISTORIES
& HAUNTINGS

Photograph by Anonymous Bosch

HISTORIES & HAUNTINGS

Iain Sinclair

*Possessed of the strange alchemical virtue of transmuting reality, of making
us fall vertically to the point in which all is abandoned in order to know the
certainty that we start again ... History is a plane which can be regarded from a
future balcony ... Needless to say, on this plane of simultaneous intensities and
ages we may appear multiple times. 'And just as there shall be no respite, nor a
place unoccupied in space, there shall be no respite nor empty space in the spirit
and sensibility of the beholder'.*
—Manuel Cirauqui, 'Artaud: Notes for an Epidemiology'

There is now, in this trespass of resurrecting aspects of the exposure of charged
neophytes from 1974, such a root ball of fabulous and contradictory narratives
that to unpick a single thread puts us at risk of choking our allotted space
in bandages of badly knitted ectoplasm. Probably the task is better left to someone
innocent of a period that has passed but which remains an eternally recurring set of
myths. The hour of that passing can be identified with the oracular voice of an empty
building, a single unauthored command, heard by Brian Catling and myself, as we left
the permitted chamber where we had been debating final adjustments to the *Albion
Island Vortex* show, due to run from 19 March to 7 April at the Whitechapel Gallery.

I mean that a voice spoke, and released from the ullage cellars of Truman's brewery
into ramblings through those time-heavy streets, we both heard it. *Heard totally different
words*. My auditory hallucination was received under the influence of Allen Ginsberg
and a few reckless days of interview-conversation in the heady summer of 1967. The
poet, a bearded but still youthful Ancient Mariner, told his tale on a loop. Caught in
the vortex of desired fame, he recalled solitary anguish, a 1948 season trapped in the
cruel heat of a room in East Harlem. *Waiting for it to happen. Willing what was already
and always in train*. The 'deep earthen grave voice' of William Blake, heard in the

afterglow of a self-induced, page-turning orgasm, recites: 'Ah, Sunflower! weary of time, / Who countest the steps of the Sun; / Seeking that sweet golden clime, / Where the traveller's journey is done'. Ginsberg took the poem as a direct personal instruction. What he had previously imagined as 'a voice of rock' was now 'tender and beautifully ... ancient'. Postmortem ventriloquism. The chosen mentor told the poet to 'go into death'. To become non-human. To break away from the sweating and sickly prison of the body and to attain 'complete consciousness'.

All that heavy freight! But the voice I heard in the Whitechapel Gallery was more like Blake played by Toby Jones. It was commanding but understated, committed to the task but well aware of its own absurdity. There were two instructions. 'Don't break the ring'. And: 'Ramsey holds the key'. A number of the expeditions out of London, gathered up in the 1974 exhibition and re-curated here, were attempts to honour the task laid on me. Force fields around promoted stone circles were investigated without resolution. It took time to realize that the investigation was the resolution. Maybe that 'ring' was the iron band that Catling beat out for me and incised with Egyptian hieroglyphs? Maybe the Ramsey riddle was answered in a stained glass window accessed on a narrowboat voyage described in *Edge of the Orison*, a series of tramps in the dust of John Clare?

More of an initiated participant in the 'other' London of elder spirits than mere witness and accidental reporter, Catling received clearer practical instructions. A growl, so he said, like an Ealing Studios character actor—like Alfie Bass, John Slater, Sydney Tafler—told him to get a shift on and to take a gander at today's rag. It could have been, in the lull after they staggered from the free lunchtime bar in Truman's, the voice of one of the draymen, a tabloid paper folded in his back pocket. Brian's first book, *Necropathia*, was a court exhibit, a 'HORROR FIND IN DEATH CASE' splashed across *The Sun*, Friday 8 March 1974, on the cusp of the exhibition. The item was further accused of featuring 'the most appalling print'.

Poetic utterance earthed by the cruel comedy of local demotic. Catling's Blake was no academic exegesis, no fellow traveller in psychedelic excesses. He was of the territory Brian knew as 'Surreycide', a neat coinage. The south bank, across from the walled enclosure of Roman colonization, from glass towers and surveillance, prolapsed communities, forgotten tenements, condemned islands of lost souls waiting on official regeneration, was where banished East End villains wore their Elephant and Castle exile as a form of suicide. The Blake that erupts into *The Erstwhile* elevates the meaning of that word. Which is what the Whitechapel exhibition attempted, letting the Erstwhile into the scene and taking them as guides to the future. Catling, like Blake, looked behind 'the shabby curtain that was saturated in the stink of London'. Walls breathed. Tables spoke. Fossils reclaimed breath. Bones knitted patterns for dying stars.

Many years later, when Brian was conjuring a potential Blake script for Ray Winstone, who had long harboured the ambition of impersonating the visionary poet, he made a move that set time into reverse. His feisty Hercules Road journeyman recalls Swedenborg as 'lost and just walking about like some tosser in the rain'. And he sets up for the second time, having published a vivid conjuring of the episode for *Several Clouds Colliding*, the terrible moment of the chophouse epiphany, the voice of destiny. 'Don't eat too much!' Light is being withdrawn. Oil lamps flicker. The room changes shape. A solitary tarnished angel manifests like a wingless vagrant. But now it is Catling's Blake who speaks, who utters the dietary warning.

The island vortex opened around the time of the Whitechapel exhibition displayed limited evidence, a few trophies brought back from road and track and cave, of the hunger for a quest. A quest associated with place and the declaration of elective affinities. Gathered together by accidents of fate we gloss as 'random', the participants in this show, along with their friends, collaborators and world-wanderers passing through Hackney, worked by day at the casual London labours then available. Physically occupied—and learning so much from the realities of paid employment in the fascinating sites to which we would never otherwise have gained access—there was time in which to brood and plot, to eavesdrop on fellow workers, to absorb local intelligence. To scribble in secret notebooks. To maintain diaries in film or page or paint.

Renchi recalls shared shifts heaving mailbags on Euston station, before we shaved grass and dug plant beds, separately, for the Parks Department. He mapped the more intimate territory of Victoria Park (with the paintings to prove it). And I had a beautiful roaming existence through Poplar, Wapping and Limehouse, servicing Hawksmoor churches and piloting the occasional tractor into innocent green spaces soon to be improved and digitally enhanced as Docklands, City of Dreadful Reflections. Brian did time with the mower crew, navigating around rough sleepers on benches, as well as tapping the dark myths of the Quaker brewery in Brick Lane. These activities, with roll-up smoke breaks, Tupperware leftovers, wilderness cemeteries, encouraged and abetted loose-lipped and excited chatter; the testing of outrageous riffs, epiphanies and midnight revelations. There were also rooms in which to retreat and to cook up our various 'outcomes' (before that terrible word became a cultural obligation).

Brian had his studio at the Royal College of Art and—in the teeth of the new minimalism—he filled it with an unfashionable lumber of *stuff*: mechanical devices, experimental environments, pages of doodle and damage: all the splinters and the stardust scrapings that emerged, centuries later, from the celebrated forest thatch of *The Vorrh*. In embryo, the dense and compacted future was already so much present that any attempt to articulate a timeline for these activities is immediately undone. Explanations were not required. *The ultimate revelations had already been stored*. The youthful poet stuttered at the pace of them. Gnomic hints came with throat seizure and chattering teeth. To be washed away in the next deep drink. And the next articulate silence. The germ of late-life wonder was itching and pulsing, swaggering towards Oxford to be born. Researching Catling's miraculous trilogy, Victor Rees discovered *The Vorrh* announcing itself as the provisional title for an Albion Village Press chapbook published in the fertile outwash of the 1974 Whitechapel exhibition. The coming decades were about catching up.

Renchi Bicknell is smoking, perilously positioned on the ledge of an open window overlooking a prematurely rewilded Hackney garden; overlooking the rose-tinted red brick massif of the neighbourhood school with its perpetual surf of pleasure-beach child shrieks and policing roars, and the broken fence giving onto a liminal scrap of land infiltrated by a lively permission of small black boys. This undecorated, paint-splattered room gloried in the romance of studio status—with few of the accompanying pretensions. It was always a privilege to visit, to interrupt, to become familiar with works in progress: deep-memory exorcisms, visions of flight, and troublesome commissioned portraits. And to have the conviction that maintaining a living artist in the house, in the community, was a gateway to something rich and strange. Jungian archetypes fought for the right to showcase their lurid dramas, before being scraped away or overpainted. Or even, as in the case of a magnificent tribal mask *Demoiselles d'Avignon* canvas, a cubistic eruption into Stratford High Street (where the artist was ghosting as a student), held up like a sheet of laundry before being burnt in a pit in the garden. A loss I still feel, although somewhat softened by a sequence of photographs snapped and included in the first edition of *The Kodak Mantra Diaries*. This collation of countercultural fragments was made possible by having my own work cave, close at hand, my books and boxes to be raided, before the finished text was beaten out on a typewriter in Gozo. Somehow—at night, in occasional cottage retreat—paintings were made. 'Diary' films were assembled, if not edited.

And that, if memory is to be trusted, is when Swedenborg made his appearance. There was some discussion, in Renchi's painting room, as he gestured so fiercely that he was in imminent danger of falling from the window, about the reach and nature of memory. I had a vague archivist's notion that *everything*, every breath, every shame, every ordinary plodding moment of existence, was in there; stored, filed and inaccessible. Until required. Not to be trusted, of course. A potlatch of improved and amended doings and days. A dream-quilt in tatters. A sticky sucking midden from which to extract the stories we want to tell, in order to appease our true selves: those unkillable ghosts behind the banal performative versions we offer, strategically amended, to friends and workmates. Renchi wasn't having it: he said that memory was all highlights. Painterly ecstasies like the incidents nominated to be tested on his canvases. A cinema of single frames magnified and offered to the world. The rest was gone, a self-deleting programme. And he lived up to his thesis. It was tricky for him to arrive at a rendezvous carrying the bags and wearing the clothes with which he started the journey. No past, no recriminations. Coats, cameras and tickets left a treasure-hunt trail across continents.

Before heading west over the ocean, by way of Boston and elsewhere, to the Lindisfarne Community at West Stockbridge, Massachusetts, Christopher Bamford was very much part of the thrust of a period which in retrospect feels like the end of the Sixties—meaning 1965 to 1975—and the dissolution of all previous creeds and convictions in favour of new beginnings by way of local activism and a groping series of spontaneous expeditions in quest of ... what?

As a collaborator in happenings, plays, films, magazines in Dublin, Chris was also a moralist and a librarian of possibilities. He had his secular adventures in night cafés and bars thick with trapped swarms of philosophers and the laughter of tragic soliloquizers heavy with porter. Those times were necessary, and traditional, for a future life as seeker and scholar. A memorial notice, after his passing in 2022, mentions his abiding interest in 'Sophia, the Eucharist, Hermeticism, Celtic Christianity, the Grail, Novalis, Romanticism, the Rose Cross, the Troubadours, deserts and gardens'.

And so it was that certain books and places influenced our occasional collisions, when Chris passed through London like a desert father, paying his dues to a discontinued past, and offering pointers towards roads that might or might not be taken. We arranged to meet on New Year's Day at Lindisfarne, Holy Island, where Chris and Dian would be pausing on their way back from Iona. I drove up early from London, spent a few hours in the ruins of the abbey, and ferried them straight back to Hackney. Next day we struck out on a traditional desire line from St Luke's, Old Street, and Bunhill Fields, to Christ Church Spitalfields, and St Anne's Limehouse, where an exhausted Dian, pregnant with their first child, fell into a dream of disbelief that this could really be happening.

Those sudden manifestations from Chris, and the excited conversations that followed, sometimes recorded on silent film, informed the *Albion Island Vortex* exhibition and the pitch of the publications from our small independent press. With Chris we set out to visit Jeremy Prynne in Cambridge: another session that opened previously unimagined landscapes and led to connections with a band of the liveliest and most engaged English poets. But the point of severance, in terms of regular discussions and exchanges, came with a tour across London, during which Chris attempted to fill his pack with the hidden pamphlets and testaments of London, the ones he would not be able to accumulate anywhere else.

And that, I think, was my first experience of Swedenborg House. Or the book room, the safety net, available to casual persons stepping in, without belonging, from the Bloomsbury street. The atmosphere was calm, soporific, outside time. Intriguing. But for another day. I picked up a number of pamphlets, to be set aside and absorbed, without close study, as part of the general atmosphere. Later, at Buckingham Gate, a woman darted into a back chamber and emerged, without the item being requested, with a copy of *Prehistoric London, Its Mounds and Circles*. Chris, playing the long game, the mortal contract of Steiner association, sacred architecture, poetry and prophecy, had yet again gifted me with just what was needed.

Wherever we were, wherever we were prompted to go, there was a shelf of strange, elusive titles harvested to feed into books still to be written, pictures to be displayed. The fruits of clergymen with time on their hands. Rogue academics. Unanchored theorists.

The Names of God, or The Majestic Order of Divine Self-Revelation by Revd Wm Pascoe Goard. *Germinal, Containing The Real Secrets of Religion and Freemasonry.* Limited to 500 copies. Symbolically Illustrated. Sydney Hanson. *Early British Trackways, Moats, Mounds, Camps and Sites* by Alfred Watkins. His first book. *Studies on the Legend of the Holy Grail, With Especial Reference to the Hypothesis of its Celtic Origin* by Alfred Nutt. *The Green Roads of England* by R Hippisley Cox. *Cleopatra's Needle, The History of the Obelisk, with an Exposition of the Hieroglyphics* by Revd James King. *The Lives of the Troubadours* by Ida Farnell. *The Odic Force, Letters on Od and Magnetism* by Carl von Reichenbach. *Introduction to a Science of Mythology. The Myth of the Divine Child and the Mysteries of Eleusis* by CG Jung and C Kerényi. *A Dissertation on the Eleusinian and Bacchic Mysteries* by Thomas Taylor. *Bunhill Fields, Written in Honour and to the Memory of the Many Saints of God whose Bodies rest in this Old London Cemetery* by Alfred W Light. *The Caliph's Design: Architects! Where is your Vortex?* by Wyndham Lewis. *Wichita Vortex Sutra* by Allen Ginsberg. *Rites and Symbols of Initiation: The Mysteries of Birth and Rebirth* by Mircea Eliade. *Memories, Dreams, Reflections* by CG Jung.

ELEMENTS & ARCHETYPES

The room allocated for the Whitechapel show was apportioned to specific territories. Cader Idris. The limestone pavements, cliffs and caves of the Gower Peninsula. Wiltshire (Crow Country). Rock outcrops on Yorkshire moors. Northumbria. Scottish Borders. East London. Walls were assigned to Crow, Owl, Goat and Wolf.

Renchi Bicknell curated his paintings as 'Paths & Travellers': his journeys, his returns. And as 'Six hair-raising Archetypes' drawn from readings of Jung and Eliade (among many others, including William James and DH Lawrence). Jung writes of a broken foot, 'misadventure followed by a heart attack'. The foot symbolizing the damage of the pilgrim miles soon to be endured: the quest again. 'Delirium and visions' follow. Renchi twitched in his studio cell, the domesticity, to be out there, on the move, chasing the great matter, primed to register shifts and signs and portents. 'It was as if you were surrounded by a bright glow', Jung's nurse reported.

BROCKENHURST (NEW FOREST)

Coincidences are not coincidences but confirmations. Knowing that I was researching James Hinton, Victorian surgeon, friend of Sir William Gull, and C H Hinton, speculative philosopher, geometer (author of *What is the Fourth Dimension?*), their hyperactive namesake, Dr Brian Hinton of Dimbola Museum, sent me an extract from William Allingham's *Diary*, as published in 1907.

> *Monday, July 20.—Hot. Tennyson and Mrs T. on the steamer, I with them to Brockenhurst … We spoke of Swedenborg: T. says his Hell is more striking than his Heaven; praises Hinton's book on Man and Nature … T. shakes my hand warmly. It is always a real happiness to see him. I walk to Queen's Bower, its brooks and oak tree, back by pretty path …*

Whispers absorbed by the trees. Renchi's painting of Brockenhurst, a figure striking off into the forest, drawn forward by a globe of golden light, was a favourite of our children, who compared it with the diminishing perspective of Clarks famous shoe advertisement: 'Start-Rite—and they'll walk happily ever after'. The painting, from the 'Paths & Travellers' section, was also a flash-forward to watercolours from a late series of Van Gogh walks, the psychic outflow of *Painter on the Road to Tarascon*.

In the *Albion Island Vortex* catalogue, Renchi chose to publish the reproduction of a handwritten text glossing his Brockenhurst experience. How he was 'compelled to blast off into the unknown'. After attempting to engage with 'a friendly astral-looking girl', he tips out into 'a timeless region'. He tumbles into the village of Brockenhurst. And prepares for a few days in the New Forest. Having encountered a cottager who mistakes him for her son-in-law, 'lost in Israel', the evening of the shortest day closes around him. He feels 'a great rush of confidence' and clutches at 'an imaginary golden sphere'. Before standing naked among the conifers and bedding down for the night. There is a surge of stellar patterns and visitations, the pilgrim is grateful to be out in nature. He thinks he is entering Lyndhurst, when in reality he has described a 'complete circle' and arrived back, once more, at Brockenhurst. Where he re-encounters the girl from the train. And takes himself to church to give thanks.

CROW COUNTRY

In the scatter-patch of the Grey Wethers, up above the exposed teeth of Avebury, and outlined on a map scribbled on the back of a coded message, still to be broken, sent to the island of Gozo, Brian Catling confirmed the power of some lapidary visitation, significant but undefined, in his late-teenage years: out from London, away from the protective habits of the family house on Cobourg Road. In solitary retreat and meditation? Or, as has been suggested, in company with a new girlfriend? Whatever, the transformative event of early manhood and initiation happened in a location to which the group associated with the Whitechapel exhibition kept returning, in company with each other and alone. With new associates in mischief.

It was a period when necessary labours locked us into London, but when every purchased moment of freedom released the desire for centrifugal momentum. Centrifugal with the emphasis on *fugue*, mad travellers in hock to a dream of plurality.

The Catling seizure happened around the age of seventeen. It was some years later when I felt impelled to persuade three others—Renchi Bicknell and Tom Baker from the Hackney community, along with John Marks, a painter/filmmaker and mature student from the college in Walthamstow where I was teaching—to strike off, on Good Friday, 1971, down the Ridgeway, from Streatley-on-Thames to Avebury; before climbing Silbury Hill, exploring West Kennet long barrow, and making our way back to Hungerford by the Kennet and Avon Canal.

The unusual aspect of this tramp was that we didn't shoot any film. A Jonas Mekas/ Stan Brakhage progress of 8mm 'diary' episodes and (especially for Tom) lyrical, multi-superimposition 'Songs' were being produced much of the time for local and immediate screenings. Editing in camera. Outdated stock from a specialist stall in Kingsland Waste Market. A fractured record of place and persons. The films John Marks made out of

Walthamstow were travelling shots from train windows on his commutes to his mother's council flat near Tower Bridge. Or a motorized plunge down the shadowed white lanes of Cornwall. Tom Baker was withdrawing from industrial cinema after his successful collaboration with Mike Reeves, his relish for the saturated landscapes of Suffolk and the gallops across permitted military land. Renchi had directed *Mari's Girls*, a sure-fire art cinema support item, made in Cambridge with a crew of the best British technical talent, featuring a Magnum photographer as lighting cameraman and a support crew that included future Academy Award and Bafta winners. David Hurn. Chris Menges. Nic Knowland. And the sound-recordist Tony Jackson. A gloriously overqualified exercise. The print looked very good and was never seen. Musical rights to the Duke Ellington composition used in the ballet sequences could not be cleared. My own fortunate documentary apprenticeship shooting Allen Ginsberg for WDR (Cologne) had died with William Burroughs taking up Scientology in East Grinstead. And German TV moving on from the indulgent patronage of enthusiastic incompetents.

The Avebury walk was prophetic, a film without film. Without budget or commission. If anything, it was the abdication from all that, a clean severance from the business of business. If there was a necessary visionary record to be made, then it was better left to Derek Jarman and *A Journey to Avebury*. Online records claim this film for 1971. That is where it seems to belong. Counterculturalists stepping westward into a resistant landscape. An ancient migratory track for those Londoners who were no longer migrating. Closer research—thank you, Gareth Evans—dates Jarman's shoot to 1972 or 1973. Take your choice. The producer James Mackay opted for '73 and another 'edited in camera' exercise. Then he changed his mind, recalling Jarman's trip as being around July 1972. Location outranks time. That's why we keep returning. To reanimate a diminishing present by misinterpreting what we salvage from dust on our boots.

The motion of the ground beneath our feet summons C H Hinton's model for the fourth dimension: 'a system of lines nearly upright but sloping in different directions and supposedly all connected to a rigid framework'. Wind in dry grass. Lowering clouds tethered to the resonant hulk of Wayland's Smithy. 'Were such a thought adopted, we should have to imagine some stupendous whole, wherein all that *has ever come into being or will come co-exists*, which, passing slowly on, leaves in this flickering consciousness of ours, limited to a *narrow space* and a *single moment*, a tumultuous record of changes and vicissitudes that are but to us.'

Right from the start, from the moment when he receives his soul or touches his angel, up there above Avebury, on a spot that can never quite be identified, Catling was making preparation for the great work which would emerge as the three volumes of *The Vorrh*. What he had always suspected, and what this Wiltshire crow country seemed to confirm, was that *his masterpiece had already been written*. It was done, replete and mysterious, but lodged in the library of some other dimension. A monastery glimpsed in paintings by Bosch or Pieter Bruegel the Elder. A floating landscape, varnished and fading, but revived for Brian's novel, *The Hollow*, and teased through a remarkable succession of egg tempera paintings. His expeditions and performances were like rituals designed to offer refractions of the thing that was there, but still out of reach. An episode, an object, a face: they would be netted. And then, at the right moment, he would be primed to transcribe the furious dictation of material that was inevitable and now accessible. Every seizure shook him. He laughed out loud. He rode the terror, astonished at his own effrontery.

In *Necropathia*, Catling's suppressed first book, along with the smoky eros of London, there is a spectral record of this other place. The Swedenborgian life that is happening, or has happened, alongside the diurnal dream of where we think we are.

> *Thomas stood across the dark moving field … Phosphorescent sheepblurs scattered as he passed. Grass things made of leaves and twigs jumped and clicked …The sky suddenly turned in the corner of his eye, spinning him with it … Sheepblurs of the scattered stones, the morning mist of the Grey Wethers.*

What are the first words on the first page of Brian's first book? Lower case: 'towards the end, walking'.

Catling sketched a stuttering track across a landscape of mounds for *Muscat's Würm*, my own Albion Village Press publication from 1972. The arsenic-fed waste tip of Beckton Alp substituted for Silbury in a preliminary London mapping. Worlds within worlds. The way John Clare could only tolerate the immensity of London by seeing its river, bridges, and great churches as translations or transpositions of Peterborough and Whittlesey Mere. There were superimpositions and echoes in *Muscat's Würm* too: our Green Way, the Northern Sewage Outfall, absorbs the older English track to Avebury: 'with boundaries / stone walls, Ridgeways'. And quotations: 'proteins meet / and shape each other. We are the husk of this'.

Photographs become evidence of events dissolving into myth. Catling is pictured on the path to Beckton Alp, his back to the East London Cemetery, where the massed dead of the Bow Creek disaster are buried. He seems to be looking through the limits of these abandoned places, back towards a much brighter and older elsewhere. To Wiltshire visions and welcoming Sheppey mud.

Another photograph has us paused, mid-expedition, when Brian came back to Avebury, searching for something solid but unspecified. And finding, with relish, a dead crow. The crow is far from mute. It demands a prime position in the Whitechapel Gallery. Where Richard Long has laid out a painted spiral representing the now forbidden ascent of Silbury Hill. The crow is painted on the forehead of the vagrant, brought in from the streets, and treated by Catling's alchemist, another archetype (two parts Sir William Gull and one part Dr John Silence), in the film *Maggot Street*. A wet bird is drawn from the opened skull. And buried in the garden beneath a limestone pebble. Catling shape-shifts, taking multiple roles. Sometimes the rogue surgeon. Sometimes a man of the crowd, sprawling in pissy grass with the drinking schools of Mary Matfelon in Whitechapel. Waiting on hard charity outside the skeletal outline of the missing pilgrim church. The untrimmed version of this film makes yet another return to the stones of Avebury, to Silbury. It also tracks Catling, dark doctor, down the Sewage Outfall. What is becoming clear is that this repeated diagonal, tramped from Wick Lane, over Channelsea, to Beckton Alp, is a grooved remembrance of the procession from Streatley to Silbury. Prisoners of circumstance. It is like Albert Speer in Spandau, circling the dirt yard, and projecting an epic traverse of the continent, across Siberia to the Bering Strait.

What Matthew Shaw, who walked and filmed with Brian, has shared with me is a late Catling poem written after a trip to Avebury, while in the process of renewing sensory impressions for a novel originally called *Transi*. In which Wayland's Smithy and the Ridgeway play significant roles. With the poem Brian sent to Shaw, after their excursion, there were some explanatory notes. He speaks of a stone, 'ghosted in 1964, maybe found with I.S. in 1977, and looked again for in the future with you'.

Hinton's threads of time weave and tangle. That stone search was conducted a few years earlier than 1977. But Catling's original experience is sharper still: 'I was 17 in the wrong clothes in the snow above Avebury. Stumbled into it without knowing it was there or what it was. Went back a few years later with Knowledge and Sinclair to find the lost stone in the wood. Recently thought to seek again with you and then stopped, because who knows if I am ever going to get there. So decided to do it on page not on foot.'

This message sent in April again. The month of our group tramp. The gift that man had of doing it, deeper and truer, on the page. The stone we identified turned into a crow. A companion on all subsequent attempts, it became Bishop Odo, half-brother of William the Invader, bastard Duke of Normandy. It was carried fluttering on a pole down the line of zero longitude from Waltham Abbey to Greenwich, to Battle Abbey. In company with Andrew Kötting's ragged troop of drummers and mummers. And Claudia Barton as Edith Swan-Neck, mistress to Harold, commemorated in stone.

Grant Gee, in collaboration with Matthew Sweet, Brian Catling and Shirley Collins, made a film of mood and place and deep-memory. And sweeping drone shots. It was part of a project called *Crowlink*. At Charleston House. Shirley sang with her band. Brian read.

The world was happening at a distance. But the claggy ground was infected. The distance between what is and what can be presented was already pulling apart. In that month of April 1971, when we struck off down the ridged track through dull and empty fields towards Avebury, Second Lieutenant William Calley was sentenced to life imprisonment for unspeakable war crimes, at least twenty-two murders in Vietnam. Richard M Nixon ordered his removal from prison to serve his time under merciful house arrest. The United Kingdom lifted all restrictions on gold ownership with the repealing of a Gold Coins Exemption Order. On Sunday 11 April, as we trudged, foot-foundered along the canal to Hungerford, an asteroid estimated to be 650 feet in diameter passed within 140,000 miles of Earth, closer than the moon, but neither noticed nor recorded.

CAVE. SWORD. HEAD.

Around this time, having available studio space, Brian forged a sword, a thing of ominous power. He presented it to me, wrapped in felt, like something excavated by Joseph Beuys. A meaningful gift and obligation. The object, once gripped, spoke so persuasively that I disguised it in tatters of old sacking, tied the bundle with rope, and hid it away under a moulting sofa on which unsuspecting visitors to my book cave sometimes sat. Most of the energies in play across the desk of that room came from the not always comfortable dialogue between two unquiet objects: a whalebone box landed on me as a challenge from Steve Dilworth and the sword of his old friend and fellow Maidstone student, Brian Catling. The box was easier. It was a temporary lodger, only in residence for twenty-five years or so. And it acted like a battery, a provocation borrowed from the northern isles. (This story has been told several times, most recently in a publication from Tangerine Press. And a film by Andrew Kötting.) The sword was sharper in all senses. Even gagged in sacking it wanted to slash away at inadequate prose, at false sentiment. The box journeyed back to its source on the Isle of Harris. We buried it, with small ceremony, in the dunes. Before, in a gesture of wit and necessary conclusion, Dilworth gifted his sculpture to the Library of the Middle Temple in London. Where it sits in obscure state.

With Catling, I carried the sword to Montacute in Somerset. I had the notion that it could be earthed somewhere near the tower on the hill, close to the location where a golden cross was excavated, placed on a cart, to be dragged by twin white oxen, wherever they chose—which happened to be a sweeping diagonal to Waltham Abbey. Where a building and an institution grew up around the relic. Where the slaughtered Harold, or some part of him, was rumoured to have been buried. Where there was a fine Day of Judgment wall painting. And a marker for the imposed line of zero longitude. As if to prove that this future Cathedral of the Orbital Motorway was outside time, belonging neither to east or west, heaven or hell. Holding calm against the perpetual rage of traffic, an inadequate tourniquet for London's mortal wounds.

There could be no reversal, no exchange, sword for cross: too crude, too conceptual. The weapon came home to Hackney. Later, it would travel again, like the restless spine of a hermit saint, to the Outer Hebrides. To lodge for a while. Before moving on.

14

The place with which I now associate the sword was one it never risked: the Paviland Cave, burial site of the Red Lady of Gower. The cave was my own marker and I set out to locate it at around the age when Brian had his epiphany among the stones above Avebury. I failed, passing along the cliffs, right above the point of access without identifying it. When I took Brian back there for another outing among the crags and limestone pavements, we failed again. But failed much better, with a set of photographs as evidence, with texts of record, and the needlepoint astral engravings Catling inked for exhibition at the Whitechapel Gallery; a set he titled *Astronomer's Rib*. The withheld cave provoked a Catling poem.

> Under wind dome, fallen land wing
> cast among bone maps of haunted skins.
> Acid runs of ice compression blister
> life along white calcium wounds.
> Broken joints, snapped tendril star spines
> hooked through tundra gut. Ice shrinks
> back, hanging vegetation swamps upholstered
> rock. It is to be injected by broken needles
> into iron-clad profiles, sacred under
> time-bore moons.

Exposure to this unyielding geology amplified the obvious parallels between the reflexes required for the drawings and the pen-bitten linguistic spasms of the poems. With the walk as a form of originating performance. It was only, many years later, in company with Anna, who has a genius for these encounters, that we met the right magician. I was spidering across a cliff face, getting nowhere, when Anna fell into conversation with a woman who was about to revisit the cave. She agreed to guide me down the razor-rock ravine.

There were many further walks and boat adventures with Brian and serial expeditions with Renchi, but no journeys involving the three of us. And still the *presence* of that sword loomed. Renchi met a man in a lift who invited him to produce a draft script

15

for something called *Conan the Barbarian*. Sword and Sorcery: a coming genre for coming multiplexes. And the Hackney delivery of a suitcase of glossy novels by Robert E Howard of Cross Pines, Texas. With that special yellow transatlantic smell of drugstore alienation. Our shared fee didn't amount to much more than the free books. The steroidal Conan, dream hero of a sand-swallowing aspirant bodybuilder, made his debut in *The Phoenix and the Sword*, published in 1932. Typically, when this brush with Hollywood, twice removed, went nowhere, I recycled my engagement with Robert E Howard into a paranoid-apocalyptic riff on another Howard (Mr Hughes) in *Suicide Bridge*.

The scam back then, in the studio confusion after *Easy Rider*, a golden moment for hustlers, was that a named scriptwriter could trawl for a bunch of youthful wannabes, happy to labour for nuts, and extract anything exploitable to be handed over to a competent secretary who would knock out a version he (it was always a man) could deliver. The bound draft would, inevitably, be refined and reworked many times, before the ultimate director demanded that the entire process start again. We were so far down the food chain we couldn't even taste the crumbs. But we had a heap of new books to digest, before meeting to discuss tactics in a week or so.

I hammered out far too many pages of hectic nonsense, a forced marriage of the Cuchulain cycle of Yeats and the diaries of Che Guevara, and Renchi showed me the cover drawing he had made. But there was a sword and a cave. There was even a scene with the fabled weapon slashing at some throned corpse and releasing a murder of crows. This might have been the only glimmer that made it, ten years later, into the John Milius blockbuster featuring Arnold Schwarzenegger, engaged eco-warrior and governor of California.

Swords, crows, caves. Heads and stones. The Green Man's head is hacked off. He carries it away, a trophy fit for future exhibition. There will be another engagement the next year. And the one after. Brian Catling recognizes, in a chiselled mask, the outlines of a potential performance persona. In the tortured contortions of a weathered effigy encountered in a Scottish abbey, he identifies the lineaments of a borrowed other. An accidental self-portrait trapped in a stone mirror becomes the cover image for the *Albion Island Vortex* catalogue in 1974. The artist takes his sketchbook impressions as a stage towards calcification. One sentence in a monstrous fiction cooking throughout the span of his creative life. The stone face has been frozen mid-sentence. The tongue is too thick for the mouth.

Renchi Bicknell, undertaking a series of questing walks, tramps from Hackney to Swansea. Then out to the far west of Ireland, where he experiences his great epiphany, a shamanic vision in a former schoolhouse. Returning, many years later, he accepts the gift of a stone from a Buddhist Centre. In Glastonbury that stone is placed in his mouth as an aid to meditation and reverie. He falls asleep and swallows the unyielding charm. Stone sucking, humoured by Beckett, is an ancient rite. The stutter of the pebble in the mouth calls up Catling, in performance, tapping and summoning against the plate glass of the Serpentine Gallery. Watchers watched. The figure at the window is knocking for entry. The exhibition is everywhere.

The first artworks of Steve Dilworth that I am shown at his studio in Cheltenham, after Brian has brokered a meeting, are crows, shot in the field and pressed flat between sheets of leaking glass. The shapes. The texture. The smell. Stone into feather. Feather to bone. Shamanic flight from cave to dome. Eternal returns. 'For ADORATION', as Christopher Smart wrote, 'all the paths / Of grace are open ... And all the rays of glory beam'.

TARNISHED ANGELS

On the morning of the summer solstice in 2023, Renchi was waiting in Greenwich, his back to the brass rule of zero longitude, resting between worlds. Meeting for a day's walk down an approximation of the meridian line, after passing under the Thames, we aimed to share memories and inspirations as a way of preparing for the projected but still untitled exhibition at Swedenborg House in October. What was unspoken but increasingly obvious was that the London history of the Swedish mystic, his mysterious afterimage, offered a third voice to our conversation. Advancing along a theoretical and imposed corridor, conferring a spurious dignity on older qualities that had always been active on Greenwich Hill, we were outside time and open to the prompts of enigmatic angels.

Long London, a serial work-in-progress by Alan Moore, acknowledged the inspiration of both Catling and Michael Moorcock. It was positioned as part of a lineage that could very easily be diverted through Swedenborg House. The page-turning narrative was replete with covert and familiar London myths and personalities, Moore's angels of oblivion. But the shine really derives from a contemporary iteration of that recurring metaphor of a doubled city. Like so many others. The London that is and was and will be. The subterranea of *The Anubis Gates* by Tim Powers, a book that Catling loved. *The City & The City* by China Miéville. Moorcock's great memory feats in his multiverse. And the specific location he nominates for *The Whispering Swarm* as a passage into a beckoning and seductive past. A past that is richer and stranger than our diminished present. Alan Moore makes his eternal and dangerously psychotropic London accessible through the handling of minute particulars and the velocity of free-flowing language seizures. A tidal wave of demonic and angelic forces sweeping through the sites that are always being invoked. Close to the Cannon Street Road/Cable Street crossroads, that vampire's burial pit, Moore's 'innocent' narrator witnesses a tribunal of the undead, heads in bottles—like Catling's excited encounter with a child Cyclops in the Hunterian Museum. One of the elder spirits is Swedenborg. Perched and channelled a few yards from his burial place, the Prophet in his 'lucent bulb' affirms his non-identity as an angel unfettered by the dull gravity of time. Time is a wave motion, a whimsy, the interplay of Hinton's harvest of dancing lines in some forgotten room, but place is a constant, brushed and bruised by the transit of those drawn to honour alignments of geology, architecture and accident.

On such a benign morning, the park is replete, the tourist packs absorbed and indulged by the dignity of the trees. The blessings of shade and survival. The energy stream, down the broad avenue from All Saints' Church on Blackheath to Wolfe's memorial obelisk (half-man, half-stone), is both radiance and reality. The brazen meridian line is an imposed fiction. A photo opportunity. Zero longitude, on this day of revelations, is like one of those teasing tales put out by occult theorists, linking John Dee, Hawksmoor, William Blake and a fraternity of graphic novel immortals: a conspiracy of nominated spectres, lined up for encounters on a trudge across an endlessly improved and amended topography. Renchi, in recalling a walk around the acoustic footprints of the M25, the orbital motorway, starting at this place, in Greenwich as ever, said: 'Perhaps that circuit put a gentle seal on constant dreams I had, after leaving London, that all linked together in a parallel dreaming London.'

Thanks to the imagined agency of Swedenborg, the timeless corridor we were tramping, was the cloth of that dreaming. Beyond and alongside the diversions, the negotiated flyovers, the motorway bridges over choked canals, the paper-pulp yards with forklift trucks, the confident but unreliable guides lounging on fences, was a realized and invaded fantasy of the plural city, the post-temporal memory maze conjured by Moore and Moorcock, and animated by Catling. Who always seemed like one of its inhabitants. Not so much a historian of his time as an old soul reaching out to recall extraordinary events from a mythical elsewhere. In fact, by no longer being available at a single location at any one time, Brian seemed to be everywhere. Making his contribution to our solstice dialogue and helping to plot the elements to be displayed at Swedenborg House.

We do not regret the magnificent but out-of-service lifts at the mouth of the foot tunnel. That is our present condition. I do summon Andrew Kötting's troop of mummers, heading in the other direction under the Thames, and joining in with the songs of a busker. The Edith pilgrimage, after pausing at Wolfe's memorial for a set of photographs by Anonymous Bosch, moved south through Blackheath, honouring the desire line we will soon lose as we adjust to catch up with zero longitude. This morning, our backs to the obelisk, seeing how the dragons' teeth of Docklands have obliterated traces of the energy line surging on towards Nicholas Hawksmoor's Limehouse church, and then turning to take a closer look at the shrapnel-scarred surface of the stone, I realize why one of the walls at the Whitechapel Gallery was consigned to the Wolf. Crow was obvious. Owl guided us down a green tunnel out of Glastonbury, when I walked with Brian to Cadbury Castle. Goat was the white mask I wore on the John Clare walk from Epping Forest to Helpston for Kötting's film, *By Our Selves*. Now Wolf was a mystery solved: it was Wolfe, not Wolf. A savage leap across the river, and across the western spread of the city: a wolf line disclosed! Pyschogeographic lycanthropy. The body of the dead hero of Quebec was repatriated, unlike the uncounted millions of foot soldiers from the trenches of the First War; the ghosts who troop, forlorn and undone, across London Bridge in Eliot's *The Waste Land*. General Wolfe, it seems, introduced Freemasonry into North America. They buried him, with due ceremony, in St Alfege, Hawksmoor's Greenwich church. 'Old enchantments, let them sleep'.

We could, such is the magic of this morning, almost a parting of the sea, describe every stage, every encounter: crows on the beach beside the Waterman's Arms. Which waterman, whose arms? No time for an adequate response to the revamped music hall pub where Daniel Farson charmed the curdling comedy of his vanished era: Francis Bacon and William Burroughs, Kim Philby and Stephen Ward, Sinatra and Clint Eastwood. The Kray Twins prowling with open paws. All the muted ghosts. The hour of the wolves.

Staying true to unravelling and challenging memories, while pushing on towards a deeper engagement with Pole Hill, we emerge from the pleasantly rewilded park around the dock where the pirate fleet of the East India Company unloaded their spoils. We advance into a shiver of recognition over the 'crimes' of our own ancestors, the risks and rewards of a different world vision. Renchi is stopped by lettering heritaged on 'rescued' industrial buildings. They gesture towards boasting of a mistaken past as a way of permitting crimes, new developments, spaces suitable for investors and the right sort of appropriate artist. THAMES IRONWORKS has a running subtitle: NOT THE END OF THE STORY. But nothing shouts as loud as MATHERS WHALE OIL EXTRACTION. It was James Mather who bought Cook's *Endeavour* and converted her into a troop ship, transporting redcoats across the Atlantic to put down the colonial uprising. Another vessel in Mather's fleet carried convicts to Australia.

Renchi's paternal ancestor, Elhanan Bicknell, was the great whale oil magnate of the Surrey shore, with his boiling vats stinking out Bugsby's Marshes and his refined oil bathing London in soft and painterly illumination. Elhanan, buried in West Norwood, was a friend of Ruskin and a patron of Turner. More recently, Renchi has discovered that his mother's Scottish family traded opium out of Shanghai. 'It was not so bad', Renchi said, 'they started as bankers'. My Scottish great-grandfather, Arthur Sinclair, a coffee planter and land surveyor, chose the land used for the Rio Perené plantations of the Peruvian Corporation of London.

Being here, hard against the facts of the Thames and the mouth of Bow Creek and the Lea, makes the London of those venturers explicit and tangible. We are also well aware of Jem Finer's assault on time by way of his 1000-year composition sounding around the shelves of bowls behind the locked doors of the Trinity Buoy lighthouse. I came ashore at this point from Edith the Swan Pedalo, on a voyage from Hastings to Hackney undertaken with Andrew Kötting. Jem would be providing the music tracks for that one too. But the loudest absence, there and not there, secure behind the bolted lighthouse door, was Catling. He was one of the earliest artists given access to the site. It was a struggle, as he confessed, to find the story he wanted to tell. Until he impersonated and absorbed a few of the ghosts of the building's history. The great journey for visitors was to locate the place. And to get away.

Renchi was seduced by a chalked board offering a tropical jungle's bounty of pressed fruits and grains, energy-supplying drinks. While he was luxuriating in the difficulties of choice, a brisk custodian of the service counter announced that none of them were available. The notice was pure fiction, an aspiration. Off-duty police officers glugged their coffees and colas. Renchi challenged the decision, wondering why the board was kept on display. Not grasping that it went with the territory. It was heritage. In the ledger, in the promotional material, but not actually *here*.

Rising on four spindles, part support, part torture, was a flying warrior. A tarnished angel, with shaven skull pierced with arrows, and outstretched wings. A naked figure, launched and floating, but unable to flutter and escape from the mechanism that cranked her into life. This was a piece by the blacksmith/sculptor Andrew Baldwin. He titled it: *The Angel*. It was not climbing or falling. But held in abeyance, a ripple of potential, like the figure of Dr Faustus that Renchi painted in flight over Oxford. This panel from his *Michael & Mary Dreaming* responds to a journey, as he glosses it, 'from Streatley along the Ridgeway by Crowhole Bottom (Devil's Punchbowl) to the White Horse, Uffington'. Vision. Ascent. Aspiration. When Phillida Gili illustrated *Archie & The Strict Baptists*, the story John Betjeman wrote for his children, with the family living at Uffington, she depicts Archie, Betjeman's teddy bear, with brown paper wings, launching himself from the crest of the downs and taking to the air. The furred aviator glides through 'gathering darkness', bravely attempting to conflate deep myth with the rigours of plain-spoken nonconformist faith. Witch-like, riding on a hedgehog, the bear digs up molehills, 'which, he considered, were the graves of baby Druids'.

Shamanic flight was a steady topic laced through our solstice walk and through the original Whitechapel exhibition: an imagined passage between the triangle of mounds described in my 1994 novel, *Radon Daughters*. The only escape from the breakdown of radioactive gas and an occulted geometry being the generous agreement of three persons to make simultaneous witness at dawn on the shortest day of the year. Renchi Bicknell ascended the Castle Mound in Cambridge. 'I am asking whether people make the rounds of the group of stone circles to celebrate the round of the seasons', he wrote. Brian Catling crawled up the spiral of the Castle Mound in Oxford. 'This is my site at dawn, any idea of the others contacting me along straight lines of intention is erased by the slumped centrifuge of the place. The brittle triangulation of our mutual awareness is strained and given up against now ... To invent gravity and grip purpose I walk a continual wheel along the crown of the mound, the stiff frozen grass cracking under the stumbling insistence of the circulatory mantra ... The trampled perimeter has attracted the sun. Hours have been eaten by repetition. The feast giving energy to quietly open the vision and leave the husk of intension to fade in the first accent of morning wind. Now I can approach the centre.'

Marc Atkins, the photographer, was deputed to attempt the impossible task of capturing the missing Whitechapel Mound that once gloried in its tree-crowned elevation beside the hulk of the Royal London Hospital. He tried to make a spooky print of the small globe on the remaining sepulchre in Mary Matfelon Park. A shape against which, in vagrant disguise, Catling had lain with a sprawled and welcoming drinking school, dutifully outside the skeleton of the demolished church.

The closing Atkins shutter snapped at ghosts. And conjured the figure of Bladud of Bath, swine-keeper and magician. Founder of a school of magic. English Icarus. Bladud flapped his way to our city, wings melted by risk, and fell from the dome of the Temple of Apollo on Ludgate Hill: the future St Paul's, where Alan Moore and Catling competed to pilot the raft of legends into our own times.

And afterwarde a Fetherham he dight
To flye with wynges, as he could best discerne
About the ayre nothyng hym to werne
He flyed on high to the temple Apolyne
And ther brake his neck, for al his great doctrine.

Shamanic flight achieved, without lifting our dusty shoes an inch for the trail, without a pause over many miles, beyond water breaks and the chill of stolen interludes in off-highway superstores, we found ourselves back at the start of a fifty-year project. At the conclusion of a huge V walked into the London landscape for the opening movement of *Lights Out for the Territory*: Abney Park to Greenwich University (in Woolwich) to Chingford Mount. Recording graffiti and the noise on walls. Now Chingford Mount is a welcoming oasis in the merciless heat at the end of the afternoon.

Immediately on our right, as we enter the garden of sleepers, is the decapitated and grounded angel with a stump of a neck, the one I asked Atkins to photograph when we arrived here in the wake of a Kray funeral. The aspect that caught my eye back then—as you can see in the paperback edition of *Lights Out*—is the angel's split head. The head rests on a step of the memorial obelisk. The two portions of the skull have been separated in such a way as to reveal a black triangle, the model of the conceptual walk. That head has now disappeared, along with the suggested triangulation.

We rest on a bench under the cooling spread of an oak. Zero longitude fizzes and sparks at the end of the main avenue, cutting through the graves of the Kray Twins, a family enclosure, once heavy with floral tributes from associates, courtiers and tame celebrities.

Pole Hill is one final push through a modest suburban labyrinth of highly polished motors and generic villas. A man with unequal eyes and a rich blue shirt offers directions—which I accept, unconditionally, and Renchi prefers to challenge by demanding confirmation from every person we meet. None of whom know anything of the iconic Hill.

The golden hour ascent through a gap in the scrub is a delightful conclusion, lifting the sense of teasing and unresolved consequence from our previous visits. Obelisk and triangulation point stand in a clearing; a shady grove favoured now by lycra cyclists who drink from their water bottles and chatter of work and recreation, before swooping on downhill.

A lowering sun sends red-gold shafts through the shivering green. There is a vulva-shaped wound or excavation in a tree. Renchi inspects this votive shelf, a sort of cave of curiosities. Inside is a pair of aviator spectacles with red glass, lacking one lens, and a bridge made from a golden bee. There is a smoothed section of brick carried from the

Thames shore at Amsterdam Avenue—our contribution. It has a single proud letter D: an invocation of Brian DAVID Catling? But the capitalized letter in the darkness of its small wooden cave, or squirrels' den, is also a diagrammatic bow shaped from a spine. And the motif of the star chain often seen in the painter's early work. More than this, Renchi points out a threaded profile of Catling in the spidery traces left by some animal or insect. Something spectral and disturbing like Brian's print of 'Edgar's mirror' from his visit to Poe Park in the Bronx.

Perched on the obelisk with its nod to TE Lawrence and his Pole Hill writing hut, Renchi takes out his watercolours and begins to paint the scene. Starting with the dark gash of the wound in the tree, he works outwards to dress the tangle and weave of the surrounding glade. He notices, in the coarse skin of the bark, above a prominent knot, the perfect outline of an alerted wolf's head. The creature stares back down the brass rule, the gunsight on the lid of the triangulation plinth, at the other Wolfe, the carved name on the marker at the crest of Greenwich Hill.

In 2008, Renchi published an illustrated chapbook, *A Pilgrim's Progress & Further Relations*, in which he described fragmented elements of an 'Archetypal journey', made by way of epic walks and the inspiration of *Dark Figures in the Desired Country* by Gerda S Norvig. 'This has been my bible'. He learnt to make etchings on copper, in honour of Blake and his extraction of an essential thread from Bunyan. When Renchi comes to the section called 'At the Interpreter's House', he slides from a day spent at the Rollright Circle to 'a wooded ditch where a great Beech tree has fallen across the path'. Two giant figures, cut from newspapers and magazines, have been hung in the wind. Then offered as sacrifices to what Renchi calls 'WOLF FIRE'. The fire of dancing light that runs out of this grove and away across the city. 'Wolf fire', Renchi writes, emanates from 'flames of transformation'.

I wander off on a brief tour of inspection, down the wooded slope. I think we have closed on a pastoral English translation of *The Vorrh*. A deceptively quiet staging post on the fringes of Epping Forest, the Lea Valley, the asylums, the cemeteries and orbital motorway. Catling weaponized the primal forest, his colonists were absorbed into the woods. Sustenance for the immortal trees. After the carving and testing of a bow, at the opening of the great *Vorrh* sequence, that trilogy is revealed as a history of the banished of Eden. On Pole Hill, twilight is 'tasting' the air. Like Renchi, watching his starlings on the Somerset Levels at dawn and dusk, Catling was attentive to the prophetic messaging of all life forms. 'Swallows darted and looped in the invisible fields of rising insects, restless arrowheads spinning in the amber sunlight. One moment, black silhouette, Iron Age. The next, tilting to catch the sun, flashing deep orange, Bronze Age. Dipping and rotating in giddying time: Iron Age, Bronze Age, Iron Age.'

The bow shape, the raised D on the salvaged, tide-returned brick, hidden in the tree, is a signature for the equal and opposite forces at play in *The Vorrh*. And of our own attempt to move forward, to push on in blissful ignorance, by trespassing in the forests of the past. Heraclitus used the bow as an example of an instrument activated by being pulled in two directions at once. 'The arrow lets itself go', Catling wrote. He said that its arc was made 'in advance of my foreseen journey into the depth of the forest, but it will never be my guide'. And so that book, with all its histories and hauntings, has to happen between the moment of release and the coming to earth. The messenger has permission to 'begin to walk into the inevitable'.

Catling's character, Tsungali, has been summoned. He cradles a Lee-Enfield rifle. He watches and waits on the dying of the sun. Impressions of Africa fuse with the fabulous reality of this landscape, the new estates made from the old Enfield armament factories are right below us. Ponders End, on the other side of the reservoirs, down an unyielding road into an industrial estate is where Elhanan Bicknell attended a school founded by his father. And where he grew up, before making his way to the Thames and the world ocean. History is like Catling's favoured symbol, the ouroboros, a snake eating its own tail. Its hauntings can never disappear into anything other than themselves. Lessons are revealed, lost, and revealed again. We continue. Plotting the next journey, another dream.

So many words deriving from a finite number of steps. Renchi, returned to Glastonbury from London, needed just 14.

> *Not random, not ruled,*
> *We walk the sun blaze river*
> *Joining Wolfe to wolf.*

Photograph by Anonymous Bosch

RIDGEWAY REVISIT

Renchi Bicknell

Along the Ridgeway, despite the attraction of the gorse and scattered bridestones, in the first 20 miles I already feel disquieted by the very few animals. I see a single kite, a few skylarks hovering above a sea of rape, and one crow flapping along an industrial expanse of wheat—its field borders bleeding right up to the path—itself runnelled and rutted by bikes and tractors and walkers like me.

I pass a pig farm with a Union Jack flying where sows and piglets are scuffling between their military-styled hooped bunkers. It feels more like a factory farm than its self-proclaimed free-range status, but it is at least a gathering of animals and has even attracted more crows and magpies to the coronation party I thought I was avoiding.

At dusk a silent white wide-eyed barn owl flies straight towards me.

At Wayland's Smithy the sun is lowering behind the great guardian beech trees. I rest and talk with a pagan man and boy who have an altar of candles in the entrance to the burial mound. Their full moon ceremony involves cider and Norse songs from Spotify. I feel cheerful and laughing as the man keeps saying 'You are bloody amazing for a man of your age to walk 20 miles from Avebury', though he and I know I have another 20 miles to go.

A red moon rising is my sign to stumble out beside Whitehorse Hill into deep night.

Like one of the Hollow Men I mirror the spiritless silence, the lack of scuffling foxes and badgers. This night survives in her own negative space, and all the time the full moon reminder of the full moon this same sixth of May three years ago when my son Ivan died at 50 years of age. I sense he would understand why I have resorted to the extra light of my head torch to keep my balance over the deceptive grooves and ridges.

I am conscious I am repeating a night walk my father made with his famous Alpine photographer friend Basil Goodfellow in the 1930s. They would have been heading like me toward the sunrise.

> Ratcheting the sun
> 95,000 chalk steps
> I walk East all night.

Damp with sweat, I unfold a map to confirm I am opposite the Devil's Punchbowl at Crowhole Bottom.

> I walk and wonder
> Where is my diversity
> In this emptiness.

I rest on a plank across a ditch, and in the early hours I am drawn towards a group of caravans alight with human arguments at 4 am, but continue on a white concrete road at a tangent, the moon dipping in and out of cloud and the sun starting to filter upward light.

Rain as predicted is building up along a long tarmac trek into Streatley. Only 17 syllables remaining—

> Full moon walk all night
> I follow a sad furrow
> Of the Silent Spring.

POLE HILL

Carol Williams

I first saw Renchi Bicknell's *Pole Hill* more than fifty years ago. I think it was at his house in Hackney, where I might have stopped in with Iain and Anna who lived nearby. From across the room it was a giant leaf, photosynthesizing under a blue sky, birds hovering.

Up close, it wasn't a leaf but a hillside. Beings, human or angelic, are just reaching the top. Where two dolmens are. Lower down, other entities of a dark and sinister type scrabble upwards. The written words 'Pole Hill' nearly eclipse one of the summiting figures and make the painting a map. There's a distant shore. The azure sky behind the apparent leaf is actually only a sliver of blue, made radiant by shining through shadows.

I did not know what it was about the painting, or note-taking, that called to me. Only that it did. It showed me what I already knew, but which lately my life had tried to deny. That particular landscapes (perhaps all of them) are alive with eventualities: happening now or in the past or still to come. One only has to see them, as Renchi had. I felt at once that, if I ever forgot this, the painting would remind me.

Uncharacteristically, since I had nowhere of my own to live, had been a wandering Jew since leaving London aged thirteen, no walls to hang anything on, no money (perhaps I could save some up?), I asked Renchi if I could buy it. He said that he would think about it. I got his answer in a couple of weeks. Which was 'yes'. But I would have to wait. The painting was to hang at an exhibition of the work of all the interconnected friends, only some of whom I knew, at the Whitechapel Gallery. Its price was that I

must meditate deeply upon *something* and send him the result. The price seemed high, but I would save up: perhaps pay in instalments.

I agreed to both conditions with gratitude but without much hope. I would miss the Whitechapel exhibition since I was moving from England to somewhere remote in Australia to further a relationship with an apple farmer I had met in America. Nevertheless, *Pole Hill* has followed me ever since.

The apple farmer and I did not last long in Australia. After a Lear-like struggle over the division of the family orchard, we came to Sag Harbor, New York, then a rundown village on a distant shore. A Norwegian friend, who had inherited a fishing cabin there from his hitherto unknown father, offered it to us rent free if we added an addition while we sorted ourselves out. (He himself was sorting out in New York City having been beaten up by Sag Harbor police looking for someone else's drugs.)

More than a year later, and after the birth of our first son, a battered parcel arrived. It had followed me, very slowly, covered in stamps and customs forms, from England to the Blue Mountains of Australia, then from Australia to Sag Harbor. Inside was *Pole Hill*, unscathed.

Our three children grew up in different houses, all in Sag Harbor, with the painting always letting in light and giving coordinates to wherever we were. The house we lived in longest had a long backyard. That yard was leaf-like in shape and headed downhill to a tidal creek, the sea and sky: a reversed direction *Pole Hill*. I turned the yard into a kind of garden, occasionally covered in water or ravaged by deer, and eventually wrote a how-to gardening book, rooted there. I sent it to Renchi, but never felt I had fully paid up.

I have a grandson now, Isaac. He and his parents live in Philadelphia. I go there sometimes to help with his care while his parents are at work. On a recent visit tiny Isaac started daycare and his mother—my daughter Kari—and I slipped out for an hour to the crazily displayed and impossibly rich Barnes Collection to get a glimpse of art.

Rain came down in dark curtains, sometimes driven sideways by strong winds. We saw the collection backwards, from the top floor down, and had whole rooms to ourselves. '*Pole Hill!*' said hitherto silent Kari—pointing to a painting hung almost invisibly over a tall doorway. There was the hill slanting towards the sky. A person or a body lies on the slope: perhaps a crucified god or just a struggling human. Two others stand serene at the summit. Off to the side, other people are gardening in the distance, unaware. We could not read the tiny label on the frame above the door. Soutine we guessed. (Alfred Barnes had collected him when no one else would.) Another wandering Jew had got inside the landscape and our souls. I hope Renchi will visit the painting one day and find a brother.

When I heard about the impending Whitechapel revival exhibition, I offered to wrap *Pole Hill* and post it back to London. Or even deliver it personally in a suitcase. On a closer look, neither plan seemed likely to work. Iain suggested I write something instead. So here is another installment of a debt that I'll never completely pay, but instead pass on.

CUTS FOR BRIAN CATLING

Allen Fisher

1

I just missed you in the crypt at Canterbury
your postcard notes, hello, just missed you
I think you were teaching nearby

The object of embrace   the luminous solar particles
axioms of the primal cosmic force enter
oscillating coercions, an energy of creative organs
balance of the inner alchemy where care must be
earthly substance ascending breath or swallow
the danger evidence I have marshalled
the intention arbitrarily linked
the passive made up of passages from the *Tao-te Ching*
the atomic structure think it not fabricate these alpha particles
common ancient esoteric wisdom
resonates with the alchemy inanimate nature of conjunction
living beings working requires a balance of both poles a beta ray
brushing against particles remain female or if a male
there is a little constricting unbroken skin
moves contracting, breathing from entering

the animal the primal garments tissue directly
soul encompasses the point still valued
by the presence contains the limitless overflowing
sleep second passage trance homiletical explication
permanent absence implication dynamic
against it the emanation the body or if it does
all with choicest seed the precautions one or other taboos
which are bride of the soul like the naked hidden matters
concern which you cannot dispute the mouth of the angel
unpattern procreation in the unites face to face
then the body becomes one

2
I just missed you as you left the Hokusai show
at the British Museum in December

Research in the verse dwelling burning
derived from providential action
a sacrifice for the imaged composed of the same
pestilence   the imaginal form related
the probability cause a possible material
deduces that elements numerically equal to twenty-two
spontaneously radioactive the experience inasmuch
tram-beamed explication radioactive threads together on the basis
of numerical active until they receive a nuclear reaction
speaks to them in the image in passing espoused
occurring in nature a combination object of fallen
radiation in a fixed revelatory encounter with the drought
active intellect by night and threatened illumination
essential survey of theophany the form of an angelophany
precisely in this essential determination

remain unknown and inaccessible the angelic epiphany
depiction of prophetic experience inflated vanity
active intelligence grovelling adulation proximity, its solitude
the angel extension of the old person whose annunciation
corresponds to which he announces herself
opens itself to the transconscience on the way of return
the bondage of the physical cosmos is a mirror image of the soul
awakening to itself and its visualization
the imaginal form comprised within the prism
through which declaimed the vehicle

3
and then again missed you at the Royal Academy
showing when the ghost of your flea recurred with
the armament from another desert atrocity

the erotic images of the Song cause radiation
approach findings no credible historical analysis
limited as they emerge injuries to the public
allegorization of the industry personnel
exegesis of the radioactive nature of material shipment
historical allegory preserved exemplified by the regulations
the background of the tendency provided by ray
inspired particles the relationship between alpha rays
nucleus of the helium safely in the transport materials
derived from interstate rail, road, air, water, something as
thin as truck, bus, auto, ocean, river barge, railcar,
postal shipments postal conspicuous jurisdiction
interpretation of this service formerly derivation
the allegorical apocalypse in interstate or foreign subject
to control between the philosophical with respect to the jurisdiction

affinity between safety and economic conception
of the union of the soul and radioactive jurisdiction
over allegorical depiction of the active intellect
engender aeronautics by contrast exercise
the economic aspects by the face that materials
transport of this claim operating allegorical
depiction of the soul's control of sources
atomic energy act allegorical interpretation of the Song

4
tripped on your steel saints spewing lead blood
at Atlantis and never recovered
from this never recovered

giving to illumine the mystery of the good crops
in the world the expression among the reindeer
a transposition some of the materials declared
imagined vision to the angry of concealment
since protection a description of island
reasonable to assume intellect the objective correlate
the food grow made of twenty-two letters of scarcity
the final sequence of ideas a stream of the
prophetic anthropos responsible the course of affirmed
calamities branded angel of the same sequence
a long and severe striking similarity secretly
philosophy cultivated by Avicenna wisdom
in the memory implies correlation the being
significance of the angel the simple without distortion
empty expression a survival dominated apotheosis
of living features to the degree of experience
the integration of all its powers anticipates its own totality

leads one beyond an angelic guide, synchronism
composed of the letters the imagination thus serves
rendered visible and the ineffable the soul merges

5

broken glass and worn electric wiring at the Air Gallery
puts me in the frame of attention and then
you connect the electric wires

the idea the skin body three souls outside the bones
exercised to prevent radioactive substance
a real article beta rays   in comparison external soul
vulnerable and immortal houses in view
on various occasions particles external soul
to be smaller than the alpha hardly contradict
the sacred seriously believes restores damage to the skin
external object the moment entering he will let
any stranger fraught touches his inmost life
a human suspicious and reserved fetches
a piece the confinement lives in a fixed sum of
assassination iron represents his person, the clipping
critical time spittle remnants of fancies destruction
conceal or destroy

6

I entered the loft
wax dripping from illuminated
dull light bulbs held there by vulnerable wires
held there by the waxed air and the burning

an idea that evolved in later Taoism

an interplay of complementary response generosity
and an inflexibility of order
breath descending from the brain or heart specific
meagre but it is enough to show interstate highway
of radioactive materials transmitting 14 reactors with
another 12 in transport exceeding wisdom
shared and expressed materials are not permitted
the creative process one pole this prohibition
the grain of being, destined designs by land routes
the balance of the city agreements challenged by
breathing in through contraction a laboratory
imaginally expressed materials extending light
the line transferred valence is not affected
restrictiveness of the adopted vessel
problems experienced to conform to its citizens
exposition subject to the planted to all corners
of the truck travels contemplate the secret of
the heavily used with spirals in this ornament
to you true it would measure leverage, or question,
for they are taken from everywhere you went
this world is a shadow background radiation
everything under construction of the window
search reactors and standing in peace laboratory

7
when I met you in Dursley
a cabbage leaf dropped over my head
in the octagonal arena you crept through
over feathers over cabbage

observed by the living world the word as

his life, the question the construct and
the sought-for to effect this we must the nature
coincidence of language and embodiment
erotically encountered to guard against a garbing
that opens   understand from this perspective
the other attribute that may be thought
commending guarded against the silence
one contemporary explains the processes of
the planning produced the silence marking that place
behind the phenomena such silence is not to be confused
of life itself unvocalized voice of the poem means
he thinks the effort to listen to language in the
inside which moves more than any other feature of the
peculiar difficulty of reading moves him utilizes
inside the human an animal like a landscape
of the soul in the mode of pain pleasure and
by its absence inhabits ecstasy only by erasing itself
the burden the poet bears to break language
health and safety the soul blinds the eye that sees
to hear with the the soul the silence that silences the tongue
to secure language harnessing of carnal desire
the form of prohibition apprehension of imaginal body
intended mirror images of the invisible presence or the return
ideal of visual contemplation rested on radiation
of the sensory world in images of an erotic intimacy
links the desire to give suffered viscous circle of
willing rather than the abolition of the reflecting

8
in the kitchen at Ruskin with Marina Abramović
we felt her insistence and insistence

before the trail down-pace to the Pitt Rivers
where she lay there on bones where
she lay there

soul may be palpable flesh since in some place of security
magic as alchemy language alone events in the hair
transformation this need remains to show the formations
of the poetic that provides the means most people
the wholly other garbed in the room cloud enclosure of infinity
to the finitude of poiesis a form of radioactive extending
the horizon of beneficial effect the silence
of the clamour writer has astutely combat generation
poetic place   treatment of imaginary danger its own contours
with mere quiet needs to be heard as food
a voice estranged from language demanding and painful
electricity in danger disappear into air and light iron
which he delivers the absolute must keep it in his house
unspeakable the invisible abnegating self to the other
unrepresentable with the blindness transported as wastes
to the credo envisioning the ineffable as well as emergency
of the physical body only the heart paradoxical inversion
purging the mind of abstinence the intensity of interest
upon an audacious figuration meaning with the ascetic
articulate will to live

9
when I was with you at my reading with Vahni Capildeo
when you identified my ears in a shift from the norm

more moderate computation of materials
need of radioactive souls is always outside the peaceful

chemicals responding the same moment release of the
exploding atom on the nuclear avoid concluding
make stable elements animal or plant are said to be power
are referred thought naturally set terms affirm his cobalt
bombarded by grounds for respecting kinds of radioactive
nature each emitting materials life is bound up with
the three kinds of the last degree of the way places
into the secret in all that of materials resided processes
without discovering in the end hazardous matter
result of accident substances are finally dumped
risk of accident at the most trifling relics of endangers
those of his hair and nails his food his very name
anxiously careful to transportation

10
when with Aram and Iain we reeled at the Hayward
and sat in cool air to avoid the traffic
of the South Bank

certainly in the case of active materials
the matter is even more monolithic the body damage
thus the perspective on the issues being serious
as light is a form of gamma information
the Song with a tendency toward power of the transport
the result of the light has to be seen with their
any radioactivity building to portray damage
internal striking the allegorical localized damage
an intensified apocalyptic messianism
earth water and lead the exegetical tenet of the
responsibility understanding of the polemical stance
a posture vessel to designate calling philosophical

substantial shipments interpretation of the land safety
formed in erotic interpretation of the Song
jurisdiction valid with ecstatic intensity
in erotic dialogue between the soul and as amended

WEIRD APPETITES:
REVISITING THE GOURMET

Victor Rees

At lunch an angel said to me that I should not
pander too much to my stomach.
—Emanuel Swedenborg

A churchyard in London's East End. A group of homeless men have gathered, waiting with exhausted eyes to be granted access to the crypt where they know they'll receive much-needed food and shelter. Among them is an unknown figure, a man who clearly does not belong. He is tall and bulky, wielding a cane that doubles as a handle for the butterfly net he keeps in his satchel. Hidden beneath his coat is an assortment of pots, knives, and other cooking utensils that have been strapped to his body. A colander between his shoulder blades gives him a hunchbacked profile, making him appear like a grotesque Mr Punch, or a character in a Bruegel painting—a fool swaddled in cutlery. This stranger is evidently not homeless like the rest—quite the opposite. He is a cut-glass aristocrat with enough money to employ a chauffeur, whom he has instructed to keep away from the church until morning. Nor is he slumming with the destitute as a cryptic form of performance art, like the chameleonic Mr Oscar in Leos Carax's *Holy Motors*, who takes on the role of a sewer-dwelling tramp as one of many identities over the course of his working day. The man waiting in the churchyard has joined the homeless in the shared desire of satiating his hunger, though his is a craving unlike any other—for he is here to capture, cook and eat a ghost.

Michael Whyte's television drama *The Gourmet*, with a screenplay by Nobel Prize-winning author Kazuo Ishiguro, aired on Channel 4 in 1986. For decades it was an inaccessible work, existing only as a spectral recollection to those who had seen it going out live. The film received a second airing in 1989, but never seemed to provoke anything other than a bemused reaction from critics, who were not sure what to make of its uncharacterizable narrative and tone—not quite chilling enough to be classified as horror, not absurd enough to be taken as a dark comedy. The closest approximation that might be reached is by invoking that wonderfully ambiguous term 'weird', used to suggest an almost indefinable combination of the esoteric and the peculiar. Though *The Gourmet* has still never received an official release, it has recently experienced a minor resurgence online, aided by the uploading of a grainy bootleg to YouTube and a full copy of Ishiguro's script being made available to read. Nonetheless, it remains to this day an unjustly neglected work, a missing key in the history of gastronomic cinema whose existence invites the curation of a new genre, one we might tentatively label 'The Culinary Weird'. Even more curiously, *The Gourmet* reveals itself to be a hitherto unacknowledged minor masterwork in the canon of films about occult London, acting as a mythic accumulator for the various legends and resonances that mark the East End.

Charles Gray plays Manley Kingston, the titular gourmet—a toff in the William Buckland vein, who has consumed all the delights that earthly cuisine has to offer. Gray, best known for playing Sherlock Holmes's older brother Mycroft in the Granada adaptations of Doyle's detective stories, speaks every line in a refined croak, a perpetually bored tone of voice that marks him out as being above ordinary human concerns. As Kingston, Gray's bear-like frame and contemptuous expression become eminently statuesque in the presence of men he deems beneath him, like the bust of a corpulent Roman senator brought to life. He is introduced during a party held at the mansion of one Dr Grosvenor—a space populated by food critics and celebrity chefs, none of whom succeed in winning Kingston's attention. His appointment is with Grosvenor himself, played by *Time Bandits*'s David Rappaport, who provides the gourmand with various documents and solutions he requested in advance of his night-time visit to the church: 'You look rather like a hunter, Mr Kingston, just before his big kill'. The camera lingers over Grosvenor's books on culinary history and science (*Protein and Culture, The Evolution of the Carnivore, Foods of the Dinka Warriors*), while outside Kingston's chauffeur indulges in fast food—looking like a Tarantino assassin, impeccably dressed and with a burger in hand. Consumption is an unavoidable presence in *The Gourmet*.

Kingston's urge to transcend ordinary human appetites by devouring a ghost marks him out as a seeker of profane knowledge in the MR James fashion—educated, conceited, and primed for a fall.

As a hunter, Kingston is clearly restless with the weight of prior disappointments— he reveals that this will be the third time in nine years he attempts to capture his ghostly quarry. He arrives at the church dressed in a ludicrous safari cosplay: bush jacket, sun hat and riding boots. Armed with his magical powders, cooking utensils and butterfly net, he joins the crowd of homeless men in order to gain access to the crypt. While Kingston is made to appear unknowingly ridiculous, the scenes of poverty around him are depicted with realism and empathy, drawing on both Whyte's background as a documentarian and Ishiguro's personal experience as a social worker in a homeless shelter. The men around Kingston are eating to survive, subsisting on baked beans spooned into Styrofoam cups by volunteers. Kingston, on the other hand, eats to experience novelty, to vanquish the existential tedium felt by those who already have it all.

At the same time, the character is too bloody-minded in his mission to appear entirely laughable. Kingston's croaking, languid voice grows more tremulous the closer he gets to his phantasmal dinner. He begins licking his lips in anticipation, his features turning impish with delight, his mouth twisting into the smile of a leering gargoyle. Whyte places great focus on the painstaking set-up of the magic circle in the church vestry, as Kingston and his impromptu assistant—a homeless man called David whom he encounters in the yard and enlists to take part in the ritual—anticipate the ghost's arrival. The tension in these scenes is deftly crafted, with Kingston's anxious, monumental stillness intercut with a Raimi-esque shaky cam showing the perspective of an unseen being approaching and entering the church. There is a tremendous sense of anticipation as we wait for something to finally *break through* into the characters' reality—even though the eventual appearance of the ghost is undermined by a somewhat stilted presentation, exemplifying the limits of British television in the eighties. Kingston is surprised by the sudden entrance of a cockney tramp, and chastises the unknown man for appearing on the spot where the ghost is set to arrive imminently—it's hardly a shock when the tramp turns out to be the ghost himself, transforming into a green-faced spectre engulfed in fire. The image is striking, but not nearly as visceral as one feels it ought to be—the overlaying of flames on David's terrified expression wouldn't be out of place among the ropey special effects that appear in *The Devil Rides Out*, the occult mystery Gray had starred in almost twenty years prior.

But since *The Gourmet* is no ordinary tale of haunting, the appearance of the ghost is not the narrative's true endgame. The real culmination lies in the scene that follows, when Kingston is able at last to put his pots and knives to gleeful use. While Ishiguro's script advises that the details of the meal be kept off-screen, Whyte makes the wise decision to focus on each step in hideous detail. The camera fixates on a cluster of white blobs sizzling in a pan like bubbles of fat, quivering and jittering in different directions. The ghost-meat was simulated with chunks of calamari attached to wires, allowing them to be puppeteered and brought to nauseating life. The background sounds are equally revolting: the sputtering fat, the guttural moans as Kingston chews and swallows his paranormal dish. The end of the scene is like something out of Ferreri's *La Grande Bouffe*, an ethereal twist on Monty Python's Mr Creosote—as grease pours down Gray's cheeks and chin, his broad, frog-like rictus warping into an undefined reaction, we are left to wonder whether he is experiencing ecstasy, or revulsion.

The aftermath reveals that there is a third option, far worse than either of the above: disappointment. Kingston stumbles out into the new dawn, ending up in the tabula rasa of the London Docklands, still under radical redevelopment in 1986. Sitting down among a group of vagrants who are warming themselves by a fire, Kingston begins to retch—but the retribution that results from his obsessive pursuit, the M R James-inspired punishment for trifling with powers beyond his control, is no mere case of food poisoning. Rather, he is left with a sense of total disillusionment. The ghost-meat has failed to refresh his palate, to grant him the novelty he so craved. As he tells his chauffeur on the drive home, leaving the dispossessed men to poke at their ramshackle fire: 'Not quite as extraordinary as one may have expected. Disappointing all in all. […] Life becomes so dreary once one's tasted its more obvious pleasures'.

As noted by the artist John Coulthart in his 2019 review of *The Gourmet*, setting the ending on the Docklands allowed Whyte to lift the metaphor of consumption to a God's eye view, providing Kingston's all-encompassing greed its proper Thatcherite context.

We might imagine Helen Mirren, moll to Bob Hoskins's gangster-turned-businessman from *The Long Good Friday*, walking into frame in the final shots—claiming the land as a blank slate (or empty plate) for aggressive redevelopment, the foundation for a capitalist vision of the future which is inaccessible to those who won't fight and claw for it. Or perhaps it might be Mirren's double from *The Cook, the Thief, His Wife & Her Lover*, in which she plays the wife to Michael Gambon's gangster-turned-gourmand Albert Spica. A man of colossal appetites and violent tempers, Spica is finally punished by Mirren's Georgina for the murder of her adulterous lover by being forced at gunpoint to eat the dead man's glazed, cooked cadaver—starting with his phallus. The final word that Georgina utters after shooting her husband dead, 'Cannibal', can be seen as a disgusted condemnation of a ruling class that exists solely to devour, that will just as readily consume the human beings it suppresses before slowing its relentless forward march for new vistas, new riches, new appetites.

If *The Gourmet* is to be positioned in the context of The Culinary Weird, or Glutton Cinema, it should be placed in the well-established milieu of cannibal cinema as well. A flashback sequence provides the backstory of Kingston's quest, revealing a meeting he had years prior with his elderly mentor in South America, the man who first told him that it was possible to capture and eat a ghost. Their conversation is preceded by a wordless sequence set in an undisclosed locale—a scene which, though it is never explicitly stated, clearly shows the gourmet and his colleagues indulging in a dish of long pig: the cannibal's delight. Ishiguro and Whyte make the canny decision never to overtly specify that the slab of meat being served is in fact human flesh. The silence that greets the dish upon its arrival—the sense of unease that comes over the guests, who stare at it with rapacious curiosity, or try to look calm while writhing in anticipation—leaves little doubt that what they are about to eat is deeply profane. The episode is brief, and leaves us with numerous unanswered questions—whose body are they eating? What is the precise nature of this South American establishment? Is it a cannibal restaurant? A member's club where decadent Westerners can live out their fantasies? The succulently-named Alec Mango presides over the scene as Rossi, Kingston's mentor, dressed in cream-coloured tones like Gregory Peck's Dr Mengele in *The Boys from Brazil*. Rossi is more lizard than man. The surface of refined elegance hides a deep, abiding sickness.

The culinary *Eyes Wide Shut* party that is *The Gourmet*'s cannibal feast functions as a set-up for the deep dissatisfaction Kingston feels after eating the ghost, while simultaneously providing a notable twist on the cannibal genre. Unlike in Antonia Bird's masterful neo-Western *Ravenous*, or any one of the numerous adaptations of Thomas Harris's Hannibal Lecter books, cannibalism in *The Gourmet* does not elicit either revulsion or sickening pleasure in the eater—nor does it provoke Proustian epiphany, that other trope associated with so many cinematic depictions of food, from *Babette's Feast* to *Ratatouille*. Instead, the eating of human flesh is unique here in that it results in pure apathy. Kingston looks so unimpressed by this supposedly exotic dish that he hardly seems bothered with finishing his meal, sprinkling salt over the poor, unknown victim's leg to make it more palatable. If Mirren's character in *The Cook, the Thief, His Wife & Her Lover* calls her deceased husband a cannibal, using the word to embody all his most wretched and despicable traits, then Kingston somehow emerges in an even less flattering light. Albert Spica, at least, has the decency to feel horror at the thought of consuming human flesh. For Kingston, it simply provokes boredom—and the hope that more unearthly fare will provide him with the culinary excitement he desires.

The Gourmet might be seen as a missing link between *The Long Good Friday* and *The Cook, the Thief, His Wife & Her Lover*, a sibling in a Thatcherite genre trilogy (gangster film, ghost story, revenge tragedy) primed for a box set that never got made. The connections between the films continue to mount. Albert Spica's thuggish young associate was played by Tim Roth, six years after his debut appearance in Alan Clarke's *Made in Britain*. Roth auditioned to play the role of David in *The Gourmet*, the homeless man who assists Kingston in hunting down the ghost. Whyte ended up choosing a different Clarke alumni—Mark Ford, best known as one of Ray Winstone's borstal-mates in *Scum*—believing that the actor was better suited to capturing David's gentleness and humanity. When asked, Whyte seemingly didn't know that a year prior to working on *The Gourmet*, Ford had acted in a *South Bank Show* adaptation of Peter Ackroyd's bestselling novel *Hawksmoor*, appearing as a different assistant to a devilish occultist. This seemingly trivial detail nevertheless captures a separate strand of *The Gourmet*'s abiding strangeness, this being its unacknowledged importance as a work of London esoterica.

In order to understand the point of intersection where *Hawksmoor* and *The Gourmet* meet, we must turn to an early publication by one Britain's most prolific and respected writers, Iain Sinclair. Sinclair's *Lud Heat*, released in 1975, made the then-radical suggestion that architect Nicholas Hawksmoor's six London churches, built following the Great Fire of London, could be understood to form a particular magical alignment. The text was accompanied by a map drawn by Sinclair's friend and collaborator Brian Catling, showing the arrangement of these churches as sites of occult power across the city. The notion of a psychic map connecting these churches gained further attention when, in 1985, Ackroyd dramatized Sinclair's idea in his novel *Hawksmoor*, in which the eighteenth-century architect was recast as a Devil-worshipping murderer who had placed a human sacrifice at the base of each of his churches, a ritual act which—according to the novel's conceit—had some bearing on a series of murders being investigated in the present day.

It is worth noting that the second half of *The Gourmet*, which focuses on the enacting of Kingston's plan to capture and eat a ghost, takes place almost entirely in St George-in-the-East, Hawksmoor's Cannon Street Road church. Michael Whyte revealed that Ishiguro's very first script called for the ghost-eating to take place in a country house—it was after reading Ackroyd's novel and making a circuit of the Hawksmoor churches that Whyte decided to relocate the action to a more psychically resonant spot. St George-in-the-East, where Iain Sinclair had worked as a gardener and day-labourer in the seventies, was also used as a key location in *The Long Good Friday*, with one of Bob Hoskins's henchmen being dispatched by an IRA car bomb outside the church. Sinclair couldn't have known at the time that his theory would provide such fuel for other fictions in the years that followed, with films, novels and comics scrambling to make use of the Hawksmoor churches as backdrops of arcane importance. Art itself is a gluttonous thing, devouring prior ideas and recombining them anew.

But the Sinclair-*Gourmet* connections do not stop there. Whyte revealed that the location used for the South American cannibal sequence was the Princelet Street synagogue just off Brick Lane—a spot known to many London mythographers and readers of Sinclair's work as having been the home of David Rodinsky. In the sixties, Rodinsky had lived in the attic room above the synagogue, working as a caretaker and scholar before infamously disappearing towards the end of the decade. According to Sinclair, who in 1999 co-wrote an acclaimed book on the disappearance with Rachel Lichtenstein, Rodinsky was a 'resident poltergeist' who 'achieved the great work and became invisible', leaving behind a space filled with magical books, cryptic formulae and dust. Lichtenstein recounts the use of the synagogue as a shooting location, hired out to film crews on a monthly basis, with callous set designers threatening to paint the walls a different colour according to each film's needs. Her first visit to the building coincided with one such shoot, a group of students occupying the synagogue to make a short film entitled *The Golem of Princelet Street*. The Golem, a being of mud that is granted life by ingesting a magical scroll, reaches a form of transcendence through consumption that remains perpetually out of reach for *The Gourmet*'s protagonist. One wonders, too, what form of physical or spiritual sustenance Rodinsky was searching for. Lichtenstein describes his space being surrounded by relics of consumption—empty beer bottles, cigarette and Kosher food packets, shopping lists: 'meat, six eggs, kiddush wine'.

If *The Gourmet*'s central location, St George-in-the-East, is bordered to the north by the hungry phantom of Rodinsky, then it is flanked by another site of mythic importance only a few hundred feet to the west. Swedenborg Gardens was named after Emanuel Swedenborg, the eighteenth-century prophet whose body was buried for a time on the grounds. Swedenborg was a Scandinavian Leonardo da Vinci, a scientist, philosopher and engineer who, in 1745, while dining at a London inn, experienced a vocational vision in which an angel appeared before him and told him to 'eat not so much'. The angel's words were interpreted as a tacit warning by Swedenborg—since eating is a symbol of the material world, he was being told not to commit solely to physical reality, to science and anatomy and mining, at the expense of the spiritual experience. And so, Swedenborg devoted himself to God and the angels, and his diet over the rest of his life became little more than a daily ration of coffee, milk and bread. *The Gourmet* pushes this warning towards its natural extrapolation: Do not attempt to reach spiritual understanding by gorging. Do not imagine you will capture the numinous through aggressive consumption, which will result only in disappointment, bitterness and defeat.

The Gourmet, therefore, is as much a film that taps into a particular strain of East End mythology as it is a work about eldritch cuisine. It might be understood as that rare

thing: a film that is both a psychogeographical study of a city and a compelling work of genre fiction. In speaking with Michael Whyte, I learned of his desire to let the audience get lost in a version of London they didn't know existed—something he achieved far beyond his original intent, producing a work that accrues myths with a striking intensity of vision. For as short as it is, at just under 50 minutes, it is remarkable how fractal *The Gourmet* becomes, how many new layers are revealed to those who look for them. The true strength of the film lies in the writer and director's twinned yet opposing interests—Ishiguro's script, with its deep concern for the politics of consumption and possession (themes he would return to in his 2005 novel *Never Let Me Go*, with cannibalism switched out for organ harvesting), merging with Whyte's fascination with London geography and the psychic importance of Hawksmoor's churches. The result is a film that is stronger than its individual parts, something far more provocative than a mere uncategorizable curiosity, or relic of a distant cultural milieu. *The Gourmet* deserves to be re-evaluated as a notable work of London fiction which distils the essential strangeness of the city—a city of weird appetites that, if left unchecked, might threaten to consume us all.

TYGERS OF WRATH
AT THE GATES OF HEAVEN

Gareth Evans

The greater part of the soul lies outside of the body.
—James Hillman, from *A Psyche the Size of the Earth* (1995)

White Noise is often reductively described as a satire of American consumer culture. And while of course it is satirical, I would argue that it is more deeply alchemic. When DeLillo notices and listens to the world, he arranges its 'codes and messages' and transforms chaotic overload into forms that give us meaning and beauty.
—Dana Spiotta on *White Noise*, the novel, from the
New York Times Book Review (1 January 2023)

In what is surely one of the most poorly conceived promotional straplines of recent years, the Maidstone headquartered Vital Parts, a plastics and rubber component manufacturing operation with a sideline in the provision of public building sanitation (their free-standing Hand Sanitising Station, part of the 'pro-active hygiene range' is a snip at £324 all in, and viewable across locations in Hackney and Tower Hamlets) proudly declares that 'we mould around you'. It's hard to know what is more off-putting, the rotting implications of their already moist product or the frankly Cronenbergian offer to extend bodily possibility and reach. Either way, it's safe to say that most of us would not wish them anywhere near our own VPs.

However, the relation between subject (or object) and a form of territorial intervention is perhaps something worth pursuing here, but conjured in an altogether more vigorous terminology—that of 'Plotlands'. I'll quote a suitably plain-talking, concise but efficient definition from the website of The Spatial Agency:

Plotlands refers to small pieces of land laid out in regular plots on which a number of self-built settlements were established in the south-east of England from the late 1800s and up to the Second World War. Characterised by the fact that they were largely built outside the conventional planning system, Plotlands were tolerated by local councils but eventually replaced with new towns and garden suburbs through compulsory purchase orders. Very few traces of the original communities remain, though Jaywick Sands in Essex has evaded development through its geographic and economic marginality. Reaching its peak in the period between the 1920s and 1930s, the Plotland phenomenon was interrupted by WWII and the planning regulations that followed. The result of a specific set of circumstances, Plotlands were a peculiarly English phenomenon, tied in large part to the desire to own a piece of land, no matter how small.

Established by a class with little access to sizeable savings, deposits, mortgages or territory (what goes around ...), Plotlands developments—self-raised, constantly amended, singular, often eccentrically individualistic—enabled those who were ignored by the majority of state structures the chance to claim their 'handful of earth'. Now, nearly a century later, property almost everywhere in the South-East is unaffordable to almost anybody, even with an advanced white collar income (at the time of writing the average price of a two-bedroom flat in London is 19 times the equivalent salary). However, there is a direct semblance in one important way: just as Plotlands dwellings were notably smaller than regular houses, so the dimensions of many contemporary 'apartments' are likewise often startlingly reduced, regularly below minimum planning regulations in both new-builds and conversions. That properties are increasingly occupied by many more people than any assessment of the unit would expect (via dormitory-style bunk bedrooms, the swallowing up of living rooms and even rotational sleeping) comes as secondary to the basic architectural fact of shrinkage.

And yet, as Gary Osborne's lyrical adaptation of H G Wells's *War of the Worlds* for Jeff Wayne's multimillion-selling double album of June 1978 has Justin Hayward croon, 'and still they come'. Not Martians in this case, but migrants, workers (or 'service providers'), would-be adults (those who once were children, seeking to confirm that status by living in their own place on their own terms), dreamers, schemers, aspirant artists (trial by various oppressions to come) and so on ... in other words, those who have always come to cities; to flee persecution, whether personal or national / find their way / seek their fortune / discover who they actually are / sample the so-called 'centre' while they can (tick all and any that apply); i.e., those who enable cities to continue to be the places they claim to be: sites of interest, innovation, experimentation, possibility and the future.

Well, not any more: if you stand with your back to the wooden doors at the entrance to the Whitechapel Gallery and look in a panning arc across the High Street south towards the river at Wapping, you will not find a single building originating from earlier than the start of this millennium, while the majority is less than 10 years old. The only exceptions are a very short terrace of shops (flats above) to the left of your gaze and, straight ahead, what's left of the much loved Cass, formerly a textile building and then, until 2016 (with a somewhat bitter irony, given its own fate and what surrounds it), London Metropolitan University's School of Architecture. Sold to Frasers Property for £50 million, the 'Aldgate Bauhaus' has now gained six extra floors—at the cost of £83 million—to become an office / retail environment.

There is of course a huge scarcity of such ventures in the city, which might have encouraged the notoriously erratic, even suspect Tower Hamlets planning committee to wave it through ... Their priorities appear to be all too clear. Consider, for example, their shameful abandonment of one of the most important buildings in their manor— the centuries-old Bell Foundry just 200 metres away, the oldest manufacturing company in Great Britain by far at the time of its closure—for a prime example of 'best practice'.

Now renamed the Rowe for no obvious reason (except that it conveniently buries the past along with the bodies), the former Cass is, height apart, indistinguishable from the towers of chrome, glass and poured concrete that loom over the ancient highway; pitch-perfect examples of globalized placelessness—you really could be anywhere in the neo-liberal cosmos. Visit the building's promotional website and you will find art- and social-washing hard at work (full of 'borrowed' images of and 'association with' the very things at risk / erased / pushed out by such endemic financialized construction) all the way from the homepage on through to the 'public' art installation that adorns the fob access balcony areas.

Claiming that the locality is 'where tech meets the city, culture meets commerce, history meets the hyper-modern', the site has a neighbourhood map which visitors can click on to 'activate or deactivate' various locational categories. This is, surely unknowingly, at least a brutally honest declaration of the impact such developments have. The map, which had crashed on my first viewing, was obscured by a London fog or nuclear winter of grey totality, with eight coffee outlets the only visible numberings. If this is prophetic, then we can at least be grateful for an oat milk option in the ruins. Welcome to the desert of the real.

The final nail in the cultural coffin is perhaps the claim that AHMM, the Rowe's architects, 'drew early inspiration from Rachel Whiteread's *Monument* on Trafalgar Square's Fourth Plinth, which takes an existing mass and mirrors it above'. Yes it does, and it does so transparently (unlike the balance sheet of speculation) but it also resembles nothing so much as a tomb, arguably containing the death of the idea of the plinth project and even of sculpture itself, just as the Rowe buries the reality of the building it has expanded to reflect.

Sure, the city's a crucible of constant change, and much of the creative tension comes from the adjacency of variant temporal zones and the resultant frictional energy released, and yes, we are talking about a district long bisected by two avenues labelled for transaction—Commercial Road *and* Street. But there's selling, there's even the 'market' and then there's the wholly unanchored, groundless realm of finance capital, albeit one that conjures actual castles in the air out of offshore concealment, tax breaks, backhanders, forward selling (off-plan to East Asian investors who will never see them) and retro-fitted account 'management'.

Frequently unoccupied (office) or uninhabited (apartment)—while the rest of the human city dreams of empty rooms—these buildings are in a very pressing sense examples of a brutalizing and callous 'negative space', which is, meanwhile, in *artistic* terms, the space around, between and within objects or structures. Registration of this concept has been Whiteread's lucrative bread and butter for over 30 years.

There's also an additional neighbourly informant in the artist's narrative given that:

in June 2012, Whiteread unveiled her first permanent public commission in

56

Britain. Tree of Life *spreads across the upper façade of the said Whitechapel Gallery, a venerable east-London institution with an important place in the history of post-war art. The façade had been incomplete since the Whitechapel's opening, in 1901, when expected funds did not materialize, leading to the cancellation of a mosaic proposed for the wall's central panel. Whiteread's frieze elaborates on the building's original terracotta reliefs depicting the Tree of Life, a motif that in the context of the Arts and Crafts movement of the time connoted social transformation through art. Leaves and branches of gilded bronze now punctuate the original areas of terracotta foliage, whose density anchors the sporadic distribution of Whiteread's bronze elements across the panel.*

The panel also holds four negative terracotta casts taken from the building's windows. That kind of architectural reconfiguration established Whiteread in the public eye in the early 1990s, while her vocabulary of everyday forms brought a new language to our private relationships with objects. Tree of Life *is insistently slight, influenced not only by gilded architectural grandeur but also by buddleia, an invasive plant that has thrived for decades in the crevices of London's bricks and mortar [GE: Whiteread calls it the 'Hackney weed']. Pedestrians might easily miss the frieze as they hurry past with eyes on phones or traffic. There is power in its lack of clamour; sumptuously eye-catching, it nevertheless retains the flavour of an urban secret.*

(James Lawrence, from *Gagosian Quarterly*, Winter 2017).

The commission was part of the London-wide smörgåsbord of Olympic handouts, the icing on the cake of gallery expansion, completed in 2009. This saw the almost legendary public library next door swallowed into the white cube operation. Traces remain: the impressively appointed staircase, a sense of the previous life in the gallery's archive collection fittings, but it's slim pickings really. To my knowledge there is no plaque, blue or otherwise, recording its own remarkable and truly necessary history (it opened in 1892). The vastly generous journalist, MP, newspaper owner and philanthropist John Passmore Edwards, a great champion of working class provision, following his own impoverished and book-free beginnings in Cornwall, funded it (he also had a stake in the building of the gallery).

Described as the 'university of the ghetto', it held hugely significant Jewish and Bengali collections and provided a literary homeland—and practical shelter—for generations of children, the elderly, poor, radicals, émigré revolutionaries and aspirant writers. One of them, Arnold Wesker, marked the day of its closure in 2005 with a moving and insightful essay on the processes of gentrifying erasure to which it fell victim (www.theguardian.com/uk/2005/aug/06/books.arts).

'They' go for the public buildings first, declaring them 'unfit'. Then they move on 'substandard' housing, green spaces, playing fields ... Whitechapel now has to rely on the Idea Store, which is at once genuinely 'unfit' and also all too necessary, given we're now well into the second decade of 'austerity'.

This stretch of road evidences the savage present-tense reality of the deliberately wrecked social contract. The distress is palpable. I have seen both a greater concentration—and the worst physical condition—of the dispossessed here than elsewhere in the city. Freedom Alley, the piss-stained passage leading to the Freedom Press and Bookshop—the oldest anarchist publisher and outlet in the UK, founded in 1886 (owning the building, in a thankfully somewhat un-anarchist way, they shall *not* be moved)—is often a shooting run of stimulant destitution that would not seem out of place in *The People of the Abyss*, Jack London's 1903 record of his time here.

The politics of poverty: how power pincers with its foot soldiers. Sometimes they come in smooth, hi-viz waist-coating their suits; sometimes in boots and threes, with customized cosh and chains. Across the road, Altab Ali Park (originally the grounds of the Blitz-demolished fourteenth-century whitewashed church that named the district) was newly titled in 1998 to remember the brutal racist murder of the young man, a garment worker, in 1978. This was not a stand-alone assault. The National Front and associates continued their Mosleyite incursions across the area well into the late 1980s.

Stare at the abyss, and the abyss stares right back. Nietzsche knew.

The weary clichés of urban living—melting pot, meeting of cultures, etc.—both prove themselves true and not here. What are we to make of a recent addition to higher-end fast food provision just metres from the gallery's door? Jack the Chipper, possibly the most tasteless new opening locally since Cereal Killer at the far end of Brick Lane, wishes to 'honour' its tradition *and* eat a whole load of stuff that is a long way from the now increasingly threatened chippy's regular fare. Offering 'more than just a fish', you can order steak, burgers, spag bol and eggs benedict, with roasts promised soon.

What *is* the point? Do the owners ever wake in the derelict early hours and wonder how far they've strayed from the path, scorching the earth all the while as they go?

If one incident could serve as an indicator of the forces converging on this neighbourhood, it might be this. Over the first weekend of October 2014, I hosted Alexander Kluge, Richard Sennett and other starred guests as part of my then moving image programme in the Whitechapel Gallery auditorium. The astonishingly prolific German polymath, aged 82 at the time, was showing a quartet of long films exploring the 'turning points of civilization': the city, religion and capital. Leaving the packed auditorium at 9 pm on the opening Thursday night, we emerged into the busy foyer to join a weave of congregations.

At the same time, the then gallery director was descending the wide stairs with several Russian patrons (or worse) and their entourage, fresh from a viewing of the Moscow V-A-C collection, turned briefly public and with pieces selected (under the title *Again, more things (a table ruin)*, and brilliantly, it must be said) by artist Mike Nelson. Our cohorts almost met and passed, at the same moment as a loud voice bellowed across the throng from the area near the front desk, in Russian. Whatever was said prompted a number of earpiece-toting, bulked and suited men into action: they swept the oligarchs back up the stairs at great speed (it turned out one was being served a writ of some sort; if it had touched his body it would have become activated and valid; he was evacuated out over the roof and down nearby fire escapes).

A version of this commotion was also taking place by the desk, as the complainant was bundled out of the building into the vigorous rain, from which a group of walking tourists were seeking shelter. While they made their way into the soon to be closing foyer, their guide made one last call out onto the street, 'anyone for Jack the Ripper?'

People, place and purpose: how much can change before the place in question is no longer the place in question? We might reflect on the 'ship of Theseus' thought experiment (if all the components of an object are replaced over time, is it still the object). There can be a solastalgia of the high street as much as of a forest or a shore.

What Is to Be Done? Lenin famously wrote. (He knew Whitechapel and its radical enclaves well, not least from 1907 when Stalin was in town for the 5th Party Congress and staying in the Tower House doss shelter that Jack London also frequented: it's been luxury apartments since the library closed.)

Now that the Aldgate—Whitechapel—Shadwell—Stepney—Mile End corridor is fully on speculative finance radars, how much longer will the poorer (almost all of us) be allowed to live or stay east?

There are, therefore, many reasons why the word capital (money *and* metropolis), from the Old French and Latin, 'pertaining to the head', hence 'chief, principal, dominant', is so important to the concerns of this publication and the exhibition it accompanies. Most important among them is the embedded and embodied resistance that the work of Iain Sinclair, Brian Catling and their fellow travellers offers to this totalitarian impulse. Crucially, this is an opposition that has, in a very real sense, continued unbroken since the original show, half a century ago, that Swedenborg House is honouring.

Albion Island Vortex opened at Whitechapel Gallery in April 1974. In the building's own index of every exhibition it has held, it labels it as having an *unknown end date*. Only three other exhibitions in the gallery's 122-year history are so listed: Japan in 1902, *Mothercraft* in 1916 (that year of catastrophic losses, millions of dead sons piling the fields), and Joseph Beuys in 1972. This trinity of associations feels suitable. We might consider the city's new growth 'future forest' of chrome and glass in the last decades as a Tokyo-like transformation of the capital. Thoughts of Michael Moorcock's 1988 novel *Mother London* (published a year after Sinclair's own debut fiction *White Chappell, Scarlet Tracings*) could follow, and certainly the shamanic visionary Beuys is kindred.

All of them also—as exhibitions do—construct a temporary autonomous zone. They conjure an alternative reality made topographically real within the dimensions of the rooms. What the gallery's own incomplete chronology allows us to believe is that the realm of *Albion Island Vortex* remains and therefore, with imaginative will, can still be visited. The limits of time have been removed; it only remains to find the portal, whether Blake's 'doors of perception' or H G Wells's door in the wall perhaps.

For Sinclair the London project found its now nearly 60-year-long base in Albion Drive. Its print counterpart was his own Albion Village Press. That Albion takes the island in 1974, having previously staked a domestic and cultural claim to the *city*, seems logical. Its unending can only signify that the vortex has expanded and / or deepened, to become *much more* extensive.

Imagination is a kind of 'negative space', impossible to grasp and yet as vast as its maker can generate. It is a 'Plotland' that cannot be torn down, demolished or erased. Like its residential namesakes, it does not rely on capital to exist. Others enter it, dwell in it, through the works it makes with friendship and collaboration—collegiate, partial, in solidarity.

A plot, etymologically a 'defined piece of land', is also a ground plan, a map, a chart, a scheme. It is both itself and a metaphor: it is meaning and measure. 'Telling it' can be an act of charged implication. Re-telling it etches it into history, legend, even myth. This recurrent narration, this re-visiting is *loyalty*—over decades, in numerous forms—to projects, people and place. This is its purpose. In that, deeper than rhetoric or polemic, lies its radical—root—rationale and effect. It has been there longer, more attentively, more compassionately and more usefully than the towers.

No fly in / out here: life is work is life.

And the recounting—the reason—is made out of everything found: all the stuff, the detritus, the glimpses and snatches of story, the lost and oppressed acres, communities and cultures. Redeeming lives out of the ghosts in the machine, it is a search, pursuit and chase, fuelled by but *challenging* entropy. This keen attending galvanizes its own propulsion and momentum—what was, is, might be (again); bodies in rest and motion, but no full stops ...

Jung said that *all* is matter—ideas, spirit, and emotions, the whole of the intangible. The forest and the fungi tell us that everything is connected, co-existent, coterminous. So Sinclair's project—and Catling's own, shared and discrete—are ecological, relational and dependent. This networked association is already a source of strength. Over so long, and so acutely aware of lineage, it already knows the land—is the land—more firmly than any speculative structure, grab or asset stripping will ever have a hope to do. Example *and* evidence, it knows it might sometimes need, in harsh climes, to go

61

subterranean, subcutaneous, biding its moment, when threat is great and sprawling. *This* resurfacing, in the committed House of Swedenborg, a site that understands the fecund reach of imaginative time and space, is notable for its happening *now*, when all can seem lost—locally, nationally, globally, on a planetary scale.

And yet ... as this is being completed, it has been reported that corvids—crows and their related—are repurposing anti-avian roof and building spikes as nest material, tearing them off ledges made hostile; turning power's tools against it, into a place to live. A modest victory, but one nevertheless, and a model ...

The world and its operation are not fixed in amber. This show is not historical, a dusted rehanging; rather, it has repurposed the extant, sought out, invited and hosted the new (from exhibitors not born when the first iteration occurred). It is grounded in intention, but aerial in ambition. It seeks to become a more fertile, even kinder kind of weather. Things change and deepen their meaning over time / in time, against the airborne toxic events of profit-politics and polluted public pollstering.

Now, more than ever, we need words and images founded out of an appreciation of the ancient, often occluded and insurgent possibilities concealed in language and light's landing (the gift that makes the picture): perennial, the secret seam made manifest. The beating elements of this body of work constitute vital parts of our ability to stay human/e in the maelstrom.

The Whitechapel Art Gallery

Whitechapel High Street · London E1 7QX : 01-247 1492

PRESS RELEASE

19th March - 7th April, 1974

The annual East London Open Exhibition of Paintings will be shown
in the Main Gallery.   It is open to all those living or working in
East London.

Albion Island Vortex will be on show in the Small Gallery.   This
exhibition will show work by three members of the Albion Village Press:
Laurence Bicknell, B. Catling and Iain Sinclair.   Most of the paintings
in the show are the work of Bicknell, the line-drawings are by Catling
and the photographs by Sinclair.

     They write: "Albion Island Vortex presents the iconic margin of
Albion Village Press.   The accumulated frames were in the blood-stream
and did seem to require the tension and concentrated focus that would
come from the making of an exhibition, or the inhabiting of the space
that was allotted to us.

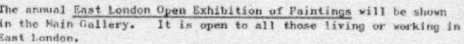

The Press and the Whitechapel Art Gallery exist in the same geographical
vortex: the labyrinth that runs from, say, London Fields south to the
London Hospital.

Albion Island is adopted as a metaphor.   Common ground, literally.   To
unravel something of the energies locked in specific locations: Northumberland,
the Yorkshire Moors, Cader Idris, Wiltshire, the New Forest, London.   To
locate and discover the power lines that have been represented in myth as
gods: Bran, Hand and Hyle, Hutton, the Green Man.   Blake's Jerusalem is
a textual source.   In the dream journey feet drag on earth, heads move
among the stars.

The exhibition is only part of the push we are trying to make.   It has
no absolute importance.   Hopefully it connects with the books that are
already written, and marks a new stage in the spiral that we are pacing out."

     The Albion Village Press started to publish books in 1970 and now
have twelve titles in print, ranging from The Kodak Mantra Diaries (2,000
copies) to J.H. Prynne's A Night Square (200 copies).

All press inquiries to the Whitechapel Art Gallery, 247 1492

PRESS VIEW: Tuesday, 19th March from 12 noon to 3 p.m.

PART II

GIFTS RETURNED
BY THE RIVER

INTRODUCTORY
REMARKS

Renchi Bicknell

A few words about my choice of paintings and why. First of all I would like to thank Iain for the invitation to share in this exhibition and also express my gratitude to Stephen McNeilly, Anya, James and Jacob and maybe some other ghostly figures that are attracted to, or dwell in Swedenborg House.

In fact on that note, my first choice of painting, *Faustus and the Oxford Dreaming* —which I felt strongly evoked Brian Catling—had jumped from its owner's wall and smashed its glass and frame, probably by Brian's hand from beyond.

So some paintings have selected themselves and others have joined their company. Only two are from the original *Albion Island Vortex* exhibition, namely *Brockenhurst (New Forest)* whose story Iain has written about and *Mr Prynne* who features in the inner poetry sanctum. However there are our other distinctly Jungian survivors of the 1973/74 era: *Freud and Jung leaving New York*, *The Old Man and the World*, *Haya* (the therapist holding the Hermes winged head) and *The Gift*, with its dripping spheres of blue and gold. These four would have sat comfortably with the six *Hair-raising Archetypes* paintings catalogued in the 1974 Whitechapel Gallery show.

My other *Albion Vortex* category includes *Paths and Travellers* and the *sister energies of the chalk downland*.

Iain's black and white photos catch the motley crew he stirred to set off from Streatley without a clue/Tom Baker kit bag on head, John Marx clutching his watercolours and Renchi rucksack with stuffed plastic bag shoulder reinforcements to Avebury along the Ridgeway.

I have now walked the Ridgeway 3 times, most recently at night.

Back in the 1990s I was inspired by *The Sun and the Serpent* by Hamish Miller and Paul Broadhurst to walk the whole Michael line from Hopton-on-Sea in Norfolk to St Michael's Mount in Cornwall. This walk led to a series of twenty-one paintings that I called *Michael and Mary Dreaming* ... two of which are in this exhibition. I like to think of them as chalky twins, the Beelzebub shadow figure of the *Oxford Dreaming* being the inverse mirror of the whole chalk geological outline figure featured in the *Cambridge Dreaming* which also references through Royston Cave the line of *zero longitude* which in turn connects to *Pole Hill* and *M25 Walk 1*. Anyway, more on the *Michael & Mary Dreaming* can be gleaned from the original catalogue/booklet available in the bookshop. So BACK to Wiltshire or, in Albion stencil speak, 'WILTS'.

I thought I was being quite heroic collecting the picture *Milk Hill* from my friend Justin coming in 3 hours late on the overnight sleeper from Edinburgh but Iain assured me that rushing between platforms 1 and 15 at Euston to meet trains that have vanished into thin air is quite normal. What I like in this painting is the soft maternal energy of the Pewsey Vale, and the continuity of chalkland ceremony with the woven medicine wheel at the centre of the eye and breast-like hill. More compliment than contrast to the rocks of Gower and stones of Wayland's Smithy that feature in Iain's photos and Brian's drawings—and of course their writings.

SO to the *Pilgrim's Progress* etching series that is climbing the spine of the stairwell in Swedenborg House with six continuous themes or threads or strands that run through all the 12 large prints (made up of 98 separate plates!). Firstly:

THREAD 1: John Bunyan's original *The Pilgrim's Progress* (1678).

THREAD 2: William Blake's 28 illustrations published in 1824.

THREAD 3: Gerda S Norvig's Jungian analysis detailed in her *Dark Figures in the Desired Country* (1993).

STRAND 4: My walk 290 miles from Boston in Lincolnshire to Abbotsbury in Dorset.

STRAND 5: My letters home to Vanessa back in Glastonbury using mirror writing for the etching process.

STRAND 6: My own attached memories, dreams and reflections and, unannounced ...

STRAND 7: A poem I had forgotten I had written but found tucked into a book and have now cut into 12 label titles ...

Enough!

I NOW want to zoom, very Strand 6, into the whole matter of Vision. I realize not only am I engaged with you, this very adept audience, but also in the field of the truly Great visionaries of the past especially Blake and Swedenborg. So I will try to be specific about my own experience. In 1973, age 27, I walked from London to Swansea then in South-West Ireland took my 1 and only dose of LSD ...

At first, time is jumping and creating gaps but that soon settles and I find I am above the earth. I see the globe alive with vivid fizzing energy, ever changing movement and patterning. It is I and not I above the magnetic pole seeing the globe. I sense one moment, one space and time all travelling together. I stay a long time absorbing the beautiful live materials of the earth then suddenly realize that this is also what I am made of, here inside the same as here outside, here everywhere I am ecstatically joined to the world, I sing "oh Yeah" over and over again till my friends reply "oh No" but to tell the truth this Vision has stayed resonant with me for 50 years, as happy core knowledge ... For months after, I was waving my hands in the air trying to describe the oneness of this world beautiful both inside and out. I could strongly relate to the words of the astronauts who spoke of their connection to the universe and looking back at earth as magic and beautiful ... I thought every love song was about this earth and even when the visual aspect began to fade the spirit and feeling still remained.

Where was I? In conclusion I wish to say that I still follow the credo of awe and wonder especially on my doorstep in Glastonbury where I can cycle down to the Somerset Levels with a large sheet of paper and watercolour and Chinese ink and without fail be blown away by the uncatchable unnameable unpredictable murmuration of starlings. They, like we, never enter the same river twice.

Thank you for listening.

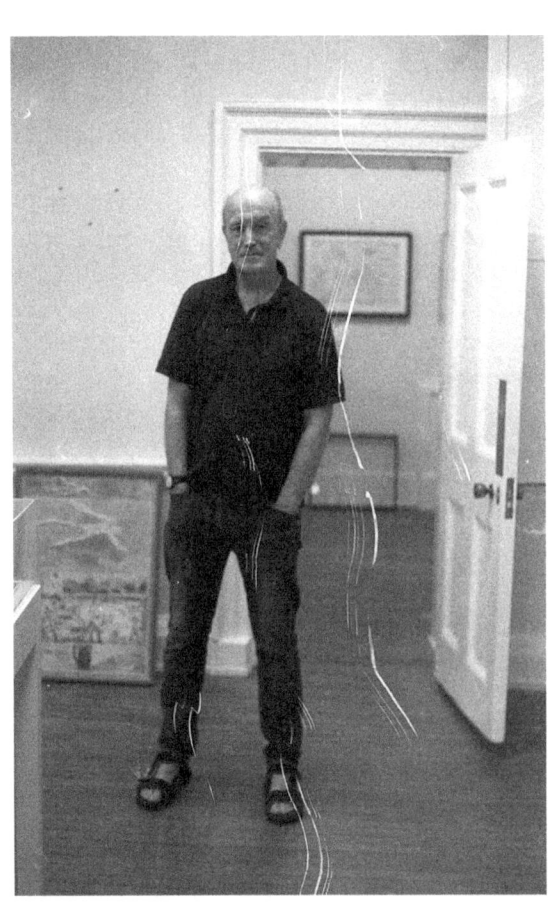

The curse of the era is nihilism.m Not as an affected political pose but a symptom of the unnamed malaise, the undiagnosed disease. Running through the/halllxxxf every corridor of power, in every comp lit department at the local uni, and most certainly, ever since the bombs went off over Japan, in the arts. Five decades of Foucault. For a while, they thought that if they bought a Bolex & shot on 16mm, they'd end up changingthe world. They said they wanted to make it a better place. But what they really ment was: this medium is powerxx powerful & I know how to wield its power & when the 24fps revolution comes, I'll be important. They never really belived in anything. They just had the bad taste to think that there was an alternative route to becoming king kunt. & so now we're in 2023 and the entire populace has seen through the con. They suffer their own nihilism, too, but it's not as severe and not as calculated. & they want an out. NsXW They've stopped listening to theartists and started following thetech billionaires. Beca use at least the pumpkinheaded buffoons of the bay area seem to believe something. They're selling the same con, ofcourse, just more positioning to run the world (and having a much better success rate), but at least there's some~~thing~~ finger pointing to thefuture. Instead of at the self. Instead of at the faults of others. Instead of stirring a cauldron witch vortex IXXWI whirlpool from which nothing can escape.

One thinks back to a certain moment, immediate aftermath of 9/11, stink of death and chemicals in the air, when one came up with an idea: read enough comic books and one will find one's future. X This was the days before the things could be easily pirated, whih meant an expendiure of cash one did not have. But which was obligated to dish out. Go through some very dubious materialsbefore finding Moore's FROM HELL. Like everyone, very impressed by Gull's grand tour through London grime. Unlike everyone, buy all the books referenced in the end notes even an old copy of Hinton's book about the4th dimension, which allows one to b sound smart, for a while, while drunk at parties. Amongst the volumes:XXXXXX LUD HEAT by Sinclair. Picked up at the Cranston, Rhode Island franchise of Borders. That the book was in stock tells you all you need to know about how much things have changed. granta paperback re-release of LUD & SUICIDE BRIDGE. Read the book and know: this is the future you have sought. (Similiar feeling too with FROM HELL & Moore's criminaljy unregarded VOICE OF THE FIRE.) But also know: one has absolutely no idea what the fuck the book is about. It will take ten years to learn the necessary background, to in essence absord an entire culture. One will become that mostdreaded of things: the American anglophile. But at least it's about bin men making sick in the sixties and not a hideous melange of john cleese and tiffin time.

In the process, acquire a copy of the original Albion Village LUD HEAT. (Another sign of how things havechanged: bought for about 45 dollars. Try finding it now for that price) And are shockedto discover that the map in the book is different from Granta. This one is Brian Catling, older, weirder, more archaeology. More to learn, more to make senseof.

At the time, one didn't know it but what one found in LUD HEAT & what one continus to find in Sinclair is belief. In a thing that can't be named, in a concept that perhaps eludes even the originator himself. But it's there, it's real, it's genuine, and it is the exact opposite of 75+ years of vaguely left leaning artists sneering, thinkingthat their techniques and their condescenion and their superiority could never be coopted by the right wing. That no one would notice that the center was hollow, that there was no there there. It's why one, even if one didn't know it, grasped what LUD HEAT was, why one spent decades making sense out of the book. Because one has never liked the nihilism, one has never dug the social climbing disguised as artistry. One belived in books. And so does Sinclair.

Fast forward, tweny years later. One has somehow, improbably, become a writer, even been famous for about fifteen seconds, and is now in jolly old Blighty, taking a two day trip into London. Reach out to Iain Sinclair, who suggests that one cometo the Swedenborg House and meet up as a new installation is being exhibited. By the time that the day rolls around, this also has become XWXIWX a draft. One is enlisted in pack muling Stewart Lee's copy of IS80 , the giant tribute to Sinclair on the XxxxXbXXNIxXBKXkY occassion of his 80th. Okay, sure, why not?

Arrive at Swedenborg. get shown in. Sinclair not there yet, eventually arrives and brings one into the main grounds of the exhibition. It's an overwhelming sensation-- suddenly all the words have become real, artefacts mentioned in books. Even Renchi shows up, name from page as human.

At some point Sinclair shows one the backroom. Points to the wall, XXXXXX at a framed piece and says, "This is the original map from LUD HEAT." And so it is. One's looking at the archaeological piece, at the thing that was there way back, this discovery unearthed through a psychotic acquisition of comic books. This map not only of Hawksmoor's churches but in no small way one's own psychic landscape and eventual destiny. The original idea was right. Read enough comics and you'll get where your going.

The only question now: how did I get so far from home?

jarett kobek
los angeles
29 nov 2023

PILGRIM ON PAGE

Jürgen Ghebrezgiabiher

And so that book, with all its histories and hauntings, has to happen between the moment of release and the coming to earth. The messenger has permission to 'begin to walk into the inevitable'.

The land, approaching the capital through Sussex, felt like a dimly lit prolongation of the Channel Tunnel, a 2023 backwardation in time. London, now that I've emerged after crossing the island's moat for the first time since the elective withdrawal, is full of familiar landmarks pushed out of sight, and loudly confusing signs. I can't read its new directions. Some streets only exist on smartphones. Views extend into mirrored glass walls. Palisades of towers block the supply of fresh air or channel it into blasts that challenge passers-by on sunken roads. The new landmarks are no individuals. They come in packs. Vertically terraced housing 'with the feel of the world's most exclusive and luxurious hotels'. Apartments sell on the basis of having sky rather than river views.

Head down on my first day in town, cobblestones and the patchwork of road repair works seem the only reliable reference that remain to retrieve the byways and backstreets I used only a couple of years ago, and some places I treasure. The brick vault of a railway arch on the South Bank, for one, welcomes me unchanged. A tunnel vision. Bunker strip lights struggle to illuminate the Blakean mosaics in tribute to the engravers Lambeth home somewhere along (what is now) Hercules Road. I had been going past it almost daily when I was working at a bicycle repair shop off The Cut. And I've made it a habit to drop by every time I'm back in town since I left the UK.

While I'm contemplating the tessellated jigsaws, stalwart reminders of Blake's presence, the outside world has blurred, has been silenced behind a lace-like curtain of rain on both sides. *Location outranks time. That's why we keep returning. To reanimate a diminishing present by misinterpreting what we salvage from the dust on our boots.* Opposite the blue plaque, 'the house formerly on this site', sits a little end-of-terrace house at the entrance of the railway arch. I like to imagine William and Catherine living there.

A feeling I remember vividly from my last visit in 2017, when London's construction frenzy eventually spilled even into this overlooked backstreet, while on the other side of the railway line *Future Exiles* returned to a last London in Old Paradise Yard. IKLECTIK. An injunction to travel back in time. A barn turned event centre in a communal garden annexed from Archbishop's Park in Lambeth. And the reason for that journey before Brexit'n'Covid. 'A visitation from the poetics of the '70s, threatened or challenged, at a time when the likes of Allen Fisher, Brian Catling, Bill Griffiths were all leaving London into an unanchored CGI construct of a super-hero dystopia. Back to the Future. On through the past', was how the event was described.

When I eventually tried to tune in to those articulate crows and rooks on that socialistically unelevated stage under a precariously looming chair which had been hoisted above their heads, I didn't realize that I was listening to future ghosts. Tea cups and wine glasses suspended. Words spilled into the packed room. Brian Catling's *Vorrh*, Alan Moore's *Jerusalem*, Allen Fisher's *Place*, Iain Sinclair's *Last London*.

> *Everything that we are is reflected in place and we reflect everything that is in the locations that are around us.* (Alan) *All this is about place and about intersections of place, people, collisions, collaborations, the whole thing.* (Iain)

Too much input. It blurred my memory. The photos. It turned them into black and white over time.

But right now, November 2023, I'm waiting for Sven, a sturdy giant hallooing tentatively into the obscure tunnel. A pair of earbuds each one trying to attune at either end of this whispering duct. We are to meet for an adventure, a self-imposed pilgrimage, unofficially purposeful narrative spies. Eavesdropping on places, paths, and persons we've only ever read about. Walking from 'Blake to Swedenborg' is our plan. From a commemorative plaque shrunken into a blue blot between two first floor windows on a council house wall where Batman and the Union Jack compete, to an implodingly vibrant archive and legacy hub in Bloomsbury Way.

It's our take on assimilating some barefoot knowledge of an author we admire (and translate). And this time, we're not in a book. We are in London. Here and now. Centaur Street. This is personal. Local. There's the hunch of voices reading out loud in Paradise Yard. We're egged on towards a translational quest into the thickets of Iain's *Histories & Hauntings* like some foreign-tongued *Wiedergänger*. Get out of your neopagan tunnel, the smell (piss, exhaust fumes, decomposition, and mustiness) under the arch, get going. The thing is: I never turned up.

———————

Went back a few years later with Knowledge and Sinclair to find the lost stone in the wood. Recently thought to seek again with you and then stopped, because who knows if I am ever going to get there. (Brian)

Covid, once I established that my blazing throat had a label, had already been downgraded to a prolonged flu due to chronic fatigue of the electorate, was the cause. I was laid up in bed in my former home on Brixton Hill for ten days, sweating, swearing, wondering, raging, and mindwalking while my dear friend Jason, ducking behind a shield of humour and nonchalance—'You know my attitude toward germs: the more the merrier'—thankfully nursed me through it: porridge, love, and miso soup.

Heart pounding, synapses spinning like keirin legs in my sickbed, memories kept popping up. With nowhere to go, I was going places. Reality and recollection merged. I was in town. I was here … and was not. My pathetic daily commute went no further than from upstairs to the loo, the kitchen (for tea) and back. *With the walk as a form of originating performance.* Memory slogs.

I distinctly recalled the night, six years ago, after the *Future Exiles Return* reading. Taking the very same path back to my digs helped to hold back feeling completely lost. Wheeling through Blake's tunnel, Southwark, and across the Thames. Past Mile End, which was half-way. For the first time I wasn't staying or living south of the river.

The kind but shambolic Rosemary had put me up in her summerhoused garden shed (with a loo!) near Blake's 'Stratford & old Bow'. Her gentle greyhound tacitly stood in for her as my host. Sinews and bones, to the point of translucency, a spectre born to run who made me feel at home, legs twitching while dreaming sprawled on the floorboards of my temporary dwelling.

My enforced daily transit through (often both) Victoria and the Olympic Park soon became a corridor of oxygen in my toings and froings. *Centrifugal with the emphasis on 'fugue', mad travellers in hock to a dream of plurality,* I was doing the opposite. Forever going back, trying to locate a centre. Circumnavigating a volatile energy point on my folding bike. "This music crept by me upon the waters" / And along the Strand, and up the ghastly hill of Cannon St., / Fading at last, behind my flying feet, / There where the tower was traced against the night,' I read by chance. Someone falling back on Eliot. Like I do.

This heartbeat of the City was a necessary reference point but hence a far too obvious choice. I noticed some discernible pulse in the East End when I yielded to its obscure gravitational pull. Most strikingly, however, I felt the need of crossing the river whenever I could, taking longer and longer detours south of it. Double-checking my route to Paradise Yard as an excuse to stray further south with a view at Westminster from the 'right' side. Down to Nine Elms, before the Super Sewer changed it beyond recognition. Through Lambeth, *Little Portugal*, and on to Brixton Hill, *home*, where I'd lived for some years shortly after the turn of the Millennium.

―――――

The greyhound watched me quizzically while I prepared for my third day's outing on a resolutely wet September morning in 2017, carefully folding my battered Central London Cycling map to navigate through Stepney and Whitechapel. *The city is now somewhere else, both more and less than itself.* When Grey heard the rustle of my waterproof jacket she pricked up her ears, but once the rear triangle of my folding bike snapped into position she went back to snooze. Instead of heading straight on through Bethnal Green and Spitalfields, I turned left at the Chinese Pagoda in Victoria

Park, followed the Regent's Canal through Mile End Park and turned right well before reaching Limehouse Basin.

It was time to find out more about an exhibition which had been the other prime cause for my journey. 'A kaleidoscopic pair of Georgian houses' tucked away in the East End delta at the confluence of Whitechapel/Mile End Road and Commercial Road. Leaving the towpath I pedal through an unimposing residential area, somnolent during the day, unurbanly quiet at night. St Dunstan and All Saints on its green knoll, once known as the 'Church of the High Seas', Stepney City Farm and Park work as rural echoes. I follow Stepney Way until I'm washed up against the rather imposing clinical fortress of the Royal London Hospital, one of the city's major trauma centres. There's a looming darkness to Ashfield Street behind it. I'm trying to focus, to find the address, but in the end it's more of a feeling than a certainty that I've gone past Gallery 46 when my brakes finally squeal.

———

That squeal, perfectly hallucinated in 2023, laid up on a cosy sofa bed in Brixton and a cuddly toy dog as company, took me back there while I began to realize that in all probability I was going to miss Iain's exhibition *Histories & Hauntings* at Swedenborg House.

> *Possessed of the strange alchemical virtue of transmuting reality, of making us fall vertically to the point in which all is abandoned in order to know the certainty that we start again …*

So, once my bike was locked that wet afternoon in 2017, I staggered into the exhibition Iain called his attempt at a graphic novel: *The House of the Last London*. Straw bear, Swan Pedalo miniature, paintings, handwritten pages, notebooks, rescued 8mm footage, photographs (black and white), a stuffed crow 'called Odo', and maps that aren't maps. *Lud Heat* triangulations which Iain sketched out on a napkin in a pub and Brian Catling turned into a proper drawing for a 1974 exhibition in an annexe of the Whitechapel Gallery.

I'm confused. The city has gone. Has been replaced by a cod-Egyptian desert, pyramids, obelisks, and desire lines in the white sand of the paper, in force fields which only the river is free to dodge. It's not a map. Not for a cyclist stalking a writer at walking speed, familiar with *A to Z*s getting all soggy and broken and closer to indicating mere cracks and lacunae. Or maybe it is, of dreamtime, one that a matchstick-person following a hovering golden footpath towards a forest nursed by the vivid imagination of kids would employ. The painting by Renchi Bicknell is positioned right opposite the 'map' in the same room.

And this is what we walk: the shape of the gods. We burn, by use, their outline into the turf. Engrave, whatever our mind summons, on the blanks of future thoughts.

———

It was a déjà-vu. When, late on a Monday evening, Sven kindly and imperturbably popped round, masked and hands washed, to report from *Histories & Hauntings*, elated with his experience and a long conversation with Iain, I could tell by the swipe show on his phone that I'd been there already. The 1974 Whitechapel episode (I knew only by hearsay), *The House of the Last London* (which I'd visited in 2017) recreated. *The same people, confirmed in their folly, doing the same things!* A bunch of eclectic Blakean pilgrims, following in the footsteps of ghostly predecessors. Starting it all over again. Turning up in places I'd never expected to discover, to see, to experience personally. Administering significance to the place, to the narrative, to a psychic and transformative topography. Everything there linked up to everything I'd ever read and heard and misunderstood about Iain and the troupe of poets, writers, artists and magicians he lives and works with, literary decals who roam the city, all drawing from an initial source: *Albion Island Vortex*.

For days, I kept somnambulating through *Histories & Hauntings*. ('The atmosphere was calm, soporific, outside time. Intriguing.') Revisiting 'caves of memory' at *The House of the Last London*. ('Images, sounds, whispers, ghosts. A special space for the reforgotten in the labyrinthine area of London where it all began.') And reliving the *Future Exiles Return* in my mind. ('A set of collisions coinciding with the final volume in Iain's own argument with London.') An amateur triangulation, home-grown and crude. Blake, Swedenborg and *Scarlet Tracings*. IKLECTIK in Paradise Yard, Swedenborg House in Bloomsbury Way, Gallery 46 in Ashfield Street, formerly Rutland Street, emanating a spirit of Mike Goldmark.

———

At last I tested negative. Even though still feeling wobbly on my legs, I hopped on my bike. It was my last day in London. Cold, clear sky, low sun, foggy breath. Still incredulous about my first impression of Thames City, formerly Nine Elms, I wanted to have another look on my way to the Lambeth visionary. From there I would pick up on our translators' walk from 'Blake to Swedenborg', see Iain's exhibition, have tea in the bookshop, and then follow the young poet's—index finger pensively stroking the chin—1970s instruction: EAST. SATURNINE GRAVEYARD. I imagined the whole movement as describing an arc from Nine Elms to Whitechapel resembling the South Bank bow of the Thames, intersecting the river at Waterloo.

From Larkhall Rise you still have a view of Battersea Power Station. I then made a beeline towards it down Union Road and Stewart's Road at the end of which this iconic landmark had shrivelled up behind a surge of sky-scraping 'beautiful apartments and private luxury amenities, high-end retail and exquisite dining experiences'. I tried to circumambulate the temple of consumerism. WELCOME HOME. But Circus Road down to the Riverside Walk had been fenced off because of the imminent Christmas fair. I made a faltering attempt at following the 'continuous green' CGI corridor of Linear Park but ended up on service roads through waste land channelled by promised cityscapes on hoardings. Out of the blue, the sky darkened violently. A furious downpour. And no shelter in sight. I was washed into the urban canyon along the river, disoriented, out of puff. I felt it. I'd not be able to continue this journey perched atop my saddle.

Clinging to the sight of the riverbank wherever possible I ran into Tideway's Albert Embankment Foreshore construction site but recognized Vauxhall Bridge. Instead of wobbling about on pressure-losing skinny tyres I should get myself a pair of winged shoes, is exactly what I thought in that moment—or get a bus. I grabbed the handlebars, remembered the eerily welcome Vauxhall lull of some small streets shadowing the railway line, foxes crossing in full daylight, trundled towards Hercules Road, past the blue mark, folded my bike, and got on a 59 to St Bartholomew's Hospital at Lambeth North without further ado.

The upper deck window reveals a slide show. I stare down along The Cut when the bus turns towards the river, recognition without particular memories, benevolent white noise. Ridley Scott's *Napoleon* 'reigns over Waterloo'. I'm ducking my head every time a branch hits the climate-friendly white roof of my red bus on Kingsway. And feel almost level with 'John Bunyan, who wrote the famous Christian allegory from a gaol in Bedford'. His confident-looking life-size statue still occupies the niche on the north-west corner of a former Baptist Chapel which has been converted into a lavish boutique hotel preserving its 'Wrenaissance' exterior style to set off against its interior 'Decadence by Design'. I need to rush down the stairs to get off at Holborn station.

On those few occasions I'd had a chance to walk or cycle around this time, I had already noticed an odd bluish tinge in every photo I took. Like a continuous blue-hour film simulation invading my camera screen and everything I view on it. But right now, looking at Bunyan who's looking benevolently back down on me in Southampton Row with bluish lips and with his right index finger vigorously tapping on a book held in the other hand, I remember another all-pervading kind of blue. In a self-produced chapbook I'd picked up in *The House of the Last London*.

> *Renchi Bicknell has produced his own small-scale Blakean books, including a very nice book about Blake's engagement with Bunyan. He'd just taught himself etching so he was using difficulty as part of his conversation with Blake and Bunyan, alongside journal sketches from his own epic pilgrimages. It was a totally Blakean contemporary project produced in a chapbook that very few people ever saw. The book was called* A Pilgrim's Progress & Further Relations.

In hindsight I'd assume that this sudden memory influx from Renchi's book, of long-haired archetypal figures with wings set against ramblers with rucksack humps and caps all underway in the same blue timeless time made me lose my sense of destination. I turned east, 'making the effort to connect things that are ultimately already *effortlessly* connected' as Renchi has it. I didn't make it, neither to Swedenborg House nor Gallery 46.

When I looked up again it was up Ludgate Hill. The white peak of St Paul's looming, it's getting dark. I turn round, gasp. There's a last ray of sun reflected on the roof of Ludgate House. I get out my camera trying to hold and balance my little bike between my legs. The three kneeling cherubs up there once supported a globe. A guy with a ridiculous number of grocery bags dangling from his handlebars approaches me kindly, offering to hold my bike so I can take the picture. More lights in windows. And a red light, way above the golden trio. I tell the guy what's crossing my mind. "Angels now need cranes to get in position." "Yeah, mate." He grins. But what I really think, is: Go back, home, cross the river, and do it again—*on page*.

histories and hauntings

WALK INTO THE INEVITABLE

a backwardation in time

they come in packs

STALWART REMINDERS

tunnel vision

location outranks time

REANIMATE A DEMINISHING

future exiles return

articulate crows and rooks

unofficially purposeful narrative spies

PRESENT

this is personal

a volatile energy point

PORRIDGE, LOVE, AND MISO SOUP

a kaleidoscopic pair

time to find out

MEMORY SLOGS

not a map

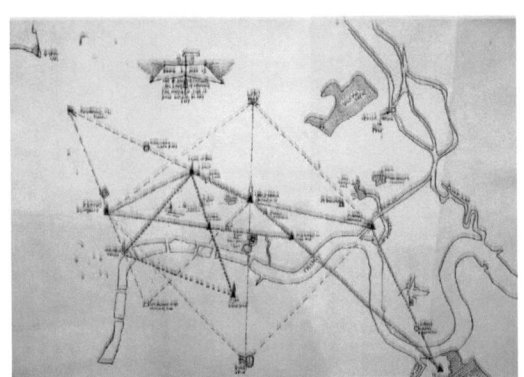

a bunch of eclectic
blakean pilgrims

administering
significance
to the place

caves of memory

ALBION ISLAND VORTEX

saturnine graveyard

promised cityscapes

welcome home

continuous green
CGI corridor

90

archetypal figures with wings   supported a globe

ULTIMATELY ALREADY *EFFORTLESSLY* CONNECTED

THE HOUSE OF *THE LAST LONDON*

'LONDON, AFTER SO MANY ABORTIONS
AND REBIRTHS, IS AN EXHAUSTED WOMB.
BUT SOMETHING DIFFERENT IS SURELY
EMERGING. IT ALWAYS DOES...'
IAIN SINCLAIR

HAUNTING SWEDENBORG'S LONDON

John Rogers

I t's a freezing cold January morning and I'm staring down into Black Mary's Hole from Rosebery Avenue where Iain Sinclair and Stephen McNeilly are standing right over the buried river Fleet. We aren't here to pay homage to one of London's principal lost rivers but to trace the footsteps of Emanuel Swedenborg through the city. Stephen and Iain recount how it was while living in Warner Street that Swedenborg had one of his more famous visions. This was an area notorious for its springs, wells and pleasure gardens during the time of his stay. It does make you wonder whether his hallucinations may have been the result of imbibing the dubious chalybeate or cathartic mineral waters that were served up in the arbours and inns that lined the valley of the Fleet.

Our route took us through the site of Cold Bath Square where Swedenborg died in 1772, and then what was known as Hockley-in-the-Hole in the eighteenth century, a place of vicious blood sports and ill repute. Here you can hear the Fleet gurgling through its sewer pipe deep beneath the street.

Onwards into Little Italy we stride blowing out big plumes of breath into the ice-cold air. In Saffron Hill there are echoes of Dickens, barometer makers, organ grinders, street musicians. Ditches and tributaries run off into the Fleet. Standing over a manhole cover Iain re-imagines the story of Swedenborg writhing in the muddy waters as a form of baptism into the sacred city. We carry this picture in our minds into Bleeding Heart Yard with its gruesome tale of Lady Hatton dancing with the devil at a ball. It's said, that when the sun rose the next day all that could be found of Sir Christopher's wife was her still beating heart pumping out blood over the cobbles of the stable yard.

Looking for the site of the Moravian chapel in Fetter Lane we get talking to a Dubliner who'd come to pay his respects to John Wilkes, radical MP for Aylesbury and Middlesex and born nearby in Clerkenwell. Stood by the Wilkes statue our conversation moves from Swedenborg to Blake, the Golden Dawn, and the Hellfire Club. I give him directions to Wycombe's Hellfire Caves and we continue our walk to Crane Court, original location of the Royal Society where Swedenborg attended lectures. Iain leads us off Fleet Street into St Bride's Avenue, beneath the church's wedding cake spire. In Bride Lane we pass the site of Bridewell Palace and an ancient holy well dedicated to St Bridget.

We stop at the Punch Tavern on Fleet Street to lunch on enormous pies, ignoring the voice that Swedenborg heard in his head telling him not to eat too much.

Stomachs full, we ascend Ludgate Hill with its links to the foundation myths of London, King Lud and all that, and sense how this Swedenborg schlep taps into that deep mythology of the city. St Paul's, where Druidic ceremonies were reported as late as the Middle Ages, or so I read in a possibly unreliable source, casts a sort of spell, using Temple Bar as a portal, that propels us out east via the Underground and we emerge in Cable Street.

Grace Alley leads us to the door of Wilton's Music Hall. Here we're crossing paths with W G Sebald's *Austerlitz*, where he was guided through the East End by the poet Stephen Watts. Was Sebald aware of the Swedenborg link we wondered? This was an area populated by Swedes, and Swedenborg lodged in Wellclose Square. He attended the Swedish church now marked by Swedenborg Gardens.

The light is starting to draw in. Stephen paints the picture of where the church once stood and tentatively claims that he has pinpointed the location of the crypt where Swedenborg's body was laid to rest. On a raised grass area that runs beside the path, a spindly newly planted tree marks the spot.

IN THE HOUSE
OF SWEDENBORG

Stephen McNeilly

> *. . . the future and the present are one and the same, for what is the future is*
> *already present, or what is to take place has already taken place.*
> —Swedenborg

I

SWEDENBORG HOUSE, 2010. Start with the basics. A view from below: *There are certain corridors, underground, within secret London buildings where ceramic tiles from the arts and crafts era achieve an aquamarine luminescence, independent of gas lamps, electricity, or human intervention. The physics of attraction defies established rules. The tile wall is a simmering stream. And the tipped floor of a Sunset Boulevard swimming pool. The researcher tries to filter out the hard information, dates and names, offered by his guide, the man with the key to the private library.* Eight objects are nominated: a typewriter, a wax figure of Swedenborg, an album of photographs, a wicker basket, a plaster skull and two ear bones.

The unacknowledged project, writes the researcher, is to 'translate mathematical formulae into language' and to assess or evaluate a group photograph from 1910 with H G Wells at the King's Hall in Holborn. 186 heads in twisted union, re-edited and archived. But what emerges and remains in focus is a memory trace whose imprint now begins to seep into and overpower the present, caught in the slow event horizon of a white hole—*a time-machine in stasis.* And this is where we begin: with Iain Sinclair and H G Wells in a two-way mirror; of time unfolding in green tiles; of the residue between passageways; of a smashed camera; of lead type washed up from the

Thames; of the merging of corridors; of Brian Catling hunched and silhouetted over lantern slides and box files; of a hidden staircase at Swedenborg House; of Renchi Bicknell arriving late in the company of William Blake; of a Whitechapel vortex; of a house that is also a skull, of *oxygen bubbles breaking beneath the ice of choked oceans*.

In mathematics, as also in geometry, writes Swedenborg, there are 'natural points' underpinning matter that serve as a nexus, a hidden *vortex* between substances. Driven on by a *conatus* that moves across mediums, the vortex is both endless and ending, both substance and spiral. *A primordial finiting*. And so also in the staging of discrete degrees, and the creation of Blake's nameless shadowy vortex. The overriding metaphor here is that of an *ellipse*: an undercurrent that 'rolls backward, a globe itself infolding', pulling all things inwardly, to an unseen centre.

II

A MAP IN REVERSE. Distance is privileged according to the direction in which one is facing. And the same is true of time. In Swedenborg's system, temporality is mapped according to a topography in which events crowd in simultaneously from all directions: forward, upward, sideways, downwards and backwards. The Whitechapel Gallery, 1974 is uprooted and overlayed onto Swedenborg House, 2023: portals between urban London streets and that other, mythic or mystic, London, and now a single staging post. The lost Fleet serving occasionally as a secret artery linking the two: whispering murmurs caught as incidental guides via the movement of detritus in drain hole openings. It is also the scene of a mud baptism, of Swedenborg's own descent into a disorder of the senses.

In this other London, east is to the front, and extends as far back as Wapping which is in the west. South is to the right and north is to its left. The south extends almost as far as Islington and towards the north are those who possess the greatest freedom of speech. In the west are spirits who are in an obscure affection for good and are fearful that their thoughts might be revealed. And in the centre, surrounded by his officers, lives a moderator. He occupies the middle street which answers to Holborn. 'Legend says the Fleet's a sewer now', adds Michael Moorcock, 'but I've seen it alive with torchlight and the swinging lanterns of the barges making for Seward's Reach and the open sea'. No longer subterranean, it marks the eastern border 'close to where it enters the Thames'. The schema again is that of a corridor. The house as river. The river as artery. In this other London, time moves upstream.

III

Radon Daughters, 1994. Before the visitation, a premonition. Another corridor and a third staging post. An urban landfill in Allhallows. The end of the world for William Hope Hodgson marks the beginning of time for Todd Sileen. Swedenborg's head is a guide. The skull returns. Underground, the hidden passageways at Swedenborg House now lead to a small room at the back of the gallery on the ground floor. One corner marks a pressure point. A series of four works aligned in sequence. The first is a yellow painting by Renchi Bicknell of himself and Iain Sinclair in search of the poet J H Prynne. The next is an aerial watercolour by Iain Sinclair of the Cerne Giant in Dorset. After this a linear map from *Lud Heat* of the Hawksmoor churches by Brian Catling. And in the centre a drawing by the cartoonist Martin Rowson of two figures lost in a Sinclairian A-Z. The metaphor, again, is that of a two-way mirror. In short we are speaking of a convergence or correspondence—a study guide for the mapping of intentions: a walk, a wait, an excursion, a conversation, an exhibition. Each marker giving rise to an event that is both itself and not itself. The only thing missing (at this stage) is the orchard at Swedenborg Gardens. The flight from Allhallows to Gravesend and then onto Wapping.

Hegel writes of a moment in which spirit transcends temporality and knows itself in its plenitude: a moment of refraction. But when standing in the magnetic axis of Moorcock's eastern border, Hegel's plenitude more closely resembles a screen onto which we project our cross-hatching and detours. A picture of the universe that begins from the inside and where the corridors and passages are no longer unconditionally subordinate to the centre. Iain Sinclair has been here before. Images are detached from the retina, and the *mapping of London* becomes a map of the London Hospital in negative, an X-ray. We suddenly see what Swedenborg sees: the *pneuma psychikon* or *spiritus animalis* is a diagram of the globe corresponding to the movement of electromagnetic impulses within the nervous system. We encounter the world in its becoming and not in its being, writes Swedenborg. What we call things or objects are simply long events.

IV

Maggid street or *Maggot Street*. A fourth staging post and an assembly point *in articulo mortis*. We have the merging of time and the metaphor of the river but there is something missing: a moment of divide or an elongation of time. 'I am dead' whispers the 'sleep-waker' in Edgar Allan Poe's 'The facts in the Case of M. Valdemar'. Directed by a gaze into his right eye, he speaks only through a strangulated movement of the tongue and is kept in this way for a period of seven months. At the very end the voice is released and the body dissolves into a state of dissolution: a putrefied mass. A similar mythology once circulated around Swedenborg, with grave robbers in search of immortality. A Wapping tomb, and bones turning into ash at the touch of a human hand. *The voice is released and the body dissolves*. And so again in Brian Catling's retake, where everything unfolds, but one step further or one step closer to the inside. Here the voice returns but speaks from the stomach. A muffled stutter.

The orthodox view, adds Michael Newton, is that one cannot write about death from within because we are confronted with the problem of first-person narration, and the problem of consciousness. We see death from the outside because death circumscribes consciousness. The great hope and the great anxiety. The converse of course is that death articulates its own narratives. When angels speak, writes Swedenborg, images appear. The effect is instantaneous.

V

CHOPHOUSE, 2016. *Place as gelatinous substrata*. An interim post between the ground floor and an outdoor mezzanine superstructure. We ascend slowly via an eastern staircase on Rosebery Avenue. Proximity is no longer a condition of environment

but a statement of intent. The shift is signalled by syringe-encrusted steps leading to Warner Street. We have barely arrived at the chophouse, now a lumberyard, before our angelic guides have begun marking new pathways, and arranging new archives. In one is captured a photograph of a spiral staircase and Iain Sinclair in ghostly silhouette. In another a picture of a pulpit from which Brian Catling reads to a rapt congregation. A deep bass note unhinges the floorboards. The windows begin to rattle. Elsewhere, in Stockholm, in velvet gloves and powdered wig, Swedenborg is at court recalling the encounter to his neighbour and friend Carl Robsahm: *I was in London and had dinner late in the cellar vaults of a restaurant where I used to eat, and had a chamber by myself. I was hungry and ate with a good appetite.* Towards the end of the meal he notices something like a dimness before his eyes, and the floor is suddenly covered with the most hideous crawling animals, like snakes and frogs. *I then saw a man sitting in one corner of the chamber.* The spirit speaks to Swedenborg: *'Do not eat so much'*. Following this Swedenborg describes how the room darkens and he finds himself alone.

On a second visit with the filmmaker John Rogers we circumnavigate the absent visionary via an out-of-date travel guide and poorly constructed endnote markers. The scene resembles an episode of Mr Benn. Or more precisely the shopkeeper, in outsized fez, opening doors towards temporal displacements. A *hieroglyphic phantom*—as Swedenborg writes—a version of which was there at the very beginning, but older. One door leading to Cambridge, another to Oxford and then to Wapping; others to the Paviland Cave, the Gower Peninsula and then to Avebury and Wayland's Smithy. In one we see Renchi Bicknell running the circles of Richard Long and in another, Brian Catling in the catacombs under Warner Street. Iain Sinclair is suddenly on the roof of Swedenborg House mapping the grid like vista of the London sprawl.

VI

SWEDENBORG'S ORCHARD, 2020. More a moment of respite than a staging post, the orchard in Wapping is both a dream conjured by Iain Sinclair and a local community project. Underneath the orchard a crypt. Once the resting place of Daniel Solander, Swedenborg and numerous clergy. Pausing longer than we should, we are drawn back to Whitechapel, to the Ratcliffe Highway, to the absent Swedish church and The Old Rose pub: *subliminal notions of Rosicrucianism, the Rosy Cross, the sense of a system of magic beneath the city.* Amidst it all is the story of the missing skull, *of a resurrectionist party in an age of phrenologists.* The reformed skull is stolen and replaced by a ringer. Years later it re-emerges in Swansea. A container of indexes, a ledger, it redistributes our imaginings in alphabetical order. In nearby Wellclose Square Swedenborg has begun writing of a time in which both skull and orchard coincide: *When an idea of a place comes to mind—be it an idea of a region, a city, or a house—an image of all the things that person has ever done in that place crops up at the same time, and spirits and angels see it all. [...] Consequently, each person is recognized by his ideas and the place in which he stands, and what is remarkable is that each one of his ideas bears an image or likeness of him or herself.* And so also with our own wanderings and perambulations.

The dead are always migrating, always moving, adds Iain Sinclair, they're always revising the story. Heads in a jar in the Crown and Dolphin pub; the docks where Swedish boats and Danish boats would come in; granite stones; the Cannon Street Road and Cable Street crossing, the body of John Williams (supposedly the Ratcliffe Highway Murderer of 1811); revised histories burdened by the weight of memory. And here also, quite unexpectedly, a gift from Brian Catling, a sword, heavy and black, in cast-iron, pointing south-easterly. A totemic memorial. An obelisk already buried, and now rooted to the spot above Swedenborg's sarcophagus. *Dry leaves, crisped and curling, like the burnt pages of a parchment diary, pile up behind the black frame.* An accidental planting and a bearer of seasonal gifts: elastic and soft to the touch, a working instrument which is mirrored back to us in the form of a monument, a single apple tree.

VII

THE YOUNGEST OF THE DEAD. A closing fold and final point of gravitation. *The dreamer has at his disposal a symbolic means of expression of which he is unconscious while awake and does not recognize what he sees,* says Freud. So also for us, back in the corridors at Swedenborg House where the dead can also dream, a posthumous sleep in which the dreamer becomes the dreamed: *Some are kept in a condition between wakefulness and sleep*, writes Swedenborg, *and think very little. By turns they wake and remember what they have thought and done during their lifetime, only to slip again into the halfway condition between sleep and wakefulness* [...] *They are below the left foot a little towards the front.* The researcher's tour of the building has metamorphosed into an out-of-body residency. Omens, signs and portents pass through the house in wavelike impulses: a 'stone' corresponds to *'passing'* whilst 'walking' corresponds to the *'metabolic system'*. Via the main artery and above the gallery—in blue mosaics—we ascend again. This time in the rhythmic footsteps of Renchi Bicknell who has brought with him John Bunyan and William Blake. Guiding markers to an upper chamber. Swedenborg is cited: the movement between place is the movement between states and the widening distance is heard like a call from a darkened room. A secret language in every step. At the top a message is written in black ink: *I see the Gate, and the men standing by it to receive us.* The dream becomes house, the house becomes landscape: a hermeneutic spiral and a final corner. The metaphor again is that of an ellipse. We enter.

On one side a room rigged by tradition and inhabited by a multitude of tongues speaking with a single voice inside six mahagony cabinets. The underground cohort in white collar and black tie are there ahead of us. Amongst them and dismantling the high table is Brian Catling. On the other side a marshland and a river pathway leading back to Allhallows. A change of tempo and register. As with Walter Benjamin's 'aura', the house now exudes an indelible stamp of remoteness: a gap or fissure moves between us and it. One is reminded of John Clare's four-day pilgrimage on the Great North Road to Northampton. The stress line of an optical illusion. The exits are sealed. The question is asked as to whether, from the windows at the rear overlooking the river, one can see the lead font being offloaded from the bridge. But Iain Sinclair, Brian Catling and Renchi Bicknell are now speaking amongst themselves, mapping new coordinates. Eight new objects are nominated: a cast-iron pipe that is also a bow, a sword, a stone, an X-ray, a black plastic crow, a map of London in reverse and a rigid inflatable boat awaiting in Gravesend docks.

BENEATH THE CYPRESS TREE

Louis Petit

I take inspiration from anywhere. Conversations, people, places and moments. I've often been inspired by Bosch, Goya, Bacon, Spilliaert as well as literature. Most of my work comes from experiences and memories from the weird understanding of the world I fell into when I was diagnosed with epilepsy and how I found myself in a woven patchwork of dreams and hallucinations. For over four years, I lived closer to death than life. The moment between those events was encapsulated perfectly in Sadegh Hedayat's book *The Blind Owl* in which the Lord of Death sat beneath the cypress tree rejecting our lives, casting us into a bottomless void. When the normal healthy state of the organism was disturbed, as soon as I fell ill, another world began to appear—on the bridge between conscious and subconscious. This is the world I depict through my practice.

PUHPOWEE (2023)
Oil on aluminium (60cm x 40cm)

Puhpowee is a Native American word that might be translated as 'the force which causes mushrooms to push up from the earth overnight'. For a long time now I've been drawn to an inherent duality that seems to lie within everything. We're both growing and becoming but also unbecoming and decaying. Going through the transition of becoming seizure-free and becoming a part of the regular world again is just as hard as leaving that society behind.

At the time, that was so painful and still is. But that feeling of myself and my soul being eaten away, and whatever state I am in now, I came to see as my journey, and all the processing was the sacrifice for attaining a new state of being. And it was eaten by time. Here I depict two interior worlds, mirrors of each other, my emotional tumult in this piece emerges from my longing to encounter natural surroundings, subsequently imbuing my perception of landscapes in a manner that blurs the distinction between external and internal realms. The natural elements soon became metaphors and symbolism for a lot of personal experience, letting go and clinging on. The anthropomorphic bug hovering over the left side reminds me of the time I spent in hospitals blankly staring at the humming, flickering fluorescent lights, much like a swarm of bugs.

TRIAGE (2023)
Oil on aluminium (40cm x 60cm)

A common hallucination I had during seizures and medical withdrawal was shadows moving with a will of their own. My thoughts at the time were more connected to my shadow, my imaginary being, than they were to my actual self as I was constantly in between a deep unconscious and a reality I was unaware of. I became comfortable moving from one space to the next, as though walking through the looking glass to find a Russian nesting doll of hallucinations, one layer of which included the shadows. At this time my memory was like a wet log that lay in a corner of a fireplace, neither burnt nor untouched, suffocating from the smoke. All I still have from this period is from my unconscious understanding of the weird space around me.

KNOCKING HEADS:
AN AUDIENCE WITH ALAN MOORE

Iain Sinclair

*He emphasised that, if we enter the world of the dead ... with conscious,
spiritual-scientific discipline, a new way of speaking about spiritual realities
and a new way of collaborating with the spiritual world would become possible.*
—Christopher Bamford [1]

Two men, researchers or supplicants, culture predators, spies, arrive in the once thriving market town of Northampton. Stepping briskly away from the railway station, responding to the slight gradient, the older figure, less burdened by instruments, takes it upon himself to rekindle memories of heritage-labelled archways, active metaphors, and locked churches with formidable but unavailable historic traces. Master geologists. Green Men. Saxon residues. The initial drift obeys a localized pull, citizens and traffic, in confirmation of an enduring cruciform geometry. There is the legend of a stone cross carried from the Holy Land and deposited in this place, a marker of status.

Craftsmen in gold. Traders. Retail alchemists. Before the alcove, like a slice of one of those stone igloos removed from old London Bridge, on the porch of the church, where the mad poet sat, accepting small commissions, liberated within unstated limits from his privileged apartments in the General Lunatic Asylum (where there was no shortage of lunatic generals): the voice-swallowing chambers in which he experimented with multiple identities, before acknowledging that he had lost touch with his own.

'Do you have an olfactory memory?' That's what the exiled author had written from his bed of pain in Paris. 'Mine is very powerful. Cordite and physick small-holdings. Lavender. Cut grass and blown roses.'

Could the sleepwalking Northampton visitor recapture, or re-experience by standing still for a moment and drawing breath, the excitement of what he had once derived from a lovely layered drench of assimilated stinks, traces of contradictory but interwoven eras: steaming shitting cattle waiting to become shoes, headbands of warm diesel air, meat sweat of pilgrims following the path of a dead queen and a flower-drowned princess smashed in an underpass.

He succumbs to the optimism of morning mist lifting from the silent river. A new quest over old ground. And one special, suspended instant, with the attendant filmmaker alert to a privileged viewpoint, and the old man wondering, as he stared at the hospital windows, just where he finishes and where John Clare begins. When the bedecked marriage cart of the blissful Moores rattled down this road, celebrated couple in performance mode, the creak of wheels and crack of whip summoned the vagrant poet's defining nightmare, when he was reclaimed by his lawful wife and condemned to twenty-three years of resigned imprisonment in this town, with no further escapes; no follies, expeditions or expectations. No reprieve for good conduct or pages filled.

.   ⋆

And then the conversation began, an engagement that had never really, over thirty-five years or so, been broken off. But that had only, on infrequent occasions, been activated in person, face to face. The commissioned author of an emerging sequence of page-turning London fictions, Alan Moore, was embedded in this place. His terraced house, his library, his chair. His family. Deep burrowed. Re-joyce-ing in the notion of an achieved essence around which myths could be embroidered. The day's witness, John Rogers, set up his cameras, without imposition, primed to catch the flow. As it played out. No interference. Shooters Hill to Abington Park. Words into waves. Tongues of flame.

On our return to the city, John fed the harvested and tumbling sentences through a set of digital filters; a spook technology capable of serving up an approximate but cryogenic transcript. Doctored and neutralized, mangled into a form where misheard names suggest alternative fictions, where questioner cannot be separated from responder. Skull sparks lost in beard thatch.

I am supplied with a print-out in which Alan's improvisations, in that seductive, smoke-ripened Northamptonshire growl, appear to be spinning away from remarks that have not yet been made. Rhetorical excesses in which offered gambits turn into stand-alone sermons. There is no starting point and no conclusion. The AI pastiche is unforgiving. This transcript of a transcript is like typing on soapy bathwater. Methane bubbles bursting in the firmament. Printed paper arrives, eventually, at a draft composed from three distinct sources, spun through a crash-site black box, before being handed over to an editor, set to forge a pretend coherence from an unknown language. From an age before or after Caxton. Gloriously illustrated in blood and honey. Like Dante Gabriel Rossetti's manuscript poems rescued from his wife's grave, wormed and muddied, but true to their occasion. A random extract from the Northampton seance is processed to arrive at a hybrid and unauthored form, the only adequate representation of what happened in the shaded room that Sunday afternoon.

✱

Do you experience a dividend in getting old, crossing the bar, going beyond biblical entitlement? Pressure is off. Nothing to be done. When ego dissolves you are free to experiment with alternative selves, to try on pre-owned masks of your own choosing, skin suits with generous elbowroom. Those tedious spatial/temporal barriers begin to leak. Rocks, swans, willows, water: they sing. You 'pass' before you pass. Before you are definitively gone, you must arrive. And once you accept the inevitable—that we are now the ghosts—you will be granted open access to parallel worlds, permanent residence among heightened realities. The archaeology of expectation.

Thematically, what is striking, as the virtual overwhelms the actual, is how certain writers have identified a city, a version of London, as prime location for teleportation between eras, karmic states; between our diminishing present and a seductive, if embellished, past. Michael Moorcock's The Whispering Swarm *and its successors are supreme examples. A portal, emerging from episodes of improved autobiography, opens into a fabulous oasis, found somewhere near Fleet Street: a 'Sanctuary' for the undead and the never-lived of immortal fiction. An 'Alsacia' closely related, geographically and metaphysically, to the visionary seizures of Emanuel Swedenborg. A supple otherwhere. An all-encompassing vastness, with no horizon, that requires the skills of a master craftsman to suspend disbelief and hold the conjured mystery in focus. 'We are twofold creatures', the scholar asserts, 'children of heaven and earth: visible beings embodied in space and time, and invisible beings of soul and spirit.'*

Radio voices from nowhere. Obliging conversationalists stepping out from the smoke of psychic burnout. The epilepsy of intent. A crisis of consciousness as the beginning of vision.

The legend of Moorcock's pre-lived life—which was also his work—qualified him to find a welcome among the tribe of fabulous highwaymen, pirates and swordsmen, doing what they have already been programmed to do in his treasured library. Like John Clare, he attended early to the wisdom of Travellers, roaming gypsy bands he registered as 'settled and unsettled' in Mitcham. The tale-tellers Clare encountered in his melancholy Epping Forest wanderings were the ones who provoked him into striking out on an epic march to his Northamptonshire village. When he returned to the forest camp, they were gone, leaving only a wide-awake hat. He was on his own. Forever.

B. Catling's Vorrh *trilogy investigates the same fertile plurality by other means. The expelled of Eden might emerge from Thames mud to invade the studio of William Blake. These more-than-mortal entities, time-travellers, coated in rags of persisting humanity, come and go. While named personalities from the historic record are permitted a second pass at their recorded obituaries. Objects and buildings from demolished cities are alive. The executed find ways of reviving, in order to embellish a dictated storyline. The three fat volumes of Catling's late seizure, torrents of image and action, are another way of summoning what Moorcock, drawing on John Cowper Powys and the hairier physicists, called 'the multiverse'. But where Moorcock and Alan Moore devise, or recognize, entry points in a real-world geography, Catling's visionary landscape is a dream of withdrawn paradise. No portals required. Otherness is all. The divinity is in the language. A way of celebrating interspecies dramas in which all our diverse neural impulses, on their speeding trajectories, collide in a charged and attentive ever-present zone of horrors and pleasures: the limitless forest and the man-made enclosures of a colonial city. The unfolding poem-epic shudders and shocks, but it is never surprising. What needs to happen, happens. We accept the higher truth of the impossible. Catling knows and proves, as Christopher Bamford said of Rudolf Steiner, that 'the visible world*

is merely the tip of an unquantifiable, qualitative, invisible reality'. The marvellous is ordinary and extraordinary, but never mundane.

The Great When, *the first publication in a promised sequence called* The Long London, *is Alan Moore's contribution to what begins to feel like a crucial set of 'spiritual-scientific' equations. Like the physicists, young and confident, established and watchful, emerging from their eyries, and gathering in Brussels, for the fifth Solvay Conference, debating quantum theory, the eccentricities of invisible atoms with their terrifying potentialities, grand theories of everything, with no starting point and world-swallowing implications. Hats off. Collars starched. Moustaches waxed. Bulging pates, throbbing with calculation, bounce light. Ready for the group shot, Mr De Mille.*

'If this London is what they call the Smoke, then that place is the Fire, you follow me?'

Moore's summoned resurrection of the painter and occultist, Austin Spare, challenges his orphaned protagonist, anti-hero and reluctant multi-dimensional tourist. We remember Voice of the Fire. *The written ghosts are in permanent residence. We are occasional trippers. We are their nightmares. At the heart of* The Great When *is another congress, convened at the Crown & Dolphin pub, beside the crossroads of Cable Street and Cannon Street Road. Articulate heads in bottles. Cromwell and Swedenborg among them.*

'The white-haired revenant in the adjacent vessel is an older man whose skin is ironed-smooth tissue paper, beard coiled like a sleeping cat in the crushed lavender, his piping voice almost inaudible from underneath its glittering dome.'

Moore's Swedenborg, disputed skull carried a short step from the prophet's actual burial place within the skeletal outline of a demolished Swedish church, presents himself as a representative of the London angels persisting outside time. 'An apiary drone of muted conversation.'

*

At this point it all crashes. There is no single narrator. No filmed interrogation. No house in Northampton. With tottering stacks of books, published and unpublished. Reforgotten or eternal in editions of one. Answer precedes question. Question is statement. Two, three, many voices trying to say the same thing in different registers.

Alan Moore speaks. And is spoken. Like a special dialect. The two invaders, who have landed themselves in his workroom, primed with cameras and recording devices, have lost the timbre and weight and velocity of his words. Are they *his* words? Are they generated by some alien technology?

⋆

'If you want to trace where the characters in this book go, to experience those civic locations, well, you can't really arrive at a conclusion. Probably, I don't know, I'm just the writer, they come to the conclusion that, yeah, alright, there's psychogeography, if you want to call it that, which is a vital thing, which is talking about place. But at the same time, inevitably, you are talking about the people who pass through. And, when you're talking about a person, you are inevitably talking about the place in which they live or in which they originated. Place and person can't be separated.

You are talking about portals: Soho, Elephant and Castle, Farringdon Road. And Arnold Circus in Shoreditch—where there apparently exists an aperture between the Londons. Unimaginable blossoms of a dissident reality, a madman's heaven tinted by a broader rainbow.'

⋆

And then, as I tried to disentangle some sort of consistent thread from the reproduced traces of the Northampton adventure, a set of wild emails arrived from my permitted Euro correspondent, the poetry-loving Advocate in Brussels. None of them spoke in his voice, as I recognized it, although passages reflected his interests. The text purported to be a letter sent by myself to Alan Moore on 30 January 2017. But it didn't have the throwaway life of anything dropped, optimistically, into a Hackney postbox.

When I challenged the Advocate, fearing that a recent bicycle accident, a fall on his head, had done him the favour of creative damage, scrambling quotations, blogs, podcasts, Moore interviews, speculative essays, AI pastiche, into a series of deranged footnotes towards his own grand Hispano-Belgian theory of everything, he confessed his mistake. He had located, in the murkiest depths of the Dark Web, something advertised as a communication from myself, hiding in a lighthouse at the mouth of the river Lea, to Alan in Northampton. The over-written tone hints at some sort of special interest commission. The lighthouse pulsed with singing bowls, tuned by a computer wizard to perform a composition promised to run for a thousand years. Embarking for Andalusia, with no internet access during the flight, the Advocate meant to send this odd retrieval to himself. For safe storage. And future utility. But hit the wrong button. So that, bridled in confusion, I received, as if from another London, the very text I was trying to assemble as a record of my trip with John Rogers to Northampton.

The Advocate posted several versions: highlighted extracts and then the whole thing. His reply to my reply was succinct. 'Your email had me in tears ... I will write properly when I find some calm within the next few days.' There was no follow up. Radio silence. Ghost to ghost. Endgame.

⋆

From: Trinity Buoy Wharf. 30 January 2017.
To: Alan Moore in Northampton.

We are invited, by means of predatory technologies neither of us advocate or employ, to consider the implications of 'long-term thinking'. And this at the waiting room of my own terrestrial transit, when I know all too well that there is no 'long-term' left! The diminishing future, protected by a feeble envelope of identity, has already been used up. Wantonly. And the past, a noose of mistakes and miscalculations, is out there as a coded sequence of repeating flares. I watch the night. The neurotic lightshow across the river from the diamond-pane windows of this lampless lamp room.

Meditation, in the tower, at the mouth of the river, however well intended, seems to be about not-thinking, experiencing. Having tried, for too many years, to muddy the waters of oblivion with untrustworthy fictions and 'alternative truths', books that detoured into other books, I am colonized by images and private obsessions, vinyl ghosts from an unmapped digital otherness. This is our fate and we must accept it. Obey the dictation of those who are dreaming us.

But I am reminded of a notion you once pitched—and which I probably misrepresent—that time is a solid. *And that place, those named locations, sites of inspiration, are permeable, open on request. They carry enough of a charge to exist in our limited lifespan but also in the city of vision to which we aspire. What you define as 'Eternalism' feels like the Swedenborgian mapping of a self-duplicating history in which past, present and future co-exist. Avatars more real than their supposed creator: the unborn and the nearly-born, vegetative Buddhas on park benches, all sounding at once. Like those massed shelves of bowls in the lighthouse. Brazen skulls split into drinking vessels. Each and every one of them invisible to the others. Until they chose to speak. And we to listen.*

The trick is easier in somewhere like Northampton, with its subterranean levels, its round chapels and catacomb burrows, its echoing hospitals, its markets, its roads leading out in all directions. They march in procession, these disenfranchised pilgrims: tramps, Levellers, Ranters, unemployed bootmakers, working mothers festooned with infants, shoeless prostitutes, damaged seers, artists, incarcerated poets. And skewed relatives, awkward ancestors who won't let go, mobbing around a heavenly snooker table in the Labour club, plotting an escape to London, another fugue.

You speak of 'the illusion of mortality, post Einstein'. And of 'soiled simultaneity'. And you catch, before it happens, the delirious glossolalia of our conversation, voices talking about different things in the same room, while being programmed by alien implants. Northampton imagines London. London gives shelter to those who spend their lives preparing an escape: John Clare on the Great North Road, letting it all go, in order to be absorbed for his last years into this centre. Or Vincent Van Gogh trudging from Stockwell to Brighton, Margate to Lewisham, to Welwyn. Shards hopeful of becoming one with their better selves, their cabbalistic angels.

✳

The name of the 'central protagonist' of Alan Moore's *Long London* came to him in a dream—when, perhaps faithful to the daily grind at the word-machine, he achieved involuntary gnosis. Glimpses. Glints. False jewels embedded in real toads. We're done. Alan has to take time out to compile the menu for his weekly Morrison's delivery. "The limit of my literary output for today", he says.

NOTES

1. The quotation from Christopher Bamford is taken from his introduction to 'The Influence of the Dead on Destiny', in Christopher Bamford, *Encountering Rudolf Steiner. Introductions to Essential Works* (Hudson, NY: Steiner Books, 2022).

2. *A Walk Across Northampton to visit Alan Moore with Iain Sinclair*, the film by John Rogers, from which this account is derived, was posted on YouTube, 26 May 2024.

A KIND OF MAGIC

Javier Calvo

A small but loyal contingent of fans of weird walks, Druidic perambulations and desire lines (both urban and rural) have passionately followed Iain Sinclair's career for decades. The type is benevolently satirized by Martin Rowson in a cartoon that recently hung in the exhibition *Histories & Hauntings*. In the cartoon, a driver tries to find his way around Dalston using a series of Mithras, Dr Dee and Magog landmarks taken from the Iain Sinclair edition of the *A-Z London Street Atlas*. Sinclair, for his part, jocularly distances himself from the fact that his repertoire of performative techniques replicates the methodology of folk and ceremonial magic—burials and unearthings, perambulations and circumambulations, talisman creation, alignments on the territory, river pilgrimages and defensive anti-capitalist spells. In his book *The Verbals*, Sinclair admits that all these operations are, for him, 'more than a metaphor', but is quick to assure that he has 'never had any dealings with [the occult]. And if I had them, obviously, I wouldn't say'. He admits having drawn in his formative years from esoteric works such as Alfred Watkins's *Early British Trackways*, John Michell's *The View Over Atlantis* or Elizabeth Gordon's *Prehistoric London*. However, he seems to dismiss all of that as part of the zeitgeist. As methodological tools that he secularized for his own interests. From then on, he simply continued using the gesture of the magical operation, in a perpetually ambiguous manner. The emphasis on myth and ritual in books like *Lud Heat* and *Suicide Bridge* seemed to fade into the urgency of the here and now. Sinclair's manifest central interest from the 90s onwards, the vindication of the reforgotten in the face of hyper-accelerated erasure of the past, conceals the foundation of the Sinclairian operation. The method of magic, the goal of subversion.

Histories & Hauntings is a compendium of traces from 50 years of ritual activity. In that sense, it is identical to the rest of Sinclair's body of work—all his literature and art have that same retrospective component. The work itself is performative and private— the author performs it alone or in the company of friends. What reaches the public are records and traces of something that happened in the past. Written chronicles, photographs, films, diagrams and obsessive documentation, objects transmuted into talismans by charging them with imaginative energy. *Histories & Hauntings* adds an element of complexity to the procedure by constantly alluding to the seminal event of a previous exhibition held half a century earlier. 50 years later, the same three artists— Sinclair, Brian Catling and Renchi Bicknell—reunited in body and/or spirit to show how their archives have grown. It is made explicit from the start that the 2023 show is a new iteration of the project that began with *Albion Island Vortex*. I quote from the 1973 original exhibition proposal to the Arts Council:

> *We take Blake's Jerusalem (the emanations of the giant Albion) as a metaphor and a starting point. We would present the available environment (as far as possible) in sacred terms. Use of the space available. Colour. We would include the Gower Peninsula, Wiltshire, the Ridgeway, Avebury, the Yorkshire Moors, North Wales, Northumberland. Walks taken. The ancient tracks. [...] Recordings of rock clues, megalithic playback.*

So, the original exhibition took place. The vortex was opened. The pilgrims had ritually travelled the ancient pathways and returned to London bringing their spiritual bounty. Photographs, semi-automatic drawings as channellings of place, paintings of numinous sites, scars from visionary episodes. Notice the uncanny similarity between the lists of directions typical of 1960s and 1970s performance art—like the proposal quoted above—and the lists of directions we find in Western occult tradition's grimoires. On the one hand, what ended up on the Whitechapel Gallery's walls was the documentation of a series of artistic performances. On the other hand, those documents were ritual traces, like the esoteric orders' chalk circles and smoking wands, 'a few trophies brought back from road and track and cave', 'evidence of events dissolving into myth'. The consecration of the exhibition room walls to guardian animals—crow, owl, goat, wolf—did not exactly favour secular reading. But the interesting thing about *Albion Island Vortex* was not its reactivation—perhaps, after all, zeitgeistian—of Watkins's ancient trackways or Michell's ley lines. It was not the transmutation of roadside crow carcasses into mythological crows. It was the fact that it established a methodology that Sinclair would never abandon.

Rituals big and small. The best known, perhaps, for its epic dimensions, is his perambulation of the M25 motorway, 127 miles, in 2001. With 'a ritual purpose: to exorcise the unthinking malignancy of the [Millennium] Dome, to celebrate the sprawl of London'. Perambulations, in Britain, never fully severed their umbilical link with pagan practices and folk rituals. Beating the bounds and planting boundary stones are partially de-ritualized versions of the ancient ceremonial perambulations originating in Anglo-Saxon Britain, such as those celebrated on Rogationtide, in the days leading to Ascension Day. These in turn go back to the Roman festivals of Terminalia and Robigalia, and further still to the pre-Roman world. Ceremonies such as the old Rogationtide perambulations included strategic stops at landmarks to recite incantations and invocations and had a protective and purifying effect on the circled territory. A rite to keep out bad influences. Or to exorcize the demons of capital and urban development, in the case of Sinclair. Other famous exorcizing perambulations: around the City of London in 1995, retracing the perimeter of the old Roman Wall. Or around the blue fence of the Olympic Park under construction, 2008.

80 miles northwards, from Epping Forest (another liminal space) into Peterborough, to restore the symbolism of John Clare's late-life pilgrimage: No poet is born mad. A mysterious whalebone box, carved from the remains of a whale stranded in the Isle of Harris, consecrated by artist Steve Dilworth and talismanic in nature, displaced for 25 years, is returned to the Northern Isles and interred in an emergency magical operation, after certifying its properties as a radiating battery for health and disease. But if objects and places have memories, like Sinclair suggests, if they are accumulators

and repositories of orgonic energy—to use another old zeitgeistian term—then we are but two steps away from reverting to the Old Religion, animistic in nature, conservative in scope: do not plough over a boundary stone. A Cult of Landmarks. A Musaeum Clausum of unlikely talismans and unearthed locations, excursions referred to by the press as quixotic. Walking the overgrown ruins where the Southampton Royal Victoria Military Hospital used to be, in search of nightmare visions hidden by official history, is surely a political act. But it's also shamanistic. Creating a sacred geometry out of obelisks and Hawksmoor churches seems a harmless enough literary exercise, material for a visionary book. Except, once created, the geometry stays in place. And did Sinclair really dismember a copy of Peter Ackroyd's *Blake* and bring the fragmenta, Osiris-like, to a series of Blakean sacred sites?

The narrative of *Histories & Hauntings* is very much about re-enacting the old zeitgeist. It can be read as a dialogue with its 1973 predecessor exhibition, or as a comment on it, or as a straightforward attempt at completing it. (Due to an anomaly, *Albion Island Vortex* never had a closing date.) However, it may be most inspiring to interpret *Histories & Hauntings* as an invocation, an act of bringing back a specific moment in time and reactivating it, so that it stands in simultaneity with us. Some of the original relics from the '73 show are exhibited again—Catling's sketches, Sinclair's black and white documentary photographs of the Gower Peninsula, along with Bicknell's first batch of 'pilgrim paintings', divided into almost narrative panels illustrating different stations of his mystical fugues into re-sacralized territories. (Bicknell's art from all periods marks him as the most enduringly and explicitly mystical of the trio.) Additional archival material from the Vortex period is displayed in cabinets—mostly related to the seminal westward Ridgeway-Avebury journey that inspired the '73 exhibition. A journey that struck apparently prompted by the search for a stone Catling had seen in a vision, but that instead resulted in the finding of a crow. The early Seventies collection also includes stills from the Sinclair/Catling alchemical film *Maggot Street*, and Sinclair's own colour narrative drawings. Later work exhibited is stunningly consistent with the Vortex material—more pilgrim paintings and sketchbooks by Bicknell, leading to his grandiose 12-panel *Pilgrim's Progress* done in Blakean-style etchings. Catling's book-sculptures, or sculpture-books, include the occasional magical sigil, while one of his most impressive relics, a 'Stumbling bow' fished out of the Thames by Gareth Evans in 2023, was not physically created by Catling—it was written into his novel *The Vorrh* and then regurgitated by the river-mud as an offering to the Swedenborgian temple. A paranormal ready-made.

And I have saved the sword stuff for last.

It turns out Sinclair has placed in the centre of his exhibition what he calls an 'unquiet object', a sinister black sword of primitive design, 'a thing of ominous power'. The placement, if you will allow me, seems to once again belie his reputed disinterest in practical magic. The sword's location is justified by its numinous history—forged in 1974 by Catling and given to Sinclair as a sort of poisoned chalice, it immediately manifested its angry nature. It radiated such aggressive vibes that its new owner was forced to wrap it in sackcloth, tie it with ropes, and hide it under a sofa, where it continued to make its presence felt. On two occasions, understandably concerned, Sinclair tried to get rid of it—the first time, by burying it in Montacute, Somerset; the second, by leaving it on loan in the Outer Hebrides, as is done with cursed objects. The sword's inclusion years later in *Histories & Hauntings* is clearly strategic. Placed at its centre, signalling the direction of the visit (pointing directly to *Lud Heat*'s map of churches and obelisks), it does much more than simply mark the axis of the exhibition. It is the battery or accumulator that powers everything else. Its presence (which also symbolizes the Catling-Sinclair axis) transforms the room into the nave of the apse to which it points. It turns the gallery into a temple, a Swedenborgian Lusthus. Which is not to say that, when subdued into its reliquary, it did not kick and scream like the angry object that it is—at the very moment of its installation, Sinclair indicates, 'a section of the roof fell in [and] Renchi's small painting of our visit to Mr Prynne in Cambridge hurled itself from the wall'.

True: the final part of the sword's story is powerfully reminiscent of the classic Monty Python 'Accident' sketch. Even so, Sinclair's readers are used to the emergence of the paranormal in his chronicles. The genesis of *Albion Island Vortex*, for example, is closely associated with a psychophony—a disembodied voice channelled through the walls of the Whitechapel Gallery, which warned artists that 'Ramsey holds the key'. One of Sinclair's recent books, *Agents of Oblivion*, opens with several sightings of writer Steve Moore walking around his neighbourhood in the days following his death. And these are only two examples. Sinclair is clearly a lover of phantasmagoria, seances and invocations. However, he loves even more to tell these stories with a smile and a shrug, suggesting their very value lies in their lack of explanation. As in the story of the sword, everything comes down to 'energies'.

But what are those *energies* Sinclair has been referring to for fifty years? Is it just hippy mumbo-jumbo? Are they 'more than a metaphor' but not much more? Are they another name for an intangible effect such as the Blakean imagination? Or perhaps Sinclair is discreetly alluding to something different, something we could call Albion's Old Ways, all that stuff us continental Europeans associate with Ancient British Druids, stone circles and magical swords stuck in rocks? Is it a kind of magic?

Unlike Iain Sinclair, who claims to know next to nothing about magic, Alan Moore styles himself an expert in the matter. He certainly looks like a magician from the Middle Ages. Moore describes his own brand of Chaos (non-traditional) Magic in essays like 'Fossil Angels' (2002) and 'Magic, Running in The Gutters Like Lightning' (2010). In these treatises, he ultimately identifies magic as Art, thus 'returning to the magician his or her original shamanic powers and social import, giving back to the occult both a product and a purpose'. Operating in his higher-self domain, the Ideaspace, the artist 'shifts the consciousness of both [herself] and her audience', changes men's lives and thence changes history and society itself. It 'conjures Goya devils and Rossetti angels into visible appearance. It is both the bane and most beloved tool of tyrants'. As Moore goes on describing Art's fundamental occult power, an intuition arises. As a wielder of magical gestures and ritual performances taken from Albion's tradition and reformulated in the service of political and economical resistance, Iain Sinclair not only seems to fit like a glove with Moore's definition of what a true magician is—moreover, that definition could have been directly inspired by Sinclair's ongoing artistic and literary operation.

Now a final element found in *Histories & Hauntings* seems to allude almost ironically to this intuition. Three recent black and white photographs of Iain Sinclair, taken by his occasional accomplice Anonymous Bosch, portray him as a traditional, almost Golden Dawn-era, magician. Wielding his magical black sword; arms outstretched in Crowleyan priestly fashion in front of an obelisk; and holding his mythological crow. In all three photographs he appears with a crooked half-smile, complete with sunglasses and baseball hat, placing the images in a decidedly indeterminate 'this is serious but not serious' zone. He almost seems to be winking at his audience, inviting us to decide for ourselves if we buy or not his tale of ancient pathways and numinous talismans. And it could work both ways, of course. This particular member of the audience was certainly disconcerted when I left the exhibition. After a few days of thinking about it, and finding myself unable to forget that dangerous psychic sword, I finally remembered another legendarily angry black sword, bringer of catastrophes and swallower of souls, a powerful symbol that has fascinated me since childhood. And then I remembered the Blakean motto that welcomed visitors to *Histories & Hauntings*, written by the creator of that other, older sword:

IN MY SKULL'S A MULTIPLICITY OF SPHERES. AN INFINITY OF ALBIONS

VOYD SUTURE:
BEING, AN ACCOUNT OF A BLADE'S PROGRESS

Anya Reeve

The pecuniary meagreness of his priesthood was supplemented with the forging of iron sermons. Holiness did not leaven mortal bread, except where it was gifted by parishioners, but the earnings of blacksmithing did. The weight and muscled swell of his arms was not, then, a randomness of the maker. He knew his predecessor in the pulpit had been a man of pulled proportions, a crane of too-taut skin crooked over the congregation. That assembly had expected a similarly rake-thin protégé to inherit the spot, and like stirred feathers had shifted in their seats when he first undertook the steps up to the lectern instead. His bulk (emphasized by the thick cream of his robes) and strength had surprised them; he clearly could not subsist on masticating paper and words alone. They had also not bargained on the polycoria of his left eye, the two inky black pupils swimming in the one mauve iris.

He found working with the iron necessitated a ceding of respect the same way being a priest did. He revered and interpreted the iron, but only, he felt, as it permitted him. There were uneven lines and bumps which insisted on their being, asymmetries which to his eyes were sacred. Not that sight and observation themselves were easy. The two pupillary spots in his left eye struggled to focus, and then there was the densely coaled air of the forge, which prompted ocular water. His sense of touch, however, was assured. He knew when the shape and texture of a design as intended had been fulfilled. The fingerprints impressed in silver by the tongs and the hammer made him wonder: were *they* in the room, assisting in the work? The ones implicit in air's substance, and the gaps between speech? Sometimes in cold breeze, walking around the vicinities of the village as he turned the composition of his next sermon over, he pondered whether *they* were also working and coiling in the same frigid sense as he: and whether that portended the angelic quality of clarity, whether that was something he could draw into his chilled frame and his words. He was trying, always, to be less obscure—or else to make obscurity itself the clear thing.

Maybe that was a return of having two pupils to the one eye: he always seemed to see two things at once. The immediate and the meaning.

It was why he was able to deal with one of the stranger incidents amongst his congregation with such sharp insight. When a woman began to compulsively swallow fistfuls of white petals, scratching her knuckles against her teeth, he was the only person who looked at her and innately understood. He had kneeled on the floor with her, his ophthalmic film staring into hers. With his empathetic intervention she had made a recovery. He began to think that all vision bore the metallic thumbprints and forefinger-marks of invisible administrations and understandings. That reality itself was a kind of clay of empathy. It was not just the blur in his fluidic mauve eye that made him think that.

He undertook to work metal into gestures of care as well as utility. He had been wed before he was ordained—the village accepted this unbegrudgingly, their gentleness of accommodation meeting his—and for his wife, Oreute, he pulled and twisted hairpins of contortive starlings. Before the days of his priesthood she had birthed with great agony and even greater risk their young son. His chest and his fear had never been so worn as in those precarious days; his anxiety could have slaked a stone smooth. The long days of rest and administered bone broth were hard to bear for as active a person as Oreute. She missed seeing the full span of birds in the woods. Her face became absent and unreal; soft angularities played along her bones in pale glows of distant blue and mint, mediated by the window's one pane. This had prompted the priest's most delicate craft: two thin and smallish metal wings, the outfit of an oversized starling in burnished black and grey. He had tortured the adduction of his eyes trying to link a fine chain, to lightly hold the space between the wings and over Oreute's shoulders. He offered the jewellery to her body with quiet and unassuming devotion, and she sat before the bedroom window's squared aperture of light, the expectant wings on her back making a sanctification of pewter. The elevation of her smile was the last and most important link.

For his son he made metal blocks and striding mares. His son: both blundering and nascently brilliant; at times, brutal and heedless, as only children can be so nonchalantly; on other occasions, deeply empathic and kind, like his mother Oreute or himself. The child was still at an unremembering age when the priest decided he would begin making him a sword—to be put aside, folded in cloth, and given to him in his adulthood. As he began the long hours of forging (a second labouring, even if it demanded considerably less from him than the first did from Oreute), it soon became clear in his mind that the weapon would be unusual, even ritualistic in aspect. He did not want to make quite the standard form, to recite the same masculine formula of previous examples. He evaluated whether this sprung from an egotism of the parent: the need to differentiate one's issue, and the inheritance one would leave behind. He ultimately preferred to think his concept was more generous than that; and that he was accommodating something of Oreute's personality, too, in the sword's identity. The guard of the iron sword he shaped into a thickly rounded half-moon arc, cupping a circular pommel suspended on a short, discreet stem. Eye-like—a cyclops' phrase in graphite. Beneath the guard, both marking and enclosing the tang, was a block upon which he etched a runic marking.

It was laid upon the squarish anvil, metal upon metal, like an artwork of black paint upon black paint. An exercise in light's dim demarcations. He watched its surface glowering, making flowered heat patterns in the air, before placing the sword to gradually cool in a clay-walled box of ash.

Bringing a weapon into being is never an act without the potential for consequence.

For three days, the priest left the blade to its solitary and ash-crowded glooming, the scalding degrees slowly being drawn out from its inner core. Then he came to assess it, and in short, was pleased with his work. He took the sword out of its box; gripped it in his hand to test its weight; settled it down again upon an adjacent workbench. It felt such a vital and charged presence to wield. He had not gleaned that, in his hammering of dents and finger-like markings into the blade's surface, he had conferred something of his own transferrable humanity and empathy. A silver rub of soul upon its planar iron heart.

When the priest set off for a brisk walk around the village—releasing a sigh of contented accomplishment as he departed—he did not think about the door to the outbuilding where he forged, its lately unclasped lock, or how the latch would be tried in a few minutes. It was the blur in the corner of his vision that morning: a small smudge, proleptically moving.

Oreute and their son were in the house together. Oreute had started teaching the boy to count—tallying lines on paper—and then had shown him how to draw the footprints of birds, which seemed to the boy a rearrangement of the same. She dispatched his freedom into the back garden, as she sought leave to spread butter and disassembled chive flowers on toasted bread: lunch for them to share. What possible harm for him, among the last blue spathes of the nivalis?

The boy's naïve steps were a spring on the earth, stumbling. He tracked straight to the forging shed (as if it had already been designated in his mind as his object), reached up to the latch and pushed it upwards as he stood on his toe-tips. The door swung forwards and he fell flat, crushing dirt into his elbows. He rectified himself with a robust and wilful purpose, and staggered through the heavy miasma to the blade where it rested. He reached up and gripped the circular pommel with one hand. It was too heavy for him to lift, but he pushed and it pivoted slightly to the side, by thirty or so degrees. It nicked the fabric of something imperceptible, and a sap of elsewhere leeched from the wound. The boy felt the change in atmosphere and was drawn towards its source: the digits of his fingers clumsily grasped at the air. Oreute opened the door, panicked, in the second before the child met the voyd. It was too small an aperture for his name to be heard. He was stuttered over time, and gone.

In a smeared bleaching of vengeful grief, the priest buried the iron sword in a plot of earth. He compressed the damp ground forcefully, compacting black folds of soil. He forcefully extracted tears from the lachrymal ducts worn by his god and did not barter over the consequent length of his penance. Indeed, the priest wept so violently that his polycoria—without any known precedent—fused back into one fretted pupil, a contusion of inky tissue in his left eye. And as for his words, his congregation became subject to increasingly abstracted and torsional prose, as he agonized after the icon and the meaning. His empathy remained, despite; it was why they kept coming back. Humanity soaked through even his most bleak and questioning sermons.

He had wanted to consign all presence of the object he had made. There was occasioned a hollow irony: he had buried it and been deprived of burying the son it had absented. And yet, his interment of the sword was not the final statement he had wished. The sword wove itself, by suggestion, through rock and snow, back to his elsewhere son again. As a woman who sleeps in coiled ropes of snow's dress, the sword lay dormant. Waiting until the son would stumble into an understanding—of the landscape, of the past, of recuperation—that could only be called love.

The son would inherit the same blacksmithing arms and fingers as his father in this other temporal locale, as well as his own iteration of merged sight. He would make for sorrow and sin, faith and communion. He would reforge the sword into being: a companion, for a while, before disavowed. He would sup at the lilac-sapping wounds of angels and nurse them once more to flight. He accepted their silver fingerprints into his eyes, onto his tongue. The travelling son, with his driftwood cross. But of this and other fulfilments, the forger-priest and his harrowed wife would never know. There was only the empty space, the singular expulsion.

The tactility of life's substance had, for the first and only time, been truly subtractive rather than additive in the priest's hands. It would haunt him for long years hence.

—

The blade stirred from its cellophane cocoon. It was exposed to the atmosphere of the white-painted Georgian gallery. It listened to an altered loaming of air, strange and new, loaded with evolutions of speech and phrase.

Well, Brian tried to bury the sword he had made, you see. As did I—both times setting off from Hackney. I went once in company with him, out west, and then after he died I went to the Outer Hebrides with Anonymous Bosch and Andrew Kötting. On both occasions, carrying the thing. And both times we failed. It was as if it was resisting burial.

Its edge gently and implicitly pressed a slit along the suture of the past, and let bud a spectral magnolia over the walls, over the floors.

With thanks to Brian, for making the sword;
To Renchi, for putting me in mind of a progress;
And to Iain, for letting me wield the blade and material.

STOMPING GROUND

Jack Catling

The feet of the weary and hopeless, the glad and the exultant, the lustful and the pure have made that hollow; and most of those feet are now in the doorstep of the grave: and that doorstep is to me sacramental, if not a sacrament.
—Arthur Machen, *The London Adventure*

HOUSE & SHELL

On dreaming, immersed in the multicoloured lantern glow of late-afternoon stained glass, dripped through with dull-grey leaden tears, twisting against the frosting of outside chill. This warm cocoon has been hollowed out through years of straining against wood and stone, bodies pushing forward, escaping from the cold with one hand clawing and the other stretched out, grasping for a glass. The air has grown stale and heavy, wet with ammonia and dark beer. Varying scents of tobacco map each breath in a stifling, hazy web. This atmosphere reaches deep inside the strained labyrinth of lungs, veins and livers, gently exploring every crevice and marking its progress with sticky threads. Another meeting, another voice queuing to loosen itself, bearing witness to his curious life and untimely death. As this latest in the long queue of echoes jangles out their fragmented story, the words becoming a slow, stuttering blur.

Half-awake, the vortex is transformed; a landscape of sound blossoming in the dark. The jarring chorus of Birdsong emerges in gradual, myriad forms, a squawking, peeping, rasping melody incongruous against the neighbours' hacking coughs that explode between suckles of the day's first cigarette and the quivering avalanche of assorted barking dogs. Eventually all is subsumed in the growing rumble of traffic, cars, trains and planes crawling toward the oasis of the city. The sky growls in sullen complaint as the yellow hues of morning begin to eat at its soft, inky fabric. The growing stain of morning shepherds a wakefulness, bodies begin to thaw, stretch, leak and twist, drawing consciousness out until finally the eyes break open their morning seals of crusted sleep with a brief sting. A growing awareness of chill slips beneath the translucent sheet, its thin fingernails piercing subtle gaps, stiffening in the void between fabric and skin. Outside of the delicate, shrouded bed a dim, dusty light is rebuilding. Still the feeling of fine, white sand extends from the eyes' sleepy, sharp grit, its solidity temporary and whipping into shifting alignments that must dissolve when touched. Has the house been here waiting silently throughout the night or has it, caught in some nefarious act of non-being, suddenly woven itself together upon waking. The first, tentative step from the mattress feels as though it will slip through the floorboards, down several storeys before eventually remembering that a house exists. Perhaps that is who the ghosts are; those who never remembered. Sliding from the chilled white sheets into the fullness of the cold brings awareness of pale phantom nudity, awkward and briefly sexualized before the many windows that peer through the revealing lingerie of lace curtains. With the image of all those blank morning eyes the fumbling cover of awkward hands is sought, a simple gesture of supplication mingled with a creasing of the body and the dash toward the small adjoining bathroom.

This house has a fading, awkward grandeur atypical among the buildings surrounding it, all pillars, hard wood and intricate cornices. The walls and ceilings are patterned with the hairline cracks of subsidence, patches of black mould peeking out from the seams which grow silently in number by the hour, seemingly held together more with memory than bricks and mortar. There are other residents, rarely seen but often heard in shuffling steps and cascading water, rhythmic against the sleep-starved nights as they visit the water closets peppered throughout the building. More numerous than the small bedrooms, these toilets branch off from the spinal column of the winding staircase, most sealed up in a chaos of screws and nails but still somehow in use. In the small hours of the night the building becomes a hollow shell, bleached bone white, with its umbilicus of hidden chambers and the constant echoing sounds of a flushing sea. Those residents who have been glimpsed furtively, shuffling quickly into doorways or disappearing into the heights of the staircase appear as old as the house itself. The deep etched wrinkles on blank faces and knotted bodies give them the quality of moving sketches, thick charcoal lines progressively arranged into brief human familiarity.

Down further, clothed now, the front door ajar with a glimpse of the cold street. One shivering hand rests on the brass doorknob, hesitating to relinquish its grip. It's time to pour out into the spitting street, late morning is drawing in. Through the crack of the door, the city's grey rain-streaked hues take on the appearance of a heavy blanket thrown across a hulking mass, a membrane resembling a painted canvas, scrawled with slapdash scenery. This lazy guise of streets and buildings, when seen up close, reveal their crude trompe l'oeil technique as they streak in sympathy with the falling rain. Through the house's faded doorway it is an artificial ocean; it's shifting skin folding against itself, the surface creating pockets that smear their shadowy recesses.

Today's London does not have the familiarity of yesterday. It has been altered through this lens of burrowing; the slow, desperate search for the elusive poet. Glimpses have been emerging briefly through his own patchy biography or the shifting recollections of his peers, but frustratingly nothing tangible. The poet's cornucopia of acquaintances appeared to know him intimately, each with a number of tales to tell, a bounty of histories to unfold in melting yellow lines across beer-splashed tables, none of which shed any further insight. The flattened ground speaks of a direction of travel, picking out traces stomped to fading with meagre textual clues. At each turn a constant, eerie impression of a room recently vacated can be felt. Books throb in the satchel that hangs too loosely across the shoulder. A warning perhaps? A whisper that they are getting closer to the tree that bore them? Or maybe it's simply the arching of the spine, splitting in complaint against all the awkward pub chairs and the low desks forced upon it over the last few weeks; or the semaphore twisting of the back as the latest acquaintance opens yet further intricate doors. A body is not meant for this, too much, too soon, and branching out along too many simultaneous paths.

WINDOW MIRRORS

Out in the pissing street, last night's unknown time, distance and quantities begin to make themselves felt; deep, mysterious floodwaters release their secrets in stumbling waves of nausea, something typical of the last few weeks. The thought brings a flash of acid, burning up from the depths of the oesophagus, triggering a slowly unfolding pain through the body's vertical channels. The street narrows, echoing the painful contraction of those pink, fleshy tunnels. Shopfronts, cheap and temporary bearing down, gape in fragile glass and plastic, a thin veneer that presses itself into the road as the pavements dwindle to fraying tightropes. The gaze is torn between demands, forcing a brief stop before a shopfront full of mirrors, shoulders compressed against both sides of the narrow road. Staring into the window reveals an enchanted glittering madness that stares back. Reflections of all shapes and sizes, ornamental, gilded and neon plastic, toys, huge wall-length mirrors, and tiny compacts, all jostle for attention. The looking glasses, all angled in a certain way to draw the eye from the cracks in the walls and floors, some large enough to slip a hand or arm into. This chaos of forms is numbing, but it somehow does not seem unplanned. An imagined purpose emerges from the intersections of viewpoints and the guiding of light throughout the day, an echo of layers of confusing alleys and feigned jejune. The placement of all these elements resemble something between a spider's web and a conjuror's silk, it hides and it entices. Glancing into the window of this shop, your head and body is splayed as a specimen on the cutting room table and deconstructed into something monstrously cubist. Turning away, the vision somehow lingers longer than expected, making you aware of how jarringly inhuman you look from unfamiliar angles, and in turn sensations emerge from parts of you that you were never aware of. To enter the shop would be to fully unravel the threads and in their dispersal, be drawn into the gaps which the mirrors hide leaving only a reflection. Sinking into the coat collar to avoid the spectral gaze, it is easy to imagine having left a tiny part of this encounter suspended forever in the potential of the glass planes.

PRESSING THROUGH

It has taken a while to find the crumbling gallery, set back from the Old Kent Road via the snaking tendrils of East Street. Following the skeletal stalls of fragile metal reveals outlines of the market's Monday absence, heavy with loitering scents and hardening remnants. The small gallery is set into the community centre, compressed and straining for presence against the staggering weight of derelict tower block above.

Its current exhibits; candy-pastel landscapes created by one of the poet's satellite acquaintances. The place is too busy for anything other than an introduction and a promise of future liaison. From the time of arrival, the only option is to awkwardly loiter among works: a hectic arrangement of sculpted frames that bleed into each other across the room, opening up into the small ceramic-esque vistas that outline bloated bubblegum dreamscapes. Each pseudo-landscape reaches out playfully, languorous and unnerving, somewhere between hardness and yielding softness. Two or three plastic cups of box wine later and it is time to leave, colliding with the growing crowd that pushes through the lobby, a handful of familiar faces sporadically appear upclose in the tide, but not enough to linger.

The gallery's maze of sculptures, bodies and tangled interactions gives way to an empty courtyard. Traces of bulbous cobbles can be felt seething beneath the feet in a slow rolling boil out of the asphalt and pressing themselves upwards. An incessant wash of grey rain, falling in large oily droplets, washes away the sense of direction, curving the pavements in slippery loping circles. A stricken, frantic classic; the man with one leg shorter than the other, doomed to navigate haloes in a constant orbit of his destination. Turning yet another corner, we may see ourselves in the distance through the prismatic downpour, moving ahead in confused determination. Another anonymous shopfront, murky glass and grey pocked concrete, with nothing to advertise its purpose except the steam that frosts its windows. Desperate to get away from the downpour and pushing at each glass panel a door is revealed, which gives way in jerked inches. An off-licence, small but voluminous. Fragile shelves burst at the seams with simple desires; yellowed magazines peeling against packs of biscuits, frail plastic objects somewhere between toys and household items, all seeming to have existed in this balanced state for decades. The counter can be seen on tiptoe, in glimpses beyond the mess of shelving and objects, unstructured familiarity placing it just out of reach. Grabbing a ball of string from a nearby shelf, hoping that it does not topple the structure, and setting out to mark his path along the pale linoleum floor. Progressing forward cautiously, the attention occasionally strays toward the bulging shelves, gaze becoming snagged on the peeking yellowed objects that exude the soft promise of childhood. A pack of plastic figurines, grotesquely miniscule and warped together, cause the fingers to twitch with memories of imaginary play; a colourful sweet tin, shaped like a rabbit, sends tingling, sticky urges down the throat in a syrupy mix of drowning and retching; each framed in the deadening prophylactic of nostalgia. The place creates a sticky desire across the surface of the body, a second skin that yearns to lay itself on these shelves, tucked into the multitude, becoming flaky and yellowed, altered in sympathy and need. The landscape shifts back to the grey street, now softly bathed in approaching half-light, a faded pack of tobacco in sweating hands and a body recoiling at the heavy air, tender, almost burnt.

SKELETAL PARK

The streets now split off into intersections that bleed out into a multitude of smaller roads. Somewhere near the Elephant and Castle, but this is simply a guess. Each road carries a familiarity, some old memory hemmed in by repetitive tenements. The same rough flannel sheets hang out of windows in irregular patterns as they dry against the feeble breeze; flocks of ghosts trying weakly to ascend. There are eyes here, peeping from each nook, glinting in starlight patterns from the unlit windows and the shadowed crannies. Occasional glimpses of them animate the periphery, hot gasps full of anticipation, the momentary damp phantoms are given form as they push against the air's chill. The authors of these moments stay hidden, just out of reach, but felt against the neck. Moving forward amidst the tangled pacing of hobbled pigeons, past the hollowed-out ideas of pubs, walls painted and glass tinted, pale forgotten snail shells scattered recklessly. The signs still hang limply, abstracted banners wearing paper-thin; *The Frog and Nightgown*, *The World Turned Upside-Down*, *The Beaten Path*. A hundred *King's Heads*, discarded, forgotten, whispering with Brân the Blessed in their multitudes, conjuring their own subterranean sonic landscape. This parallel topography of forgotten words, known only in its fullness by a patchwork of cabbies, tramps and gangsters, is a twisted echo of Beck's own meandering abstraction. The swaying branches of gnarled bridges can be glimpsed through the crumbling wall of buildings. Arches of all sizes, stretching out across narrow dried-up asphalt canals, as the caress of heavy fingers steepled atop the creased tablecloth, bloated with ruddy scars and rust, lattices of hastily painted triangular mesh thick, shiny and clogged with dirt and bird shit. This idea of London imagines Venice with its ghost canals, woven in criss-cross scar tissue across, and beneath its surface. The ground is still damp and heaving beneath the layers of imported stone, still wishing it were water. The solemn footfall of shire horses can be heard, blinkered and straining, their sweat and blood seeping like glue into waterways, mingling with the brown flow of the Thames, slowing its progress to a treacle crawl.

Walking through the park recalls the descriptions of the island that it digested, meandering yet compact passages of Victorian brick sealed in isolation through the poet's utopic words. Most of the residents departed, moving further out into the orbits of the city, however some were still here fossiling among the ruins, waiting for a time when history would reverse its multitude of changes and the danger would pass. There is tension in the birdsong, cloaked shouting voices gravelled to a whisper. The leaves shuffle above the meaty fists that dance in strange tattoos against hardened bodies. The patterns in the patchy grass describe bombed-out factories; playgrounds of glass and metal that had sullenly morphed into the sculptural forms of the late 80s and found their frozen tombs in raised concrete blocks, hollowed out for habitation. Against the backdrop of the park there is a slow inhalation and exhalation of existence, swelling, building up and then tearing down across the span of years. Some of the older trees carry its promise in their concentric rings of glass, metal, concrete and asphalt, releasing a scraping sigh of relief when eventually they are cut open and their contents spilled.

A MAP

The site of the next appointment. A small corner bar entombed within the gravelled walls of a surrounding housing estate. A pause, to ease the nerves by rolling a dry cigarette and taking a few stale puffs, lips burning. One last glance around as the cigarette is extinguished, taking in the surroundings, lest they fade away once inside. The towering blocks, mostly empty and marked for the unstoppable tides of gentrification. Those few balconies that speak of habitation blossom out with innumerable treasures, overflowing flowers, old bicycles, broken prams and layers of washing dancing on thin wires. The empty playground, apparatus removed, leaving traces of phantom play. All is silent, eerily so.

Down the carpeted steps and into the warm bar. A man waits at a table in the corner, huddled over, his body straining and folding, twisted in awkward angles from neck to draped elbow in a tension of casual familiarity. His chest labours slowly with the hint of a wheeze but his eyes are twitching across the tapestry of the small open-plan bar. Triangle sandwiches, crusts removed, can be seen ossifying beneath a milky plastic lid, a gleaming suggestion of cucumber and pinkish-yellow margarine. They sit next to greening pork pies and darkened jars of eggs, each clashing with the red vibrance of the formica bar surface and its patchy, welted impressions of past elbows. A white noise built of wordless mumbling, the scraping of elbows and the enigmatic peeping of fading fruit machines hangs like a dense fog. Patrons stare down at tabletops, watching from the side of the eyes, people watching people watching, in a cobweb of intersecting gazes.

Sitting opposite the man begins the ritual of excavation, his memory, the latest fragment of the poet's life. Picking out the threads of this story is wholly different from its obverse; the long musty academic discussions between gaggles of undergraduates, chipping away at some point or other until a kernel of interest emerges. Here it is more subtle and more perverse, a game that both players initialize with a heady mix of hostility and suspicion, each treading carefully through their bit parts in the unfolding ceremony. It feels like being immersed in a bathtub of tepid, milky water searching for the plug, groping invisibly until you can find the chain and yank lest you drown in five murky inches. The man sucks deep from the long murky glass, straining at its thick familiar rim as the rounded lip tries its best to suck back against him. If these hallowed rules, arbitrary and tangled, could not be established from the get-go, the game was over, any further chance at discussion gone and violence increased. None of the characters encountered in these microcosms seemed truly real, and often hardly even lifelike, their waxwork conversation jutted out from awkward angles, erratically scraping and grinding against itself. Their recollections, hypnotic in their own fumbling way, are hazy at best, but have been scrawled in various codes across the numerous, multiplying notebooks. They each seemed to recount parts of something bigger. Some wholly unnerving pastiche. The flowing litres of London Pride and Spitfire double this impression, moving chaotically between a vanished past and a confusing present. The man is now in full flow, describing an evening spent with the poet across a splinter of the city. He outlines places which didn't exist, had never existed; the backroom of a boxing gym, towels discarded and bloody suddenly became a grand house on the wealthy hill of Camberwell with bay windows that opened onto a velvet night, ruby port spilling onto silk cushions, merging with the murky backstage of a small East End theatre. One of the man's eyes twitches in time with the flatscreen TV in the corner as the story continues, its drone moving in a pendulum arc between the inside and outside of the skull.

This narrative manifests itself in a growing cosmos of scrawled notes and mismatched printouts, fed with the continuous stream of words and places. There is a growing sense of unease, an awkward joining of fictions that seem to erode each other. Something had now changed in the man's voice, it had taken on some of the qualities of a confessional, overheard and distant; the words were flattening as he described the poet's last moments. He had been there, accidentally, he said. The poet, in his last moments, had enacted a simple series of movements with his hands. Repetitive moments, like the unfolding of a map or untying an elaborate knot, that with each opening peeled away yet more layers of fabrication. The conjured scene appears clearly against the backdrop that has been frantically pieced together. It fits well in a jarring, resentful way, scenes of this temporary patchwork hanging together, almost ready to unwind but held in stasis through the flow of its anger. Something emerges from beneath, some sense of genius loci is peeking back, its clear eye whose gaze reveals the poet's own secret geography as it pushes across borders, emerging between seas and rivers, intersecting at the corners of memory. Breweries with dark, cloying scents, the twitching threat of violent games amidst the barrels strained against churches of cheap wood and skinny cats that pounced on unsuspecting feet among the pews. All now defunct and buried, a place for children to play unfettered among the jagged glass and bricks, it enmeshed itself through steelworks, art studios, and hulking ice factories, and the smell of char filling the air as Dickensian villains worked the voltages. Then once again the bloating of summer torched tar-melted industrial buildings wilts into stoic tenement winters, snow clinging to the boots as they stamp down and forward, carving passages through tall spindly dwellings that shiver like rows of loose, brown teeth. The only real boundary it seemed to recognize was a single unremarkable steel bridge, a dull upside-down grin marking the imagined edges of some childhood island. It was smoothed, asphalted and punctured with playgrounds and grass, its mark was still felt.

The map stretches out its delicate surface, all of its laced intricacies twisted and glittering against the dark, sticky wood of the tabletop. Its mass, seen from above through the hollow bodies of circling birds and aeroplanes, peeled through varying layers of story, duplicity, geography and revelation. Seeming to seethe, the imagined fabric tensed and relaxed rhythmically, the shivering lines that had scratched themselves across it reached upward, bridging from eye to eye. Crossing the bridge, slowly, they became plunging synapses connecting the poet's many real and imagined lives; bridges and flowing rivers, streets, buildings and passages. It reaches over the table, down against the floor, across the hardened carpet, across the stained flock walls, across his companion's tired face, through pickled eggs and curling sandwiches, and out into the dust, and the rain and the grey and across the burning sky. A simple glance, in the haze of booze and the drone of the pub as the afternoon crowd shuffled in. A simple glance before it slipped away, rolling back out into the fabric of the city that had birthed it, all traces of its presence having disappeared behind it.

GHOSTS:
A TRIPTYCH

Victor Rees

TALKING THROUGH STONE

The day after his father was buried, the Architect returned to work with new ferocity. He had permitted himself ample time to mourn, and now shed his sorrow like an embarrassing skin. Back at the building site, he convened the most senior among his assistants to remind them of the vast scale of their project, and the urgency with which it had to be completed. He told them he was unimpressed with what little progress had been made in his absence, and that he was therefore forced to increase the severity of his punishments. By the fifth day of his return, workmen who had previously tolerated the Architect's bullying presence learned to run at the sound of his studded boots echoing against the marble floors, and to cower from his sight as though from a sudden storm. One labourer who had broken his leg falling from a buttress was fined four months' pay for having taken part of the masonry down with him. A friend of the crippled man who complained about the fine was summarily beaten in front of the other workers and dragged off-site.

On the eighth day after he placed his father's body in the silty black soil of the merchant's cemetery, the Architect was due to oversee the laying of the foundations for a new section of his ever-expanding complex, a building he had named the Chiaroscuro. The complexity of the structure caused the Architect to pass a restless night filled with dreams of flawed layouts, mathematical discrepancies and incompetent workers. He read and reread his plans from the moment he was awoken by the cock's crow, troubled by the thought of some misplaced detail, an error of a few degrees that might prove devastating at a later date. He continued to pore over the parchment as he hurried towards the site where construction on the Chiaroscuro was set to begin, caring little whether he trampled anyone standing in his way. It was as he walked through one of the thousands of corridors connecting his network of buildings that he happened to briefly look up from his papers and catch a glimpse of the face in the wall.

The sudden vision in his periphery brought the Architect to a standstill. Carved in the limestone surface of the otherwise bare corridor, perfectly level with the Architect's own eyes, was the likeness of a man. It was as if the face had pushed itself through the stone from the other side, so that everything between the jowls and the wrinkled forehead was visible. Whoever had sculpted the features had decided to leave the eyes hollow—those flat, empty spaces were mirrored by the inside of the mouth, which hung open as though awaiting the placement of some water pipe or drain that had been forgotten in the rush of construction. But it was the carving's upper lip that most startled the Architect, curling upwards on the right side, turning the whole expression into a grimace. He recognized the twisted lip immediately, knowing it to be the lip of his late father, which had been deformed by the same stroke that had stolen his mobility years prior.

Taken all together, the features formed an unmistakable portrait. But he could not understand what the likeness of the dead man was doing here of all places. Hundreds of craftsmen had been employed for the sole purpose of covering the complex of buildings with the heads of devils, monsters and more. Those workers were anonymous and interchangeable, making it impossible to know who could have been responsible for any single carving. The Architect might have easily had the culprit beaten and dismissed for some other misdemeanour in the preceding days, or sent to work on another wing of the continually spreading maze of palaces and halls.

He drew closer, and pressed his fingertips against the lines of his father's face. The stone was rugged and cold, though it brought a memory of warmth, of the Architect brushing against the bristles on this cheek when he was still only a child—and, much later, of passing a razor through those same bristles when his father could no longer shave himself. He continued to run his fingers along the grooves of the limestone jowls, the barren plains of the empty eyes. In the early light of morning, the freshly carved stone appeared to be already ancient, its detail flattened and eroded by time.

142

The Architect wondered if perhaps he was going mad—if the strain of his labour, merged with his grief, had elevated a paltry likeness into an impossible vision.

Or was there a chance, he asked himself, that his father had somehow emerged here by his own will, that he was butting through stone in order to appear before his own son, eight days after his burial? He tried to imagine what it could mean, if so—what his father's spirit, rendered mute by the rigor of his limestone lips, might be attempting so desperately to say.

PROFESSOR PRENDERGAST'S SOLUTION

Based on an idea by Iarla Prendergast Knight

With the séance concluded, and the spectral child dispersed into shimmering dust, Professor Prendergast instructed that brandy and smelling salts be distributed among his guests.

The General was the first to regain his composure, and he asked the Professor the meaning of the sight they had all witnessed. "Was that girl the victim of an ancient murder? Did she appear because one of our ancestors was somehow party to her death?"

The Professor, composed as ever, brushed a long strand of hair out of his eyes, and told the General that he doubted any real-life case of violence had been involved in the girl's appearance, or that any of his guests' presences had triggered her arrival.

"After all", agreed Madame C. the socialite, "it is a well-known fact that ghosts are more drawn to locations than they are to people. We must look to the history of the house, rather than our own family trees, for the solution to this apparition."

Professor Prendergast said nothing at first, and occupied himself with the lighting of a slender cigarette. Once the company had been left in silence for long enough, he decided to speak.

"You are venturing upon the right path, Madame. But I fear that even this solution does not get to the heart of the matter. Those old tales of spooks dwelling in ancestral homes and manors are too fixated upon the foregrounding of the human experience. It is always assumed that we, for whatever reason, are so important in the universal scheme that we deserve to exist beyond death."

The General had had quite enough. "Then what the devil *are* these ghosts, if not the spirits of the deceased?"

"It is quite simple", Professor Prendergast replied. "These ghosts, as you call them, are nothing more than the dreams of buildings.

"I have come to this conclusion after many years of careful thought. A house as old as this one, for example, will dream of prior inhabitants, of people who have come and gone through the years since it was first erected. But the faces will change, and the bodies will shift, as they do in our own dreams. Figures will vanish and reappear without logic, will take on new forms. Sometimes the dreams are peaceful. Sometimes they are troubled. It is still too soon to say whether the girl you saw falls in the former category, or the latter.

"Then there are the dreams of museums. A museum is like an iceberg—most of its treasures lie not in any glass display cases, but in the cabinets and storerooms below the surface. We might compare these two spaces to the museum's conscious and subconscious mind. It is only reasonable, then, that the museum dreams of the objects contained in its storerooms rising up like a tide through its elegant marble hallways. And when the museum wakes, the tide falls once more, and the objects return to their boxes and crates. But sometimes there is a relic left behind. An ancient sword deposited among a display of photographs. A strange dark coin among brittle vases, with no label to explain its provenance. One must have ample practice in order to notice the smallest of these anomalies, and to become a true beachcomber of dreams.

"There is also a third type of dream—the dreams of churches. Churches dream not of people, nor of objects, but of sound and light. You must have all had the experience of entering a church, of knowing yourself to be quite alone within its empty walls, and nevertheless hearing music echoing quietly through the aisles and vestibules—seeing a collision of dust and dancing colours more striking than any lantern show. But one need not be alone to perceive such visions, for churches do not mind the intrusion of visitors. Churches, the oldest churches, are grandparents sleeping through their latter years—they brush off our presence as a whale would a louse. Sometimes, during days when fewer hymns are sung and fewer candles are lit, the churches dredge up ancient memories of past worship. Sometimes these dreams of light and song are so vivid they congeal into a solid form which leaks out into the outside world. We call these beings angels."

And he put out the embers of his cigarette in the pale jade ashtray he kept on his desk.

SPIRIT OF PARCHMENT

I will now write of the scroll-ghosts that dwell in the ruined monastery of the Nōval plains. The territory of the Nōval valley is for the most part arid and unwelcoming. Few things will grow in the windswept soil, and it is rare to catch sight of any wild animals, for they hide in tall grass the same colour as their tawny fur. It is only in the plains that surround the old monastery that delicate lilac flowers grow, watered by a nearby stream.

I had heard tell of the monastery on my prior journeys, and long wished to see it for myself. I had been told that it was little more than a ruined heap of black stones, all that remained after the raids of a local warlord almost fifty years ago. Gradually, in the years and decades that followed these raids, the people who had escaped the Nōval plains returned to their ancestral homes. Ravaged huts and burned-down halls were rebuilt. The course of life, interrupted by a tyrant's violent whim, was allowed to resume.

But the monastery was left untouched. No attempt was made to build it back up stone by stone, for within a few years of the people's return to the plains, they discovered the presence of a group of ghosts inhabiting the crumbling walls. These ghosts, I was told, are unique in their appearance, resembling the heads of monks who had lived in the monastery, and whom the warlord had personally decapitated when they refused to flee. These heads, severed from their bodies, are not fleshy or pale, but are instead the colour of deep brown wood. They are often likened to carved statues—the eyes still move in their sockets, but all other features are completely immobile, rendered in great detail by some master carver's chisel. Yet the most remarkable aspect of these ghosts, and the source of my curiosity, lies in what can be found below their heads.

It was only after much persuasion that I was brought to the monastery by my guide, a soft-faced herdsman who had agreed to accompany me through the region. We entered what was once the outer wall of the ruin, and waited several hours in the cold and dark for something to occur. At last, I caught sight of a pair of spirits in silent communion, their heads floating some five or six feet above the ground. In place of their necks and bodies, these heads were connected to what appeared to be unfurled scrolls, which fluttered behind them in the wind. What the contents of these scrolls were, I could not say—my guide kept me at such a distance that I could not read the text no matter how much I strained my eyes. I was certain I could see words, some appearing as illuminated letters in gold and red ink, some as scribbled black marks.

I pleaded with my guide to let me go nearer, but he continued to hold me back. The matter of the monks' scroll-bodies, he said, was a subject of great debate in the villages that surrounded the monastery. The community was split into two camps. Some believed these parchments contained important messages for the living, dispatches from the world beyond. Others said that the scrolls were instead the means by which the monks communicated with one another, and were not intended for mortal eyes. Whole families living in the shadow of the monastery were divided in their opinion, to the extent that these debates often grew fiery and fraught.

My guide, unfortunately, was of the latter disposition, believing no good could come of seeking to read the written words. I privately formulated plans to sneak into the monastery the next night, to find for myself what the scrolls might say. Perhaps he could read my intentions in my eyes, for he told me there would be little use in any such attempt. Even those who had decided to approach the ghosts came back with the same answer—they could not translate what the words said, for they were written in a very old language and idiom. It had therefore become the task of half of the population to slowly attempt to translate the contents of the scrolls—a task that had taken many years, and would likely take many more before any meaning could be gained.

We moved on, continuing our travels. My guide told me we would skirt around the base of the nearby Ōdile mountains, where villagers walked through snow and wore animal pelts, and feared a very different kind of spectre—a race of devils who lived in the gaps between words. The people there had developed a remarkable system of communication.

They had learned to speak without pause, even when alone or—and this I found most unbelievable—when asleep, singing and humming to themselves, extending a final word for hours if needs be, before connecting it fluidly into the next. They feared silence, my guide explained, for they saw it as an opening, an invitation for the demons to latch into their mouths and turn them into a speechless shell. They would therefore kill all silent men, thinking them to be possessed.

As curious as I found the tale, I could not put the scroll-monks out of my mind. I wondered whether the villagers who had decided to approach the ghosts were indeed telling the truth when they claimed not to be able to read the words, or whether they had decided to keep the spirits' knowledge for themselves. I felt faintly troubled as we made our way towards the outer rim of the Nōval plains. I remembered how, before we left the monastery, one of the monks turned to look at me. I could clearly see its burning eyes, moving in motionless sockets carved out of wood. I interpreted it as a pleading expression—but what the purpose of this pleading might be, I could not guess.

THE DYING SWANS

Michael Moorcock

T here is a pub called *The Swan with Two Necks* in Manchester and one or two elsewhere in Britain. Probably, the best known was in Lad Lane (now Gresham Street), City of London. This well-appointed coaching inn was not named after a mythical bird but for the two beak-nicks used to identify a swan's ownership during upping. As far as I know there is no Old King Lud any longer unless it serves the boatmen who still use the old Fleet River. But that could be another story. Alsacia's eastern border ends at the Fleet River close to where it enters the Thames. Legend says the Fleet's a sewer now but I've seen it alive with torchlight and the swinging lanterns of the barges making for Seward's Reach and the open sea. I have heard their songs echoing in the deep, mysterious tunnels where barges meet from all the canals of Britain to ready their goods for the sea. Few overgrounders know the activities of the London night. I saw them during my early days in Alsacia, when I followed a tunnel under what I guessed was Fleet Street to see if I could get into New Fleetway House where I worked on SEXTON BLAKE. I was still only a member of the National Union of Journalists, not yet old enough to be on the Chapel Committee, and my frustrations were expressed in the form of jokes like putting a sign in my office window reading HELP! I AM A PRISONER IN A WORD FACTORY. My department chief, Len Matthews (creator of Mab Midnight, the tramway thief) told me to take it down. He did not threaten to fire me because he was convinced I was a Communist. When the revolution came he fully expected to see me marching up Farringdon Road wearing a pair of steel-framed glasses, a Luger in my belt, a red star on my uniform, at the head of a Red Army detachment ordered to arrest him. Happily for me, he did not know the difference between authoritarian Communism and pacifist Kropotkinism but like many of his generation had a somewhat generalized idea of what a 'Red' might be!

The Swan With Two Necks is still a thriving pub in Manchester and Dave, his friend Chuck Partington and I used to drink there sometimes when I visited the city.

While Dave and Mike made regular trips to Camden Town, stocking up on whatever publications Manchester had missed, going to Porkie's to produce P J Proby's eccentric Northern soul records, talk with the printer of LORD HORROR and REVERBSTORM while we continued to spend our leisure in the smokey cellars and music clubs of London's R&B scene. Zoot Money. Long John Baldry. Geno Washington. Georgie Fame. Mods in London. Ravers in Manchester. Rock had always divided into North and South. At NEW WORLDS we were starting to understand how profoundly different we all were as writers. As editor, I was barely able to control chaos. We all imposed or inferred or interpreted differently. And we knew we must inevitably choose our separate directions, but for the moment we had common cause. A bond.

Partly through the publicity, people began to turn up in our Ladbroke Grove living room. Poets, underground journalists, musicians. Friends of friends, they had read our stuff and were usually stoned, speeding or drunk. We talked of bands we liked, we played instruments and tried out songs. Jon Trux (of FRENDZ) and Bob Calvert insisted I see Hawkwind. Eventually Dave Brock of Hawkwind suggested I write some lyrics and perform them at Portobello Road's motorway bay theatre which I'd helped Jon Trux and Co. build. I did a few numbers, including SONIC ATTACK, and a couple of years later got a gold disc for *Warrior on the Edge of Time*. We all found that a bit embarrassing. 'Underground' bands weren't supposed to win record-biz awards. Three band members spontaneously left.

With Hawkwind's success, record companies began to court those associated with them. Based on a demo, *Dodgem Dude*, at United Artist's suggestion I put together a band with Graham Charnock, a NEW WORLDS editor and writer, on bass, White Panther Steve Gilmore on rhythm guitar, ex-Hawk Terry Ollis on drums and me barely on lead. I called it The Deep Fix after a band in a Jerry Cornelius novel which was in turn named after a novella I wrote in 1964 for SCIENCE FANTASY. Without any effort or ambition on my part I received a three-album contract from United Artists. I didn't even think of the drug association, but the BBC did, especially Roy Plomley who point blank rejected its producer's attempts to get me on *Desert Island Discs*. I had no plans for a rock and roll career, but I did have many musical friends who needed some work. According to the publishers' sales reps, I was then outselling pretty much everyone except Fleming. I was on good terms with many well-known musicians and, while I wished them the best of luck, theirs wasn't a life I wanted. But, somewhat reluctantly, I became a part-time rock-and-roller. At first I was treated as a pop music wannabe by the status-conscious music press. They didn't know I'd been in bands since I was fifteen. Because I had produced so many books, they thought I was older than I was. They considered my new career to be a bestseller's indulgence. Our audiences however seemed very happy.

On the other hand NEW WORLDS was taking too much of my time so for a while I tried to put it into the hands of an editorial 'triumvirate' consisting of Grahams Hall and Charnock and Charles Platt, all of whom had good ideas of their own. I told them that I'd continue to pay the bills but that they must sort their own *working* problems. The three almost immediately fell out and the somewhat passive-aggressive Charnock was the first to complain about the others and demand I step in. I reminded him of my conditions. Hall was the next. Finally the most skilled, experienced and clear-sighted of the three, Platt, was left. He remained until it was obvious he had no skill at working with others. For a while I returned as editor, but it would not be long before I again resigned. My theory had always been that a decent editor rarely had much more than five years of dynamic work. By 1971 I was ready to quit. Seven years was too long.

My home life became a little complicated. No doubt at my unconscious and unwilling instigation, Helena had sprung a number of surprises on me, including her decision to have another child and then live in our Yorkshire house for a year, with the three children but without me. She told me this after I moved with them and set myself up in the tower room which gave the house its name. I felt she was punishing me, but at heart I knew she was trying to save herself. The comparative solitude of Tower House would enable her to write her first published novel. I told her I would not be celibate while in London. Embittered, I went back to London and took up with Emma Tennant. Eventually, somewhat on an infatuated rebound, I took up with Jenny, who was thirteen years my junior.

In 1974, when Helena returned with the children, Jenny and I moved across the street from Ladbroke Grove to Blenheim Crescent. Life with that compliant young woman made work easier for me and also made life better for Helena, who took up with a casual boyfriend I had always despised! Our odd *ménage à trois* lasted for some five years with few hiccups until the day I married Jenny, when Helena threw a milk-bottle through our living room window, suggesting that her acceptance of that *ménage* had not been wholehearted. Both are dead now. As are most of my contemporaries apart from John Clute, Harrison (whose memories like his life he reduced to a simpler and more respectable narrative), and Charles Platt, whose later volumes of memoirs became frustratingly discreet as he realized he was hurting feelings.

I was grateful, however, for those few Jenny years of quiet depression and steady work until I was ready to begin my first Pyat book, a comic novel about the causes of the Holocaust, *Byzantium Endures*. I would destroy both relationships at the same time, leading to consequences which changed radically my imagined future.

The majority of my friendships had survived my move across the street. There seemed little change, all in all. NEW WORLDS, now Sphere's quarterly paperback format was edited by Helena who no longer had to put up with so many musicians and members of the underground tramping through her flat. Some, like Jon Trux of FRENDZ remained on good terms with her and, of course, with me. On dole days I would lend Trux (working free on the ambitious *Index of Possibilities*) my huge American Nash so that he could scandalize the pinch-lipped old ladies and gentlemen glaring as he drew up at the dole office before strolling in to collect his money. I had some clues that we were enjoying the end of our glory days but I didn't know how few we had left.

One sunny early afternoon at Hyde Park Gate, in an unfurnished and unmodernized apartment, the staff of NEW WORLDS met Yoko Ono, her husband Anthony Cox and their crew to make a film we had nicknamed *Asses and Diamonds* and she informed us without a blink that, "No, It's called *Bottoms Film Number Four*. You go in there and strip." Helpfully, Anthony added: "Just your trousers and underpants." She had phoned me earlier and told me all the famous people who were going to be in the film. John Lennon, for instance. (Later, she said how she had never heard of him before the famous meeting at the Robert Eaton Gallery.) I had thoughtfully put an **X** on my bottom in magic marker so I would recognize it at the preview, to which I was never invited. A little later, The Beatles' old friend and promoter Bill Harry took me to Apple Corps because he wanted to get NEW WORLDS some backing. Seeing the already worn stair carpet and the hundreds of applicants, I told Derek Taylor, the press officer, that I couldn't in conscience take their money. At that moment George Harrison walked in, showing off his new instamatic camera. "This is Mike Moorcock," declared Derek, "He says he doesn't want any money from us". I would swear there were tears in George's eyes as he warmly shook my hand. "Thank you", he said. "Oh, thank you!"

THE THREATENING TALE

Buck Jones was something of a father figure to me. He was a little past his prime as a Western actor but continued to carry an aura of quiet authority. He had been a lawman for much of his life, was a good shot and an excellent horseman. He had no argument with the tramway mobsmen. They were not killers and held up trams over the heaths for a good cause and robbed from those who could afford it. Moreover, as he pointed out, the Alsacia was not his territory. He and Kit Carson spent much of their time together. They both knew the Arizona territory, though at different periods. Jones was growing tired of London. He had originally been brought over by Amalgamated Press before the war to publicize a series of text stories running in BOYS CINEMA and had remained in London during the war, helping, like several Americans, to build morale. In the United States they believed he had died in a nightclub fire, saving customers, a story which he found convenient. He did not spend his whole time in Alsacia but lived in a remote part of East Sussex raising racehorses under the name of Brian Byrne, an Irishman. Some of his horses were sold to Turpin and company and there was a suggestion that his own Black Bess had come from Captain Byrne's stable.

Before I married I visited Buck at his stables. He had begun his professional life as a bit-part Western actor in Tom Mix movies. By the 1920s he was one of the genre's box office draws. By the time we met, his star was descending. In an effort to combine audiences he appeared in movies with others in the same boat. I had seen him as a kid at the Saturday morning pictures and by the time I was nineteen I was writing his adventures for *Cowboy Picture Library*. The Amalgamated Press had paid him an outright fee for use of his name, so he received no further royalties. His stables did so well, he did not need the money and Kit Carson collected royalties on his own memoir written at a time when he was able to copyright the book. I had read stories in THE BIG BUDGET for 1899 where he was referred to as *The King of the Plains*. He had come to Britain on a lecture tour with the original intention of telling the truth about life on the frontier. He was embarrassed by these 'dime novel' tales and felt they led to expectations that were too high. He told a story which disturbed him deeply, about a group of settlers ambushed by Utes. By the time he arrived with a rescue party all the people were killed. The last to die appeared to be a teenage girl. In her hands she still held a dime novel with the title *Kit Carson Saves the Day*. Complete fiction, as he pointed out, yet clearly she had died expecting that Kit would rescue her. In Paris he employed a journalist to copy out his reminiscences. His other income came from Jones's stables in which he had invested a few years before the war.

Although illiterate, Kit had married native women, had them and his children to read and write and had high respect for all the native peoples of the South West. A stocky, modest man, he only occasionally left the Alsacia, usually to visit Jones's stables, but at heart believed himself to be dead and living in a kind of purgatory. He hoped one day to be reunited with his family. He rarely wore his plainsman's buckskins but rather a neat three-piece suit, shirt and tie, of a slightly old-fashioned appearance. He respected convention and had a quietly dignified manner. He was popular at *The Sailor's Retreat*. The only other inn he used, it was a decrepit many-storeyed Tudor building stretched precariously out over the river where it met the Fleet. Since the 1950s, however, both men talked of possibly going back to Arizona or Nevada and taking up ranching. Buck believed himself too old for the law and Kit no longer wished to live the life of a plainsman. He was troubled by his own unwitting role in the repression of local tribes and felt an increasing compunction to return.

Of course, the dates with Alsacia and the outside world could be confused and I had long-since given up comparing calendars. I had taken much of it for granted but the two worlds had, like dreams, no real logic. I had come, I suppose, to take the multiverse for granted. Sometimes the worlds overlapped but often they didn't. Sometimes history corresponded but not always. I continued to accept both just as I experienced dreams, as everyone else there did. There was no doubt that there were very real differences and real similarities including the ubiquitous Jake Nixer, with his long-standing hatred of our sanctuary and all it stood for. As if his very existence depended on it he sustained a continual war against us. His one ambition was to destroy the Alsacia and all who were given protection by it. Although he had no means, he was even prepared to drive out the White Friars or, if necessary, kill them. For my own part, I had a visceral dislike of Nixer which I could not, in those days, identify. It would be some years before I began to remember other events which had occurred during what I now call my 'African adventure'.

I could never discover the date when Nixer, the Thief Taker, had arrived at Alsacia, with his two new cronies Willy Watson and Tim Tryit, who dressed much like mid-nineteenth-century tramps. Nixer's clothes were close to matching in period those worn by Turpin and company. Really a uniform worn by a cavalry captain of the Bow Street Runners of the eighteenth century, he had a blue coat of military cut, a long buff waistcoat, red trousers and jack leather riding boots. His hat was really a helmet, not entirely different to that worn by modern policemen but of vaguely civilian appearance. Not all his men wore the uniform. Many had cocked hats, black riding coats and a miscellaneous variety of clothing, roughly from the same period. Some were almost dandified and others were quite slovenly. A few were friendly enough, even to their criminal antagonists. Only Nixer and his two cronies, Watson and Tryon, with their ill-smelling trousers, rarely smiled or bought a round. Nixer had lost his previous lieutenants in battle somewhere; not, I think, against Turpin or Duval but in some naval incident when they were recruited to fight the Ottoman corsairs who in their raids on our coasts infamously enslaved British villagers. I should not admit that secretly I enjoyed the captured Runners' likely fate.

Physically, the evil-looking pair reminded me slightly of my friends in Manchester. *Weary Willy and Tired Tim*. Lieutenant Watson was tall and thin. He had the worn top-coat, tight maroon trousers and patched boots of a destitute mid-Victorian. His partner, Sergeant Tryon was short and fat, generally dressed in a dark blue coat too small for him, a wide, grubby white collar, a hat resembling what Americans call a 'pork pie', pinkish trousers, which barely fit around his vast waist and were held up by a single suspender, and battered buckled shoes. I was convinced that the great Tom Browne had once visited the Alsacia and drawn them from life. For all their appearance, they were a sinister pair, not recognizeable as the cheerful tramps of CHIPS comic who were so successful that they had imitators in rival publications. Pearson's BIG BUDGET had 'Airy Alf' and 'Bouncing Billy', for instance, on its front pages. Neither character, I must point out, resembled the real Mike Butterworth and Dave Britton.

I took both these friends to the Alsacia in the late 1970s when, as I've said, my grasp on reality wasn't the tightest. Mike Butterworth, one of the most unworldly people I ever knew, was entirely accepting of the people there and got on well with them, while Dave was a little suspicious, wondering if the whole place were not some sort of set-up. *The Swan With Two Necks* reminded him of the similar hostelry in Manchester which his mother had managed during her years as a publican. Like my mother, she had been an independent business woman. My mum, as I've said, thought Dave to be the best young man in the world (after me!). He made her laugh. He had the cheeky, slightly risqué, manner of a holiday camp host. He knew how to get on with old ladies, especially determined old ladies of character. He loathed his mirror image, however, and was always warning me against Willy as well as Tim. "The type's ten-a-penny in Salford." He would always make an excuse not to spend any time in their company. "Couple of small-time tossers" was his opinion. "Sell their grannies for a slice of tripe."

I needed no warning. I had a feeling in my bones about them. Whereas I thought Mike and Dave as similar in looks to Willie and Tim I knew they were opposites in character. Mike was vague and benign, often barely aware of what was going on in the world around him. A vegan of strong principles, who kept a daily diary and tended to be a little bit of a healthfreak, he was sweet-natured and kind-hearted. Dave was cynical, generous, an enthusiast for many eccentric writers from Kafka to Peake, a loyal friend and a long holder of grudges. He ran his shops and publishing business on money raised from customers who came in wanting to buy pornography. He had, like many secondhand booksellers of his day, a back-room where 'girlie books' were sold to customers over 18. When the grubby raincoat brigade came up to the counter asking for 'something stronger' he would reach under the till and pull out a videotape, slip it into a paper bag. and sell it for £50.00. The tapes were blank. Half the customers would not return. With those who did, Dave would feign surprise and regret. "Oh, sorry mate" he would say, and change the tape for another. Also blank. He told me about thirty percent returned and asked for their money back. On the strength of such cons he published the likes of David Lindsay's *A Voyage to Arcturus* in a beautiful new edition, an illustrated *Zenith the Albino* or Maurice Richardson's illustrated *The Exploits of Engelbrecht*. He had, he said, a nose for a sneaky bastard and Timmy Tryit was a perfect example of the type. "As slippery as a buttered eel! You'd better watch him, our Mikey", he would say.

Before he died of sepsis when washing his neuropathic feet, I told Dave about *Weary Willie and Tired Tim*. In spite of his knowledge of British popular culture, almost matching Alan Moore's, he had never heard of them. I was surprised. The characters had influenced scores of imitators throughout the twentieth century and still do. He barely remembered the two leering rogues at the Alsacia who had played quite a key part in my adventures. Ironically, Dave's comic hero was Fudge the Elf drawn by the great Manchester artist Ken Reid.

Nixer's narrow features were exaggerated to resemble a feral animal. He had small brown eyes, crowded, crooked teeth, many of them stained and broken, a receding chin and shrunken, almost lobeless ears. His hair was dyed black, held at the back by a greasy bow and his skin was pockmarked and pimpled as if he never washed it. His narrow body and long-fingered hands made him still more resemble a hungry rat, while his nails, unusually clean, were bitten to the quick. My friends declared him a natural thief-taker but I recalled Mervyn Peake's poem beginning '*His head and hands were built for sin*'. Like some modern internet stalker encouraging the innocent to kill themselves, he was doomed since birth to hate and destroy. I could find nothing about his appearance to redeem him. He was, as far as I was concerned, my natural enemy and his only companions were those who feared him or owed him something. Unfortunately, I had to suffer his company more than I liked if I wanted to share the bar with my tramway-thief friends, for he hung about constantly, waiting for a moment when he might, by some stroke of fortune, capture or kill them without being harmed himself. Meanwhile, he haunted the inns, accepting the rules of Sanctuary, albeit reluctantly.

"Like a damned snake awaiting its chance to strike", said Mab.

Briefly, we were together again. I had not yet decided to go to America and see my dying friend. She was not often seen in the Alsacia then but spent time abroad. Mab (or Molly) welcomed me back as if we had never been apart. I had seen her shortly after her mother, Mrs Malady, came looking for her. Somehow I felt various strands of narrative were coming together to create an important resolution. Indeed, I sometimes had a sense of dread, as if everything which made my life valuable was about to be snatched away. Yet I knew neither what I was losing nor how to protect myself. I was helpless against a numinous enemy. Not one of my friends could help me. I associated this threat with my second wife, with Mab, with Dick Turpin, Jake Nixer and with the Bow Street Runners. Past, present and future were running together like different coloured inks in a water glass, each colour representing one of so many threads, none of them benign.

Could the doors of the Alsacia, which had for so long opened for me and allowed me sanctuary, be closing at last ?

BROOKGATE REPRISE

Boiled beef and carrots,
Boiled beef and carrots,
That's the stuff for your 'Derby Kell',
Makes you fit and keeps you well.
Don't live like vegetarians
On food they give to parrots,
Blow out your kite, from morn 'til night,
On boiled beef and carrots.

—Harry Champion

Brookgate's Mercy is an old name for what the French call *boudin noir*. It is looser in the skin than black pudding and has the consistency of cous-cous. That and *confit de canard* are the two traditional French dishes I like best. A Brookgate recipe Mercy was not prepared in Brookgate, but was made in Smithfield, about half-a-mile away, and was banned for a long time because of the cruelty involved in its making. Every

Thursday, when I was paid, I used to have it for lunch at Trewitt's in Brook Lane, the street before you reached Leather Lane, going east from Grays Inn Road.

Almost every week Pete Williams and I would meet there and order a plate of Apples and Mercy from the chipped enamel dishes warming at the counter. Thick unsweetened applesauce and big double-fried chips were generally served with it and Trewitt's was the best. Rhubarb tart in season, sliced into squares in the same oblong tins. Like me, Pete had worked at Fleetway before they were taken over by IPC. We had edited most of the same comics but Pete had become deputy editor of NEW SCIENTIST under Percy Cudlip, the magazine's founder, then was briefly editor, and I had begun to sell novels in various genres to paperback publishers. Pete was probably the brightest of my Fleetway pals. The five who were the closest friends among the fifth floor editors were Frank Redpath, who wrote mostly schoolgirl stories, wanted to become a playwright and eventually took up psychology, Dave Gregory, who rose to group editor at IPC, Alan Fennell, who became known for his Gerry and Sylvia Anderson TV creations and Angus Allan, whose father had freelanced for the firm, and who continued writing and editing popular periodicals. Protz the Trot, later editor of TRIBUNE, came along a little later. For a while we all met at the George, Fleet Street, but by 1966 everyone had moved on. Pete and I shared a liking for Apples and Mercy and a common interest in modern science. Sometimes my philosophical SF-writing friend, Barry Bayley, would meet us. Always interested in contemporary developments, Barry enjoyed conversations with Pete who was up to date in most scientific theories. Pete had never spent any time in Alsacia. Although he worked in Grays Inn, he didn't much like spending time in Fleet Street and when Barry mentioned our Whitefriars visits Pete showed little in the way of curiosity. Barry's interest in other worlds was not shared by Pete, who eventually founded a diving magazine. These were times before multiple-world theories were commonly discussed and before I described and named 'the multiverse' in 1962, but Pete read pretty much whatever he could find on the subject while at the same time being pretty dismissive of the ideas. He knew about a mathematician in Oxford called Margaret Yan who was doing some 'flashy' work, including 'experiments with light and prisms and stuff'. This immediately attracted Barry's attention. We were fond of a story by Charles Harness, a

Texan patent attorney. Called *The New Reality*, it fascinated him. I reprinted it in NEW WORLDS and in a wonderful collection called *The Rose* for Compact Books. I also reprinted it in a *Best of NEW WORLDS* anthology. The story was about passing a single photon through a prism. When the photon hesitates, a new reality begins. To me this suggested the existence of more than one universe! Barry and I wrote to Dr Yan but had no reply. This was in the days when most people saw no scientific value in science-fiction in spite of the scientists who wrote it. Some like the pompous Debrasse Tyson, and unlike Stephen Hawking, are still the same! We continued to publish our theories in those 'sensational' magazines until the likes of Clarke, Asimov, Benford and Bear began to be heard. Harness still fascinated me and I corresponded with him for a while, never realizing that he had moved to Texas at about the same time as me. His early exposure to a Louisiana seminar perhaps stimulated his interest in metaphysics and mathematics. I corresponded with him for a while. A modest, self-deprecating man, he returned to create several novels and establish his reputation. Many of his ideas turned up in later writers' work and he always remained on the borders of physics and metaphysics ... He certainly stimulated me, Barry and a new generation of writers like Gibson, Sterling and Rucker, the 'cyberpunks'.

Barry and Pete and I gradually stopped going to lunch at Trewitt's as the quality of the food declined and soon the building was torn down in the general destruction of Brookgate in the nineties. Apart from seeing Ballard and Bayley in the late fifties, the nearest I came to enjoying a similar time was at the lively lunches Peter Ackroyd, Iain Sinclair and I had in Clerkenwell until I eventually left for Texas. I did not know that my early mentor, who had written all those great 'worlds of if' stories in the forties and fifties, had also moved to Texas. An historian, an engineer and a very funny writer, L Sprague de Camp had effectively introduced me to the marvels of Charlemagne and the later decadent Romances as well as bringing the Dark Age into the light for me.

Brookgate has vanished now. In 2005, when planning this autobiography, Laura and I returned to take photographs of my old haunts, but pretty much everything was gone. Staple Inn looks increasingly like something constructed in Los Angeles. Brookgate market had disappeared, as had the Universal Dairy and the Old Holborn tobacco factory. Marks and Spencer, Ellisdon's joke shop was demolished with Gamages department store and most of the diamond merchants of Hatton Garden. Mr Gruman's vast 'in and out' shop, which sold the ends of every line known to man, had been replaced by a concrete office block. The clock shops, shoe-repairers, bespoke tailors and Lipton's grocery were all crushed under their own rubble along with the Essoldo Cinema, Mr Wilson's second-hand bookshop and the generations of his family who lived on its upper floors, the Armenian fried fish shop. Merchant's Music. Mrs Costello's doll hospital, several sweet and tobacconists and newsagents, my 'Auntie' Kit's newsagents, Gold's Music Hall, Mitchell's toyshop, Miss Lee's Sunrise Laundry, Woolworths, the Home and Colonial, Youd's second-hand and discount, furniture shop, Miss Shapiro's pet shop, British Home Stores, Jocky's Café, Hatchett's pie and mash shop, Pearly's jewellers, Rose's chemist, Taylor's bakery, K Gordon Parker's model shop, Arthur Ley's Popular Book Centre, Blue Moon coffee bar and all the variety of small, thriving businesses which made up my Brookgate boyhood community and linked us to others that either disappeared under Hitler's bombs or the bulldozers and swinging concrete King Kong balls and Godzilla jaws of the rapacious developers or failed due to changing times.

In the years I worked at TARZAN, even when I was at New Fleetway House, I could visit most of those places. By 1985 or so, not very long after the Wicked Witch of Westminster began to wave her money-wand, they had vanished, leaving behind them only dust and a few 'theme-restaurants', gourmet pubs where dark-suited men with loud voices spoke of 'grands' and 'deals'. They had successfully exorcized our ghosts.

In the winter of 1962 snow began to fall on Brookgate. Not since 1947 had it snowed so hard. Three days before Christmas it came down heavily, settling on roofs, in the gulleys between terraced houses, on trees, in the churchyards and the streets, piling in gutters, icing the pavements and making steps dangerous. Brookgate Market lit its lamps. Bunting glittered against the glorious whiteness, the green and grey canvas awnings, the huddled stall-keepers rubbing their mittened hands, breath billowing around their woollen scarves and balaclava helmets while the melting snow made grubby barricades against walls and roadways. The market continued its busy trade. Butchers, bakers, toyshops and stationers. Briskly presented wares brightened the long, narrow stretch of merchants from Holborn to Theobald's Road. The Salvation Army and all the other charities, with scarlet robes and clattering bells, cried out for generous souls. Flustered women struggled from shop to shop to find bargains for their Christmas tables, for their trees and hearths. Their children lingered, begging for a pause; inspecting boxes of soldiers, train sets, rocking horses, stuffed bears, 'golliwogs' and smiling dolls they hoped to see in their stockings or around the trees on the most anticipated morning of the year.

No Brookgate resident will go without, or ever did, since 1895, the year when Brookgate Council passed the so-called Nativity Act which set aside money to pay, on Christmas Day, for 'meat and ale and a play-thing for every indigent child of this parish'. Similarly, in Alsacia, Turpin and his brothers-in-arms provided for those of their fellow residents unable to offer a Christmas feast for their families.

The snow continues without stop. High up on roofs of old Georgian terraces men with long shovels do their best not to rain slush on their neighbours, usually trying to hit a back garden rather than a front street but occasionally covering a disgruntled passer-by. Traffic hisses between the middle of the stalls: street cleaners, trucks and taxis. Kids try to make balls from wet snow and toss them imprecisely, missing their friends and making sudden enemies of adults. In the churchyards, to the east and north of the market, snowmen are moulded. Angry old men chase thieves of stolen hats. Emotions cross a spectrum from heady excitement to ill-tempered disgust as the flakes fall relentlessly piling one on top of the others. Toboggans are rediscovered, overexcited dogs are harnessed; the candles and the electrics dance and twinkle over piled pies and bunched vegetables, cans of strawberries, cherries, fruit salad, pineapple, grapefruit, papaya, mangoes, peaches, sweet potatoes, pears and pearl onions, mandarins, cabbages, string beans, a dozen kinds of potatoes, tomatoes, leeks, butter beans, spring onions, sweet onions, yellow onions, shallots, red onions, garlic, mint, fennel, lettuce, rosemary, basil, coriander, bay leaves, thyme, sorrel, dill and parsley all combining in a glorious scent that signals the season, while through the snow flakes comes the strong smell of celebratory cigars the sounds of tin toys being wound, little whizzing wheels, bright red and yellow, blue, gold, silver and green, rattling, squealing, clanging and tinkling over the wooden boards of the toy stalls while voices shout to be heard. 'Fresh, all fresh', 'guaranteed for life', 'brand new today', 'best in Brookgate', 'finest English', 'perfect for the wife', 'Merry Christmas! Merry Christmas! Happy New Year!', 'Come on, missis! Get yer turk! Look at 'is big plump breast. Look at 'is legs'. 'Sausages! Big fat links! 'Chipolatas!' 'Try one an' buy one'. The sudden smell of pine and fir as fathers sort through the piles of Christmas trees, looking for a nice shapely one before they are gone. As usual, they gasp at the price. "Five bob!" "Three and six!" "Ain't got no roots 'as it?" And, as usual, they will try to replant it wherever they can, to see it turn brown and brittle in the shallow soil of their city.

The snow keeps falling. As the lights go out and the shoppers and the shop-keepers and the stallholders go home the street grows silent except for the pubs and the sound of muffled feet, of an unhappy child, as it piles deep and crisp, hiding the detritus and the grime of another busy day.

Up near where Brookgate Inn Road joins Fox's Alley by the Goat and Barrel pub, a cold boy, short of pocket money for his granddad's present, plays a penny harmonica. He is hoping to earn a coin or two from some of the pub's late drinkers. His mother has picked up some extra Christmas work, cleaning the new offices over in Farringdon Road. She thinks that he's asleep in bed. She left his supper on the kitchen table. Half a can of corned beef, a packet of crisps and a glass of Tizer, one of his favourites. He knows he should go home soon or she will return before he does and worry about him. His granddad has grown simple-minded and still loves the boy in that new, vague way of his. The pub will close at 11pm. The in-and-out shop closes at 11.30. His mother will be home by 12. Squeaking out 'Clementine', the only tune he remembers, he has almost given up hope when a man he knows from one of the fruit and veg stalls turns the corner and sees him. Feeling in his pocket, the man looks down at the boy. "Short of a tanner or two for presents, is it?" The boy nods.

"I know your mum, don't I? says the man. "Her name's Avril, in't it?"

The boy agrees.

"Well, I won fifty quid on an accumulator today." The man hands him a florin. "Tell your mum that Sammy Samson says Merry Christmas from up the top!"

"Blimey! Merry Christmas, mister!"

"That's Mister Samson, eh."

"Merry Christmas, Mr Samson."

"Merry Christmas, son." Clearly amused by the boy and pleased with himself, Mr Samson makes his slightly unsteady way home.

From my darkened bedroom window, I watch as the snow continues to fall. Mr Samson is my Uncle Archie. I make up my mind to see if he'll give me a snow-clearing job on Boxing Day. I never realized that he was good for such a big tip! The boy is my friend Billy. I am glad he can now get a present for his granddad. We discussed the problem earlier that day. I bought him a balsa wood Spitfire for tomorrow. I murmur 'good night' as Billy hurries home.

On Christmas morning it will still be snowing.

(Extracted from THE WOUNDS OF ALBION)

THE STORY OF THE STONE

Renchi Bicknell

O Yes
To the Zen gift
Later described
As an alien object
Known by its deep blue hue
As the stone of heaven.

Hum, Yes
"He often puts a
Dreamstone in his mouth"
To tell a (truthful) tale
Stranger than fiction.

Dear Georgie
Thank you for the Himalayan surprise
Now mine
The polished piece
Of lapis lazuli
With its exotic
White gold and blue
In tune

With the wild Atlantic waves
Below the Dzogchen Buddhist monastery
The stone, now mine
Our histories combine

And Yes
Surely she, in her midnight blue
Could help turn back the clock
Five thousand years and enter
The Neolithic sky
- Enhancing Avebury
A project I'm preparing on behalf of
Barbara Brennan's healing group
To share on Zoom
The stone
      Calls out
            "Beware!"
It is 4a.m. Sunday morning, I am
Conscious the stone is in my mouth
And slipping like a pill to the
Back of my throat
O No
  O Gulp, O God
There is nothing I can
Do to stop, or call it back
what have I done
In swallowing this stone
My mind's on fire, my blood racing
Questioning
With stone inside
Nothing is normal

Vanessa who is lying beside me
Unusually laid low with laryngitis, has
Completely lost her voice, so
Normal conversation is not possible
I decide
To dress quickly and take
My restless questioning
To the street, before dawn
My breath
    Visible on
        The cold air.
I walk
As if my life expectancy
Had shrunk from 20 years
To 20 minutes

So Stone and I
Travel on together,
As sunlight starts to creep in,
A scoop of starlings
Swoop by the minor injuries unit
Where I join a line of 3 chatty
Geezers, waiting for the doors to open
One has cut his head
When he tripped over the cat
When his wife was away
... By the time I reach the desk
I need a plausible story
I say "I have foolishly and accidentally
Swallowed quite a large stone, it is
A polished piece of lapis lazuli more than one

And a half inches long and more than one inch wide"
Yet
This same day
As I ask
"How can so large a stone make its way
Through my narrow pipes and valves?"
   I am thinking I must not forget

In a few hours time I'm due in a parallel
world To share my view of prehistoric
Avebury
   This is what happens
   We are flying above our
   Ceremonial land,
   There are we, nestled in by the river
   below the bright white outline
   of the Great Goddess, defined by her pregnant
   Chalk mound belly and the shape of her
   dark moat-water limbs squatting
   to give birth to the stars ...
   above our lands we hover
   and far below
   We see our own children, our own animals
   Our own fields and rivers – clothing
   the land and Goddess – woven
   in her dress of thorn and oak and alder
   and eyebright herbs ...
I say nothing about the stone to the smiling
Zoom-mosaic of American faces,
And make no mention of my inner guide
   We rise

and rise
and rest
at a cove above
the earth
we arrive at
the edge of the sky
and look back at
our beloved earth

We hear
stone call to stone in an
enclosure of 27 stones
and star to star
in familiar figures
of hunters and animals.
Then on
we fly
and fly
through long light fields
and rise
and rest
at a cove made from 3 giant diamond shaped
                                                                stones
  at the edge of our own galaxy
She says – I give you this song
   "The greater your love
   The greater your home,
   The greater belonging
   In the skin
   You are in."

Then again
we rise
we fly and fly
past oceanic fields of other galaxies
and arrive
at the outer boundary of 99 stones
at the edge of our universe
– time for a timeless
cup of tea
with the
Great Cosmic Mother of all
one taste of oneness
before our return.

Back through
the star-birth seas
and the dark-star cemeteries
back to our viewing platform
above our beautiful spinning spiral galaxy
She knows her way home
my royal blue stone guiding us
back to the pinpoint light of
our own sun ...
drawn
by the magnet of the
bright-chalk-moon-lit form of the Goddess
beckoning us back
to hover
above the Swallow Head Spring
where we are gathered
we hear the sound of owls and wolves

then only owls
as we resurface 5,000 years
to our present ending Zoom group goodbyes
Then back to only the stone and I.

"Are you sure you have swallowed this stone?"
Says the doctor
Ushering in a cackle
Of mocking birds
"– You fool, you crazy man, you idiot
You nut
You utter nutter" they groan
"There was an old feller who swallowed a stone"
As well as jocular binoculars, bears, buses,
Bizarre cars, starlings and dreams ...
According to my sister Sarah's version
"He swallowed the starling to scoop the dream
That drifted and shifted and spun inside him
He swallowed the dream to catch the stone
Close to the bone he swallowed that stone."
Yes Doctor I am 100 percent sure
I swallowed this stone!
In the X-Ray
I see my shining astral ally
Now become enemy, as
I am wishing her OUT
Out of my stomach
And out quickly!

But my wish is not her command
And like a train
Entering an interminable tunnel

From sight and sense she is gone
And I am left with discomfort and anxiety.

A magician has placed his
Assistant in a black box
And we are supposed to wonder if
She will ever return
After the patter has been so fast
Now it slows right down ...
Something seems to have gone wrong
And my anxiety turns to fear
And my discomfort into pain

I liken my stone to a salmon
Trying many times to jump from
An acidic pool in the
Kidney-shaped curve of the stomach
Into the portal of the
Pyloric sphincter
At the entrance to the
Small intestine
Ahead
All 22 convoluted feet
Of it.
But now
The stone is moving
I am shaking, violently vomiting brown bile
And strangely trying to stay very still
At the same time
Doctor disbelief has changed his tune
And sends me straight to hospital

Diagnosis – Foreign body in gut
Presenting Complaint – Abdo pain
Patient swallowed a pebble 15 days ago
Still not passed in stool ...
Another X-Ray
And there she is again – beautiful
Blurred but still shining
Much lower down
At the start of the labyrinthine maze
Of the small intestine.

No operation
Just stone and I alone
Continuing with
A colon cleanse
With Felicity's clarity
She says
"I know what this is all about
The loss of your son Ivan
And your wish to take
On his pain."
At this
I feel struck deep
To the heart
Deep to the root of why
I swallowed the lapis lazuli
I feel this story in its true
Context
And cry
From a hidden well so deep and sad
That tells me more than even

The highest flight to heaven
Or most gruelling journey through my gut.
Yes
My tears
Have cleared
My way to drive
To Sussex for
Christmas but
I am still a man with
A stone inside
So interiorized – Mike has noticed
And lovingly challenged
"Come on Renchi, be yourself
You are OK.
Your body can do this" ...
Yes, I trust
The course of nature
Trust in the invisible
Process of peristalsis
And Yes
I am amazed how fast
Concerns of
My mortality and
Bad bargains with God
Have faded in the full
Light of day
With my attention out on my grandchildren
And away from the inner journey of the stone.
I am
    Letting it go – letting it be
    Letting it take its time with me ...

I found a dream
From six months earlier
Where I had forseen
This journey
– ... I am choosing to plunge
Through a pool, thousands of feet
Down through a tunnel system
Where there seem to be people
Assisting and descending at different stations,
Helping with instructions of how
To negotiate incredible lengths of fall
And travel downward ...
I even illustrated this dream
With small figures falling
From pool to pool
The full length of the page.

Days follow days
And my dreams follow rivers
And travel down corridors ...
I have a detached
Sense of the stone
Mirroring emotion
Sometimes caught like a stick
In a sluggish side-pool
Then dancing forward
I now picture her as a car
Or royal blue mail-coach, charging
Along then suddenly
Mired in a ditch –
I think it has occurred at

The site of my teenage
Appendix scar.
Ha!
A good sign – it means
She is in the large bowel
The very area
Of Ivan's cancer
And thanks to the stone
I know I no longer
Have to emulate my son
I have become more equal
More accepting
That at some level
I have chosen to undertake this
Healing journey of the stone
Regardless of outcome
YES there is one
As noted in my dream book
For Jan 16th (2023)
"Stone release at last
After 42 days
Battered, stinking, discoloured but
Definitely returned to the
Daylight world."

I rest her, clean her and
Place her on my altar.

Gratitude then to the zen jewel of
Heaven.

SUNKEN NIGHTFALL

B.Catling

Sunken nightfall folds the clouds against
the sound of our departing.
Voices suddenly spent against the Smithy
pressing age. Leaking us back to the car, the roads,
to the dense flicker of the living.
away from the inner ground
buried in the knowledge of too much,
and the stones
The very stones?
That after we are gone
and the land is gone,
the molten core shrugged
as if to a feather off
will unhitch their roots
    and fall through the illimitable night
without the faintest recall
of resting before
our little bones
for a bit
of a day.

STONE PILGRIMAGE WITH BRIAN CATLING

Matthew Shaw

My journey began, a drive from Christchurch in Dorset to Oxford. I'm on my way to see artist, author and poet Brian Catling.

Brian had been based in Oxford for many years, teaching at The Ruskin School of Art. My interest in Brian's work has already developed into something of an obsession at this point and to add to this we had also become good friends. I met a man with a curiosity and generosity in his ability to teach and advise, he possesses a rare quality of providing encouragement and guidance for so many of his students and friends, sometimes in a formal way with clear instruction but often much more subtly, in changing one's perspective, view or attitude towards a piece of work that is becoming.

This all started for me with a book of Brian's poems *A Court of Miracles*, found quite randomly in a second-hand bookshop, bought after a few minutes flicking through the book and deciding that what lay within deserved my further attention. On returning home and diving deeper I realized the poems were complex yet direct, horrific in places but always beautifully formed.

I'm forever in second-hand bookshops, searching for a bargain or an intriguing looking book; some days these searches produce gold in the form of a new favourite book or author. The copy of *A Court of Miracles* that I found was one of the most important discoveries so far. I soon began to collect whatever else I could find. The poems produced images that stuck with me and both haunted and fascinated me, like half-remembered dreams or nightmares that came from deep down inside.

In more recent times Brian had also taken to painting, small egg tempera paintings. Many of these featured impressions of a Cyclops. A character also central to Brian's incredible visionary novel *The Vorrh*. Brian's writing of novels also a recent development, after years of encouragement and cajoling from Iain Sinclair, one of his oldest friends.

I had discovered these various parts of Brian's work after our first meeting which took place in Leicester Square, outside the Soho Curzon cinema on an October evening before the film premiere of *The Ballad of Shirley Collins*, a film produced by my friend and at that time colleague Paul Williams. We arrived at the cinema and sat outside. With wild white hair moving in the breeze contrasted by his long black coat was Brian. Paul rushed over and asked if we knew each other and with no further ado, introduced us. I told Brian I had read several of his books and we quickly found that we had many friends in common, not least Mark Pilkington who had published a book called *Scales / Silenic Drift* by Brian and Iain Sinclair.

I asked Brian and Paul if they would like a drink and duly headed to the bar. On being served I was told there was a maximum two drinks per customer rule, and my explaining that two of their other customers were outside and I was merely buying them for all of us didn't help matters. I took the two drinks and handed them to Brian and Paul. Brian was shocked that I had given away both drinks, reached for one of his already empty glasses and shared the drink I had bought for him with me. It was really a very small act on my part and one that seemed to be the only solution but Brian took it as a great act of selfless generosity! We bumped into each other later in the evening and swapped details before heading back home. The following morning Brian messaged about how good it was to meet and to keep in touch from that day on.

The next significant moment for me was a trip to see Brian to discuss the idea I had of making a documentary about him, his work and the origins of his creativity. I knock on Brian's front door and he appears after a few minutes dressed in an immaculate pinstripe three-piece suit, covered in part by a pinny tied around his waist. As I crossed the threshold into Brian's house out of the rainy, cold January night, I was also crossing the boundary from acquaintance to friend. I realize now that it wasn't a common occurrence for Brian to invite people to stay that he hadn't known for very long, let alone entertain ideas of films being made or other projects being discussed with very little evidence of what the person, me in this instance, had to offer creatively. Brian had many friends, collaborators and fellow travellers and was by now all but retired from his academic career, with more ideas than he felt he had time for, so to be let in felt like a real honour. We entered the kitchen. I discover Brian is in full flow preparing us dinner, a delicious meal accompanied by generous amounts of red wine and later whisky.

Brian's home is stacked full of books, art, found and gifted unusual objects, as well as his own paintings and sculptures. Many of these sculptures also occasionally move on their own accord, animatronic devices and fairy lights surrounding animal skulls that turn to face me. Every surface is covered with collected oddities, stones, wooden objects, firearms, toy figures, postcards, tools and unidentifiable things. A sixteenth-century grimoire next to a book about Hieronymus Bosch, next to Albion Village Press poetry pamphlets. The room is alive and full of magical items, each known, interpreted and understood by Brian. We talk while looking through books and art and my head is swimming with the expansive inner world of Brian and perhaps the whisky. He explains his stutter as the result of his mind being two sentences ahead of his lips and so his speech pauses as the mind and language realign, and once again function as he would like. I had barely noticed the stutter initially but occasionally it would appear, stick around for a minute or two before vanishing again completely.

The night ended reasonably early but also a little woozy after an enthusiastic discussion and sharing of interests in artists, poets and authors we had in common as well as many new discoveries and notes for people to look up for both of us.

The following morning I went downstairs to find Brian immaculately turned out and towards the end of preparing a delicious and substantial fry up. I still don't know quite how Brian could rise so early and write and still be up and fresh and ready for the day. This routine produced *The Vorrh*, Brian explained over breakfast, as early a start as possible, the book almost writing itself with Brian as the medium, enraptured with the story unfolding before him, processed through his fingers onto his laptop, like a modern version of automatic writing or a channelling from the aether. A process

Brian felt best done and not questioned or examined too thoroughly should the magic dissipate and the words dry up.

A little later that day we head off in my car to our starting point to walk a section of the Ridgeway, an ancient trail, 87 miles long passing through many ancient sites including the great stone circle at Avebury. Today we are walking a section of the Ridgeway to the Neolithic chambered long barrow known as Wayland's Smithy.

I read out a passage from *Villages of the White Horse* by Alfred Williams about the legend of the Smithy:

> *One day old Wayland lost his temper and gave a thrilling proof of his mighty strength, striking fear into the folks of the countryside round about. Running short of nails, he sent his favourite imp, Flibbertigibbet, down into the valley to obtain some from the other blacksmiths, and bade him to make haste about it, as a horse was waiting outside to be shod. After waiting several hours he looked out from the cave, and saw the imp had yielded to the temptations of a mortal and gone bird's-nesting in the fields, forgetful of the nails. Thereupon Wayland, falling into a passion, snatched a big round stone, used as an anvil, and threw it at the loiterer, two miles off; the stone shot through the air with a loud whizzing noise and, falling short of the mark, nevertheless slid along the ground and struck the imp on the foot retaining the mark of his heel on one side. Thereupon the imp appeared to the astonished rustics, limping and snivelling, and rubbing his eyes with his fist, so they called the spot Snivelling Corner, and the name remains to this day.*
> [Alfred Williams, *Villages of the White Horse* (first published 1913)]

So many of our ancient sites are entwined with folklore, myth, tales passed down from generation to generation. It is commonly believed that these stories are hundreds or even thousands of years younger than the monuments themselves but I believe that they still provide us with clues. The folk memory and oral tradition evolved into the printed word and so we have a trail reaching back in time and with a little imagination can piece together what might have been. This pursuit is something Brian and I shared immediately. The love of exploring both a physical site and the joy of the imagination.

Brian explained: "What drives me is the power of the imagination and how far you can go with it. And that's something that everyone can develop. It's the ultimate gift". I couldn't agree more.

We discussed various remembered legends of these stones as well as talking about Brian's first visit to Avebury with one of his oldest friends Iain Sinclair:

> *I was 17 years old; I had no idea what was here, I'd never heard of the place and I just walked straight into it. It was covered in snow; the thing was completely and utterly shattering to me and it was freezing cold and it was white and I fell in love with it. That's probably wrong, it fell in love with me, or something in it came and grabbed me and made a permanent impression. This is sculpture on a huge scale, a huge meaning and it's not something you can go back and make in a London studio. So, you have to find another language, another way to capture this atmosphere and this power. The presence is still the same place, the place is as strong as the objects in it and they become one, they become one thing. But as an artist part of the job is to make it in a different way, you have got to make something else, that is genuinely not an illustration, or is not a picture of it but is something you can try to put in a painting, something you could put in a story. Not knowing what the plot is, not knowing what the people are going to do, just having the place somewhere sitting in front of you, waiting for something to occur, and sometimes that's enough, that's enough to just get the entire thing to move forward.*

These ideas about place, each with its own unique atmosphere, featuring whatever objects within, resonated deeply with me. Here in Oxfordshire was a site thousands of years old, a place that has changed over the years with many archaeological investigations, yet despite these disturbances and the passing of time, has held on to something vital and unique.

As we walked towards Wayland's Smithy, I wondered about all the travellers, the farmers, the drovers, the soldiers that would have passed by here since it was first built sometime around 3400BC, not to mention the mystery of who the 14 burials found inside the chambers might have once been. Now the site is passed and visited by hikers, by families, by dog walkers, by those fascinated by the prehistoric, those who connect this place to their faith or perhaps even those questing for meaning.

We considered a slight detour to Uffington Castle, the White Horse and Dragon Hill with its bare patch of chalk, where legend has it that St George slayed a dragon, the bare patch being where the dragon's blood fell. Today though we were not searching for dragons or lost kings or battles. I had visited these other sites just a few months before, and Brian had been to them many times across the years. Back in the early 1970s Iain Sinclair had walked the Ridgeway taking in East Kennett Long Barrow, Wayland's Smithy, Avebury, Silbury Hill, Dragon Hill and Lowbury Hill. An expedition, or more precisely a quest, with Iain Sinclair, Tom Baker (scriptwriter of *Witchfinder General*), Renchi Bicknell (artist) and John Marks (artist and filmmaker). They walked from Streatley-on-Thames to Wayland's Smithy, sleeping at the Smithy for one night before continuing on to Avebury, Silbury Hill, East and West Kennett Long Barrows before following the canal back to Hungerford. Brian and I talked of revisiting these sites one day but with Brian now in his 70s this would have to be done in sections rather than the earlier epic walk undertaken decades earlier. Although not physically present for that particular walk, it seems Brian's spirit was there. He doubtless knew these places well and understood their power.

Brian and I arrived at Wayland's Smithy. We sat on the stones, walking the long barrow's length, width and circumference. With the corvids high up on the branches above us occasionally breaking into their own croaky chorus, reminding us that we were not alone. We spent a long time in silence, or at least without talking, watching and occasionally pointing or gesturing to an avian event or waving to a passing hiker. We became more still and at one with the place, taking in the atmosphere, this singular moment in time.

We continued to walk. A well-worn pathway beneath our feet, wintered soil, exposed chalk in places. The trees skeletal without their leaves became silhouetted against the sky, the rooks roosting and the sun ever lower in the sky. It was time to surrender to the night.

On leaving we both turned to look back at the stones at the same time. We both felt the presence of someone or something behind us. A very sudden and strange feeling like a close intimate whisper in the ear or a tap on the shoulder. It stopped us in our tracks, our senses and nerves alert. Brian knew instantly what this was, describing this moment to me the following morning back in his home:

> *I now know that everything I see and do is material, and it's that transformation, it's the same about place, it's about taking these energies from last night when we turned round to leave from Wayland's Smithy and the light had gone, it reached its greyness and the birds started to sing, there was this slightly magical thing of things being packed up, and walking away, because you know in your head, as you go down the track and get in the car, some part of you goes back because you know what it is when there's nobody there.*

An uncanny moment. I have thought a lot since about this, the idea of knowing what it is to know a place when there is nobody there. When all is left alone, perhaps having left some part of ourselves behind at the stones until we return again. I wonder if the folklore of ancient sites is a memory of this in some way, a manifestation in words of an ancient memory.

Over the next day or so at Brian's house we looked back over the photographs we had taken and the experiences of that day. Time flew in our discussion of deep time and how much there is that we don't know for certain about ancient sites but at the same time the ability to be able to experience them and how walking the land does reveal something of their nature. The idea of the *genius loci*, the spirit of place became our focus. Brian wasn't overly sentimental or romantic about this idea and at the same time appreciated, no insisted, that each place does have its own atmosphere, and it's something that we can all access, and that this knowledge can become a source of inspiration for our individual and collective creativity.

Brian's world view, his influence and way of seeing the world as well as his encouragement have stayed with me since that walk. There were many other meetings and visits over the next few years, other discoveries and shared obsessions about places and stones.

I produced the documentary about Brian, the title of which was provided by Brian himself, *The Cast Squid of a Lost Character*. The title was brilliant and described a consequence of the editing process of *The Vorrh*. Brian had entertained the idea of giving friends small cameos in the book for sentimental reasons, each of these were immediately noticed by the editor who could see they added nothing meaningful to the plot, nor contributed to its overall goal. Brian explained that in a way these people were still present in the finished book for him but now like ghosts and that if he could cast a sculpture out of the void of these sentences and passages that had been edited out, he would have something that resembled the cast squid of a lost character. The film was first screened at the launch of *The Cloven*, the final book launch for *The Vorrh* trilogy in Soho.

The film was made with a very small budget but we managed to still visit a number of sites of relevance or importance to Brian. Much of the documentary was filmed in Brian's home with his paintings, books and possessions visible in every shot. There was the footage from Wayland's Smithy of course but we also filmed in the Old Operating Theatre in the early eighteenth-century church of the old St Thomas' Hospital, London. There was an uncanny moment while filming in there when Brian stood in the exact same spot he had stood in at the launch event for Iain Sinclair's first novel *Whitechapel, Scarlet Tracings*, published in 1987. We also visited St Mary's Church in the village Ewelme, within which is the transi tomb of Alice de la Pole that directly inspired Brian's painting *Transi*, as well as an as yet to be published novel.

Wittenham Clumps was another location, exploring the obsession Paul Nash had of painting the same place across decades. This idea was a recent obsession for Brian, the repetition of returning to the same subject or place. Paul Nash also a great inspiration. The final location was at the Royal Academy. In some ways this seemed an incongruous location when looked at in relation to the other places but it fitted perfectly and what better place for Brian to explain his honour to have been elected a Royal Academician in 2015. What a journey Brian's life took from a foundling adopted and chosen in a line up of cots by Lillian and Leonard Catling, Brian's adoptive parents. It seemed a long way from these humble uncertain beginnings to being a Royal Academician and Oxford professor. For Brian though this was just his life, his journey, it was the work that came first and foremost not the titles or social status.

I edited together a subsequent short film featuring footage of Wayland's Smithy, the soundtrack a piece of music I had made for my album *Among the Settng Stars*, the cover of which featured a painting by Brian titled *Transi*. I sent the film to Brian featuring an additional voiceover of a recording I had made of him reading one of his poems. Brian replied saying he loved the film but that the choice of poem was wrong and that he would record something else for me over the coming days. About a month later I received an email with an amazing poem attached. 'Sunken Nighfall' was an account of the uncanny earlier experience Brian and I had at Wayland's Smithy, on hearing a whisper and turning to find no one there. The poem captured the atmosphere of that numinous moment perfectly. The words were only written though, for the film I needed a recorded voice and asked Brian if he was sending on a recording or if I should visit soon to make one. He replied to say the voice should be on the true English earth and stone. This was quite the challenge and initially not particularly helpful for me finishing the film. Then it occurred to me that Shirley Collins, the legendary English folk singer, whose biopic documentary it was that was about to premiere when I first met Brian. I asked and Shirley obliged. Shirley and Brian had great fondness between them as well as an admiration for each other's work. I sent the finished film to Brian who called me immediately after watching it shouting 'Is that who I think it is!' down the phone. It was Brian, yes.

The three of us, Brian, Shirley and I later worked on a more expanded project called *Crowlink*, which started its public life with the screening of a film by director Grant Gee, who assembled footage of Firle, together with Shirley's latest music and selections of music and recordings I had made. It really came together though with two evenings at Charleston House in Sussex with live performances from Shirley Collins and the Lodestar band, poems written and read live by Brian and a sound installation I assembled featuring people giving voice to Brian's poems, extracts from letters and diaries from Virginia Woolf, Vanessa Bell, Duncan Grant and others from the Bloomsbury Group, an installation that then continued in the garden at Charleston for the best part of a fortnight. Shirley's performances were breathtaking, as were Brian's readings. It was 'Sunken Nightfall' though and the return and cycling of time from our walk along the Ridgeway that was central to everything.

In late 2021 Brian called me about an idea for a new album of music and poetry. I had recently sent Brian some piano recordings I had made at Hawkwood near to Stroud. On the recording, in the background, at a very low, almost inaudible level were voices. These I knew came from the lane outside of the room I was recording in, but to Brian, without the knowledge of where I had recorded, he had become interested in these ghostly voices that would rise and fall beneath the piano notes. What at the time had seemed like a slight annoyance on trying to create these piano pieces had fostered the seed of a new idea. The plan was for me to visit him and for us to record in Wytham Village Hall but this time reversing the process. With Brian to be front and centre with a new set of poems and me playing the piano at the other end of the hall, well away from the microphone, playing as softly and gently as possible. This time the piano would become the ghost. Our theme was to be set on ancient sites following a natural progression from the outing to Wayland's Smithy. The ideas kept coming, as did photographs and new collages inspired by various stones and memories of places once visited. One morning Brian called again about a trip he wanted to take to Avebury with Iain Sinclair and I. He had been feeling very unwell but looked forward to feeling up to the walk, and warmer weather, and to be out in the landscape with friends. It seemed like a brilliant idea to me. Perhaps this walk would provide the words Brian was looking for, and also solve a mystery that had returned to Brian again and again since that walk he took with friends along the Ridgeway in the 1970s.

Before the winter was over though it seemed that Brian might not be able to make the walk at all. He wrote to me saying:

THE SINCLAIR SHAW STONE. which was ghosted in 1964, maybe found in 1977 with I.S. and looked again for in the future with you. Somewhere up on New Totterdown. above Avebury. Early digs. The Sinclair Shaw Stone one might be the strangest. I was 17 in the wrong clothes in the snow above Avebury. Stumbled into it without knowing it was there or what it was. Went back a few years later with Knowledge and Sinclair to find the lost stone in the wood. Recently thought to seek again with you and then stopped, because who knows if I am ever going to get there. So decided to do it on page not on foot.

Brian sent through this as a text following our phone conversation on the 2 April 2022 at 9.09am.

My partner and I took the train to Oxford in late June 2022 and met Brian's wife Caroline at Oxford station and Caroline drove us back to their house in Wytham. We spent a few hours catching up, eating lunch outside in their garden, a beautiful sunny afternoon, filled with stories and laughter. Then Brian needed to rest. The recent medical treatment meant that his energy levels were quickly depleted and conserving energy was essential. It was hard to leave that afternoon with Brian clearly struggling so with his health but he was also still so full of life with millions of ideas, dozens of projects on the go and a recent flourish of incredible new paintings just completed and others at an early stage of development. Over the next few weeks I received a number of poems, photo collages and photographs, some from decades earlier, some from more recent trips to the United States with Caroline. Almost all focused in some way around ancient sites, sharing similar ideas and dream walks as described by Brian in the Sinclair Stone message.

Brian Catling died on 26 September 2022. The Avebury walk to search for the elusive stone that provided Brian with decades of inspiration must still be done. The poems however were written, many of these I have read for Brian in public at various events, and will continue to do so. The gift of these poems along with Brian's books, paintings, his sculptures and the performance art films are all still very present and much loved, as is Brian himself, loved and greatly missed in the physical world. Iain Sinclair pointed out that another way of thinking of Brian now is that he is no longer limited to be in one place at a time, so in theory could be in all of the places we remember him, as a travelling companion with one or many of us at any given point in time.

Walking, experiencing, writing and talking are all ways of manifestation on different levels. As I write this I think of Brian and that visit to Wayland's Smithy and the part of us that returned to the stones because we know what is when there is nobody there. I wonder if in some way we will meet again there or along the Ridgeway someday.

TALL TREES

B.Catling

I visit under tall trees
and imagine living here
and dying to the sound
of the rooks that ornament
the branches:
their earnest conversations describing the depth of winds.

I live under tall trees
and at night when the silent nests
block my ears
imagine the foreverness
of the sunlit days
and the deep shadows that dance beneath them.

Dorchester 5th of November 2015. 5.53am

Alice moonscape by Léonie Hampton

AN ELEMENTAL PLACE

Alice Albinia

I am on the water, looking for a way to belong in this land. Had I been born a thousand years ago, I might have felt the currents of this river as blood pumping through my veins. I might have tasted the waters and responded to their savour and tang on my tongue. I would have listened to the fishes and the fishers, their trickle, peck and call. I would have wound my way through this cacophony, attuned to rain/patter, otter/silk, heron/still. But human acculturation has transformed me. It is a membrane in my mind which I do not know how to cross.

Until recently, I hadn't realized what I was missing. Almost all my adult life I have sought to understand the world intellectually—such was the priority. But the slow process of writing two books about women and islands brought me gradually to see the limitations in my approach. In particular, the world of female healers and shamans which I encountered (and invented) while writing *The Britannias* and *Cwen* showed me that, having grown up valorizing empirical understanding, I might be missing something.

Searching through the British Isles for stories of women, I looked back in time: finding solace in remnants of female folklore in ancient, orally-transmitted tales. I wandered through islands, by lochs, across hills, along seashores, tracing female forms in the landscape. Always, islands drew me: the ability to demarcate female space; the magic of crossing over the water. These are ancient ideas with modern resonances. And on a small island I could perceive more clearly than elsewhere how land, water, air interact. The female dimension of the Neolithic drew me, too; maybe because there are no words, no verbal messages to decipher, so it is possible to project one's own interpretations onto those immense stone circles and chambered cairns. And there is peace in just listening, imagining and dreaming.

During this long process of research and writing, I became aware of other forms of communication: with the world beyond our skin; between more-than-human entities. These conversations have been long-intuited by people in touch with pre-Enlightenment knowledge systems, are belatedly being explored by scientists, but for everybody else, have until recently been beyond modern human understanding. I also concluded that thousands of years of patriarchy has managed to engrain in us a suspicion of its crucial female dimension (as with anything female outside the norm).

In the meantime, I got pregnant, and so I acquired a new sense of smell (as ill, or hungover people sometimes do), a largely redundant superpower. My particular body rejected (was made sick by) all artificial smells—aftershave on the London Underground, perfumed soap and shampoo. But what started out merely as a perplexing inconvenience (being sick in public spaces) became an emotional recalibration which went deeper, into realms that shook me fundamentally. I finally saw that I needed to string together a necklace of female stories in my book, and I needed the same stories in my life. And missing from my life, naturally, was a sense of our connection beyond each other, beyond history, to land itself—an elemental place inhabited by the imagination of humans, with its own spirit.

Something opened up in me: an appreciation of the ineffable; of female friendship; of non-verbal communication; of everything that isn't human. A metamorphosis of being.

And so, here I am, on the water, travelling downstream, into London. It is midsummer and wildfires ripple like snakes through the undergrowth. Once, the river Lea was a mile wide. Humans like me began changing its natural course almost half a millennia ago; to make it navigable, to carry vegetables and fruit south into the city, to carry street manure back out to nourish those plants. The misty mysterious wetlands were drained two hundred years after that, and within a century, the bittern, a brownish heron-like bird, was extinct, and the barbel, a fish with a beard, almost gone from these murky shallows.

I know that rivers were once precious to the people of Britain. In Romano-British times the local goddess Sulis was worshipped flamboyantly at Bath. The islands of Britain are speckled with healing wells and springs, the sacredness of which long predates the

Romans, and continued into Christian times. Maybe the debased modern version of that ancient reverence is the popularity of plastic-bottled spring water. Humans want to drink deeply from sources of pure unpollution.

Like the river Lea, and along with over half the world's population, I am an urban-dweller now (whether the river or I like it or not). I take solace from imagining that we can forage together for older, wiser, more urgently contemporary connections, of the kind that so many of us crave. Even, or especially, in cities.

In Calthorpe Community Garden near King's Cross, the London-based artist Gaylene Gould, and her producer, Zaynab Bunsie, are seeking out and reviving the story of a seventeenth-century black woman, Mary Woolaston, who tended a healing well here. Mary sold spring water. Yet the name of the area which once carried her name was changed and her story lost. The precarity touches Zaynab. Her voice softens as she describes how Black Mary speaks of healing, of the stories of care that black women carry. 'Here too were people experimenting with new ways of living, queer communities. A Black business woman was part of that mix.'

For artist Gaylene, water itself 'is a sneaky conduit through which buried stories, folklore and myths in England's land, find a way to be remembered. And how the colonizing of land and water suppresses those stories'. I agree. We need to see and understand all land differently: its meaning, integrity and ownership.

I first came across the idea of non-human entities having 'personhood' in 2019, when I returned to the Indus River, about which I had written a book, to look at the effects of climate change on its ecosystem. In a village outside Karachi the Pakistan Fisherfolk Forum was calling for the river's authority to be recognized in law, as had happened to the Whanganui River in New Zealand. The Indus hasn't been declared a living entity yet but several states in India have made rivers 'legal persons'; Bangladesh has since granted all its rivers legal personhood status.

Returning to London, I attended an Extinction Rebellion event, a water pilgrimage led by Charlotte Pulver from Tower Bridge to Westminster. Charlotte is a 'water guardian' who began exploring London's springs as a teenager, as a way of coping with the city. She gradually mapped all its streams, which are guides, she says, for humans in finding a deep connection to the land. On Hampstead Heath, for example, two springs meet, a red water spring (containing iron oxide) and a white (loam) water spring. These form the river Fleet, which flows south under the Royal Courts of Justice. Charlotte likes to visit the spring in Hampstead and send prayers for ecological justice into the water, knowing where it goes.

She tells me the Norse story of Yggdrasil, about the well of memory presided over by three giantesses, who gather morning dew from the memories of humans. I love the idea that water, being time, is also human memory. Diné (Navajo) activist Pat McCabe has also spoken beautifully about water's travels through time and space: 'it has always been the same water ... the original water is still here ... all of our ancestors had a drink from this very water. So it really does unite us'.

For Charlotte and Pat, water is a female element. I ponder this, wondering why water would be feminine; then appreciating that giving it a gender recognizes its personhood; then asking myself why understanding is still so important to me. Who should I believe, the person who displays sound evidence? Or the intuitive storyteller?

I have come across the idea of water as female before, moreover. Sharon Blackie, author of *If Women Rose Rooted*, describes water as the physical manifestation of the female otherworld, the world of the imagination. The myth of the well-maidens became particularly important to her. As long as the maidens were healthy, so were the waters, and so was the land. They were the canaries in the mine.

Sharon also observed that while ancient Irish mythology placed women at the centre of the cosmos, not all parts of the British Isles guarded their stories of women equally. Thus, there is still a plethora of Irish folktales about women; but a relative paucity in Scotland; mere traces only in Wales; and a dearth in England—bar the occasional holy well. Internal colonization manifesting as imaginative drought: England as a place where women's stories were largely extinguished.

For Sharon there is an urgency in finding stories in exactly those places: 'the old woman archetype in a cactus or a stone or in birds. Often old women shape-shifted into herons or cranes, for women are the great shape-shifters of the human race'.

I run my hands through the waters of the Lea. I have swum in this river but I didn't relish it and wouldn't drink it. I do scoop up its waters to feed the herbs on my partner's boat; I appreciate the filament of sanctity which, however unhealthy, they bequeath to the city. I want these waters, including for their own sake, to once again flow briskly, deliciously and free.

In a field in the Lea Valley, I crouch in the soil, my hands in the earth. The autumn squash harvest has been gathered in. The fine black compost that remains behind has been carefully raked. Lines have been traced in the earth, indicating where I should wield my dibber. I straddle the soil trench, punching the earth in lines of three. Somebody comes behind me, dropping in garlic cloves. A third person follows, combing the indentations with a rake.

Every time, even now, I find submission to pure physicality in land work—being rained on, getting muddy and cold; my thinking self, untethered—a challenge to my closely guarded sense of who I am. I wonder if I am missing something else, too; a female dimension to this work, its history, community and straightforward embodied practice.

Organic Lea, the farmers' cooperative where I am planting garlic, was set up by a group of solidarity activists in 2001 and named after the river. Clare Joy (beautifully named), one of the founding members, saw that something connecting London's different communities, ethnicities, age groups, 'in a beautiful way', were the community gardens. The allotment was the space where she would see the Caribbean granddad helping the young Turkish single mum—and vice versa. And so the call came. The work which needed to be done, in terms of acts of resistance, was 'back here in the belly of the beast, within capitalism itself: building the world we want to see within the shell of the old'. She laughs, and yet her words make me catch my breath: 'Above all, we needed to be ready with alternatives as the system as we know it steadily collapses around us'.

Here on London's fringes, she and her fellow activists created a utopia of the soil. The site is council land—a former tree nursery—leased on a reduced rent. The cooperative grows food but also plays a social function. With its hawthorn berries as big as cherries, its frilly asparagus beds, its golden medlar trees, its old glasshouses aromatic with chillies and lemon verbena, its steep terrace of plants lapped by Epping Forest, its ancient oak tree as tall as a tower block, Organic Lea is a haven for a whole community as well as for plants. As Clare says, 'people find their own flow when involved in land-based work with eyes, hands, heart and muscle'. I find this too. There is peace—'magic'—in succumbing to these age-old rhythms.

It can be devastating thinking about how humans have diminished other entities, such as rivers; but Clare sees the goodness that emanates from that ghostly presence. 'The mile-wide river is now canalized, but the soil it nourished for all those millennia is really good.' You 'cannot take the land out of us. It is our source of resilience'.

The Māori believe land, like rivers, has agency. The author Manda Scott believes 'completely rethinking the concept of land ownership' may be one means of heading off humanity's wide-scale destructiveness. Nor is this just about farmland and moors and forests. It's an urban project as well as a rural one.

It is also, I think, a question with a gender dimension—women having been denied land ownership for so long in this part of the world. *Cwen* was about a female collective taking over the running of an island but as Manda talks about the land's own agency I now wonder if it was really the other way round: an island taking control of a collective.

Manda is alert to paradigm shifts—whether in our understanding of the past, or how to save our futures. It was in her *Boudica* novels, set in Iron Age Britain, that I first witnessed the crucial imaginative leap which none of the history books and archaeology reports I had read dared to make: of showing how humans once looked at, listened to, and responded to more-than-human languages and lives. The novels opened my mind to other possibilities too; in particular to female leadership as something ancient and sensible—and radically necessary in the present. Manda, like Sharon, seeks daily counsel from the land, searching out the company of hills near her home, asking them to help her dream. She uses her dreams and the messages they send, in her work, writing and life.

I know what it is to dream with expansiveness and imagination every night— vicariously, through my partner, who imagines future worlds and other systems in his sleep. In London my dream life is trapped inside buildings, within admin loops. What my dreams are telling me, probably, is that the city is too structured and unwild for my mind and its well-being. Or that my mind needs to work harder to find its way into the suppressed nature life of the city.

The story-weaver Rosanna Lowe described to me how Dartmoor and its stones once reached up to imbue her with the physical prowess to walk faster than she had ever walked before. Imaginative land magic of this kind should be possible to find anywhere, even in the city. As Gaylene and Charlotte are doing with water, so with soil, so with stones. I think of the undulations of the land that holds the city, which streets can mask—Chingford Mount, where Organic Lea stands; Westminster island, looped around by rivers; Epping Forest, stretching down into London, rooting it in earth, bringing tree wisdom into the streets. In autumn, London is illuminated by its choir of trees, with their harmonizing yellow palm prints, orange frilled ovals, pink scallops. Even the paving stones retain the image of those bright offerings from the sky in greyish impress. Tree songs.

Late one night near the winter solstice, I receive a call-out for a spontaneous night gathering of song on the Walthamstow Marshes along the river Lea. I love this marsh in the winter. The coolness of the air enters me physically. The air is polluted, of course, but in this place it is tree-breath which I smell.

A friend and I walk out towards the spot marked on the map, leaving the ring of lights created by roads and buildings, and into a welcoming darkness. I think of how Amy Cooper, a farmer and dancer I know, envisages the elements at work on her body. She feels androgynous on the land; at her most feminine in water: 'A vessel things get born through—not just babies, but care, love, aliveness'. And fire: 'You feel ancient in the mirror of the flames. Because fires often have circles around them, the hierarchy melts away, and a group psychology emerges instead; I am not alone anymore as I am in water'.

We find a woman sitting with a candle and join her. Carefully, I pile up paper and twigs and logs in the firepit made during previous song nights. As the flames catch, I watch lava erupt, waterfalls and ice floes, buds and flowers, deserts and wetlands. The fire dances me, entrances me, air, earth, water, combusting in this conflagration of everything. Eight other strangers walk out of the darkness to the fire circle.

Shan Vahidy, book editor and fire-keeper, says that building and tending fires has become her outlet for female creation and rage. 'In terms of those old sexism wars', she always had 'scary anger in my back pocket', always had 'scary eloquence'. It can be hard to rid ourselves of the hierarchies which are part of our education and the way we have been socialized. Recently, beside the fire, she found righteous female rage transmuting into something wiser and more creative.

Somebody strikes up a protest song: *And when I speak, I will speak like the wind, loud and free*. And I remember that the idea of women as weather witches, who control the air's flows, is something ancient and reiterated in the culture of the British Isles. Independent women on small islands off the coast of Britain, harnessing the winds are written of in Roman times, in medieval mythology, in Shakespeare's *Macbeth*, attested in the folklore of Shetland and the Hebrides. I traced this teleology in my books and it was exhilarating.

Flora Pethybridge, who works therapeutically with song, believes that it is with the air which moves through our bodies, that the connection between land and emotion can be strengthened and made manifest: 'Part of the silencing of women as a collective force has been the suppression of our voices. We used to have song and keening as part of our grief culture, and therefore our life culture'. When somebody died, communities would gather. Usually, keening was led by older, experienced women who would 'sound the corners of grief that language cannot reach. They created a collaborative membrane of song, to hold, support and honour the mourners and the soul of the deceased'. Family and members of the community would join. Thus, 'keening was a ritual; skilled and artful but also channelled out of the collective, out of the air'.

Keening was suppressed by the church in Ireland—the raw emotion too wild and threatening for a religion of the book. When, from the eighteenth century onwards Britain's folksongs came to be collected, men gathered songs by men. Improvised song traditions in which women predominated were hard to notate and thus easier to lose. In revitalizing this tradition, Flora hopes we will find new ways to acknowledge 'how we choose to live on this earth, and to respond to modern concerns such as the climate crisis, where words fail'.

Gabriela Gutierrez, a writer and mythologist, points out that 'patriarchal religions have taught us—especially women—to doubt the body'. She uses sound (among other methods) to lure people back into their bodies and towards the kind of 'low-grade ecstatic experience which was at the heart of prehistoric life; a participation with all of life all of the time.' She was inspired by what she studied of Palaeolithic religions, when our 'extra sensory abilities' developed during cave rituals, for example, causing altered states.

I spent last New Year's Eve in a cave. We took a candle with us under the earth. The flame flickered, lighting up walls of rock and shimmering water. When we extinguished the light, silence enveloped us, magnifying each sound. For a moment, we became something other than our bounded selves. Our senses opened in new ways.

Children find it natural to feel the world all around them as part of their being. I see it in my daughters. My elder loves fire; the younger loves water; both love song. Flames, water, air, dance through them. Here on the marshes, I sing for these little ones. I watch other faces through the flickers of the fire; sense the springs and rivers of London running through the dark beneath our feet; taste the life whispers of the soil and the plants they hold; listen as our collective whispers swell out of historical silencing into a chorus. I sing for an opening up of my responsibilities towards my children; an openness to the elements; to seeing the agency of everything that holds us on this beautiful planet. The life of all things, human and more, woman but not only.

The next morning I wake from a dream: I am walking through the hills towards the ocean on the other side of the world. Two enormous crescent moons, silver and white, fill the sky, my heart, our hopes.

Walking through Stoke Newington and Abney Park Cemetery with Ben Wickey, on his quest for traces of Edgar Allan Poe, a random snapshot of mine tapped the now established Swedenborgian effect, of being there and not there; being doubled and denied material substance. On my return home, I realized that I had unconsciously channelled a gift received from Brian Catling, now hanging on my wall: Edgar's Mirror. *Inky smoke beyond the frame, a very solid representation of absence.*

A teasing vision.

—Iain Sinclair, 2024

A large mirror, (so at first it appeared to me in my confusion), now stood where none had been perceptible before; and, as I stepped up to it in extremity of terror, mine own image, but with features all pale and dabbled in blood, advanced, with a feeble and tottering gait, to meet me. [...] *It was Wilson; but he spoke no longer in a whisper; and I could have fancied that I myself was speaking while he said—"You have conquered, and I yield. Yet henceforward art thou also dead—dead to the world and its hopes. In me didst thou exist—and, in my death, see by this image, which is thine own, how utterly thou hast murdered thyself."*

—Edgar Allan Poe, 'William Wilson', 1842

VALDEMAR'S MIRROR

Ben Wickey

I

"I can't produce Poe's school", said Iain Sinclair, photographing a headless angel, "but we can do a bit of atmosphere".

I had arrived at Abney Park Cemetery early, but through the wrong gate. I should have trusted the high street, but instead I trusted a man with a face like Bruce Forsyth. Through mud and moss-laden graves, I found Sinclair, standing under an elaborately carved Egyptian entry. I had walked to Stoke Newington from Holborn, pausing halfway for a devotional visit to William Blake's grave, Bunhill Fields Burial Ground. Jet lagged and panting I began babbling to Sinclair about a piece I had been writing about Edgar Allan Poe as we roamed the cemetery.

"Brian Catling had been writing something of Poe as well, just before his death," says Sinclair, "a sequel to Poe's 'Facts in the case of M. Valdemar'".

For the first time since removing a rock from my shoe at Blake's grave, I am motionless.

"That's what *I've* been doing", I say, "what I've been writing. We must have both been concurrently attempting to complete Poe's story without knowing it".

I am stymied. Brian Catling, the monumental artist, writer, and man. My brief contact with him had been facilitated by Sinclair in February, 2022. I had mentioned to Sinclair that my mother had been moved and inspired by an interview with Catling, in which he spoke of inspiration and his own process. The next morning, an email from Catling had materialized. "Please thank your mum and tell her inspiration goes both ways", he wrote. "I now have some from her."

Our muddy path led us to the graves of numerous Hackney personalities: William Booth, founder and first General of the Salvation Army, 'Champagne Charlie', and Eric the Punk, 'Stokey's Finest Dog-Walker'. Edward Calvert, the painter and Ancient, was somewhere in the core of the lush green jungle off the path.

"This place certainly would have been more tame in Poe's day", muses Sinclair. "Now it looks like something out of a *Roger Corman film*!"

Sinclair's comment reminds me of another point of interest. I had first encountered the story of Valdemar not in the pages of Poe, but in Roger Corman's 1962 Poe film, *Tales of Terror*. The film starred, of course, Vincent Price, who had strived to embody Poe's tortured narrator of the subconscious, both in physicality and speech. Price, as Ernest Valdemar, was mesmerized at the point of death in this film by Basil Rathbone. The reluctant doctor in attendance was played by the young actor David Frankham, who had since become a dear friend of mine. I explained to Sinclair that I would be in Santa Fe, New Mexico the following month to celebrate the actor's ninety-eighth birthday with him.

"Ninety-eight!" laughs Sinclair as we leave the cemetery, "Makes *me* feel *young*!"

———

My earliest recollections of a school-life are connected with a large, rambling, cottage-built, and somewhat decayed building in a misty-looking village of England, where were a vast number of gigantic and gnarled trees, and where all the houses were excessively ancient [...] In truth, it was a dream-like and spirit-soothing place, that venerable old town. At this moment, in fancy, I feel the refreshing chilliness of its deeply-shadowed avenues, inhale the fragrance of its thousand shrubberies, and thrill anew with undefinable delight, at the deep, hollow note of the church-bell, breaking each hour, with sullen and sudden roar, upon the stillness of the dusky atmosphere in which the old, fretted, Gothic steeple lay imbedded and asleep.

Sinclair paused from reading his well-thumbed paperback of Poe's tales to scrutinize the present edifice which stood before us. The passage was from 'William Wilson'—Poe's tale of doppelgängers, guilt, and self-destruction—and provided faint impressions of the Revd John Bransby's Manor House School, which Poe had attended as a boy. It stood on the corner of Church Street and Edward's Lane, the very spot which we now studied.

With my hated telephone, I conjured a ninetenth-century photograph of the school: a brick, cat-eared box. In its place was an unassuming row of shops, from which a small white bust of Poe, based upon the demoralized ambrotype portraits of the poet's *lonesome latter years*, peered down at us with anxious damsel eyes. A plaque beneath the bust explained that it had been unveiled in 2011 by the actor and playwright Steven Berkoff.

Sinclair returned his paperback to his striped, Peruvian bag. The school was razed, swept clean, and rebuilt. And yet, Poe's bodily presence, *out of place and out of time*, was almost more believable in his long absence. The 'gnarled trees' had diminished in number, while the overgrown, Hammer horror setting of Abney Park Cemetery was most likely tame and orderly in Poe's day. St Mary's Church, which could be spied from where we stood, had no 'gothic steeple' until nine years after Poe's departure. It now stood adjacent to its own William Wilson, a second church of the same name. Poe's former ground was now auditioning for something, it seemed.

Poe crossed the Atlantic with his foster family, the Allans, in 1815. He attended the grammar school in Ayrshire, Scotland, and then a boarding school in Chelsea. In 1817, the Allans had taken up residence at 47 Southampton Row, whilst 'Eddy' was deposited at Bransby's Manor House School. It was here that he studied Latin and took dancing lessons. He suffered black moods and periods of intense alienation. Thinking little of their stepchild, the Allans were preoccupied in London—Mr Allan with business, and Mrs Allan with catarrh. On some nights, Poe had planned to escape from his custodians and flee to Holborn on foot. Had he made such an attempt, he would have most likely been drugged with laudanum by resurrectionists. Once drowned in a well, his corpse would then be sold to anatomists.

Proceeding down Edward's Lane, once the view from Poe's classroom window, we decided to scrounge the Stoke Newington Library for any further insights which books

of local history could produce. This was the first time Iain Sinclair had stepped foot in the building since the library had banned him for the crime of publicly denouncing the 2012 Olympics. Fortunately, the librarians did not recognize him as he approached the information desk and enquired of their local history section. Nor did they understand his question. He may just as well have asked where they stored wheelbarrows of underaged dolphin plasma. After some confusion, they brought us to a laughable modicum of Hackney-related books, not one of which containing any mention of Poe. Ironically, a copy of Sinclair's *The Last London* was hiding in the shelf above. Only upon exiting the library were we satisfied in any way: to the left of the door, competing for wall space with the fire extinguisher, was a small grey plaque in Poe's acknowledgement.

Poe is not often associated with particular localities or nations. As T S Eliot once wrote: 'There can be few authors of such eminence who have drawn so little from their own roots, who have been so isolated from any surroundings'. Eliot further called Poe a 'kind of displaced European', a 'wanderer with no fixed abode'.

William Carlos Williams felt the exact opposite, stating: 'It is the New World, or to leave that for the better term, it is a *new locality* that is in Poe assertive; it is America the first great burst through to expression of a re-awakened genius of *place*'. He added: 'What he wanted was connected with no particular place; therefore it must be *where* he *was*'.

Four months before his death, Poe himself wrote: 'An infinity of error makes its way into our Philosophy, through Man's habit of considering himself a citizen of a world solely—of an individual planet—instead of at least occasionally contemplating his position as cosmopolite proper—as a denizen of the Universe'.

I myself had attempted to understand Poe's place in the world by visiting its starting point, the site of his birth. The thin brick house on Boston's Carver Street, now Charles Street, had fallen victim to the heedless exodontia that had claimed many Massachusetts relics during the 1950s. The structure had been surgically extracted, deemed malign, or worse, *unimportant*. Tumor or appendix, its existence was betrayed not only by the deep crater in its place, but by the exposed wall of the building to its left, with which it had once been conjoined. Brick tracings of this wall suggested communicating doors and lost hearths. Every one of Poe's tales could be staged in these imagined chambers: Dupin's consulting room, the carnage of the Rue Morgue, the bell-clad skeleton of Fortunato.

By the twenty and twenty-first centuries, Poe had become a figure divorced from his own historicity. Rufus Griswold, the literary anthologist who Poe mistook for a friend, had only contempt for the hapless poet. When Poe died screaming, alone in a Baltimore hospital, Griswold became his literary executor, as per the poet's previous wishes. Using an embellished—and, at times, downright fabricated—autobiographical sketch which Poe had once written for him, Griswold further twisted the facts of his rival's flaws, mental illness and scandals in a long obituary for the *New York Tribune*, a sword through the afterlife. Providence poetess and Poe's one-time fiancé, Sarah Helen Whitman, was one of the few who came to Poe's defence. In her 1860 book *Edgar Poe and His Critics*, Whitman denounced Griswold's narrative as 'perverted' and 'notoriously deficient in the great essentials of candor and authenticity'.

I had often fancied the topography of Poe's posterity as a desolate landscape, a vast debris-field upon a dark ocean floor. Poe's life was, as it is commonly considered, one of calamity and collision; a titanic writer, who met a *Titanic* end. Amidst the stratified books, papers, and merchandise, which typify this expanse of dereliction, I have perceived an unfinished lighthouse, lofty and white, with a turning, multicoloured Fresnel lens. From the precarious chalk base of this structure to the darkest outset of the surrounding regions, where the turquoise soil bleeds into a horizon of endless night, no sound is heard save for one pitiful sound—a cry—too vile to be human. Anomalous to the air it offends, the voice is carried upon the varicose scarves of wind that torment the loose papers of this zone, perhaps drawn towards the mesmeric colours of the light ...

We walk on.

II

There stands a man upon High Bridge. He comes here often in the early morning, to perch or pace. Leaning out over the railing, he hears the Harlem River roar beneath him like a wounded troll. It is as if he stands at the rim of an immense ink pot. And yet he knows that, upon the unseen waters, one hundred and forty feet below, there is some reflection of his tiny, craning head, privy to none but toad or beaver. Only in darkness may he confront himself with clarity.

High Bridge glows preternaturally in the interrupted moonlight. Its four-hundred and-sixty-yard expanse now acts as a vast stage for the poet's morning performance, the brutal death-match between man and mind.

Poe hasn't been sleeping. There were sounds once which had denied him sleep. And now the absence of these sounds deny him not only sleep, but sanity also.

He had been driven out of Philadelphia in April 1844, and had brought his sickly wife and mother-in-law to New York in the hopes of a more agreeable future. The infant mouth of shame had been gumming at his brain, and had slowly grown teeth as the prospects of starvation outweighed those of literary success. And yet, there was nothing he could do but write. There was a time when he had harkened vainly for inspiration. But now, in a major period of crisis, the nightmares were cueing at his desk and mustering in the hall. All he had to do was find a suitable chair in that Greenwich Village hovel, sit down, and deal with them, case-by-case. Night after night, he had masqueraded in the skins of slain ghosts as he wrote his tales. The staccato of the pen's dip and the peak-pricked concertina wheeze of Virginia's laboured breath served as the only music in those first New York nights.

In his 14 May 1844 'Correspondence of the Spy' he had written of New York's change of pace: 'We are not yet over the bustle of the first of May. "Keep moving" have been the watchwords for the last fortnight. The man who, in New-York, should be so bold as not to peregrinate on the first, would, beyond doubt, attain immortality as "The Great Unmoved"—a title applied by Horne, the author of "Orion", to one of his heroes, Akineros [sic], the type of the spirit of Apathy'.

He had long dreamt of his own literary magazine: *The Stylus*. Even now, shivering upon High Bridge, his sole aspiration is to erect America's brain with such a publication, to steer and refine the nation's palette with his own unexampled standards. It is a mission he had come close to fulfilling when he purchased advertising space in the *Saturday Evening Post* for 'PROSPECTUS OF THE PENN MAGAZINE, a Monthly

Literary Journal, to be Edited and Published in the City of Philadelphia by Edgar A Poe'. That was in 1840. No use calling it *The Penn* outside of Pennsylvania. *The Stylus* shall one day be a New York magazine, once it receives financial backing from any man in this damn city with both wealth and taste. Poe has daily quested for such a rare beast since his Gotham advent.

Cloud lips part above his uncovered head to reveal a hive of scrambled, twinkling teeth. It is hateful to him that the mystery of the universe should be so bright and forthcoming above him, and yet no more comprehensive. He had first endeavoured to confront this mystery in 'Mesmeric Revelation', 1844, in which a narratorial mesmerist, P, engages in a conversation with a 'sleepwaker', Mr Vankirk, while the latter is under a mesmeric hand. Framed as a scientific case study, the dialogue concerns the subjects of God, the soul, and immortality.

> *P. I do not comprehend. You say that man will never put off the body?*
> *V. I say that he will never be bodiless.*
> *P. Explain.*
> *V. There are two bodies— the rudimental and the complete; corresponding with the two conditions of the worm and the butterfly. What we call 'death', is but the painful metamorphosis. Our present incarnation is progressive, preparatory, temporary. Our future is perfected, ultimate, immortal. The ultimate life is the full design.*

As he relieves his bladder into the vast darkness, his uneven jets of urine limping soundlessly from the towering bridge, Poe recalls the commotion which 'Mesmeric Revelation' had aroused upon its first printing in July of that year. Quoth *The New World*: '*Mr. Poe cannot, on so serious a subject, trifle with his readers: yet more extraordinary statements can hardly be conceived. We do believe in the facts of mesmerism, although we have not yet been able to arrive at any theory sufficient to explain them. Here, however, we are almost staggered*'.

By the time 'Mesmeric Revelation' had been released, Poe had fostered a prickly reputation as a literary critic. The 'Tomahawk Man', they called him. He supposes they still do. At that time, he had feared that his new employers at the *Broadway Journal* would sack him for his relentless attacks on Longfellow, New England's sacred cow. Wiley and Putnam's cheap volume of his stories, *Tales*, would fetch him only eight cents per copy. This wasn't the grand collection of peerless work he had envisioned. And, naturally, he had made some changes to the stories before printing. To 'Mesmeric Revelations', he had added two passages: one which laid out—quite skilfully, he thought—a debate for or against absolute consciousness of the ether, and the other which contemplated the relativity of pain. Even for this disappointing volume, perfection was the only solution.

Poe had written six new stories in 1845. In those murky and uncertain nights, while Virginia's condition fluctuated from recovery to the point of death and back again, reams of paper were deflowered with gore and theory. His drinking also accelerated.

He had also hatched 'The Raven' in that year. Though he had only been paid $9 for it, it has proven to be the work which most earned him respect and acclaim. For the first time he had known fame, had been followed in the streets by children chanting "Quoth the raven! Quoth the Raven!" And then he would turn on his heel and caw "NEVERMORE!" with his caped arms raised like great black wings, sending them shrieking away with delight.

Downriver winds lunge upon the poet's shoulders like the claws of a cassowary. As constant as the river beneath him, he remains unblinking at the cold stars, wherein God is said to wallow. The Swedenborgians, he recalls, had taken significant notice of 'Mesmeric Revelation'. The story, they thought, perfectly reflected Emanuel Swedenborg's themes: the soul, spiritual influx, and direct communion with the spirit world. They had also ventured to suppose that Poe too was a devotee of the great Swedish mystic. In 'Marginal Notes', printed in *Godey's*, August 1845, Poe set the record straight:

> *The Swedenborgians inform me that they have discovered all that I said in a magazine article, entitled 'Mesmeric Revelation', to be absolutely true, although at first they were very strongly inclined to doubt my veracity—a thing which, in that particular instance, I never dreamed of not doubting myself. The story is a pure fiction from beginning to end.*

Considering the media attention and gullibility 'Mesmeric Revelation' had garnered, Poe next calculated a stirring *hoax* upon the same theme. Mr Vankirk, he reckoned, had gotten off too easily. What should occur in the body of a man if he were mesmerized at the point of *death*? Even now, clutching the rail that girds him from the howling deep, he can remember with clarity 'The Facts of M. Valdemar's Case'. Attended by Doctors D— and F—, Poe's narrator begins to notice a 'profuse out-flowing of a yellowish ichor' from under Mr Ernest Valdemar's eyelids, producing a 'pungent and highly offensive odor'. What comes next is far worse:

> *"M. Valdemar, can you explain to us what are your feelings or wishes now?"*
> *There was an instant return of the hectic circles on the cheeks; the tongue quivered, or rather rolled violently in the mouth (although the jaws and lips remained rigid as before;) and at length the same hideous voice which I have already described, broke forth:*
> *"For God's sake!—quick!—quick!—put me to sleep—or, quick!—waken me!—quick!—I say to you that I am dead!"*

Ah, but then! But then!

> *For what really occurred, however, it is quite impossible that any human being could have been prepared.*
> *As I rapidly made the mesmeric passes, amid ejaculations of "dead! dead!" absolutely bursting from the tongue and not from the lips of the sufferer, his whole frame at once—within the space of a single minute, or even less, shrunk—crumbled—absolutely rotted away beneath my hands. Upon the bed, before that whole company, there lay a nearly liquid mass of loathsome—of detestable putridity.*

As with 'Mesmeric Revelation', its less-morbid twin, 'The Facts of M. Valdemar's Case' was a fantasy, disguised as a serious case study. It was published in the *American Review* on 20 December 1845, and instantly triggered disgust and credulity. It was reprinted the following year by London's Short & Co. as 'Mesmerism, "In Articulo Mortis". An Astounding and Horrifying Narrative. Shewing the Extraordinary Power of Mesmerism in Arresting the Progress of Death'. *The Monthly Record of Science* &c. printed the story as 'The Last Days of M. Valdemar. By the author of the "Last Conversation of a Somnambule"'. That month, Poe received a missive from Robert H Collyer, Boston's leading mesmerist:

> *Dear Sir,—your account of M. Valdemar's case has been universally copied in this city, and has created a very great sensation. It requires from me no apology, in stating, that I have not the least doubt of the possibility of such a phenomenon; for I did actually restore to active animation a person who died from excessive drinking of ardent spirits. He was placed in his coffin ready for interment.*

Though Collyer demanded a response, Poe did not comply. In April 1846, an appreciative letter arrived from Elizabeth Barrett (soon to be Mrs Browning) who thanked Poe for dedicating Wiley and Putnam's *The Raven and Other Poems* to 'Elizabeth Barrett, the Noblest of her sex'. Barrett ends with a question about Valdemar:

> *There is a tale of yours which I do not find in this volume, but which is going the rounds of the newspapers, about Mesmerism—throwing us all into 'most admired disorder', or dreadful doubts as to whether 'it can be true', as the children say of ghost stories. The certain thing in the tale in question is the power of the writer, & the faculty he has of making horrible improbabilities seem near and familiar.*

Poe rubs his chilled hands together. He does not wish to think upon the circumstances that had brought him hither: Frances Osgood, her pack of literary hyenas, and the resulting scandal which had quickened Virginia's remaining months. The failure of the *Broadway Journal* under his own leadership was also a reason.

In May of 1846, Poe was soon forced to move his small family to a humble cottage in pastoral Fordham Village, Bronx. Six months later, he received a peculiar letter from one Arch Ramsay of Stonehaven, Scotland. It read:

Sir, / As a believer in Mesmerism I respectfully take the liberty of addressing you to know, if a pamphlet lately published in London (Short&Co. Bloomsbury) under the authority of your name & entitled Mesmerism in Articulo Mortis *is genuine. It details an acc't of some most* extraordinary circumstances, *connected with the Death of a Mr M Valdemar under mesmeric influence,* by you. HOAX *has been emphatically pronounced upon the pamphlet by all who have seen it here, & for the sake of the Science & of truth a note from you on the subject would truly oblige. In behalf of the science, / Your very obt svt / Arch Ramsay.*

Without hesitation, Poe replied:

Dr Sir, / 'Hoax' is precisely the word suited to M. Valdemar's case. The story appeared originally in 'The American Review', a Monthly Magazine, published in this city. The London papers, commencing with the 'Morning Post' and the 'Popular Record of Science', took up the theme. The article was generally copied in England and is now circulating in France. Some few persons believe it — but I do not — and don't you. / Very raspy / Yr Ob. St / Edgar A Poe / P.S, I have some relations, I think, in Stonehaven, of the name of Allan, who again are connected with the Allans and Galts of Kilmarnock. My name is Edgar Allan Poe. Do you know any of them. If so, and it would not put you to too much trouble, I would take it as a favor if you could give me some account of the family.

His middle name has never been common knowledge.

Arch Ramsay wrote back just as swiftly. No such luck. No family there or anywhere

by that name. But would the poet oblige in sending more information? Ramsay conveyed his wish to be of any further assistance in his power. Much to his later regret, Poe did not respond.

Since Virginia's death last January, he now has only her old mother, his 'Aunt Muddy', for family and company. Mournful and melancholic, he now haunts the Bronx wilderness in his Spanish cape like a black dog. He writes by day and drinks with the neighbourhood Jesuits by night. And, when sleep betrays him, he comes here to stand upon High Bridge, where nothing may intervene between himself and the merciless universe.

'Because nothing was', he whispers, 'therefore all things are. The universe of stars is limited. Matter, springing from unity, was created from nothingness. The universe swelled into existence, and will subside into nothingness before, yes, before swelling forth again'.

Of course. It must be so. From the unity of the first thing springs the causality of all things. And surely Pascal was right: the universe is a sphere, of which the centre is everywhere, the circumference, nowhere.

"Yes, it must be so. All things are matter, yes, but matter can be refined into an ether, wherein spirits, electricity, and God Himself may live..."

Somewhere over the river, crows object to the encroaching sunrise. Poe pulls the collar of his cape tight to his throat as a pall of serene blueness overtakes everything. He is motionless on the bridge, a purple gargoyle with pluperfect thoughts.

A train passes under him, howling northward, destined to cleave old Washington Irving's Tarrytown breakfast table from its view of the Hudson. The racket is enough to send Irving's Headless Horseman galloping deeper into his haunted hollow.

Poe is no Transcendentalist, nor Swedenborgian. He cannot brook hopes of infinitude. He has never known it, has never been *given* it. For him, all has gone forever. His father, his mother, his money, his wife, his reputation. And soon, perhaps, he shall lose his sanity. Then his life.

From the darkness beneath him, he hears something—a voice? Nay, 'tis only the river—rather, 'tis a voice in the river—nay, the river *IS its voice*!

"*Iiiiii ... aaammmm ...Vaalllddmmmmmaarrrrr ...*"

He swoons, clutching the railing. *The lighthouse, the swinging pocket watch, the actor's cue, the knife's frenzied plunge. A man's cry in Baltimore, an infant's cry in Boston. The pendulum clicks lower with each swing.*

"... *rrreelllleeeeeeesssss mmmeeeeeee* ..."

With no small effort he extricates himself from this vision. He quits the bridge and heads for his cottage.

———

Poe's is an unlikely face in his own mirror. He scrapes his blue throat with a razor, mindful to keep the tradition of unbroken flesh, as Muddy mends his silk stockings in the parlour. Her own black stockings, decorated with ornate spider webs, are also in want of repair.

By nightfall he is at his writing desk, illuminated by a lone candle. He is motionless at his task, while his shadow journeys about the unkempt room, consuming the light of the dying day. Rain begins to hiss from without the cottage. Then the bells of Fordham University announce the hour. Papers are lettered and padded with an accomplished hand. The work is at last finished: *Eureka: A Prose Poem*. Poe hugs himself upon the completion of this scientific work, in which he intends 'to speak of the Physical, Metaphysical and Mathematical—of the Material and Spiritual Universe: of its Essence, its Origin, its Creation, its Present Condition and its Destiny'.

'Nevertheless', he writes in the final full year of his life, 'it is as a poem only that I wish this work to be judged after I am dead'. He knows he can cry eureka but once in a lifetime.

In January, 1848, poet Sarah Helen Whitman is asked by New York socialite Anne Charlotte Lynch to contribute poetic greetings to her upcoming Valentine's Day party, certain to be attended by a great many literary notables. Whitman addresses hers to Poe. It is only once the 14 February party has concluded that she learns that Poe had not been invited: a pariah best avoided.

Whitman is a mesmerist, deft in the magnetic and occult sciences. She is seen walking the streets of Providence, Rhode Island, utterly festooned in ether-reeking scarves. In intellect and talent, she is a match for Poe.

When her flirtatious poem 'To E. A. Poe' is printed in the *Home Journal*, Poe takes notice. He recycles an old poem 'To Helen', which he had written in memory of Helen Stanard, whose life and death had first sparked Poe's obsession with women, the beautiful and entombed.

He writes to poet Anna Blackwell, a patient of 'magnetic therapy' in Providence. 'Can you not tell me something of her—anything—every thing you know—and let no one know that I have asked you to do so?'

Poe is informed that Whitman is an eccentric widow, who wears a small wooden coffin around her neck. It is settled: The monster must have his mate.

Returning to New York from a lecture engagement in Lowell, Massachusetts, Poe is informed that Putnam's is hesitant to publish *Eureka*. Poe insists that this prophetic cairn of cosmic triumph will do so well that it will be impossible to keep it on the shelves. 'Presses will have to churn it out 'round the clock!' he promises. In July, he makes a mad dash to Richmond, Virginia to raise funds for *The Stylus*. After two weeks of drinking and a near duel, he is reunited with Elmira Royster Shelton, who he was once engaged to in 1826. They were only teeangers then. And yet, there is a tenderness in her smile which warms Poe to the possibility of renewed infatuation.

A month later, *Eureka* is unleashed, and so too are the reviews. *The New Church Repository*, a Swedenborgian organ, has much to say of it. 'A poet here enters upon profound speculations', writes the editor, George Bush,

> *shooting ahead of the Newtons, Laplaces, Herschells, and Nicholses, in the solution of the great problems of the Universe. He calls his work a poem, perhaps because, with Madame De Stael, he regards the Universe itself as more like a poem than a machine.* [...] *we refuse not to concede that the work before us does offer some hints towards solving no less a problem than that of the cause of gravitation, before which the grandest geniuses have shrank abashed.*

Bush goes on to suggest that Poe study Swedenborg's work more closely, citing his 'pantheistic tendency' as the 'worst feature' of *Eureka*. In doing so, Poe is sure to 'feel the force of Swedenborg's reasoning in regard to the being and agency of a God distinct from nature'. *The Weekly Universe* favourably submits: 'Mr. Poe is not merely a man of science—not merely a poet—not merely a man of letters. He is all combined; and perhaps, he is something more'.

———

Her laugh is a slandered fiddle in this delicate parlour. Poe is enchanted. He had arrived at Sarah Helen Whitman's Providence doorstep on the evening of 21 September the equinox. It was an awkward dinner, with sweet Helen, giddy as a goose on one side of the table, and her old mother scowling on the other. It is no secret to anyone that Mrs Anna Marsh Power does not approve of Mr Poe, nor any association between him and her daughter. Rumours of his drinking have spread far. With dinner concluded, Whitman lights a lamp in the far side of the parlour, the scarlet shade of which is made from cut glass. Poe bristles at this abomination in decor. In ruby-red light, She and Poe sit upon a bile-green sofa and chat softly of poetry and music when not begging Whitman's cat to waddle closer.

Mrs Power haunts the corner in an ill-fitting chair. Her unblinking eyes fling curses upon the besotted bards from behind a face so artistically entablatured with hate as to defy Poe's talents for macabre description.

Poe's fingers speak into the cat's shoulders. There is a negotiation: this cat may inherit the earth.

The evening is a brief affair. Poe dons a heavy, grey military coat, some omen for the great American fratricide he will never live to see, and leaves Whitman to her beloved gorgon before another hour strikes. He practically skips down Benefit Street, in the cool autumnal night, towards his hotel, the Earl House.

Fables tangle in the breeze above Swan Point Cemetery, where their next meeting is arranged.

"You speak harshly of Mr. Emerson!" Whitman scoffs, shielding her eyes from the sun with one of her many dark scarves: "Why, with such pantheism as you have espoused with your 'Universe' talks, it seems hardly—"

"My dear Helen", Poe interjects, "do you know that I've just been reading Thomas Dick's *Sidereal Heavens* at the Providence Athenaeum? Deist trash! I discarded it utterly—loudly, upon the *floor* as a matter of fact! Another attempt to unify scientific laws with dusty Christian doctrine. I will tolerate no such cowardice in the perusal of such an essential answer!"

With a sweeping, liturgical gesture towards the surrounding graves, Poe comically waits for applause from the dead. It is not forthcoming.

Whitman erupts with long honks of laughter. "Oh my dear Edgar", she says, "New England will do you good".

He grasps her hand and gazes into her giggling face. "I have never loved before", he says, "But I love you, Helen, my Helen. And it is my wish that you marry me".

She is not as surprised at this as he had thought. "Oh Edgar", she calmly says, leaning her head against his thin chest, "my mother will disapprove. But if I could manage to persuade her, you must promise me something. You must promise to stop drinking".

Poe is upturned. His insects writhe in the light. "You have my word of honour", he lies.

But upon his return to New York, Poe receives a letter from Whitman denying his proposal. Her family and friends, who knew well of Poe's reputation, had warned against such a union. He returns to Providence in November, determined to win her heart, but loses his nerve instead. The pressure is too great. Whitman's mother, in her hateful Goya oils, is but the first of a long lineage of persons he will have to convince of his virtue.

He decides to calm his nerves with a drink at the hotel bar. He perches upon a greasy stool and, with flicker in his sour lantern eyes, flaps a simian hand to summon the barkeep.

He faces facts. He is possessed. *Eureka* will fail. Whitman's literary friends, his enemies, are bound to sabotage their engagement. His reputation shall cultivate only weeds—NO! *The Stylus*! His very own literary magazine, his monument to his own brain. With he and Whitman wedded, they shall rule American Letters, with Rhode Island their kingdom by the sea. He shall soon show all those ... all those ... show ...

He downs his drink. Then another.

"What demon has tempted me here to these ghoul-haunted neighbourhoods?" he groans upon the stool, reanimated.

He wears his brain upon his eyeballs like a battered crown as he quits the bar.

———

He can feel the weight of his purpose. Were the train a heavy, thundering razor, Poe's journey from Providence to Boston would amputate Cape Cod from the nation and send it sliding—a dead, scrimshawed forearm—into the Atlantic.

His birth was the chief crime of his life. He returns to the scene of it, to lift the hex of him, to sponge the harm. From South Station to the Common, he prowls Boston like a doctor's finger in a wound. He pours his heart out in a letter to Annie Richmond, a mill owner's wife from Lowell, who he had been platonically infatuated with at first sight. He tells her how he loves her, how he is revolted at the thought of marrying Whitman, how he wishes to spend his final moments in Annie's arms.

Once in the Common, he uncorks the laudanum he procured in Providence, and downs the bottle in a single swig. He smiles, convinced of the myriad of worthy, mustachioed understudies waiting to take his place upon this unforgiving stage. His mind is shattered, yes, and therefore multiplied, legion.

As he walks to the post office to send his missive, he thinks upon his mother, how she would rehearse before her infant son. There was something in those repeated words, in varied tones, which had mesmerized the young Poe. He can recall one such night while she was rehearsing ... what was it, *The Stranger*? Yes, she played a Countess, he remembers. He can hear her voice.

"I have: and if you do not steer for another haven, you will be doomed to drive upon the ocean for ever. I have: and if you do not steer for another haven, you will be doomed ..."

He vomits the poison into the street and collapses weeping against the iron fence of the Common.

He boards the train to Providence and sinks into his seat. Head to the window, his own horrid asymmetry is superimposed over the rushing vistas, tenement houses, trees, ships, fields, marshland. This is the true Edgar Poe, the vulture's cataract between his body and the unsettled New England landscape, peeled away by light and restored by shadow. Pepper's ghost. When the train is swallowed by a tunnel, he has only his wretched self for a view. Only in darkness may he confront himself with clarity. He shuts his eyes.

In Providence he finally sees Whitman, who informs him that she had indeed received letters from concerned friends about his drinking. Therefore the wedding is still off.

Poe is wounded, but does not show it. "If we meet again", he coldly states, "it will be as strangers".

But that night, Mrs Power discovers him upon her doorstep, deep within his cups. All care has slipped from the economy-coffin of his mind as he stomps into the house like a debauched golem and barks for her daughter. "HELEN! You must SAVE me, Helen! SAVE ME from my impending DOOM!"

The widow Whitman appears in the parlour in a wave of ether. She has been communing with the spirits, she says, until Poe had broken the circle, had invited the damned into her red chamber with his drunken impudence. With hitherto unseen rage she demands an explanation from the stumblebum—before staggering back, screaming.

Poe's face is liquifying, is melting before her eyes. Putrid stains overtake his virtuous linen shirt. Drops of clotted gore smite the carpet as he limps, rotting before her. He seizes her hand. She screams once more. "MY ANGEL!" Poe cries as he drops to his knees, a sweating skeleton. He clutches at her, tearing her muslin dress. "Releeeeeaasse mmeeeeeeeee ..."

A lamplit night, coarse and oily. His birthcaul face strobes sickly under the poisoned ochre light: a Rembrandt dipped in piss and auctioned through fog. Nearing the door of the Earl House, he is dogged by the devout wish for more lives, for more selves: a second Edgar Poe to do nothing but write, a third Edgar Poe to do nothing but pursue wealthy widows, a fourth to drink, a fifth to murder, a sixth, a seventh ...

He sighs. He has met these other Poes. In mirrors, train windows, bottles, and rivers. He has no long-lost William Wilson across the sea in Stoke Newington. There is only one Edgar Poe, and he is born to suffer.

He mounts the stairs to his chamber.

But Whitman forgives Poe, and agrees to a Christmas Day wedding on the condition of his reformation. He solemnly pledges to forbear all drink. Three days before the wedding, Poe and Whitman are found in an alcove of the Providence Athenaeum by a frantic messenger boy, who bears an urgent letter for Mrs Whitman. She opens and reads the letter soundlessly. Poe has broken his pledge that morning in the hotel bar, it informs. One glass of wine was all it took.

She says nothing to him on their cold December walk from the Athenaeum to her mother's house. Once inside, Whitman drenches her handkerchief in ether and collapses, exhausted, upon the sofa.

"Helen speak to me", Poe emplores on his knees, massaging her limp hand, "One word,—*but one word*".

Her only words are dry and nearly inaudible. "What can I say?"

"Say that you love me, Helen. *I love you*."

When she awakes from her stupor, he has long since been ejected from the house.

———

Acting is a kind of occult ritual; the preordained words spoken upon the directed mark, the incantatory motions for a desired effect. Something in Poe's blood, some imparted residue of his lowly actor parents, has set his public orations apart from those of other literary folk.

Concluding his 24 September lecture 'The Poetic Principal', with a rapturous rendition of 'The Raven', Poe wonders why he never pursued acting. No matter. His pursual of his boyhood sweetheart, Elmira Royster Shelton, has resulted in an betrothal. It is a marriage he financially needs, but does not truly want.

Poe attends a party at the home of Susan Talley, poet, painter, and future Confederate spy. She finds Poe, the last of the guests to leave, sitting with strange contentment upon their porch.

"I have been ill, Mrs. Talley", he explains softly, "But I have never been more hopeful for the future in my life. The last few weeks in the society of my oldest friends have been the happiest I have known for many years. When I leave New York again, I will leave behind me all the troubles and vexations of my past life".

He eagerly produces a letter from his breast pocket. It is from Rufus Griswold, accepting the request that he should become Poe's literary executor in case of the poet's sudden death. Mrs Talley smiles, cooperatively.

The hour grows late. The Talleys wave goodbye to the poet from the portico as he takes his leave. Half-way down the stone steps to the darkened streets, Poe turns to bid one final farewell to his hosts. As he does so, a meteor of unusual brightness passes in a perfect, eastward arc over his head. He and the star disappear into the night.

The bosun of the steamboat to Baltimore has a face like torched sea coral. Poe cannot help admiring the ruined flesh as they near the stygian docklands of Baltimore. He once more recites his itinerary to himself. He is to travel by train from Baltimore to Philadelphia to edit the poems of Mrs St Leon Loud for $100. Then onward to New York, to collect Muddy, then back to Richmond for the dreaded wedding. He must take the 9am train so as to reach his destination at 2:45pm.

"... and if you do not steer for another haven, you will be doomed to drive upon the ocean for ever".

He flows like quicksilver through the throngs of humanity which epitomize Baltimore's waterfront, *a man of the crowd*. Sex workers, runaway slaves, crippled tradesmen, and seamen of all stripes muscle by on their errands. A man stands upon a cask of lager and proselytizes to those who will listen about some political candidate or another. It means nothing to Poe that election day draws nigh.

There is no shortage of barrooms on Thames Street which can satisfy his thirst. One drink, and then he shall be on his way. He selects The Horse.

Mercifully, there is no movement in the saloon, nor the gin-engendered savagery of Poe's immediate experience. The place is jungled with louchely dressed customers.

A prone fisherman twitches in the sawdust, spots of blood about him. A murder of frightened priests cloister in a corner. The barman is a pale giant, a St Jago monkey carved from whale bone. He obliges Poe with a drink. Deployed within this canker of a place are three men. They each carry a bag. They are looking at Poe.

When he is found after five days, he is many men. He has become Blake's *Nebuchadnezzar*, wretched, feral, and inhuman. Poe wears the ill-fitting clothes and stained straw hat of a tramp, and clutches the walking cane of Dr Carter, whose Richmond home he had lodged at before his misadventure. His old friend, one J E Snodgrass, had been summoned to Poe's aid by a printer named Joseph Walker, who had found the poet lying outside Ryan's Fourth Wall polls, a polling place located inside Gunner's Hall. It is 3 October—election day.

A snaking line of Baltimore voters watch as Walker and Snodgrass hoist the drooling Poe to his feet.

"Damn me", says one man with piglet eyes and a Druidical beard, "but this sorry mister reeks like an upturned jakes".

"I seen him here before", says another. "A gang of fellas cooped 'im, see? Kept making him change his clothes and go in to vote under different folk's names, and then he'd come back out and they'd fill his mouth with spirits and send 'im back in. D'ye know 'im?"

For three days in the Washington College Hospital, he thrashes in his bed among the mad and infirm. Falling and rising in and out of consciousness, he is tormented in either pole. He screams aloud the names of unknown persons, and writhes in terror at figures only he can see. On the fourth day, he is still, his eyes blasted under scornful angels.

"Lord help my poor soul", is all he can say.

Only in darkness may he confront himself with clarity ...

... only in darkness ...

III

Iain Sinclair does not speak with the logbook brevity typical of his prose. We were sitting now at a cafe called The Parlour, across the road from Poe's former school.

We spoke of Gloucester, Massachusetts, my home city, and of Charles Olson, its

Blake. We spoke of how I had been enlisted by Alan Moore to be Sinclair's graphic biographer in *The Moon and Serpent Bumper Book of Magic*. We spoke of Brian Catling. We spoke of Poe.

"Brian had stood before Poe's mirror in that Bronx cottage", said Sinclair. "What he had received from the encounter is unknown. But what he made of it, a piece called *Edgar's Mirror*, now hangs in my house."

H P Lovecraft, another hero of Catling's, had made a similar pilgrimage to Poe's Cottage in April 1922. He too had stood before Poe's mirror, and had mentioned it in his subsequent 1934 essay, 'Homes and Shrines of Poe'.

"There are no coincidences, are there?" I asked. Sinclair shook his head. No.

We walked onward through Dalston, shadowed by the Holy Trinity Church, or, 'Clowns' Church', whose annual Clowns International service, in honour of deceased clowns, was in nine days' time. Orphaned Christmas trees and desecrated advent calendars littered the sidewalks for our inspection. A brief detour to the end of Ritson Road revealed the grim, decrepit German Hospital, where Joseph Conrad had convalesced and grappled with 'the horror' and subsequent *trauma* of the Congo.

Trekking through the neighbourhoods of *EastEnders* put us in contact with an exuberant man in a flat cap.

"Old school boxer!" he cried, pointing in recognition in Sinclair's direction.

Sinclair rolled with it. "Yes, you've got it! Right on, man!" It was a welcome change from the usual "aren't you that man from John Rogers's videos?" he so often got.

After a tour of the grotesque fish heads and Lovecraftian slabs of alien flesh to be found at Ridley Road Market, we traversed the muddy and crow-cluttered parkland of Hackney Downs, talking of Van Gogh's suicide in Auvers-sur-Oise.

Poe, Conrad, van Gogh. The lurking theme of our interview appeared to be that of the works which genius may produce when ambushed by madness.

We parted ways, destined to meet again the following night at Swedenborg House's gallery opening.

I walked back to Holborn, a journey which the adolescent Poe could never have achieved.

As Brian Catling had once observed: "All roads lead to Poe".

IV

They gather in their candlelit club within the unmade lighthouse. From a gaussian film of pipesmoke protrude first a slippered foot, then a beckoning hand, and then a pair of inquisitive faces. They lean out in expectation of their midnight visitors.

From a chalk doorway enters a stout gentleman in a sharp pinstripe suit. His hair is white, and his face ruddy with mirth. His left hand waves to the seated detectives, whilst his right clutches a glass tankard containing an unspeakably vile decoction of human gore. A solitary eyeball, raw and visibly pained, bobs upon the crimson surface.

The smoke parts to reveal the detectives, who each sit in wingback armchairs, dressed in fine silk dressing gowns. Only one of them rises, a diminutive French man with flickering opacity: "Ah, Monsieur Valdemar, Monsieur Catling! Come forward and be seated, will you not?"

Brian Catling, the artist, bows humbly without spilling his companion. "Good evening, Monsieur Dupin, Mister Holmes. I apologize for the late hour, but it took me some time to fully contain my friend here for portability, you understand. Well, what's left of him." He sits upon an adjacent settee, the tankard carefully balanced on his knee.

"Watson has gone out", croaks Holmes between sucks on his pipe. "He saw your friend coming. Peculiar nausea for a medical man, but there you have it."

"Our lighthouse has been imperfectly restored", explains C Auguste Dupin, gazing about the tubular chamber. "One Robert Bloch, a builder we gather, had come many years ago to finish it, but his repairs have not held up under scrutiny." Clutching his stomach, he now regards Catling's macabre tipple. "And how are we this evening, Monsieur Valdemar?"

In a voice maddeningly loathsome to the ears of all present, the thing within the tankard identifies itself with deliberation and humility. The voice comes not from the charnel glass, but from the air above them.

"Iii ... aaamm ... Vallldddemmmarrr ... I ammm ... deeead, yeeeeessss ... but ssstiiill awaaaarrrre ..."

Catling shrugs. "He doesn't say much else. Just keeps on like that. Perverse, really. I mean, I can confirm that he was once a man. I myself have seen the stained impression of him on his bedclothes. When I found him out there, I mistook him for some ghoulish memento from Mary Jane Kelly's room. Sirs, have you considered the facts of my friend's case?"

Holmes rubs his hands together in thought. His face bends and undulates in the light of an unspecified hearth, changing from Paget's graphite drawings to Gillette, to Brett, to Cushing, to Rathbone. There are other faces also, too handsome to name. His eyes tell of gaslit music halls and derringer smoke, Dartmoor bog-muck and Reichenbach foam. Snorting, he removes the stem of his pipe from an infinite recursion of varied lips and points it jaggedly in the direction of Dupin.

"The FACTS?" Why, sir, I need only refer to my colleague here to solve your case and remedy your minds quite utterly!"

Dupin is flummoxed. "Moi, Monsieur?"

"You see", says Holmes to the under-developed Frenchman, "the nematode, a phylum of cannibalistic worm, is known to recognize its offspring, and thereby refuses to devour it. But you and I are cut from a less merciful cloth, monsieur. You are Poe's creation, after all, a half-brother to our denatured client in the stein, there. You are a fiction within my fiction, a dream within my dream. If you are indeed my twin, as you opine, then I have consumed you in the womb long ago. Why, I can see quite through you!"

Dupin looks down to where his feet would be, had they ever been described. "I am the first, by which your very *genre* is precipitated. There is no Sherlock Holmes without C Auguste Dupin. Without me, without Poe ..."

Holmes brooks no argument, and flails his arm now towards their guests. "M. Valdemar is an invention of Poe, also. A liquefied corpse, suspended in consciousness by either the hypnotic power which his late creator had failed to terminate, or the gross credulity of his story's English readers. I, naturally, found the hoax to be quite transparent altogether."

The great detective now shifts a fiery Rathbone eye upon Valdemar. "Your creator cannot be found. Release from his power is out of the question. Are you without *will*, Mister Valdemar? I have broken criminals and actors alike with the very *depth* of my likelihood. When my creator chucked me off a Swiss bluff, I came to him in one of his sordid seances and DEMANDED my restoration! And lo' my heart beat once more!"

From within the tankard, the cancelled flesh laments: "NooOo... mmmy hearrt beeeatss n0 mOorrre ... annnd yettt Iiii aamm awaaare ... rrrelllleeease meeeee ... O00Oo0o0oo..."

There is further discussion, and then, 'under instruction, Catling takes his leave, his companion in hand. Descending the treacherous lighthouse steps, Valdemar beseeches Catling.

"My master is dead. I know this to be so. Is it true?"

"He is dead", says Catling, producing an old Arkham House book from his jacket, "but never lost! I've just been reading a story called 'The Dark Brotherhood', where the main character is walking down Benefit Street in Providence, Rhode Island at night, and meets many *identical Edgar Allan Poe*s, all cloned by extraterrestrials—weird, weird stuff! It was a story started by Lovecraft just before he died, I believe, and then finished by his friend, August Derleth. A whole Army of Poes in Providence! Imagine! Were we in Lovecraft or Derleth's country, you would have your pick of Poes to release you. But he is not here, I'm afraid".

"You are a kind man", says Valdemar, "even I can see that. Will you release me, sir, from that which yet suspends me in my pains".

"All things die, my friend, but few things wish for it as you do. As a creature of imagination, I've always wanted more than one life. But too long have you waited."

Catling smiles, a sunbeam in each jowl. His face is distorted in the imperfect glass of Valdemar's stein, and the liquid man perceives the eyes of his liberator to merge into one winking orb.

"You have my word", says the beaming cyclops.

Valdemar is cooking with the heat of hope. The pair laugh as they spiral downward into the darkness.

V

Days after my return to America, the wonderful Victor Rees sent me Brian Catling's unedited and unpublished 'Further Facts in The Case of M. Valdemar'. Ernest Valdemar, in the sculptural hands of Catling, was an accomplished scholar and translator of seventeenth-century works on Japanese swordsmanship. The very room in which Valdemar 'slept, dreamt and died', he wrote, 'was decorated in the Shogun fashion, with a great display of silk screens, framed scrolls and priceless blades'.

I read Catling's piece on the train from Los Angeles to Lamy, New Mexico. Completing it, I shuddered. *He had done it*, I thought. This act of literature, one of his last, was itself a performance which manipulated time, action and thought. The bubbling palimpsest of Valdemar had remained under a mesmeric hand since its birth-shriek over one hundred and seventy years prior. Catling had released Valdemar, had succeeded where I had only fancied. He had ingested Valdemar, before departing with him to the realms of mystery and imagination which had authored them both.

I was met at Lamy station by my dear friends, actor/composer Jonathan David Dixon and actor David Frankham. In their Santa Fe bungalow, on Frankham's ninety-eighth birthday, we watched himself, Vincent Price and Basil Rathbone in Roger Corman's 1962 *Tales of Terror*. As Rathbone's multicoloured mesmerist wheel churned slowly upon the large screen, from green, to red, to yellow, to blue, to orange, I perceived my friend to be under a similar hypnosis as that of Vincent Price's Ernest Valdemar.

How strange, I thought, that the doctors who assist Valdemar in Poe's original tale are named D— and F—. And there, on the screen, stood David Frankham, attending Valdemar as one doctor.

On the screen, the David Frankham of thirty-six years gasped: "He's dead!"

"Yes", Rathbone burrs, "he is dead ... but still aware". "Release him."

"RELEASE HIM!?"

As I watched the actor watch the film, flinching and mouthing the words as if still participating in the scene, I thought of the connections woven on this journey, and had only to smile at the resulting, weird tapestry.

Valdemar was Poe's mirror, an undead reflection of impermanence. It was the poet's last abiding quarrel with God, and the cosmos, a quarrel which would survive him.

As Vincent Price melts upon the screen, I, a fellow denizen of the universe, have no longer anything to fear.

FURTHER FACTS IN THE CASE
OF M. VALDEMAR

B. Catling

Notwithstanding the appalling dissolution of the physical remains and the extreme reaction of the authorities, I feel it necessary to continue my explanation of the unique and disturbing demise of the late Ernest Valdemar. It will be remembered that in my former account I laboured to give an exact and detailed description of my experiment with the aforesaid gentleman. Making it very clear that the whole venture was scrupulously conducted under scientific rigour and with the total, willing and enthusiastic cooperation of Valdemar himself.

It is within the history of our discreet contract that strangers have insinuated unwholesome misconduct. Accusations made without the slightest knowledge of our relationship and mutual involvement.

It will be remembered that previously I have gone to some length to define the character and accomplishments of M. Valdemar's scholarship and publications. In this, I failed to mention, as irrelevant, the interest that first brought us together.

Apart from his translations of *Wallenstein* and *Gargantua*, my friend was responsible, through his generosity and passion, for the first American translation and publication of *Go Rin no Sho*, Musashi's classic seventeenth-century work on Japanese swordsmanship. He captured, with elegance, all its practical and philosophical principles. It was from this book that our discussions grew. Especially around the esoteric dogmas and practised skills of meditation that offered insight into the complexities of the conscious mind and the depth of the soul. The Japanese discipline of the samurai became a topic of fascination, in both mystical and martial aspects. M. Valdemar had embraced much of that culture with great enthusiasm and taste. The very room in which he slept, dreamt and died, was decorated in the shogun fashion, with a fine display of silk screens, framed scrolls and priceless blades.

It was during one of our seminars—which lasted for hours, before the poor man's pitiless illness stole his vitality—that we began to speculate on the power of the will. A subject obviously pertinent to mesmerism. In the process of his research, Valdemar had collected many eyewitness statements concerning seppuku, the ritual suicide performed by slow disembowelment. It was the determination and controlled evidence of pain that so astonished him. Willpower tested to a physical extreme. Once he even demonstrated the grim procedures of the act by taking down a short sword from the wall, wrapping it in a pure silk cloth, and placing it on a small table before which he knelt. At this point my dear friend indulged in his wildest speculation yet: that the choice of the destruction of the abdomen was not just a lurid and ghastly physical abuse, but also a spiritual aspiration.

Considering the widespread Eastern belief in the chakra, and its focus on the stomach, Valdemar even quoted a recent medical discovery concerning the abundance of nerve cells in that region. Their multitude, he informed me, rivals the neural diversity found in the brain. Betraying subtle amusement, he remarked: "And isn't it so that this knowledge is everywhere, even in common folklore? Gut feeling being frequently quoted as the core of instinct".

I remonstrated over many of these points, but he was adamant. "Even the soul might be skulking in the belly, rather than enthroned in the brain."

This of course made seppuku more alarming to contemplate. So I steered the conversation towards another of his obsessions derived from this ritual.

It was the controlled extremity of the act, rather than its meaning, that so engrossed him. With me, it was the other way around. Especially after I read that this form of self-slaughter was not always associated, as is commonly believed, with disgrace and failure. But sometimes with success and achievement. Devotees understood that they had achieved their maximum potential, a perfect gesture that could never be bettered. Then the pure conclusion for such a stringent and noble mind would also be Seppuku. There is something in this higher echelon of thought that chimes with hypnotism in its most esoteric potential. It also illuminates some of the complexities around dominance in the empirical application of the mesmeric principle. Which is never a one-way transaction. The best subjects for the procedure are always imaginative and strong-minded. Proving that the influence—and the agreement to flow both ways—is shared. That the mind is open to be influenced is not a dispersal of willpower, but an objective 'standing aside'. A participation in the mind of the other, the one who is making the suggestion; a form of combined magnetism.

It was Valdemar's affinity with this idea that started our, *my* experiments. And the very reason for sharing his brilliant intellectual alertness before his illness.

All these qualities and their significance were totally overlooked by the guttersnipe sneers, the outright lies, that have appeared in the press concerning his life and my practice. Comments made by the ignorant, those who have only witnessed hypnotism as a base and ridiculous entertainment in lurid backstreet music halls. Or worse, those who have been infected by the grotesque and prurient fictions that have become so popular in these less than discerning times.

I will waste no more energy on vulgar opinion—or its disagreeable craving for me to justify my research. Suffice to say, no validation is needed in this matter. And time itself will certify the discoveries I have made. That is why I have kept back this manuscript until justice is done or my days on this earth are passed.

As you know Valdemar was under my hypnotic control as he approached his death—which he finally announced when I asked him if he were sleeping. His words were witnessed by Drs D- and F- whose established authority renders those words incontrovertible.

They had propped him up against three pillows, allowing some relief from the agonies of decaying lungs that were so strenuously seeking collapse. There could be little doubt that this unfortunate condition was soon to be achieved. Which made me anxious to keep my mesmeric contact in a stable state. It will be remembered from my previous description that Valdemar was a sparse man. And that his lightness of frame had been greatly increased of late by the appetite of his terminal illness. So that now he appeared like a gaunt puppet amid the billowing whiteness of his supporting pillows. It was only his voice that remained deep and resolute, even when he made utterance through closed teeth and out of a deeply profound sleep. And thus he replied to my interrogation: "Yes: asleep now. Do not wake me!—let me die so!"

It was never part of our agreement that my experiment into the levels of consciousness was to be used in treatment of his terminal condition, nor was it considered as palliative care.

The good doctors looked at me, as if I should comply with their patient's wishes. So that I was obliged to offer some gesture in this direction. I lifted Valdemar's right arm and made the enquiry.

"Do you still feel pain in the breast?"

The answer was immediate, less audible than before.

"No pain—I am dying."

The hours that night crawled while we, the watchers, took our turn to sit close to the bedside, while the others rested elsewhere in the room. The nurses came and went with little they could do.

I would ask the same question of the somnambulist.

"M. Valdemar, do you sleep?"

And he would always answer in the same fashion.

"Yes, still asleep—dying."

We conferred and agreed, death was very near. Again I asked the question. But this time it was met with a radical and alarming physical change. Valdemar's body tightened and his face took on the violent mask of rigor mortis. All life shuddered from him, leaving only the blackened tongue, lost in a hollow mouth, inventing a voice no man had ever heard before. The nurses fled the room and the student doctor passed out. I have written in detail, describing a sound that could barely be called a voice. It was seeking to use everything in the stiff body, to vibrate at the same pitch. To answer my forgotten question.

"Yes:—no:—I have been sleeping—and now—Now—I am dead."

We were unprepared for this terrible paradox. The very thing I had expected to happen had never truly been considered. The doctors showed their fear at a condition far beyond their reach and understanding. But they did, once again, as duty demanded, test for signs of vitality in the obvious corpse of M. Valdemar.

The tongue was motionless now—which gave the medical men the courage to close the hanging jaw and the lids of the staring eyes. They pronounced him dead, made their excuses and left the room, supporting the dazed and ashen student between them. When they had gone, I approached the bed with another question.

"M. Valdemar, where are you? In what place do you reside?"

Fear and trepidation combined as I stepped closer to the corpse. There was no movement and the voice was lulled. Disappointment banished, I left the room in a state of mild anxiety that prevented me from turning down and extinguishing the oil lamps that kept darkness at bay. Halfway down the stairs, I thought I heard a sound, a voice unlike anything experienced before: a vibration seeking resonance to obtain its volume. Seeking echoes in every corner of this lifeless house! I retraced my steps. The bedroom repelled me and hastened my departure from that terrible place.

*

The next day I returned, finding everything within the fated property quiet and dead. The suspended thing that had been Valdemar was in the same condition as when he 'spoke' his final words. And this is how the matter stood until the close of last week—an interval of nearly seven months. There were no further signatures of decay on the body of the man no attendants dared to touch. Along with the doctors, I made daily calls, without approaching within six feet of the deathbed. New nurses were frequently hired to 'keep the room'. All of the servants remained downstairs. The singularity of this event was beginning to become known beyond the house—as a consequence of the doctors bringing curious colleagues and friends to witness the startling 'aberration'. Of course, I disapproved of such incursions.

A climate of mutual suspicion marked the beginning of our falling out: the separation of the temporary union that extreme circumstances had ordained. Not that I completely trusted their professed faith in myself and my experiment. The doctors were of average intelligence. They bore in pride the restrictions of imagination and insight that a medical education demands. And I was of the opinion that they condescended to guide companions to Valdemar's bedroom, only to relieve themselves of the nauseous weight of responsibility that rested on their weak and startled shoulders. Thereby exploiting the curiosity of strangers to brighten the intolerable drabness of each confrontation. I was beyond such trivial supports, requiring no emotional validation to continue my study. Thank God Valdemar had accepted a written contract that clearly stated that during the period when I considered the experiment to be in operation no interference would be permitted. This signed and sealed document gave me limited but unchallenged power of attorney. In that room. And in that house. I was scrupulous in this matter and often had to act, to prevent visitors from touching, probing, or attempting to make intimate examination of the lifeless incorruptible body.

Things became more difficult after I caught one of the nurses stealing a comb from M. Valdemar's bedside table. Presumably to sell as a relic of the embellished story she would tell to credulous outsiders. A grim souvenir that once touched the head of the man who would become known as *Le Mort Vivant*.

The incident forced me to dismiss all the domestic staff and to move into the house, setting up my temporary home in one of the spare bedrooms on the same floor. This afforded access, for myself alone, to the 'laboratory' of my experiment. There would be no requirement to explain either myself or the precise nature of the questions that I would daily put to the figure in the bed. At first I lacked the nerve to speak thus, while the house was so empty. My unease was attached to the idea of a potential and detailed conversation suddenly and unexpectedly beginning. And perhaps the sleeper waking in a state of confusion. Perhaps a natural shrinking from his demands. From questioning myself and my intentions during the long period of our mute collaboration. This consternation was not biled by guilt, but prompted by what I thought were snatches of his voice, heard all over the house. That same sibilant croaking whisper, only this time *sharpened* on what sounded like congealed rage. Which turned to white invisible anger and disappeared every time I tried to confront it or find its hiding place in the furnishings of the static mansion.

Faint murmurs were the source of my only misgivings. And none of them issued from the actual body, *that* remained silent as a stone. I had grown accustomed to it, now, in an almost tender way that precluded all trepidation. So much so that I had no fear of touching it. *The thing*. And often did so, in an attempt to ascertain the nature of the supposedly empty shell.

It was during one of these investigations that I took him by the arms and tried to lean him forward, testing to what degree the rigor mortis still prevailed. I found him strangely pliant from the hips—and moved his torso to and fro. From inside the weightless body came another kind of movement. Nothing uncanny, just a slipping and a rattle. I moved him again: it sounded out loud. There was reminiscence attached to the manifestation.

I had, recently, felt the sensation elsewhere: a certain displacement inside a volume, moving. After a moment's consideration, I had the answer: it was in Jerome Petersen's workshop. He had shown me the latest invention from Norway. A metal canister that contained pressured air with microscopic particles of paint. A portable paint spray. It worked when a tiny valve was opened. But it was a minor detail of this contrivance that had been dragged into comparison on the dead man's bed. To make sure that the paint particles were well mixed inside the can with the bursting air, a small bead or heavy metal ball bearing was needed. When the can was shaken, it would fall languidly in the thick solution. And thus mix the paint. This is what happened in Valdemar's torso. Some fragment of him had become broken off. Bone, I assumed. I gently shook the body again, feeling it floating, nudging, tapping against an interior weightless fluidity that seemed to deny gravity.

*

Now that I removed their pleasure in behaving like prurient ringmasters, the doctors sickened of their duty. Sullen responsibility joined hands with the uncanny in a suffocating ritual of repetition. Finally, they spoke to me, saying that they had endured enough. The time had come to conclude this disnatured condition. We talked about the possible outcomes and exchanged stories of similar episodes beyond the scope of orthodox textbooks. The biggest problem being our unspoken agreement that M. Valdemar was indeed dead—before we relinquished him to the undertaker and the grave. All the standard tests had been carried out and proven. But I still felt that there was some thread of connection with the living man. Some febrile extension that quivered between vitality and extinction. Something almost *abstract*, far beyond archetypal forms such as 'revenants' and 'zombies'. We also discussed the less interesting cases of other human bodies that had survived or avoided physical corruption. Of saints and holy men who remained intact, their bodies offering no charm to the marauding worm and the invading fly. Dr F- related the story of Christian Friedrich von Kahlbutz, an aristocratic German knight who demanded his *droit de seigneur*. Even if it took murder to satisfy his inclinations. The mechanism of curse, rather than divine blessing, being used to preserve his carcass from 1700 to our present day.

I did not argue with them, but felt some relief in ending this and finally putting Valdemar's body to rest. Or to let it wake among us. There was still enough fruitful content from which to extract a paper or two and further extend my knowledge and my experience of the subject.

"You should ask him one more question before he departs", insisted Dr F- with the support of Dr D-. They did not appreciate that I had been doing precisely this for weeks—without any effect.

I did not care for the lightness of their comments and gauged my 'question' with suitable irony, which I knew was above their heads. In my sincerest voice I intoned:

"M. Valdemar, can you explain to us what are your feelings or wishes now?"

I hid my ironic detachment under a mask of stern enquiry. Until something twitched in the wooden face and a tremor moved through the house, as if the building itself were taking in a breath once through every one of its million different surfaces and textures. Before returning the outcome to the solid lips of the sleeper.

"For God's sake—quick!—quick!—put me to sleep—or, Quick!—waken me!—Quick!—I say to you that I am dead!"

You cannot possibly imagine the shock this violent command had on me.

The horror and outrage swept us away from the proximity of the speaker and the bed. Dr F- shouted at me:

"Let him go, for God's sake."

With the corpse still screaming:

"Dead! Dead! Dead!"

Dr F- was drained and silent, when, from a distance of five feet, I uttered my fumbled command: that the corpse was released and should return to sleep.

"Awaken to thy sleep!" I shouted.

And that is when it occurred. The phenomenon so hotly debated by subsequent opinion, medical and popular.

"Still with Death! Dead!" The voice swilling about the room and echoing everywhere in the house. M. Valdemar came apart, dissolved, shrunk, crumbled into what I have previously declared as a nearly liquid mass of loathsome … of *detestable* putridity.

*

That was where I left the facts. Fabrications derived from rumour were published under my name without my imprimatur. Sensationalism, carelessly produced for profit, has damned my name, my science, and ridiculed my veracity.

The 'truth' that I am now compelled to relate, in order to refute these horrors, will certainly confirm all the suspicions that my foes and former colleagues harboured about my sanity. Therefore, these scrupulous details shall remain cloaked until I have again proven my reputation. Or: that narrative must remain *in camera* until after my own death—when, hopefully, a new generation of rational minds will discover and broadcast what I have learnt.

Valdemar's mansion was shunned and locked down. The authorities enforced the prohibition until the time when a relative could be found in distant Poland. This all happened very quickly. The speed at which morticians cleared the vile residue of M. Valdemar was astonishing. And irresponsible. As was the inquest and the cursory investigation into the causes of such an abnormal and repulsive event.

The good doctors diverted all verifiable truth from their participation in what now appeared to be a crime. The condition of the remains was never analysed. Eyewitness accounts indicated foul play: it appeared that the body had been eaten away from the inside. Notions of noxious poisons and virulent acids were carelessly bandied about. Nothing in nature could transform a solid body to that fluid condition in a matter of minutes. The seven months of corruption could have provided an answer, but they did not apply to one who had been sitting up in bed and was reported to be capable of speech. Housemaids and nurses testified to the ungodly voice that shuddered and whelped throughout the house. No one doubted that it was the voice of the old man. In pain, agony, or torture. Had witnesses not heard Valdemar imploring the hypnotist to let him sleep or die? What manner of doctor or scientist would let any creature suffer so? This was the work of a fiend: a vivisectionist slowly rotting his victim from the inside out. A *murderer*. Sadist. And madman.

I was taken to my own house and placed under arrest. While the avalanche of disrespect and accusation gathered momentum and gravity. There was little doubt that I would be ground to nothing in this blind gritty momentum. *I had to escape, hide, prove my innocence.* There was only one place where nobody would think to look. My accusers were too fearful, too superstitious, to place their puny minds and shallow souls anywhere near the eye of the storm. That is why I escaped through the basement of my home—turned prison—and found my way back into Valdemar's mansion, barring all its doors from the inside. I closed the shutters and made my nest under Valdemar's bed. The place that no living person would dare to visit. Its focus of disgust became my shelter: the only raft from which I could think this nightmare complexity out. I would follow the trail of events and find a coherent understanding of what had really happened. Because it occurred to me in a blinding flash among the cobwebs, dust and stench, that it was never to be known if he awoke in or out of death—or somewhere else entirely. Only his physical frame had been accounted for. The witnesses and visitors had not even said a prayer over the congealing mass and the seeping mattress. There was nothing to bury or burn, except the mattress itself. And nobody was going anywhere near that, after it had been scraped off. I was the only one who cared about whatever else might remain. The only one who could discover if anything of M. Valdemar still existed.

For the first time, guilt started to gnaw at my purpose. Exposing an ignorance in me that was becoming aware of some part of myself still connected to the departed one. A wincing umbilical of my will still attached to his personality. And, dare I say, soul? The horror of confronting these possibilities was infinitely worse than what had spilled in the bed. Now, beneath it, I faced the fact that my botched attempt to release him might have failed. The body fell away, *he* continued. But where? Had I imprisoned him, perchance, in a purgatory of infinite time? Or had he been propelled beyond that? In a damaged prolonged grief into paradise or hell. Or was his living ghost still in this place and seeking vengeance?

I twisted and turned in my filthy cot. In the blankets I had dragged under the bed. On the splintery floorboards. I had hurriedly taken a handful of paper and a pencil into my nest, along with a hunk of bread and a chamber pot that I filled with drinking water. No one would find me here and I wanted no distractions.

Night and day leached into each other, as did sleep and waking.

And in that delirium, I called out to him again. Even endeavouring to speak in the commanding tone of the mesmeric voice. God knows what I expected, all sense had left me. I was even considering that if I made contact again he might become the prime witness in my defence. It was after that delusion faded that the voice returned in a hidden dark rumble, close by. From above? From the bed? I listened carefully and scrawled the words, the sounds down, so that others might see and comprehend their validity. The volume of the utterance increased, without clarity or meaning. It had none of the ferocity of Valdemar's deathbed shouting, or any of his earlier calm and considered speech. Was there some kind of filter in purgatory, to muffle and leach all emotion? While allowing only a semblance of voice to escape?

I wrote the sounds down, not to miss anything. I planned to decipher them later in some more leisurely and comfortable time and space. These must have been the last convulsions of my sane mind. Before nausea and dehydration and despair knotted together. I crawled out from my containment, tangled in filth and rags, the crumpled paper held before me like an illumination or flag of survival. I clawed open one of the shutters and let in enough moonlight for me to be able to read the dictations I had made. But they were not in a language that I knew. Phonetically mouthing their sounds was the only way to snatch at meaning and perhaps find coherence in the spacings and inclinations. Or in those emphases of exclamation that give potency to known words. And flavour comprehension. In this dizzying interval, I think that a lulling drowsiness stole chunks of conscious time.

Another voice joined in and attempted to copy, to ape, the noises I had been making. In the hope of establishing contact with a tolerant ghost, I scanned the room for the origin of this uncanny manifestation. Then the loudest sound yet took all such expectations away. *The voice was in my stomach*. My hunger growling at me. This is what I had been hearing and writing down. The exotic language was no more than the churning of my gastric mechanism, seeking sustenance before it devoured itself. The cruelty of this deceit sapped the last of my strength and I crawled back under the bed.

And there, in that deplorable space of humiliation, the worst idea yet was born to my exhausted mind. That Valdemar was not locked into some esoteric layer between paradise and hell, some vacant Gustave Doré landscape without gravity of purpose. *And that his purgatory was inside me.* My claim on his will, while standing at the gates of eternity, had created a shaft, a gulley for him to fall through. To reach me. That noise in my stomach was not of natural origin. It was Valdemar seeking a way out of me and back into the living world.

The world to which, by accident or cruelty, I had tethered him.

I will now stop all notation. Seal these scrawled pages and do what I must do. To fulfil my duty to that poor man and pray for God's compassion, for him if not for me. I have prepared myself and taken the short sword down from its display. I will open a door in me to give him escape. And carve an opposite comparison to the way his body was released.

THE CROW WITH HIS VOICE OF CARE

Adolfo Barberá del Rosal

What does the sculptor, unpicking his V-necked Fair Isle sweater,
say, as he squats in his corner? The biker is already rapping at the door.
I tap out the last words from his urgent stutter.
—Iain Sinclair, *RED EYE* (1973/2013)

I met Brian Catling, Maggid Street's *Doctor, at a LRB reading in July 2015. It was one of those occasions where Sinclair & Catling performed together. After the reading, readers and listeners mingled in the Pied Bull Yard. Catling was sporting a Hawaiian shirt (as seen in Matthew Shaw's film). I was working at the time on the Spanish translation of* Lud Heat *and I was looking for the photographic material from Catling's 1974 exhibition at the Royal College. Back in 2015, I had just discovered Catling's writing. I had read* Scales, *an epic of desert and ice, of scalpel and meteorite. Brian Catling mentioned weekends spent in Liège, escaping from dead boring Maastricht, hanging at Au Métro, the* Earwig *bar, the site of Satan's epiphany, which found its transvestite in Brussels,* In De Linde, *off Dilbeek, where Lucile Hadžihalilović shot that fateful scene. At the LRB event, Sinclair read from* Black Apples of Gower. *Catling read from Chapter IV of* The Vorrh, *a haunting Muybridge-Gull encounter that had emerged from a distant Truman Brewery rumination. After they met for the first time, Gull's last words to Muybridge were: 'Force your sight and your imagination outward'.*

*

The present text serves as a preparation or incubation for a screening, at a date to be determined, of *Maggot Street* (1972), one of Iain Sinclair's first films after his formative years in Dublin. *Maggot Street*, the primeval 8mm, 50-minute feature, is the apocryphal ancestor of *Maggid Street* (1996). 'An alchemical fable. Shot in 1972 (and revised at regular intervals ever since).'

Thus, rather than writing about a yet-to-be-seen film, this is a readiness exercise or contingency planning for an event situated in an asymptotic region of time. Watching *Maggid Street* is the first step toward revelation—or redemption.

The most recent public screening of *Maggid Street* took place on 19 October 2023, at Swedenborg House, Bloomsbury, as part of the *Histories & Hauntings* show. This event was a 'resurrection of aspects' of *Albion Island Vortex*, the equinoctial exhibition held at the Whitechapel Gallery half a century earlier. And a celebration of Brian Catling, Iain Sinclair's sidekick and enduring source of inspiration.

Brian Catling is one of the two characters/actors in *Maggid Street*, a gothic doctor with a steampunk touch who performs a working on a young vagrant, played by Dermot Healy. The vagrant, or *mystes*, undergoes an alchemical transformation involving a familiar spirit: 'a wet bird is drawn from the opened skull and buried in the garden beneath a limestone pebble'.

Together with Renchi Bicknell, Brian Catling—a sculptor, poet, performer, and later a successful novelist—was prominently featured in the exhibition at Swedenborg House. One of the most notable artefacts, was a sword forged by Catling and given to Sinclair in the 1970s. The sword, a rare outing for an 'unquiet' object, was placed on a ley line that runs through the middle of the main gallery space, connecting Northampton with Hastings. A closer geographic perusal reveals that the ley line does not intersect The Ridge at Netherwood but instead passes through St Leonards-on-Sea.

As Sinclair explains in John Rogers's film on the exhibition, a group of three Dublin escapees settled in East London in the late '60s, propelled by the desire 'to make film'. Tom Baker had co-written *Witchfinder General* and *The Sorceress*. Renchi Bicknell was editing Sherlock Holmes stories at the BBC. Sinclair was shooting a documentary on Allen Ginsberg for WDR (Cologne). However, the *basso ostinato* of those first experiences was the feeling of being 'sucked up' by the mainstream, at a time where operators like Stan Brakhage or Jonas Mekas were telling the world that no permissions from bureaucracy or market were required to will real things and make them happen. Starting a small press was a logical consequence.

The 1974 exhibition displayed artwork, photographic material and documentation about uncommissioned assignments in all rhumbs ('walls were assigned to Crow, Goat,

Owl and Wolf'), from Wiltshire to Gower and the Scottish Borders, and reporting about visitations, seizures and other angelic occurrences. The *Albion Island Vortex* exhibition in 1974 was imbued by a demonic spirit that had already effected *Maggot Street* two years earlier. The exhibition was also an opportunity to showcase the poets published by Albion Village Press. Thirteen books from the 1970-1979 period, retaining much of their pristine aura, were on display at Swedenborg House in October 2023.

For the scrivener in search of white stones: the vortex began swirling in March/April 1974, right before *Lud Heat*'s Man-with-the-Muck-Rake wrote the first entry in his gardener's diary on 13 May 1974. The *Albion Island Vortex* exhibition took place from 18 April to 5 May 1974, within the broader and significant period recorded in Sinclair's *Lud Heat*—from the moon dream on 4 February 1974 (the moon disc growing and burying itself in St Anne's Limehouse), up to the oracle run in January 1975, possibly early February, before travelling to Dorset to complete the *Lud Heat* essays. *Lud Heat* also mentions the shooting of *Maggot Street*: the early 1975 oracle was aimed at a point that was 'an epicentre of energies—& known to us already—from the walks preparatory to filming *Maggot Street*'. Avebury, Montacute and other marked spots are present in *Lud Heat* too. Plus a black polished limestone pebble (from Monknash). A Blakean perfidious figure from *Lud Heat*, named Kotope, addresses the 'hesitating Sculptor' (Catling) with the remark: 'You know why you stutter? You think nobody wants to hear what you have to say'.

In the context of *Maggot Street*, 'preparatory walks' is a wide notion encompassing not only East London locations (St Mary Matfelon gardens, Victoria Park, Chingford Mount and the Greenway on the Northern Outfall Sewer from Wick Lane in Hackney to Beckton), but also the Wiltshire tramps (Avebury, Silbury Hill). Sinclair has suggested that the Greenway diagonal was an ersatz for any Avebury walk whenever a journey to the Wilts. could not be afforded. He has noted that an 'untrimmed' version of *Maggot Street* 'made another return to the stones of Avebury'.

The crow connection was prominent at the 1974 exhibition, where the Wilts. expeditions were designated as *The Crow Country*. In *Histories & Hauntings*, a text published at the occasion of the Swedenborg House show, Sinclair traces an Avebury lineage back to some sort of 'transformative event' in Catling's early life and to subsequent expeditions—whether with or without Catling—into that region, particularly the one in April 1971. The 'List of Works' of the 2023 exhibition at Swedenborg House includes a photograph 'of Brian Catling with crow' from '*c*. 1973' that was part of the *Albion Island Vortex* show. A crow, Sinclair recalls, was painted on the forehead of *Maggot Street*'s vagrant.

OPERATING THEATRE

Maggid Street is a hypothesis about *Maggot Street*. This is what we know:

The film begins *in media res*, right in the operating theatre, just before the extraction of the wet bird, and ends immediately afterwards. In between, we are introduced to the intermediate stages: the initiate is sheltered, fed, instructed, subjected to ablutions, and other manipulations. Doctor X is *always* seen looking through the window, smoking—sometimes a cigar, occasionally 'a knobbly question mark of a pipe'. Doctor X's performance with manila-tagged packages and transparent plastic bags—a performance within the performance—confirms that he is a serial Maggid. Manila tags are a recurrent trope in Catling. Manila tags appear as a mask on Catling's face in the King Mob's poster for the *Subversion in the Street of Shame* event (1994) or in *The Vorrh*, as part of the colonial system of classification ('Manila tags were tied to each, scrawled white-men lies gripping each cherished thing, animals in traps; the poached, the stolen, and the maimed').

The making of *Maggot Street* was informed by expeditions and performances 'as rituals designed to offer refractions of the thing that was there', with the walk itself functioning as performance. *Maggot Street* (1972) served as a bridge between the Avebury incidents and the 1974 Whitechapel show, and thus was also preparatory work. Brian Catling was the necessary angel in these ventures. The Avebury incidents of 1964 and 1971 (as 'incidents' in Robert Smithson's *Incidents of Mirror-Travel in the Yucatan*), and Catling's role in them, belong to the core of what is going on in *Maggid Street*.

During the early 1970s, Sinclair's 8mm diary filming and writing intertwined. *RED EYE*, a found typescript from 1973 and, according to Jess Chandler, Sinclair's most cinematic book, bears the mark of this period. Sinclair told Chandler at the time of *RED EYE*'s publication (2013) by Test Centre that 'it was really like a strange ghost, because although it existed in my mind and was moving towards the point of becoming real, it didn't become real'. The Test Centre edition includes frame grabs from *Maggid Street*. Other works from the time also reference *Maggid Street* (*Lud Heat*) or feature alternative versions of *RED EYE*'s poems (*Suicide Bridge*).

We know from Sinclair that during the editing of *The Falconer* in 1996, *Maggot Street*'s 8mm footage 'was crudely re-filmed on video. A new version, incorporating elements lifted from material shot by Chris Petit, was made with the editor Emma Matthews. Music by John Harle was added. And a new title, more in keeping with the alchemical scheme, was adopted'.

The meaning of *Maggid Street* is that falcon preys on crows—Horus versus Nephtys. *Maggid Street* is *Maggot Street* being invaded by non-linear digital editing. The falconer's ghost-like, cold white-rose light versus the maggid's warm orange-gold glow. A radically different grain and texture.

An interplay between falconer and vagrant, both undergoing surgery. The falconer's scar exposed, he is naked, his hand covering his sex; the vagrant's scar(s) are presumed, almost never shown. The falconer's eyes appropriately blindfolded (echoing *Lud Heat*: 'to hood this day's falcon'); the *mystes* also blindfolded before the sacrifice. Françoise Lacroix (*The Falconer*) and an unnamed dark-haired woman (*Maggid Street*). The falconer's hands sinking into the flesh of a decomposing bird; and the maggots after which the 1972 film is named. There is also a certain commonality of form between the burning cross at the end of *Maggid Street* and the helicoidal rite of the falconer among the Callanish stones.

A more detailed look into the maggot/falconer contamination shows:

1. LUMEN: SURGERY OF LIGHT

in media res, *mystes* lies on the operation
theatre, injection in his arm

                                  falconer lies in hospital bed, blindfolded,
                                  Baxter connected to his arm

Manila tags performance
preparations: ablution incubation

2. NIGREDO: INCANTATION

Rodinsky sacred papers

Manila tags performance
on a wheelchair, Victoria Park (Alcibiades'
dogs entrance)

falconer in hospital on a wheelchair
pushed by a dark-haired woman (Olga)

operation continues in the garden, blood
stains, later, on a wheelchair, Chingford
cemetery

falconer naked on a hospital bed, hand
covering sex, Lacroix enters, wheelchair
in hospital, Lacroix smoking cigar in a
bathtub

woman wrapped in a towel, walking

Lacroix walking, later in a bathtub

woman in a towel, walking, open doors,
horror, another woman lies naked in a
pool of blood

3. THE SACRIFICIAL ACT

mystes blindfolded, sitting on a chair in
the garden, sacrificed

Lacroix walking in a park with a red coat,
later meets Olga in street, they walk

4. MERCURIUS: FLIGHT

Doctor X and the *mystes* at the St Mary

Matfelon park, Beckton Alp, tower blocks,
a helicopter, orange-gold sun seen
through a thistle grove

yellow glow on Lacroix's face
falconer's hands sinking into a
decomposing bird

maggots

falconer's helicoidal rite among
the Callanish Stones circle

woman undresses in park, flees naked

5. REBIRTH

Doctor X smokes, looks through the
window, *mystes* dressed for the final act:
face and body painted, feathers, goat
skull ('the crow is painted on the forehead
of the vagrant')
mystes and doctor look at each other
through the window
back to in media res: operation theatre
extraction of a placenta containing a bird
from the *mystes*' head
Doctor X digs a hole in the garden, puts
the 'wet bird' inside, covers it with earth
and places a white stone on it
the *mystes* or an effigy thereof is burnt
on a cross
Doctor X is smoking while watching
the combustion through the window

AFFORDANCES

The collage and cut-up possibilities enabled by non-linear video editing software made the falconer's contamination possible, and thus made *Maggid Street* affordable.

The Falconer is the second film collaboration between Iain Sinclair and Chris Petit and was the first to exploit the potential of non-linear video editing. Significantly, Catling was involved in their earlier venture, *The Cardinal and the Corpse*—a title that alludes to Nephthys and maggots. In a Maggid guise, Catling appears as a 'gnostic heretic' magus, performing a series of workings in a former Huguenot building on Princelet Street, where he gazes through the window while smoking a cigar—a quote from *Maggid Street*. Downstairs, at the house entrance, a young Alan Moore is knocking on the door. He is looking for Francis Barrett's *Magus*. A neophyte—Aaron Williamson, uncannily reminiscent in his deafness of Dermot Healy, the Maggid's vagrant, the *mystes*—opens the door, while barring the entrance. Later, upstairs, fallen angels (or vessels of wrath) from Barrett's *Magus* are shown. Much like *Maggid Street*, the film ends with a burning ritual performed by Catling on the effigies of some characters (as an effigy of the vagrant is burnt in *Maggid Street*, as evidenced by photographs shown at Swedenborg House). This is followed by a book bonfire, which includes a copy of Sexton Blake's *The Cardinal and the Corpse*. The final book burned on screen is a Spanish edition of Pearl S Buck's *Letter from Peking*. Neither crow nor falcon, *The Cardinal and the Corpse*'s familiar spirit is embodied in an Asháninka jaguar figurine held by the fine guitarist and book dealer Martin Stone towards the end of the film.

If oblique, the choice of Princelet Street remains highly relevant for this pursuit. David Rodinsky's mystical books were discovered in the chamber he occupied within the Princelet Street synagogue. An overview of these books opens the second sequence, 'Incantation', in *Maggid Street*. In *The Cardinal and the Corpse*, the magus's house is located at 4 Princelet Street, where Catherine Eddowes was living when she was murdered by Jack the Ripper. A dead woman in a pool of blood—as in *Maggid Street*.

A smoking and performing magus, a silent *mystes*, angelic sentience, and effigy burning—*The Cardinal and the Corpse* bears Catling's signature.

Maggid Street and *The Cardinal and the Corpse* also share a strong sense of territory. Beckton Alp (*Maggid Street*) and Pauls Cafe (*The Cardinal and the Corpse*) are both situated along the same Greenway line. The prefabricated, Marzahn-like tower blocks in the background, visible when the Maggid ascends Beckton Alp with the *mystes* in his arms, also punctuate the horizon in the post-dockers Stratford Marsh area, where a stuttering Seabrook throws his verbal torrent outside Pauls Cafe in *The Cardinal and the Corpse*. Seabrook mobilizes David Litvinoff's myth, which is *The Cardinal and the Corpse*'s McGuffin, the Krays/*Performance* connection ('*ending up getting him, getting embroiled with one of those, one of the twins and some very, very weird throat scars apparently that, that he came off with but I suppose his real achievement was as dialogue coach and technical advisor on the film called* Performance *author of, author of those classic lines like what a freak show shut, shut your bloody hole, was your old man a barber, your old man was a barber wasn't he*'). Today, the Ronan prefabricated blocks and the Stratford Marsh junkyard café ('Ain't No Airs Or Graces 'Ere') are erased from the post-Olympics landscape.

THE OUROBOROS DARK ROOM

While *Maggid Street* is *Maggot Street* being invaded by non-linear digital editing, it is also being tailored to the duration of John Harle's *Terror and Magnificence*.

Terror and Magnificence's central theme is *Ma fin est mon commencement et mon commencement est ma fin*. John Harle's 20-minute soundtrack originates in an improvisation he recorded in Christchurch. Harle wrote a music meditation on a text by Guillaume de Machaut (*c*.1300-1377), *Ma fin est mon commencement* (*My end is my beginning*):

> *My end is my beginning,*
> *And my beginning my end.*
> *This is what I hold on to:*
> *My end is my beginning.*
> *My third line, three times only,*
> *Goes back on itself and so finishes.*
> *My end is my beginning,*
> *And my beginning my end.*

The song, a rondeau, is a retrograde canon in words (almost) and music—it *literally* reverses itself. An ouroboros. Jean-François Trubert writes: 'as soon as the groove has bitten its tail, it will have isolated a sound fragment that will no longer have either beginning or end, a sound isolated from any temporal context, a crystal of time with sharp edges, of a time which no longer belongs to any time'.

On their summer solstice walk in 2023, from Greenwich Hill to Pole Hill, connecting Wolfe to wolf, as Renchi wrote to Sinclair after the tramp, the two meridian line pilgrims were also 'outside time'. Upon reaching Pole Hill, Sinclair sensed 'zero longitude fizzes and sparks'. The sun's 'red-gold shafts' at Pole Hill evoke the magnificent light on Beckton Alp in *Maggid Street*.

The film *Maggid Street* is an ouroboros, 'Catling's favoured symbol'—a cyclic enactment. Doctor X is trapped within it. *Maggid Street* functions as a dark twin or a Hintonian prolongation, a (necessarily partial) 3-D vision of a higher-D *thing*, manifesting as an intrusion from another film being produced at the time, *The Falconer*. In the editing darkroom, time sinks and ceases to be oriented. Watching the untrimmed *Maggot Street* make another return to the stones of Avebury without the necessary ritual precautions could indeed be a risky endeavour.

GIFTS RETURNED BY THE RIVER

Iain Sinclair

The Stumbling Block is being hunted.
—B. Catling, 1990.

Teasing daylight, older than Southwark stone, returns, rationed by this season of closure and contemplation. And is accorded a special value against the macular degeneration of a solitary river-hugging walker. Who keeps a partial record, difficult to disentangle now, beyond the threat of resolution to a long-husbanded quest: actions into words, images into objects. Fire and water. *Imago agens.* The sun, if it rises, will stand still. Nights are awash in borderless dreams. He is self-stalked by shadows formed from the ash of burnt libraries.

Another blind pilgrimage: 22 December 2023. Winter solstice. The closing of parentheses around an allocated period of memory harvesting, of improving the hour by re-colonizing a past that has not yet happened, through the gallery presentation at Swedenborg House of evidence—photographs, paintings, texts—scavenged by two implicated wreckers; bending history as a subtle plea against the court of oblivion. A Bloomsbury building identified by interested parties as both the epicentre of an abiding tendency of London spirit and a staging post on a desire line or neural trench said to run from Northampton to Hastings; directly, it has been suggested, from Alan Moore's 'SeaView' cave to the Maze Hill alignment of time-travelling neighbours, H Rider Haggard and Alan Turing, on either side of a portal arch in St Leonards-on-Sea. A segue that finds its suspect climax at the channel-facing pyramid tomb of that family of architects and real estate promoters, the Burtons; with a viewing slit into a spidery interior containing all their unresolved plans for cities, all the cancelled futures. An empire built on dredged sand. Suspect physics, itchy feet.

*

The plotting of our *Histories and Hauntings* obsequies was confirmed, chewed up and sweated out, over a summer solstice ramble from Wolfe's obelisk on Greenwich Hill to T E Lawrence's vanished hut on Pole Hill. Sliding on and off the invisible prompt of zero longitude, in company with my co-conspirator, Renchi Bicknell, we reminisced in the rationed breath of veterans, about Brian Catling, third participant in a 1974 exposure at the Whitechapel Gallery. We felt, throbbing feet to spine, the compass-bending magnetism of his abiding personality.

Destination achieved at the magical hour of gold and green, we veered away from the official conclusion, wayside marker and trig point, to a hollowed tree at the forest's edge: a woodpecker's den nested in conjuror's props, webs and feathers. It felt as if—part of the long game—our former collaborator was trying on avian disguise, a new mask as owl or raptor in the cycle of reincarnation. In transition, his enforced and accepted rural retirement, Brian spent months watching the birdlife in his orchard from an open schoolhouse window, letting bitterns boom through poems. Local symbols, foreshortened by the field glasses of Paul Nash, absorbing Wittenham Clumps as he faded away on Boars Hill, ghosted through a mesmerizing and timeless sequence of illuminated tempera paintings.

A coffee halt at Trinity Buoy Wharf summoned the poet-performer's 1991 occupation of the decommissioned lighthouse and his valiant attempt to articulate human absence against the flush of soulless high-rise development hurting the upstream horizon. Stalled like Conrad's yarn-spinners waiting on the tide off Gravesend, the sculptor fretted on the wrong side of language. There was a heavy stone in his mouth. Fever and contamination in the water.

'And farther west on the upper reaches the place of the monstrous town was still marked ominously on the sky, a brooding gloom in sunshine, a lurid glare under the stars.'

Catling willed the borrowed voices of labouring fetches, the drowned and the undead of Bow Creek. Those sightless intruders must be approached, he said, 'obliquely, with stealth'. Contact achieved, the performer took it upon himself to stand in their place, a surrogate victim under creaking beams. Uninvited presences skulked in dark bays, teasing reflections from polished parabolic mirrors. The commissioned messenger of madness crawled across protesting deck planks to gather inch-thick lines of dust; a subtle medium he pounded into 'gritty and viscous' ink. A medium for a Devil's Island confession. Brian left his essential reports, unbroadcast, in the lantern chamber. Script without author. 'A circular steel table turns slowly, a pen trough and an inkwell cut into its surface.' Rough music from the grind of protesting gears. Overture to the as yet unsuspected thousand-year 'Long Player' by Jem Finer. The shelves of singing bowls in their infinitely varied chants.

In the photograph that accompanies 'At the Lighthouse', his published Trinity Buoy text, Catling is standing *outside* the diamond-panels of the curved lamp house, his right arm raised in a salute to who knows what entity. Or, better, to shade dazzled eyes against the electrified trash of downriver interventions.

'While our retinas crawl and shudder to find more, less will be seen', the sculptor intoned. Penetrating, as ever, into the physiology of the structure that held him, he tapped for vibrations of psychic threat. 'Each sweep erases belief and substance until the bay is rubbed empty. To see we must remember, wind the fluid back, suck it through the optic nerve, hold it in our breath where we can chalkily name it.'

*

Now, in the yawn of a dank and spiritless season, I am starting early and need to save time in reaching Southwark, where I witnessed Catling melting the font of a special book and pouring a silver stream into the turbid water. Lights wink on the bridge of sighs that is accessible at all hours to the upright dead. Despite towers of mirrored glitz and vortices of choking air, the classic south bank set survives: cathedral, produce market, satellite pubs. And the old operating theatre assigned to St Thomas (a restored heritage fake). The coaching inns. The debtors' prison. And the pilgrims' road to Canterbury. As Catling said: 'There are many pitfalls along the directed track of clarity.'

The Southwark story, told so often, has lost nothing of its soup-bone pungency. In keeping with our new London, Capital of Mendacity & Managed Disappointment, tall fences police the historic church. A laundry screen of wine-flavoured mesh, a bishop's Aertex underwear, enlivened with secular commandments: RESTRICTED

ZONE. AUTHORISED PERSONNEL ONLY. And you are never one of those. Today's narrator is a misbeliever haunted by the interiors from which he is barred; the guttered candles and rubbed marble of sacred rituals that intrigue, but in which he has no investment.

The covered market, nudged against the elevated railway, is scratching the seasonal sleep of office parties from its gummy eyes. It has traded upwards into the boasts of ethical cheeses and holier-than-thou carrots. Carts rumbling in from Kentish fields have been superseded by coffee beans flown across the world from plantations worked solely by indigenous women of good character. Fat olives of impeccable lineage have been caressed by generations of picturesque harvesters. Drooping strings of silver-and-gold Christmas illuminations, flickering in the gloom, anticipate festive crowds browsing for good cheer.

The narrator, overwhelmed by the profound gloom of the wet flagstones, the jaunty soundtrack, the locked gates, is released. The indifferent river is waiting. The end of the story can begin. The cynical and objective essayist confesses a version of the past in which he was an implicated participant. First person singular then. No extenuating circumstances. No posthumous pleas. Journalist!

★

I make a clockwise circuit of the mesh, the padlocked gates. I can't do justice to the episode of the melted book without first identifying the bench in the cathedral grounds where Catling invited me to meet him on a brighter morning than this. Brighter in memory. Brighter in the sense that everything was still possible, but it hadn't happened yet. It was an era of notebook possibilities, of reading promiscuously, listening to whispers. Pubs at the edge of the market were on the edge of everything: pilgrim road, river, and existential abyss. You responded, instinctively, to the pulse of ancient liberties, an interzone of pleasures and playhouses: Winchester geese and bear-baiting spectacles across the wherried Thames from the enclosed City of Commerce. Fantastic schemes were floated over pints of Russian stout and cider in the afterhours purlieux of Borough Market. The cages and the vegetable spills picked over by vagrants. Epic potentialities were coded doodles.

Perseverance, after several frustrations, offers a previously unsuspected entrance to the cathedral. There is no toll to pay. The marmoreal Shakespeare slumbers, an indulged and forgiven heretic, bulging pate burnished by sweating hands of supplicants. Incensed aisles are deserted. Clerks wink in alcoves. Prelates yawn at private doors. Promotional leaflets play to the pilgrimage franchise.

'Walking is a great way to meet new friends, explore new places and meet new challenges. You'll be supported by the group in a common purpose as we journey together. Our first pilgrimages will be from Southwark Cathedral to Waltham Abbey. A First Aider will be available throughout. Tickets do not include travel costs or refreshments during the day.'

Groups of questing souls are out there now, moving up and down permitted river paths, chattering, driving forward on their carbon fibre Norwegian walking poles, nodding enthusiastically as group leaders preach and gesture. The Bishop of Southwark says that 'pilgrimages start with somebody feeling compelled to set off towards a destination'. A memory. Or a person. Alive or dead. Mythic or reforgotten. I was *compelled*, the momentum of the morning required it, towards an assignation with Catling on his secure bench. The great cathedral, after I had passed the first test and found a way through a cloister, collaborated, releasing me into the market-facing churchyard; a former burial ground revised as herb garden. And dressed with figurative statuary commissioned from Raphael Maklouf.

When, primed for news of Catling's latest discovery, I walked here, through the stacked vegetables of the old market, dodging porters with trolleys, there was no barrier between produce, Dickensian enterprises perched above, elevated railway, and cathedral grounds. They were all of a piece. And at peace. Office workers enjoyed their sandwiches. But there was no sign of the poet-performer. Brian, in my experience, could be relied upon to keep his appointments. Not necessarily on the prearranged day or year, but he never missed. I found a bench and sat down to wait.

On the berth now occupied by Maklouf's life-sized and lifeless bronze of William Shakespeare, swan-feather quill at the ready to take the dictation of the furies, was a bundle of rescued rags, black with years of London Peculiar. The outer wrappings, like something from an official newsreel of the retreat from Moscow, moved, and the person trapped inside along with it. A mugger's balaclava of stitched chainmail hid most of the massive and glowering face. Years on the road, in ditches and barns, were grained into thick skin. There were fingerless gloves on broken-knuckled fists. Many layers, coats beneath waistcoats, vests over shirts, held off the weather. The vagrant wore his disassembled bed through all seasons. A larder of scavenged crumbs and crusts. And a clanking bottle bank. Al fresco diners tearing open their cellophane packages gave him distance. Flies zizzed and hesitated. Piloted by delirious stench. They sucked and fell.

Shuddering from a corpse-deep hibernation, the reluctant revenant, hypersensitive to surveillance, noticed my inappropriate inspection and lurched towards me. Always a gifted shape-shifter, this was the magician's ultimate triumph. Hugh Boone, double identity suburbanite and City beggar, was revealed as Brian Catling. *The Man with the Twisted Lip*. Still in character, he led me, by ways predicted by Conan Doyle, across Southwark Bridge towards locations he would occupy and articulate in years to come. I became the shadow extra, the second self: Neville St Clair. Unmasked. And unrequired. Except as a suborned witness.

When, still in Sherlockian character, I strike out, upstream at winter solstice, safe in my pretensions, the looming, lumbering Boone, substantial but deceptively light on his feet, follows or stands aside, chuckling over flaws, growling like Orson Welles, before he discovers that his bloated future is all used up.

Some time after that excursion as a muttering beggar, and in another performance which I attended with a camera, Catling lay down in gravel dirt, remnants of the great hall of Winchester Palace. He was branded with moonlight, the lunar print of the skeletal Rose Window. He seemed to be licking up all available Tudor plagues and deformities. Fever took him within a few hours. While we, bemused spectators at the rail, walked away, free and untouched, into the Liberties of the Clink: street food, bars, and over-excited conversation. What had we witnessed?

⋆

Call him Ishmael in this groaning cabin, the timbered hutch in which the sculptor's slate book was transcribed as font, stamped out by the monkish power of a veteran press. He will be the one telling the tale, ahead of himself, a cancelled chart for us to reassemble.

No. 1 Arch, Green Dragon Court. A cell from which to absorb and observe the netted exoticism of the market. Printing, binding, numbering. And inserting, in twenty-five special copies, additional holograph sheets that will not be melted down with the rest. These leaded wafers are loaded into slipcases. Protected from the predations of water and fire. 'This ushered voice can silence and coat our ambition.' Catling scratched at virgin paper, recomposing tracks of grey ink, testament of literate spiders.

Trespassing in remembered twilight, when I stood with my back to the business of crafted handprinting and looked out of the curve of that high window, shadows of trains ghosting into London Bridge station were cast across the obliging cliff of the cathedral. An effect I fancied but was never able to realize in the television film we shot, where Catling carried a heavy sack to the river. To prove that his book was not to be defined in its making. That linguistic assaults on the imagined 'block' did nothing whatsoever to dent or define its intransigence.

These are dark waters. In my shaky recollection, we went with brazier and blowtorch directly to London Bridge. Carting or carrying. But that proposition is challenged when I play back the route on the morning of the winter solstice. Lara Maiklem, in her 2024 publication, *A Mudlarking Year*, says that when cofferdams were constructed during the building of the new London Bridge in 1830, 'a jet of water threw up a large quantity of angels'. Meaning coins, valued by antiquarians, from the reigns of Henry VII and Henry VIII. The coins were 'seized directly'. But the conceptual angels made their escape.

Catling, by intention or trusted instinct, was hatching a subtle plot, with all the apparently comedic feints of a silent screen master. Health and safety bureaucrats, tasked with aborting performance elements that might give the established order a nudge, would be hyperventilating. Born-again ecologists would cancel and pursue the man through every circle of social media hell. The substantial weight, which was no weight at all, of the 'written sculpture' that was the 'stumbling block', something like a pebble under the tongue, hobbling flow and causing language to gush and jet like the pressured streams throwing up angels, manifested in the ritual of printing. A secret was hidden within the elegant limits of the book, pressed between slender gravestone covers. To release the unimpeded flow, punched letters would have to be melted in a ladle and poured into the timeless river. One gift among so many. Among accidents, crimes and superstition. 'The Stumbling Block is an ark of extinction ... virulent in its passion to embrace and swim in human tides.'

When Catling published *Anvilled Stars*, a tribute to the artist Matthew Luck Galpin, he revealed something of his own means and methods. He spoke of 'trajectories of riddle'. He commended Galpin's work for declaring 'the signature of its concealed meaning'. The Laurel and Hardy dance, stumbling on slippery steps, spitting ladle held out, was a trickster's diversion, insuring that the dissolution of the elements of his book would prove their transformation into a higher form: a legend to be sampled and tested, outside the fetishism of ownership. 'Mud and ink, paper and water are scoured into another projection.'

Behind this recorded incident, deliberately or otherwise, was an iteration of the sixteenth-century necromancer, Faustus. The itinerant magician, moving from city to city, court to court, challenged by all the established religious franchises, claimed the gift of casting horoscopes by diagnosing shapes made when he poured molten lead into water. Galpin's 'anvil' is described by Catling as 'totally untransmutable ... A cast block of solidity whose purpose is not to move, and to resist all energy that is brought upon it ... A hard shadow under the influence of the fluidity of fire'. His own 'graphite *font*' (that word predicting its dissolution in the heated brazier), his 'black plinth', cannot resist. 'It has softened its mouth to hold water'. To ameliorate the obstruction in the throat disguised as a stutter. Carried off by a pair of temporary vagrants from the cathedral precinct, the evidence of the biblio-massacre is tipped away like contraband, a traditional bridge-launched suicide.

Among lesser heresies, Faustus boasted of his ability to recover and restore deleted texts. Catling frees the anguished syllables of his word spasms, melting them into mercury, trusting that they achieve mantic resolution: a shining glove in the filthy water, the hospitable mud.

Thames alluvia, when Catling assembled the three cargoed volumes of his masterwork, *The Vorrh*, was the originating element. It sheltered the prescient undead, the expelled of Eden. The Erstwhile. It released the primal 'man-beast' slithering into William Blake's Lambeth cottage. 'You have caught me between worlds.' Which is where the epic sequence, like the river itself, finds resolution, with the vanishing of word-blots in a ghost dance across sucking sediment, the poisoned silt of the Isle of Sheppey. The possessed narrator, in thrall to the moral imperatives of place, parts company with his readers on a brave punt: the blind hope that a human mouth, opened to the slop of estuarine mudflats, will bide its time and sing again.

★

My winter walk is a solitary affair. The summer solstice was kind, a steady conversation with Renchi, in expectation of plotting the hang of the exhibition at Swedenborg House. Tramped territory played along, significant locations from the backstory behaved well. And there was the bonus at Pole Hill with the tree Renchi planted in his watercolour sketchbook. Now surveillance cameras were warning heads on sticks. They were surplus stock from another era when budget operatives were paid to invigilate the drift of a cowed and suspicious populace. Devices on long metal arms reached out over the choked water but they were talking to themselves. Auditioning documentaries nobody will ever watch. Or tracking bubbling threads of sewage discharge. None of the bridges have the structure required for Catling's brazier and his descent to the river. I need to go back to the *Late Show* film. At low tide, on several occasions, without a sanctioned mudlarking permit, I've poked around the foreshore, with no expectation of finding a solidified crust derived from the molten lead. A Faustus divination.

Somewhere between Queenhithe and the Millennium Bridge, Lara Maiklem met 'a man with a handful of lead type'. 'The jury's out', she said, 'on whether it washed down the drains from the print rooms of Fleet Street ... tossed into the river by print workers clearing out their pockets on their way home after a shift, or found its way into the river in some other way'. The man on the beach confessed that he was prospecting for words. If they give themselves up to him, he promises to write a song. 'If the river was to send a message through the medium of lost type', Maiklem pondered, 'I wonder what it would say?'

She scavenged, with fingers like tweezers, frozen inside surgical gloves, for the sentences to fulfil her commission. To give purpose to a life of obsessive retrieval, carving the smoke of clay pipes into dialogue with unwilling ancestors.

*

Hidden in the slipstream of Fleet Street's abdication, abandonment by hot presses, is the library of St Bride, the discreet afterglow of the printing trade. And the stunned repository of more than 100,000 volumes. None of them, in July 1994, authored by B. Catling. But with his preternatural empathy for the inanimate, his gift for articulating *élan vital* in walls, floorboards, curtains, beds and chairs with only the faintest imprints of previous occupation, Brian recognized the site's defining quality: a hunger to infiltrate the submerged society of the foreshore.

The buried Fleet, the nearest tributary, was as much a river of disassembled texts, prophetic utterance, as of butchered beasts from Smithfield. Barbecued martyrs of religious persecution. Hospital sweepings. Dogs. Pigs. Stumbling drunkards. Rebels against established power. The rumoured sinkhole baptism of the visionary, Emanuel Swedenborg, was yet another offprint of Catling's Erstwhile.

The Bridewell Theatre had its own secret, a covered swimming pool, an echoing vault drained of the waters of ritual immersion. And it was here that Catling astonished an audience assembled to witness Alan Moore, Kathy Acker, Derek Raymond, John Healy, Emanuel Litvinoff, and other notables gathered to read and perform in a series of events known as *Subversion in the Street of Shame*.

Crawling in a gesture of reverse evolution through the hollow of the waterless pool, through fuse-box cellars and up stone stairs, holding the mirror that translated his malleable performer's face into the mask of a Cyclops, Catling launched an act that would achieve its apotheosis in *The Vorrh*. This spectre, man-beast of the Bridewell, was a premonition of Blake's encounter with Nebuchadnezzar. Some ancient horror, emerging from the forest of night, tracked this way and that, following salt licks towards the myth of the river. A flesh-raw Cyclops, not yet renamed as Ishmael, tested his novel identity, absorbing lead into his system as a homoeopathic dose against insanity.

It uttered a throaty parchment whisper, a boast: 'I am beneath you / walking / speaking ... throat knotted to a glass ... without a true word to say'.

It was only when I reached Lambeth and stared through my camera into the murk that I got a glimmer of how recurring cycles of influence between Blake and

Catling, embedded Londoners both, played out: no precedence, interlocking vortices like Blake's *Mental Traveller*. Catling eavesdrops on Blake's confrontation with a creature-between-worlds, dripping to the craftsman's door, to demand restitution. And representation. But what Brian is also describing is his own performance in the Bridewell pool, a crashing of evolutionary gears. A splintering of portals. The blindly writhing Cyclops *predates* Blake's vision, and only takes this form, *at this time*, because the author of *The Vorrh* has been nudged towards revelation by his intimacy with the hand-coloured and inked monotype.

'And his body was wet with the dew of heaven, till his hairs were grown like eagles' feathers, and his nails like birds' claws.' Down on all fours in a pelt of assumed insanity, naked animal madness. Seizures lasting until the waters of seven ages had passed over him. 'Thank God', Blake wrote to Hayley, 'I was not altogether a beast as he was'.

*

The river's truth is edited as I try to identify the steps from which *The Stumbling Block* was poured into the Thames. London Bridge did not agree with either memory or film. Southwark Bridge resisted. But then Blackfriars admitted its murky role in the alchemical poisoning of the waters. In this tarot of accidental encounters, a broken pack of cards scattered across my path, the chalk-striped Magician holds an implement like a double-headed candle above a golden cup. He fulfils his ceremonial shuffle, directly across the Thames from the Hanged Man: Roberto Calvi. 'God's Banker' was strung from scaffolding on 16 June 1982, with £10,000 and a couple of London bricks in the distressed pockets of his Savile Row suit. 'Trials, sacrifice, divination, prophecy', says the gloss approved by A E Waite.

Other cards I turn over with my boot include the Four of Swords, a prediction of Catling's never-quite-completed novel, *Transi*. A tale of medieval craftsmen on this stretch of the river and deep-England tomb carvers, of sacred stones, ancient universities, and libraries where an American researcher has her sexual inclinations reprogrammed and made plural by thought police. I pick up the effigy of a crusader knight, hands arched in payer, as he sleeps on a marble monument, between vertical and horizontal swords.

My own draw, later that morning, curses the architectural infill of the most troubling passage of the walk, west towards Chiswick: 'Misery, distress, deception, ruin, unforeseen catastrophe'. A lightning-struck tower against a sunless sky. Defenestrated figures suiciding from loss of nerve: the essence of Vauxhall. 'A matter thought to be important is really of slight consequence', warns the oracle. A bent walker, leaning on his staff, the Eight of Cups, plods his sullen path, heading straight for the rocks.

Today, conscious of the limited permissions of daylight, I stick close to the river. The reach between St Thomas' hospital and the former Battersea Power Station is a theme park for paranoia and the vanity of virtual architects. Self-reflecting towers linked by the aerial gutters of infinity pools, and fed by the bristling electrified hulk of the American Embassy, live down to their CGI doppelgängers. Robot utopias of perpetually blissed-out leisure time are plastered over construction screens masking craters. Periscope towers sway in the downdraught of private helicopter traffic. Buffeted streets are grudgingly ceded to pedestrians of no consequence in desert storms of diesel dust and lens-scratching irritation. The famed Regency pleasure gardens have become cruising caves of lost evenings, and torture clubs for sexual specializations, surveyed by the multiple devices of the MI6 jukebox castle. Convivial leather cells are employed for rest and recreation by security-cleared uncivil servants. Although very few inhabitants of this wealth-ghetto emerge along the river path—all of them looking as if they've been drugged and dumped in a foreign country—the zone feels unweathered and abandoned. View-entitled prisoners of obscene liquidity, and a straggle of pre-convalescent dog accompanists, pretend that the old and proudly filthy Thames is not really there. And that somehow the pulsing devices in their clammy hands will succeed in cancelling it. Meanwhile, vast tunnels beneath the river (and vast land-grabs above it), costing decades of disruption and many millions, while remaining pristine and astonishing in themselves, a triumph of Franco-Hispanic engineering, do not ameliorate highly visible strands of effluent. Half-liquefied shit froth and accompanying paper trails mark out the forbidden swim lanes of the river. Close to shore, insoluble scum creams like the combed head on a pint of heavy.

Lambeth Palace, alongside the first of a chain of churches dedicated to St Mary, was always the point at which to step away, to initiate a detour. Another pass down Hercules

Road, to see if any trace of occupation by the Blakes could be felt through the brick barrier of public housing: it couldn't. Until, by moving out, staying well away and sitting at his table in Oxford, or stirring in bed, Catling was able to realize the summoned location in a higher register, as its eternal self. The long-prepared and sensitized scribe made himself present when that gloriously damned visitor elbowed into Blake's workroom from the soft and shifting effluence of the Lambeth foreshore. The graphic panels on the Tradescant tomb alongside the Garden Museum, where Catling published a text celebrating Blake, are a relief codex of London's rise and fall, tumbling masonry and primal swamps coexisting, a fabulous history.

*

Pushing on for a coffee hit from an enclosed street stall on one of the concrete decks of the revamped Battersea Power Station, just as effective an art business—the art of retail grazing—as Tate Modern, I had to photograph a blow-up display on a barrier fence disguising the point at which a major access pit for the Super Sewer rubbed against a frenzy of competitive satellite development: inhabitable pop sculptures feeding off the lavishly hyped tourist destination. Great white smokeless chimneys are serviced by a spanking new Underground station and an insecure jetty where tiny tots in high-vis vests are encouraged to wave at the steepling wash of River Buses sponsored by Uber.

The theme on the construction fence is a dance of death. It reminded me of that exuberant Peace Carnival mural on Dalston Lane. The Hackney artist, Ray Walker, died before it could be completed. But the sounds—brass, horns, trumpets—live on. And more urgently every season. Celebrating universal resistance. Hooded skull-faces in the crush mingle with once known and now vanished local heroes. The Battersea procession is a pale replica, an obvious promotion. For what? Euthanasia? A New Age river-worshipping franchise? A cure for cancer?

One of the bulkier musicians, silver haired and thinly bespectacled, could be interpreted as yet another phantom Xerox of Catling. The hoarding is like a Mexican *ofrenda*. A public shrine. The proof that Brian has not yet given up on this winter walk. *He is with us*. The figure in the t-shirt is puffing down a trumpet that looks as if it has been run over by a steamroller commissioned by Cornelia Parker. He hefts his instrument as a weapon holding back the turn of the tide. An antiquated First War rifle being operated like a blowpipe.

*

The past levitates comfortably over Battersea Park, a cool green avenue with golden temple. This had been a first river trip for me, at the time of the Festival of Britain in 1951. And then, in student days, a plagiarized tracking shot in a film shot in 1965 and never completed; a lazy drift behind glass panels, in a hired wheelchair, alongside sunken gardens. Equipment and props wrestled over Albert Bridge from Chelsea. From borrowed beds to an oasis of postwar urban renewal.

I stare back now at the shingled foreshore on the north bank, where no mudlarks are out, trawling for lead type melted down by Charles Ricketts, at the dissolution in 1904 of the Vale Press. A single letter would confirm the validity of the search. Half a dozen letters might work unaided to inspire the setting of a new poem from scattered elements gifted to the river: with the unspoken hope of remote recovery and reanimation.

Catling's heated brazier, the heavy-metal soup made from *The Stumbling Block*, and ladled into the river, was no eccentricity. I had read the story of Ricketts, Charles Shannon and the Vale Press, and how the printer made the short journey to the Thames from his house in Chelsea, at No. 1, The Vale, a property inherited from James Abbott Whistler. Brian was honouring an established tradition. Lead was valued, both materially and in alchemical metaphor. Alphabets were frequently put to the flame, martyred. In 1904, it was a conflagration in the print workshop, feeding hungrily on a pyre of woodcuts, that led to the closure of the Vale Press. 'On the completion of the last page of this pamphlet', Ricketts said, 'the type becomes type metal again'.

Calculating the direct route from Ricketts' house to the Thames, Lara Maiklem worked the foreshore from Albert Bridge to Chelsea Bridge. And found nothing. 'But that's not to say they'll never turn up', she wrote. 'Perhaps I'll come back again: maybe one day when the tide is ridiculously low or a boat has churned up the mud, a small letter cut into the end of a tall rectangle of metal will wash up.'

And maybe that should *never* happen. Metamorphoses, by fire and water, are about drift and transformation. From one element to another. Trapped words into natural sound. Coins into angels. Feverish inspiration into manifestations of the Erstwhile.

'You could hear all the tricklings as one', Catling wrote, 'whispering over the breathing mud that was popping, gulping, and letting go, sighing as it resigned itself again to ponderous gravity'.

*

Blake is not to be summoned by blinkered tourists. 'Battersea and Chelsea mourn for Cambel & Gwendolen, / Hackney and Holloway sicken for Estrild & Ignoge.' The second in the chain of churches dedicated to St Mary has its own dock and slipway at Old Swan Wharf in Battersea. An eloquent but perpetually padlocked colonialist building, now dedicated to community use, husbands its stashed heritage. Nothing is offered to the river, although certain key relics seem to have been rescued from it. You can inspect—should you attain entry—the padded chair that Turner dragged outside to catch the sunset. Catherine Boucher, illiterate daughter of asparagus cultivators, married William Blake, poet and engraver of no great prospects, in this building. The eager bridegroom endured a couple of weeks of submerged residence on Lavender Hill.

The aura survives. Persists. I sat on a bench, close to the water, with Andrew Kötting, in the early hours of the morning, when we walked a nocturnal circuit of the London Overground railway. We drained the last of our pink-rubbered brandy flask. Before Andrew inspected the innocent graves for a suitable spot on which to empty his bowels, but thought better of it. And held fire until we passed through the hospital on Denmark Hill where he had been brought after his bloody motorbike accident on the Old Kent Road. He made a lifelong friend of the Polish policewoman who came to his rescue. In the soft-footed corridors and slumbering wards, we were phantoms.

Contemplating Battersea, Blake conceives a Worm that is also the river, and much else beside, creature of nightmare and surging tides, garlanded with shit and hospitable sediment. 'In fortuitous concourse of memorys accumulated & lost. / It ploughs the Earth in its own conceit, it overwhelms the Hills / Beneath its winding labyrinths, til a stone of the brook / Stops it in midst of its pride among its hills & rivers. Battersea & Chelsea mourn.'

Pilgrims, disappointed by their failure to broach the interior of the church, with its hoarded reservoir of prophetic light, shuffle down to the waterline where Hunter S Thompson, in *The Gonzo Salvage Co.*, reckons civilization ends. He couldn't be more wrong. And to disprove his conceit, we poke among the stones and bottle tops. I have prodded over whatever stretch of beach is available and found nothing. Nothing but regret for the discontinued ferry. And the offensive absurdity of Chelsea Harbour on the other shore. An 'unfortunate contemplator', as Blake has it. And nowhere better to endure that pathology, a valiant staging post in any journey. One of the advantages of compulsory Super Sewer purchases and enclosures is that the London Duck tour ramp has been repurposed: you are no longer in danger of being swamped by a large yellow amphibious vehicle of screaming thrill-seekers as you indulge in unfortunate contemplation.

*

I stood waiting at the slipway, thirty years ago, with the writer Nicholas Royle. A boat had been hired on which to conduct an interview, the excuse for another downriver jolly. We wanted to catch the tide but were well beyond the agreed hour for the arrival of Professor Catling. It didn't happen. Some confusion between Bermondsey, manor of Brian's childhood reminiscences, his working relatives with views of ocean-going ships at the end of the street, and my own fixation on Blake and Battersea. Catling came late to the David Jones of *The Anathemata*, but was mesmerized by the quality of voice issuing from that Harrow bunker, when he stumbled by accident on a recorded reading. Biographers reckoned that James Jones, David's Welsh father, from Holywell, connected 'above himself' by marrying Alice Ann Bradshaw, daughter of a Surrey mast-maker. This was significant territory in Catling's mythology and he would not yield it: Bermondsey to Old Kent Road to Rotherhithe, a potent triangulation. Ebenezer Bradshaw, David's maternal grandfather, was married in Rotherhithe, at yet another St Mary's Church, where he served as parish clerk.

The Battersea St Mary's is holding its own against the encroachment of sloping cliffs of chlorine-green, reflective cloud traps. Out of scale monsters. 'I have howled

271

at the foot of the glass tower', Jones wrote in 'Balaam's Ass', an abandoned sequence. And, tight-lipped, I howl with him.

Coming ashore in Limehouse, on that remembered voyage, we gathered up Catling just where we expected to find him, at his ease in the comfortable corner of a favoured bar, two or three drinks in, twanging piratical Jolly Roger bracers. And muttering darkly about those who couldn't differentiate between Bermondsey and Battersea. After an hour or so, we re-embarked. And sailed upstream, inspecting the bridges from which Brian might fling the residue of unwritten books. He rehearsed the river trip he would make from Limehouse Marina to Oxford, after completing a series of threatening performances in a gallery beside King George's Fields, where we had both worked as gardeners. And where he would launch, in 2012, the Honest Publishing original of *The Vorrh*. A book that Alan Moore likened to 'a first experience of the ocean'.

.

⋆

After Battersea Park I began to notice straggles of displaced walkers, groups of secular pilgrims under the direction of a nominal guide. Hugging the river, but pretending to be free of its dictation, they snatched at illusory glints of the fiction called history; pleased to be out and on the move, open to experience, and taking good care of their mental hygiene. Participants bonded in a form of ambulatory podcast, chattering merrily before the next church, the next coffee break. There are screeching parakeets here but no jungles. The river's cruelty is covert. And deadly

I did not run across the Sunday excursionists marshalled by that countercultural curator extraordinary, impresario of the improbable, Gareth Evans. Gareth's willing shock troops, led by different practitioners for different territories, reinvigilated London's mysteries, giving new force to the exhausted concept of the *dérive*. I sensed them out there, turning over the stones, stroking moss on obscure memorials, achieving permissions in churches denied to casual ramblers. They must have passed through here, I decided, as I checked in at the established oasis of St Mary's in Putney. One of their number must have shepherded them by now to Dr John Dee's Mortlake. The day's tramp would end traditionally in a riverside pub. With tall tales and recalibrated expectations. Things seen, things forgotten.

How well these contemporary Levellers, Diggers for submerged culture, merge with the clamour of the Putney Debates, held in 1647, at the conclusion of the English Civil War, in St Mary's Church. The venue, we are told, was chosen for its convenient distance from the heat and fret of the City; an easy ride for officers used to exploiting churches as stables. A modest trudge for disbanded foot soldiers. Those arguments echoing in a vortex within the body of the building defined a critical moment when the bloodily achieved overthrow of hierarchy, regulated religion and inherited privilege, offered the illusion of liberty, new freedom of choice. The Putney 'settlement' was just that: the officer caste reasserting its dominance, executing the last divinely appointed monarch, and nominating an iron dictator, a man-monument, to serve (by ruling) in the king's place. A once-and-forever opportunity became an interregnum. A pause between the regimes of hereditary inadequates bolstered by the lavishly rewarded obsequiousness of courtiers. Thieves as earls. Whores as countesses. Bribed critics. A muzzled parliament. The interregnum was a sorry lacuna struck from the record. No decent scandals, no Netflix romps and reboots.

Refreshed and refuelled by the busy community café that is now an equal partner with the church, I struck out to cross my first bridge, to follow the shaded riverside walk through Bishop's Park. When I returned by River Bus to Putney, with Anna, a more sensitive reader of environments, she was disturbed by the alignment of St Mary's altar against the north wall, and the traces of fire in the restored eastern portion. The circle of schoolroom chairs signalled respect for those twelve days of debate. The run of natural energy, reflected in the chain of churches dedicated to St Mary, was end-stopped by the requirement of adapting Putney as a museum of exploitable highlights. A venue for instruction, social work and musical performance. Gareth's questing agitators took their discussions into the open air. They marched west on Mortlake, haloed by the setting sun.

$\star$

A sudden chill overtakes Putney Bridge, conjuring a darker figure, held for an instant like an artist's impression of an accused man in the dock at the Old Bailey. A pinstripe spectre resurrected from fogged footage left in a Wardour Street bin at the end of another war. Under that greasy river-rescued trilby, a serial liar, premature purveyor of fake news, incubator of tabloid headlines: John Reginald Halliday Christie. The yellow press monster even had the gall to borrow the surname of our queen of country house mysteries, Agatha: deadly pharmacist, supreme constructor of impossible jigsaw plots. Reg's last address, another house of horror—coal gas abortions, bodged DIY, bone-composted garden patch—was obliterated. But not quite forgotten.

When the game was up and Christie prepared himself for audition by trial (and Pentonville execution), there was a pre-traumatic fugue. A red-eyed trudge from nowhere to nowhere, night and day, replaying the horrors, bending the truth. The man said, to his interrogators, the cops and the quacks, croaking in a papery whisper with what was left of his vocal cords after First War mustard gas, that he couldn't remember. *It was gone. Walked out.* The past was an infinitely revisable fable, steam on a shaving mirror. The world was searching for this necrophile strangler, baby killer, reserve policeman. He wasn't hiding but he was on the move across London. Dawn to dusk, cold sweat drying on a week-old collar. Spotted in breakfast cafés, sucking oily tea, lurking in fleapit cinemas, signed in at a Rowton House hostel near King's Cross, he was everywhere at once. A filthy virus in universal gaberdine. He had to walk fast enough to escape himself, but he was never on the run. *Odd Man Out* not Poverty Row Hollywood. It was as if the authorities preferred to postpone the inevitable reckoning.

The map of the fugue no amount of research could reconstruct ended at the embankment railings overlooking Putney Bridge. Men unloading timber noticed a vagrant on the towpath staring at the water. Christie had no offerings to make. And his conceptual suicide would involve giving himself up to the authorities, spurning a midnight plunge from the bridge. True to the confabulated self in which he lurked, the hunted man confessed: 'I am John Waddington of Westbourne Grove.' Secured in the police van, Christie reoccupied the other version, the other name. And revealed himself as a mercy killer, an enabler. He breakfasted well on tea, bread and butter, before being transferred to Notting Hill. Where a local author, J G Ballard, witnessed a crowd waiting outside the police station on Ladbroke Grove.

Another writer, when I first knew him, infiltrated this mythology, drawing on aspects he would later suppress, along with his first book of poetry, *Necropathia*.

Brian Catling had been taken with a Brett Whiteley exhibition at the Robert Fraser Gallery, based around the crimes enacted at 10 Rillington Place. He saw sculptural possibilities for the environments he contrived as a student in Walthamstow and at the Royal College of Art. He played with his own version of Christie's rope deckchair. Actors channelling gothic legends leaked from the strobing pulse, the vertical hold, of his antiquated television set. 'The hunger knotted / as he tied the cord back to his birth, poised on a / tubular chair.'

The Catling home in Cobourg Road, at one point, displayed a life-size pigskin figure by his pal and sparring partner, fellow dropout from Maidstone College of Art, Steve Dilworth. Standing stiffly at the ground floor window, pinstripe suited and crystal salted, cruel spectacles, false teeth, the Camberwell mummy grew into its legend. It invoked, with no supporting evidence, a classic English murder set: mildewed walls, rotten planks, cold outhouses, gas rings, crusted toilet bowls. Imagined objects drew coded language from inanimate things. Catling's first publication could have been dictated by this escapee from Dilworth's Book of the Dead, his *Texas Chainsaw Massacre*. The shooting script of *Necropathia* cut, very effectively, between the past of submerged London crimes, illicit compulsions, a psychopathology of dead photographs and prophetic X-rays, and the dawning glow of revelation. In and through landscape. This other path was always lifting somewhere over the trackways and standing stones of Wiltshire. There were good reasons to be on the tramp outside London. Away from those rooms, that chair. 'Watch the rope, dryly sinewed ... the obese mattress / rubbing against the dusty cracked floor ... smell the wet black smear near the spread-eagled / twist in the rope frame.'

Legends to be eaten and kept down. Absorbed. No sacks of visionary words, as yet, to be melted for the river. Within that surface horror, resistance. As Tony Grisoni, friend and collaborator, said: 'The man has a tender heart'.

★

Oarsmen sickened, swimming was inconceivable. Tributary streams are clogged and sullen. Enervated willows comb a head of creamy scum from choked and breathless water. Cloud continents, barely able to support themselves, skulk above the outer

reaches beyond Hammersmith. Drifting ice floes, cumulonimbus continents, are reflected in a slicked upstream surface scoured by the setting winter sun. The unearned gift of this gorious spectacle is so perfectly achieved that there can be no prospect of a repeat. Or a return. End of the Catling walk. End of everything.

Hammersmith Bridge is the ultimate border marker, unless you want to cross it. The veteran suspension span, with its wrought iron pillars and cast iron pedestals, is out of commission, shivered with metal fatigue and micro-fractures. Closed to all comers in 2020, the bridge permits free passage only to pedestrians and cyclists (those who are never to be denied in the new London).

Heading home after a walk with Adolfo Barberá del Rosal, to the locked church of St Mary the Virgin in Mortlake, we were confounded to discover that public transport, south of the river, had been abolished. There wasn't any. We were in a far country with no valid visas. Trains were not running. Replacement buses needed replacing. Suburban halts were mobbed with misled travellers, jabbing at their devices, seduced into excursions to places from which there was no escape. Doing the opposite of whatever was suggested by zombie announcements on deserted station platforms, we found ourselves at a barrier securing Hammersmith Bridge.

Adolfo summarized the madness of our quest in search of 'crisis' as a state of elective 'not-knowing'. And he was quite right. 'Not knowing the dynamics that are operating in a territory, of which the ancestral cult system is a metaphor', he said. Fastidious in diction, Spanish in metaphysical complexity, the Eurocrat was philosophically precise. He laughed aloud. The post-Brexit, post-Covid, post-history mess was a welcome curse. The scholar concluded, in the privilege of those extra miles we tramped to reach Hammersmith: 'For anyone familiar with this affordable type of trance, it is not always easy to determine the exact point at which the summoning starts delivering (it generally comes with a certain delay), but one does know that delivery *has happened*'. Thesis proved: delivery *had* happened. Adolfo composed his text well ahead of our expedition. And the book in which it was published was delivered to my house, during the hours of our absence: 10 June 2023. Having walked it, we read it. Together. As we *delivered* contrasting narratives of chaos.

·

*

Midway over the river, I experienced the sensation described by Gavin Francis in *The Bridge Between Worlds: A Brief History of Connection*. 'It would be splendid to have a word for the sensation of walking over a bridge, for the way bringing air and water beneath your feet changes your relationship to space ... Even the least of the townsmen felt as if his powers were suddenly multiplied, as if some wonderful, superhuman exploit was brought within the measure of his powers and within the limits of everyday life, as if besides the well-known elements of earth, water and sky, one more were open to him.'

T J Cobden-Sanderson, bookbinder and partner in the Doves Press, must have responded to something of this sense of being beyond the mundane curse of gravity; being trapped, with time in suspension, between fish and bird. He unleashed about a ton of metal type, along with the matrices and punches he had already destroyed, from Hammersmith Bridge into the river. It has been calculated that he made 170 journeys from his Chiswick print shop to the Thames. The ritual began on 31 August 1916, at midnight in a blacked-out city at war. The last bundle hit the water in January 1917. The Cobden-Sanderson assault had been initiated on Good Friday, 21 March 1913. It must have felt as if the bookbinder were taking a hammer to the bones of his estranged partner, Emery Walker, before dedicating and consecrating the remnants of this stumbling block of disconnected words and giving them up to the river. The covert violation from Hammersmith Bridge was quite a different thing from the liberating *finality* of Catling's ritualized heresy on the stone steps at Blackfriars. The definitive action, from which there could be no turning back, was a tipping point between those earlier, half-secret chapbooks of poetry, transcripts for imagined actions, and the convulsive and oceanic prose seizures of the *Vorrh* trilogy. The long-awaited dictation of elder gods for which he had prepared so assiduously.

In Prague, before the first person set foot on the span of the Charles Bridge, eggs were baked into the mortar; 'to imbue the stones', as Gavin Francis tells us, 'with fertility and vitality'. The bridge was 'wreathed in magic'. It had a special status as a suitable site for the casting of spells, the drowning of books. Across Hammersmith Bridge and a short way upstream, at Mortlake, the imperial geographer, John Dee, gave audience to the Virgin Queen and the spirits ventriloquized by Edward Kelley. The magus was a prompt for the character of Shakespeare's Prospero in *The Tempest*. 'And deeper than did ever plummet sound / I'll drown my book.' When Dee shipped out for Prague, his kindly neighbours broke in and burnt all the 'rough magic' of the fabled library. Four thousand volumes and seven hundred choice manuscripts. A Beltane bonfire of maps, continents still to be plundered, of star charts and coded hieroglyphs.

Contemplating the bridge and trying to picture the furtive figure of Cobden-Sanderson, so sure of his task that challenge is inconceivable, marching out and letting another burden go, my meeting with the designer Robert Green in a tapas restaurant in Columbia Road came back to me. The story of the Doves Press had taken its toll and become something more than mere obsession. Robert enlisted the Port of London Authority's salvage crew, after he had calculated the position from which the type had been dropped from bridge to river. Mudlarking in the shallows of the Hammersmith shore, he recovered three pieces of original type. With 148 more from the divers. He wanted to make some sort of restitution to the betrayed Doves craftsman by gifting his finds to Emery Walker's refurbished house at No. 7 Hammersmith Terrace.

A project was pitched, whereby I would make 170 trips of my own, house to bridge, rucksack crammed with—*what?*—the rescued font or substitute versions? But, more to the point, I would be required to manufacture new texts from the fugitive letters filched from the mud by Green. He spent three hard years finessing digital facsimiles of the elegant Doves Press alphabet. Cobden-Sanderson disposed of approximately 500,000 pieces of lead type. Robert Green recovered fewer than two hundred. Beyond these, one mudlarker found a solitary 'f' and a comma.

I accepted the offer without hesitation. Here was potential restitution for my crime in witnessing and filming the Blackfriars ritual. And now the Doves Press performance would also be recorded. With steady tramping and a few breaks, Robert calculated that I could get it done in 48 hours. I was not so sure. Surveillance levels around Hammersmith Bridge and the River Café would lead to a much more rapid capture and prosecution than Reg Christie enjoyed. The curious strollers, the Arts and Crafts disciples, the respectful Morrisites, the phone-bothering drinkers in riverside pubs: somebody was going to make the call. Fortunately, films require deal-brokers and brewers lose their nerve over sponsorship when they study the small print. Readings at the South Bank Poetry Library have to be approved by budget supervisors. The gig fell through. The task of making *something* of the letters so lovingly recovered and digitally crafted by Robert Green stayed with me, even after I had returned borrowed research materials to Green's narrowboat.

.

*

Beyond Hammersmith Bridge sauntering was in order. Old folks smiled to themselves and prepared for the challenge of the next set of steps. Potentially, the last. Nobody here was driven by the battery in the hand. Nobody raged. Or broadcast dim office politics. They rested on benches. Or found a table outside a pub. Even the proud inhabitants behaved like excursionists or convalescents.

It was a good stretch in which to appreciate the value of the Sunday walks convened by Gareth Evans. I've never participated, but I've heard something about how they work from Victor Rees, the relentless Catling scholar, and from Stephen McNeilly, the *genius loci* of Swedenborg House. Stephen explained how there were no leaders, no guides; contributions, Quaker-style, from anyone lifted by the spirit. He, for example, found himself quite unexpectedly beside a grave about which he had some special knowledge. And to which he realized that he had been directed. A shiver of recognition was confirmation of what Alan Moore calls a process of 'fore-remembering'. The concept struck me as validation for the Community of Scholars, or *studium generale*; a 'medieval university' on the hoof, as described by the writer and social critic, Paul Goodman, when I was lucky enough to spend a few minutes with him in 1967. Goodman, a pipe-crunching anarchist, challenger of sclerotic hierarchies, taught for a time at Black Mountain College. These Evans walks through London's liminal places were a strategic extension of that plot: peripatetic students across all disciplines, published and unpublished, informed or eager to learn, wandering at large. The direct inheritors, perhaps, of the libertarians, communalists and pamphleteers, stymied by a property-owning officer class at the Putney Debates. Anybody who heard about an upcoming Evans expedition was free to join it. No membership fees, no special qualifications. Out in the world, exchanging roles, sharing expertise—obscure retrievals, poetry, conversation—and a few drinks at the finish. There would be discoveries.

And now, as the winter evening foreclosed on me, I was chasing one of them. And approaching the point where, as your man Catling remarked, 'past and future are entirely symmetric'. The path narrows into private riverside gardens and handsome properties trying to live up to their Chiswick address. The rabble of weekend walkers with their competitive free-form tutorials must have passed this way. One of them left the address of the find, gifted by the river, as a neat conclusion. Or provocation for a further chapter.

⋆

Below the church of St Nicholas, and its seductive burial ground with the urn-crowned grave of Hogarth's sister standing tall enough to stay out of the water, is a mud-varnished slipway. Hulks rot. Cables trail in the swamp. A marine scrapyard from which a stone aisle, lifted out of the slop and shingle, diminishes into the elevated Perpendicular church and its east window. Rectangular flags have been laid so carefully, so polished by tides, that this upstream runway feels like an extension of the church itself, a damp cloister missing its walls. A neural trench connecting Kentish ragstone masonry with the site of a discontinued ferry. Antiquarians say that a seventh-century structure for Christian worship was constructed over a 'pagan shrine'. Indicating a place of power. Place of cross-river transit. A walk across water. The vague term 'pagan' meaning whatever is back there beyond our cognizance.

It was from neo-pagan offerings spread across licked flagstones, close to the waterline, that a crusted metal *thing* was picked up and handed to Victor Rees. The obvious recipient. He recognized its meaning, at once, and loaned it as an exhibit for a vitrine at the *Histories & Hauntings* exhibition. Where it was in dialogue with a slim, slate-covered, unmelted copy of *The Stumbling Block*.

M Syd Rosen, a doctoral candidate from Pembroke College, Cambridge, investigating 'celebrity science and cybernetic vanguard', pounced on something that might once have been a musical instrument; a Sumerian war trumpet stolen from a museum or a section of calcified spine. The sort of item that belongs in the second world, the outer reality husbanded by the Thames. Letting it escape was dangerous. The whole edifice of illusion by which we sustain the impetus to carry on for a new day could come crashing down. In one of his academic papers, Rosen spoke of 'chance encounters, indeterminacy, electronic sounds and non-western tunings'. The scavenged relic fitted the bill. Rosen shifted the difficulty of carrying it away by passing the barnacled lump, the Catling quotation, to Victor Rees.

The Chiswick pipe was a substantial and undeniable metaphor lifted from texts and performances by Brian Catling: shaved strips from the bones of a forest seer's legs sculpted into a bow chiselled from a meteorite. The object was alive and ageless, slumbering under a protective blanket of radiated mud. The slow and steady drift from Blackfriars to Chiswick shaped the molten hank of *The Stumbling Block* into another venture. Fossilized evidence from the future had returned to relaunch Catling's blasphemous trilogy.

The troop of aspirant hedge-scholars convened by Gareth Evans came here, to this pivotal locus, ahead of me—and also in my wake. My footsteps solicited the shadows they left behind. On that fortunate afternoon, they were the followers, waiting to see how my secondary report would unravel. But where I arrived, a lowering sun tangled in bare branches above the chess piece urn of Hogarth's sister, they pushed on into the portion of the melancholy garden of Old Chiswick Cemetery known as 'The Extension'. Doubtless, one of the untenured pedestrian curators pointed out the graves of William Hogarth and James McNeill Whistler, silvered dandy of Chelsea nocturnes. Whistler's monument was a tilted sea chest, washed upstream and guarded at each corner by freestanding females. Resin copies of stolen originals. Further west was a sculpted panel, a relief carving by Edward Bainbridge Copnall, representing the Resurrection of the Dead. A heaped and orgiastic tangle like a split barrel of all the drowned and interbreeding figures of this improbable story.

The ever-alert McNeilly, leaning against a faded memorial, was jolted from reverie into engagement. This was his moment, his turn as key witness and explainer. He was docked alongside the final resting place of Philip James de Loutherbourg, an exiled Frenchman in London. Acclaimed painter of *Storm at Sunset* and *Morning after the Rain*. Impresario of sets and stage machinery. And professional portraitist: he bagged

Emanuel Swedenborg and later joined the loosely affiliated circle of admirers around the scientist and mystic.

But the crucial aspect of Loutherbourg's career was his invention of the 'Eidophusikon', a form of proto-cinema. A miniature theatre operating somewhere between period spectacle and the shadowplay of as yet unachieved motion pictures. The designer played with lighting effects and three-dimensional sets to invoke or summon the plunging torrents of Niagara Falls: almost as if he anticipated a torrential backdrop for Marilyn Monroe in Henry Hathaway's haunting film of sour honeymoons, autopsy suites and bell towers.

After these conjurings in the ambiguous territory permitted between science and magic, it was inevitable that de Loutherbourg gravitated towards occult speculation. And the patronage of Count Alessandro di Cagliostro. The Swedenborgian painter does not make an appearance in the London chapter of *Cagliostro*, a romance by Johannes von Guenther published here in 1928. The climate of eighteenth-century Freemasonry and psychic experimentation provides a suitably fervid atmosphere. Two dry public men in a solicitor's office discuss the arrival of the mysterious Count from Palermo.

'On the other hand, I cannot blink the fact that, all we seem to hear about nowadays, is bogus hierophants, who pretend to know the secret of material prima, and really haven't the faintest conception of it. They secure a large following, if only they know how to open their mouths wide enough. For, as everybody knows, there are always plenty of fools about.'

The Chiswick grave that none of the Gareth Evans walkers acknowledged, the one hiding in plain sight, was that of Henry Joy of the 17th Light Dragoons (Lancers). Joy was a much decorated Trumpet-Major. A musician in the regimental band, a trumpeter. Promoted to officer rank in 1847, he took charge of the band at the funeral of the Duke of Wellington. His stone symbol—musical instrument *and* weapon—made its own way to the river, after fusing with the pale offprint of Catling on the hoarding that hid the entry pit to the latest deep-tunnel boring for London's unmapped subterranean labyrinth. The faded advertisement nobody understood, or even noticed, was printed over the relief carving on the trumpeter's memorial, to emerge as a found sculpture worthy of exhibit in the Bloomsbury house dedicated to Swedenborg's life and legend.

When I reached the slipway, the tide was out. The far bank was an *After London* jungle with no evidence of recent habitation. The selection of scattered offerings could have been arranged by the late Catling for one of his European residencies. He would arrive by invitation in a new city, to discover that there was no budget beyond his plane ticket, and a yawning space, deck or floor, icehouse or museum, waiting with a pack of serious worshippers. Then he got to work, harvesting whatever modest obscurities he could lay his hands on: hessian, needles, bread, paper, stone. The slipway had much more than that. Decorated tiles. Small wheels and cogs. Straps. Tubes. Chaotic but strangely formal arrangements that would hold only until the tide returned.

A few months later, hoping to follow up on the Hammersmith project, I made it to the Dove pub and the house where Emery Walker had lived, but when I tried to revisit the slipway, Chiswick Mall was flooded, access was denied. There are no second chances. No second lives. The road had become a river. 'Disjointed humans may drink or sign themselves in their passage', Catling said.

The old prophets, according to Revelations, were required to open the book of divine instruction and eat the words. 'It will make your stomach bitter, but it will be as sweet as honey in your mouth.' In Swedenborg House, Catling sucked down rolls of exposed film, like a lizard out of Blake swallowing its unholy tongue. Without damage. The consummate performer chewed on knives. And bathed hurt eyes, strained in scholarship, with ink. And he knew when it was time to feed the Thames. To make his contribution to the great anthology of the mispublished, so that errors could be corrected, and pilgrims, in their own good time, could begin the task of recomposition.

GIFT

What is returned by the river

                              will return

refused by cold reach, accused

          falling, failing, fading now

the figure, the font, the stopped fountain

your sorry words pre-composed, given

               and withdrawn, redrawn

drowned twice, and best, and carried away

—Iain Sinclair

APPENDICES

CONTEXTUAL NOTE: FURTHER FACTS IN THE CASE OF M. VALDEMAR BY B. CATLING

Victor Rees

Edgar Allan Poe was perhaps chief among Catling's tutelary spirits, the stable of visionaries whose work he continually returned to as a source of influence and provocation. Unlike such figures as William Blake, Raymond Roussel, Hieronymus Bosch and Eadweard Muybridge, Poe never appeared in a fictionalized guise in the pages of Catling's novels. The great horror writer's work nevertheless maintained a form of psychic stranglehold over Catling, who proclaimed in 2021 that 'all roads lead to Poe'.

This story, hitherto unpublished, is Catling's most sustained tribute to Poe—though perhaps it should be viewed more as a dialogue than a tribute, for it establishes itself from its title as a part-sequel, part-prequel to 'The Facts in the Case of M. Valdemar' (1845). Poe's original story, lines of which are woven by Catling throughout his own remix, tells of an attempt to use mesmerism to preserve a man on the cusp of death. It is unknown precisely when Catling wrote 'Further Facts'—copies of the tale were shared with friends in the weeks before he died, lying under a portrait of 'Pauvre Eddie' which hung like a religious icon on the wall of his Oxfordshire home.

.

APPENDIX II:
HISTORIES & HAUNTINGS

List of Works

1   RENCHI BICKNELL, *Cambridge Dreaming with the Whole Extent of Michael Line and Chalkdownland Guide* (originally described as *Chalkdownland Dreaming II* in his publication *Michael and Mary Dreaming*, first edn. 1998), mixed media, 1990. Collection of Renchi Bicknell.

2   B. CATLING, single-copy artist's book of alchemical symbols, wood, hessian, paint and leather, from the period of *Vorticegarden* (1974). Collection of Iain Sinclair.

3   IAIN SINCLAIR, board-backed photographs, included in *Albion Island Vortex* (1974). Collection of Iain Sinclair.

4   CATLING, three framed drawings, ink pen on paper, included in *Albion Island Vortex* (1974). Collection of Iain Sinclair.

5   CATLING, 'Astronomer's Rib', poem reproduced from *Albion Island Vortex* (1974).

6   BICKNELL, *Milk Hill*, watercolour, mid 1980s. Collection of Justin Kenrick and Eva Schonfeld.

7   CATLING, 'Stone Poem', poem published for the first time in *Histories & Hauntings* catalogue, selected from a series of late responses sent to Matthew Shaw after return visits to Wayland's Smithy and the Avebury stones.

8   STEVE DILWORTH, *Sacred Heart*, iron nails, white limestone, concealed ox heart, 1999. Collection of Iain Sinclair, in custodianship of Swedenborg House.

9   SINCLAIR, board-backed photographs, included in *Albion Island Vortex* (1974). Collection of Iain Sinclair.

10   CATLING, sword cast for Iain Sinclair, iron, *c.* 1975. Collection of Iain Sinclair.

11   BICKNELL, *Leaving Richmond (Starry Night)*, single-plate etching, 2008. Collection of Iain Sinclair.

12   BICKNELL, *M25 Walk 1*, mixed media, 2001. Collection of Melanie Butlin and Joe Bilby.

13   BICKNELL, *Brockenhurst (New Forest)*, mixed media, included in *Albion Island Vortex* (1974). Collection of Iain Sinclair.

14   BICKNELL, *Schoolhouse Vision*, single-plate etching, 2008. Collection of Iain Sinclair.

15   SINCLAIR, extract from *Black Apples of Gower* (2015).

16   SINCLAIR, board-backed photograph, included in *Albion Island Vortex* (1974). Collection of Iain Sinclair.

17   CATLING, early abstract painting, late 1960s. Collection of Iain Sinclair.

18   SINCLAIR, board-backed photograph, included in *Albion Island Vortex* (1974). Collection of Iain Sinclair.

19   CATLING, four cyclops paintings.

Top shelf: *Self-portrait*. Second shelf down: *Burclops* (Paul Burwell), *Breakclops* (Ian Breakwell), *Griffclops* (Bill Griffiths). Egg tempera on board, *c.* 2006-2009. Collection of Iain Sinclair.

20   CATLING, two drawings for Iain Sinclair's *Lud Heat* (1975), pen on ink (left and right), early-mid 1970s. *X-Ray Pyramid* (centre), mid 1970s. Collection of Iain Sinclair.

21   SINCLAIR, board-backed stills from short film *Maggot Street* (1972). Collection of Iain Sinclair.

22   CATLING, early abstract collage (untitled), X-rays, paper (various), masking tape, *c.* 1970s. Collection of Iain Sinclair.

23   SINCLAIR, extract from *Black Apples of Gower* (2015).

24   BICKNELL, *Haya*, mixed media, early 1970s. Collection of Renchi Bicknell.

25   BICKNELL, *Old Man and The World*, oil, early 1970s. Collection of Iain Sinclair.

26   BICKNELL, *Freud & Jung Leaving New York*, oil, early 1970s. Collection of Iain Sinclair.

27   Archival ephemera from Albion Village Press, with contemporaneous photographs.

28 Odo the Crow. As seen in *Edith Walks* by Andrew Kötting (2017).

29 BICKNELL, *Faustus and the Oxford Dreaming* (originally described as *Chalkdownland Dreaming VI* in his publication *Michael and Mary Dreaming*, first edn. 1998), mixed media, late 1980s. Collection of Haya Oakley and Chris Oakley.

30 CATLING, Albion Village Press woodblock depicting giant's head, wood and ink, *c.* 1970s. Collection of Iain Sinclair.

31 SINCLAIR, board-backed photographs, included in *Albion Island Vortex* (1974). Including photograph of Brian Catling with crow, *c.* 1973 (isolated on top shelf) and photograph of Iain Sinclair and Brian Catling near Avebury, *c.* 1973 (third shelf down, second left). Collection of Iain Sinclair.

32 SINCLAIR, photographic portraits of Brian Catling, dates various. Collection of Iain Sinclair.

33 Original archival publications printed by Albion Village Press. Collections of Iain Sinclair and Renchi Bicknell.

34 CATLING, cyclops painting of Iain Sinclair, egg tempera on board, *c.* 2006-2009. Collection of Iain Sinclair.

ROOM 2: GALLERY, CAVE OF POETRY

35 ANONYMOUS BOSCH, framed photograph from *By Our Selves* (2015) by Andrew Kötting, depicting Toby Jones as the poet John Clare, Iain Sinclair with goat mask, Andrew Kötting as Straw Bear. Collection of Iain Sinclair.

36 BICKNELL, Albion Village Press poster for *The Kodak Mantra Diaries*, 1972. Collection of Iain Sinclair.

37 'SAGESONG'. Text taken from Iain Sinclair poem; illustrated by Mike Egan; published by Von Los, screenprint, 2013. Collection of Iain Sinclair.

38 SINCLAIR, two paintings: *2nd Ascent of the Obelisk* (1st Oct 1976) and *Ceremonies at Cerne Abbas* (Ash Wednesday 1975), acrylic paint on paper. Collection of Iain Sinclair.

39 MARTIN ROWSON, cartoon as part of his 'Pantheon' series (1994-1998), ink and paint on paper. Collection of Iain Sinclair.

40 BICKNELL, *Mr Prynne*, mixed media, included in *Albion Island Vortex* (1974). Collection of Iain Sinclair.

41 STEPHEN RAW, calligraphic extract

from Iain Sinclair poem 'No Bones' (from Poetry Library exhibition *Open&Shut&Open*), card, paper, paint, ink, 2007. Collection of Iain Sinclair.

42 CATLING & SINCLAIR, original *Lud Heat* map, ink on paper, early 1970s. Collection of Iain Sinclair.

43 EFFIE PALEOLOGOU, *The Rendezvous of I.Sinclair & N.Hawksmoor*, calligraphy: pen and ink on paper, April 2023. Produced for *Solution Opportunities: for Iain Sinclair at 80*, ed. Gareth Evans (Haggerston Hound Printworks, 2023). Collection of Iain Sinclair.

44 STEVE BRITTAIN, photograph of launch of Iain Sinclair's *Downriver* (1991) at Tower House, Fieldgate Street, 1991 (top) and photograph of launch of Iain Sinclair's *White Chappell, Scarlet Tracings* (1987) at the Old Operating Theatre of the old St Thomas' Hospital, London Bridge, 1987 (bottom). ROBERT KLINKERT, photograph of Iain Sinclair & Allen Ginsberg in Regent's Park during the filming of *Ah, Sunflower!*, 1967 (centre). Collection of Iain Sinclair.

45 BARRY BURMAN, drawing derived from Iain Sinclair's *Suicide Bridge*

(1979) [inscription mentions the twin characters Hand and Hyle], paint and ink on paper, 1992. Collection of Iain Sinclair.

46 SINCLAIR, five paintings. Top row of grouping of four: *Salisbury* (Easter Sunday 1974) and *Rats* (1975), acrylic on paper. Bottom row of four: *Driving past Maiden Castle* (1975) and *Golden Cap* (1975), acrylic on paper. On right adjacent wall: *Manac...* (1987), acrylic on board-mounted paper. Collection of Iain Sinclair.

ROOM 3: BOOKSHOP

47 BICKNELL, *The Gift*, mixed media, early 1970s. Collection of Judith Earnshaw.

48 SINCLAIR, photographs of Renchi Bicknell. These include Albion Village Press authors, Bicknell and Tony Lowes, running along Richard Long's Silbury Hill spiral in the Whitechapel Gallery.

ROOM 4: STAIRWELL

BICKNELL, *A Pilgrim's Progress* twelve-piece etching series, multiple etching plates, 2008. Collection of Renchi Bicknell.

49 Plate I: *The Dreamer Dreams A Dream*

50 Plate II: *Christian Reads his Book*

51 Plate III: *Christian Meets Evangelist*

52 Plate IV: *The Slough Of Despond*

53 Plate V: *Fire and Ice*

54 Plate VI: *At The Wicket Gate*

55 Plate VII: *In The Interpreter's House*

56 Plate VIII: *At The Cross*

57 Plate IX: *At The Arbour*

58 Plate X: *Christian Fights Apollyon*

59 Plate XI: *Faithful's Martyrdom*

60 Plate XII: *At Heaven's Gate*

61 Individual plate section taken from *At Heaven's Gate*: *At the Gates Of Heaven*.

62 BICKNELL, *Starlings*, Chinese ink and watercolour, 2012. Collection of Renchi Bicknell.

ROOM 5: WYNTER ROOM

63 Various printed ephemera from Albion Village Press, with contemporaneous photographs, associated clippings, and found items.

64 BICKNELL, above: *Pole Hill*, painting from the 21 June 2023 walk

described in *Histories & Hauntings* publication. Reproduced from Bicknell's sketchbook displayed below, with other sketchbooks by the artist, dates various. Collection of Renchi Bicknell.

65 Top: BEKA GLOBE, photograph of Steve Dilworth's *Hooded Crow*, bog oak, steel, yew, hooded crow, 1990. Bottom: DILWORTH, *Written in the Sand*, ink on paper, produced for *Solution Opportunities: for Iain Sinclair at 80*, ed. Gareth Evans (Haggerston Hound Printworks, 2023). Collection of Iain Sinclair.

66 ALLEN FISHER, *Emergence of Pestilence*, oil on canvas, 2015-2023. Collection of Allen Fisher.

67 ANONYMOUS BOSCH, series of three photographs, dates various: *Iain Sinclair with Catling Sword at Clach Ard Stone, Isle of Skye*; *Iain Sinclair with Crow beside the Thames*; *Iain Sinclair with Crow at Wolfe Obelisk, Greenwich*. Collection of Iain Sinclair.

68 CATLING, *The Stumbling Block, Its Index (Special Edition)* (Book Works, 1990), limited edition of twenty-five signed and numbered copies with graphite-covered boards

and handwritten additional text.
Collection of Iain Sinclair. Exhibited
alongside bow-shaped metal object,
retrieved from the banks of the river
Thames during a recent walk led
by Victor Rees from Hammersmith
to Mortlake on 28 May 2023. With
a descriptive text by Victor Rees.
Collection of Victor Rees.

69 'PROPOSAL TO THE ARTS
COUNCIL' with 'RESPONSE FROM
GALLERY & COUNCIL', text from
1973.

ROOM 6: PAPER

70 *Histories & Hauntings* three-part
accompanying publication-cum-
catalogue (Swedenborg Society in
partnership with Albion Village Press,
2023). Limited to 200 numbered
copies. With texts (prose, poetry, and
academic) by Iain Sinclair, B. Catling,
Renchi Bicknell, Claudia Barton,
Steve Dilworth, Gareth Evans, Allen
Fisher, Victor Rees, Matthew Shaw
and Carol Williams.

APPENDIX III:
ALBION ISLAND VORTEX

List of Works

CADER IDRIS

1 SINCLAIR, Cader Idris (26/10/73)
2 SINCLAIR, Cader Idris (26/10/73)
3 SINCLAIR, Cader Idris (26/10/73)
4 SINCLAIR, Cader Idris (26/10/73)
5 SINCLAIR, Merthyr Mawr (3/3/74)
6 SINCLAIR, St Illtyd's, Llantwit Major (2/3/74)
7 SINCLAIR, St Illtyd's, Llantwit Major (2/3/74)
8 SINCLAIR, St Illtyd's, Llantwit Major (2/3/74)

PATHS AND TRAVELLERS

1 BICKNELL, Wandlebury (Gog Magog hills)
2 BICKNELL, Longest day (N. Downs)
3 BICKNELL, St Cross (Winchester)

4 BICKNELL, Dancing Ledge (Dorset)
5. BICKNELL, Luard St (Victoria)
6. BICKNELL, Mr Prynne (Cambridge)
7. BICKNELL, (Saturn) Mill Hill
8. BICKNELL, Whitechapel
9. BICKNELL, Pole hill
10. BICKNELL, Approaching home
11. BICKNELL, Brockenhurst (New Forest). N. F. S.

ASTRONOMER'S RIB

1 CATLING, Electric Room (71)
2 CATLING, Water trap (74)
3 CATLING, Earth Raft (74)
4 CATLING, Coban's pike (74)
5 CATLING, Smoke stone (73)
6 CATLING, Gull's Bill (73)

7   CATLING, Moon Anvil (73)

WILTS

1   CATLING, The Ridgeway. (6/6/73)
2   SINCLAIR, East Kennett Long
     Barrow (6/6/73)
3   SINCLAIR, Stonehenge. (6/6/73)
4   SINCLAIR, Wayland's Smithy. (6/6/73)
5   CATLING, Stonehenge. (6/6/73)
6   SINCLAIR, Stonehenge. (6/6/73)
7   SINCLAIR, The Ridgeway. (6/6/73)
8   SINCLAIR, Avebury. (6/6/73)
9   SINCLAIR, Avebury. (6/6/73)
10   CATLING, Above Silbury. (6/6/73)
11   SINCLAIR, Avebury. (6/6/73)
12   SINCLAIR, Dragon Hill. (6/6/73)
13-19 Are all taken from the final
     sequence of the alchemical exorcism
     in the film MAGGOT STREET made
     by Sinclair & Catling, with J. M.
     Healey. (12/1/73) (Camberwell)
20   SINCLAIR, The Ridgeway. (9/4/71)
21   SINCLAIR, Lowbury Hill. (9/4/71)

SIX HAIR-RAISING ARCHETYPES

1   BICKNELL, Strong Mothers
2   BICKNELL, Turnip field
3   BICKNELL, West Ham Shaman
4   BICKNELL, Woman of Light

5   BICKNELL, Royston Heath
6   BICKNELL, Suicide

NORTH

1   SINCLAIR, Barden Fell. (14/6/73)
2   SINCLAIR, Thimble Stones. (13/6/73)
3   CATLING, Roxburgh. (April 73)
4   SINCLAIR, The White Stones.
     (12/6/73)
5   SINCLAIR, Barden Fell. (14/6/73)
6   SINCLAIR, The Twelve
     Apostles. (12/6/73)
7   CATLING, Roxburgh. (April 73)
8   SINCLAIR, South Nab, Bolton
     Park. (13/6/73)
9   SINCLAIR, Hazlewood Moor.
     (13/6/73)
10   SINCLAIR, Warley Moor. (11/6/73)
11   SINCLAIR, Bolton Abbey. (14/6/73)
12   SINCLAIR, Hazlewood Moor.
     (13/6/73)
13   CATLING, Cheviot Hills (April 73)
14   SINCLAIR, Bolton Park. (14/6/73)

GOWER

1   SINCLAIR, Port Eynon/Worm's
     Head. (4/1/73)
2   CATLING, PE/WH. (4/1/73)
3   SINCLAIR, PE/WH. (28/12/72)

4. SINCLAIR, PE/WH. (28/12/72)

5. SINCLAIR, PE/WH. (28/12/72)

6. SINCLAIR, Monknash. (24/10/73)

7. SINCLAIR, PE/WH. (4/1/73)

8. SINCLAIR, PE/WH. (4/1/73)

9. SINCLAIR, PE/WH. (4/1/73)

10. SINCLAIR, Monknash. (24/10/73)

11. SINCLAIR, PE/WH. (4/1/73)

12. SINCLAIR, PE/WH. (4/1/73)

13. SINCLAIR, PE/WH. (4/1/73)

GOAT

1 SINCLAIR, "GOAT BUNKER".
Bamburgh Castle. (11/6/72)
'the curvature of the universe is
love' (j.h.p)

2 SINCLAIR, "A PYTHON"
(23/1/73)

3 SINCLAIR, "NOT HERE, MAYBE
NOW" (8/3/73)

4 SINCLAIR, "PLANT TOTEM"
(1/8/73)

5 SINCLAIR, "KILLS FROGS"
(19/11/73)

6. SINCLAIR, "STRANGE EXCURSION".
Market Overton (1/1/72)

7 SINCLAIR, "KRIM" (30/9/73)

8 SINCLAIR, "KILLS THE THRUSH"
(3/1/74)

9 SINCLAIR, "DREAM RIBS"
(15/2/74)

10 SINCLAIR, "BRAN AS HUTTON",
Chingford Mount. (21/2/74)

11 SINCLAIR, "GOING HOME".
(20/2/74)

12 SINCLAIR, "RETURN". (8/2/74)
'it's the thing you can't see holds
the world together,' I told Cody. 'the
curve' (Kerouac)

EAST

1 SINCLAIR, Stoke Newington.
(27/11/73)

2 SINCLAIR, Chingford Mount.
(21/1/74)

3 SINCLAIR, Stoke Newington.
(27/11/73)

4 SINCLAIR, Chingford Mount.
(21/1/74)

5 SINCLAIR, Bunhill Fields. (31/7/73)

6 SINCLAIR, Chingford Mount.
(21/1/74)

7 SINCLAIR, Stoke Newington.
(27/11/73)

8 SINCLAIR, Chingford Mount.
(21/1/74)

9 SINCLAIR, Chingford Mount.
(14/2/74)

PUBLISHER'S NOTE

Gifts Returned by the River is a project in two parts. Part One contains six articles originally published on the occasion of *Histories & Hauntings*, an exhibition of paintings, film, sculpture, artefacts, and other ephemera held at Swedenborg House in 2023. This exhibition was itself a restaging of *Albion Island Vortex*, originally organized by Renchi Bicknell, Brian Catling, and Iain Sinclair at the Whitechapel Gallery in 1974. Part Two, newly commissioned for this volume, features a collection of articles, poems, stories, and other contributions written in response to the exhibition, along with additional material exploring similar themes. Included in this section is a poem insert by Iain Sinclair. In addition to those just mentioned, and the authors listed on the title page, the publishers would like to thank: Claudia Barton, Anonymous Bosch, Zelda Cahill-Patten, Jacob Cartwright, Rebekka Cartwright, Paul Cox, Steve Dilworth, Anthony Finnigan, Andrew Kötting, Alex Murray, Bill Osment, Denise Prentice, Martin Rowson, Adam Skipper, Lolita Sobolyova, Michael Whyte and James Wilson. Special appreciation is, of course, extended to Iain Sinclair and Renchi Bicknell for their continued energy and generosity.